The

# Player

and the

# Pixie

by L.H. COSWAY & PENNY REID

Caped Publishing

Made in the United States of America

Print Edition: April 2016
Print ISBN: 978-1-942874-17-1

## DEDICATION

In no particular order: yoga, dogs that hump your legs without even buying you a drink first, and the bubble butts of rugby players everywhere.

And to the city of Tulsa, where a second love story was conceived.

# Chapter One

*Peace comes from within. Do not seek it without.*

-Lucy Fitzpatrick (also, maybe Buddha).


**\*Lucy\***

FLESH WAS A strange color for nail polish.

I understood black (for the Goths) and even gray to a certain extent, but flesh? You were just painting your nails the same color they already were. It was like dying your hair red when you were a ginger.

Pointless.

I stared at the selection of colors in the cosmetics section of the local department store, trying to resist the urge to pick up that oh-so-tempting shade of canary yellow and shove it in my handbag. *You don't need it. You don't need it. You don't need it. Material objects are transitory. The joy they bring is momentary and hollow . . .* Strangely, my mantra wasn't working right then.

So, you've probably already guessed my secret. I had an addiction . . . or maybe a compulsion was the better word.

I was a thief. A shoplifter. And the mere sight of consumer items small enough to conceal within the confines of a purse or a coat pocket gave me twitchy fingers like you wouldn't believe.

It was abhorrent, I knew that, and I struggled daily with my guilt. In fact, I'd been doing so well in my attempts to quit. To be a better person.

Six months ago I'd moved to New York to begin a new job as a celebrity photographer/blogger/YouTuber, and I resolved to stop. It was my chance for a fresh start. I hadn't stolen a single thing in all that time. Yes, the Big Apple remained untouched by my habit for five-finger discounts. And yet, there I stood, just itching to steal that flipping ridiculous bottle of nail polish.

I knew the reason why, and her name began with a J. That would be Jackie Fitzpatrick, my mother, and provider of inferiority complexes everywhere. It was summer and I'd come home to Dublin for a visit, see my brother and his fiancée, meet up with some friends. The problem was, I'd committed to staying at Mam's for the duration. I was only back a day before she started in with the usual comments.

*When are you ever going to meet a man and settle down?*

*Those baggy jeans do nothing for your figure.*

*Going out with you when you're dressed like that is embarrassing.*

*No man is going to want to marry a girl with so many opinions.*

*Have you considered coming with me for a Brazilian wax? Men love it when you're smooth.* (I'd blushed like a maniac after that one.)

*Would you please do something different with your hair? Looking at all those colors is giving me a headache.*

So yeah, even though it was wrong on so many levels, stealing was that hit of relief I needed in order to deal with my mother's constant criticism. In fact, I'd come by it rather by accident. One day I'd been on the phone to her while in a deli, she'd been berating me for something, and I'd been so stressed that I'd walked out before paying. An odd relief hit me when I realized I'd stolen, even if it was inadvertently. After that the compulsion grew and grew, until it was completely out of control . . . it was getting out of control again.

My need for relief won out over my feelings of guilt. I snagged the bottle, dropped it discreetly into my bag and turned to leave. I'd just stepped away from the aisle toward the exit when a voice called, "Hey! Wait."

My heart began to race and heat flooded my cheeks. I'd been caught. It wouldn't be the first time, but still, it didn't get any less embarrassing or anxiety inducing to be found stealing. Nothing else for it, I turned and was met with a pair of eager brown eyes. Those eyes belonged to a young guy, about my age, and also an employee of the shop. I waited for the expected spiel. He was going to ask me to step back inside so he could search my bag, and then the humiliation and shame would follow. I most definitely deserved it.

"Lucy? Lucy Fitzpatrick?" he asked hesitantly.

I glanced from side to side. How did he know my name? "Uh, yeah."

He smiled. "I'm Ben, Ben O'Connor. We went to school together, remember? I used to sit by you in History."

Now that I looked at him properly, I did remember. I think I asked to borrow his pencil sharpener once. It was a surprise I could recall him, because normally I had a memory like a sieve. I actually had to use tricks sometimes in order to recall people's names. For instance, when I first met my new friend in New York, Broderick, I kept envisioning him in a brown hat with helicopter wings and a long trench coat. That way my brain could make the connection to Inspector Gadget being played in the movie by Matthew Broderick, hence my new friend's name was Broderick.

"Oh yeah," I smiled, while on the inside I was crapping myself. Had he seen me taking the nail polish? "I remember now. It's been a while.

How are you doing these days?"

"Great," he replied with enthusiasm and I tried to return it.

"That's good. That's great."

He nodded and slipped his hands in his pockets. "Yeah."

A few seconds of awkward silence ensued and I wanted to leave. Ben was being friendly, and he seemed like a lovely guy, but I was still panicking over the nail polish. Stupid tempting canary yellow. How was I supposed to resist such vibrancy? *How?*

"You look different these days," Ben said finally.

I laughed nervously. "Different good or different bad?"

He shrugged. "Just different."

"Must be that sex change I put in for," I said and winced. I always made weird jokes when anxious.

Ben gave me a consolation laugh but he clearly didn't see the humor. I didn't blame him. I was so odd sometimes. He cleared his throat. "So, you know I'm a massive rugby fan, right?"

My stomach dropped a little at his question. For a second I thought he might be chatting me up, but no, this was about Ronan. I loved my brother to pieces, but his career meant that people often wanted to be friends with me because of who I shared DNA with. Kind of depressing, but I always tried to look on the bright side. Outweighing negativity with positivity was the key to a happy life, and being related to a famous person brought with it many advantages. I always tried to concentrate on those. Plus, I was a naturally happy and bubbly person when I wasn't dealing with my mam's undermining influence.

"Oh, you are? That's cool."

Ben nodded. "So, do you think maybe you could get me into tonight's party? I'd love to go and meet the team. Seriously, it'd be a dream come true."

The Irish squad had just played their last game of the season, and tonight there was a celebration going on to mark the occasion.

"Um, I'm not actually sure I can swing that, Ben. The party's in a couple of hours," I told him honestly.

All of a sudden, Ben's expression changed. He no longer appeared sheepishly polite. Now he seemed cynical – cocky even. He stepped forward and narrowed his gaze. "Get me into the party and I won't tell my manager about the nail crap you just stole."

My heart pounded and I swallowed harshly, stunned by his sudden personality change.

My attention flickered to the older man who was manning the service counter. It was ridiculous, but I felt a bit like crying. Sometimes I was so naïve, so gullible. Ben wasn't lovely. He was trying to blackmail me. I didn't cry, but I felt like it.

"All right then," I told him. "I'll make sure your name is on the guest list."

I turned to leave.

"With a plus one?" Ben called after me. Negative thoughts tried to flood my mind but I pushed them back, repeating a few lines from the *Tao Te Ching* I often used while meditating. Ah, that was better. I was calmer now.

"Yes, Ben, with a plus one."

***

ON THE WAY home I dropped the nail polish into a charity collection box. I knew it was a weird thing to donate, but I thought maybe the bright color would put a smile on some poor woman's face. I certainly didn't deserve to keep it. I rarely kept the things I stole—giving them to charity or people I thought needed them.

Later that evening, I got ready for the party. My dress was cream lace, sort of floaty, and I wore my hair down with a single daisy clip at the side. I was sitting in a VIP room at the back of the venue with my brother, his fiancée Annie, and a couple of Ronan's teammates. We were enjoying a few bottles of champagne and discussing the success the Irish squad had enjoyed during the year. Mam was elsewhere, socializing with the other team mothers, and I was glad. I just wanted to enjoy my night without her saying something about how unattractive or embarrassing I was.

We were all having a great time until the door swung open and Mr. Tall, Blond and Up Himself walked in. That would be Sean Cassidy to those not in the know, Sleazy Sean, as nicknamed by the rugby club. I tried to always see the good in people, but he and my brother didn't have the best relationship. Not only had Sean slept with Brona, Ronan's ex-girlfriend, but he was also universally acknowledged to be an arsehole.

It went against everything I believed in to say, because I liked to think everyone was redeemable in some way, but Sean just wasn't a nice person. He actually seemed to be proud about the fact, like he wanted people to dislike him.

The conversation died down, everybody casting surreptitious glances at Sean who swaggered his way up to the private bar and loudly ordered a bottle of bubbly. That's actually what he called it, but speaking of *bubbly* . . .

Almost of their own accord, my eyes wandered over his broad shoulders, muscular back, and down to what must have been the most perfect bubble butt I'd ever seen. You know how sometimes male athletes develop those really defined, rounded but masculine derrieres?

Well, Sean Cassidy was most definitely rocking one of those, and I couldn't resist the urge to ogle it. It was pure muscle and simply bite-worthy.

I snickered to myself when I realized I'd almost commented on it out loud. Okay, I'd officially had too many glasses of "bubbly" as Sean so douchebaggedly called it. He must have heard my snicker because his attention landed on me. He stared at me for a second, arched a condescending brow, then dismissed me all in an instant, returning his attention to the bar.

*Huh.*

After about thirty seconds everyone went back to their conversations, trying their best to ignore Sean. Ronan had told me once that Sean was the kind of person who thrived on attention, so ignoring his presence was probably the best course of action to take.

It was my own fault I couldn't stop staring. We'd never spoken before. In fact, I'd only ever seen him from afar at parties like this one, or on television when there was a match on. But right now he was close, close enough for me to realize just how devastatingly and legitimately handsome he was: light blue eyes, a strong jaw, nice lips, attractive nose.

*Sigh.*

Why were the beautiful ones always such pricks, huh?

He leaned back against the bar, having uncorked the champagne bottle and poured some into a glass. He wore a shit-eating grin as he stared right at Ronan, holding the glass to his lips, his pinky popped. I knew he was getting to Ronan when my brother muttered to Annie under his breath, "Is he fucking shitting me?"

Annie sat beside her fiancé, wearing a gorgeous blue dress and looking worried. She quietly placed her hand on Ronan's thigh in an effort to soothe him.

Sean just kept on smiling while Ronan became more and more aggravated. It was only another minute or two before my brother finally snapped.

"All right, Cassidy, you've clearly got something to say, so say it," Ronan announced loudly. "And put your fucking pinky down."

Sean's lips moved in something akin to satisfaction as he wiggled his little finger. "What? This pinky? Do I challenge your Neanderthal notions of masculinity, Fitzpatrick? Or do raised pinky fingers turn you on?"

"Don't give me that. You're about as gay as a Snoop Dogg music video. Now spit it out."

Sean gave Ronan a bored look then cast his eyes across the room to one of the new players, an American guy named William Moore.

He pointed his finger at him; his index finger, not his pinky finger. "I know you're fixing to have this hillbilly replace me. Well, let me tell you right here and now, it's not gonna happen."

William was built like a brick shithouse and came from a small farming town in Oklahoma. His mother was of Irish descent and he originally played for a semi-professional team back in the States. William was also one of the kindest, most well-mannered men I'd ever met, so it irked me that Sean was targeting him.

It seemed to be irking everyone else, too, and I noticed a number of the guys bristle, their postures growing stiff. Sean wasn't doing himself any favors by calling out William. Everybody loved William.

"You're being paranoid," said Ronan. "No one's looking to replace you, Cassidy. Despite the fact that we'd all like to shove your head down a toilet most days, you're unfortunately talented. It's the only reason we put up with your piss-poor personality."

Sean didn't seem to hear the veiled compliment Ronan had given him, and instead focused on the insult. "That's funny, because your girls have a history of finding my personality irresistible. Or maybe they just find you lacking." His glacial eyes slithered to my brother's fiancée, "It's really just a matter of time."

Ronan stood from his seat and took a step forward. Annie tried to grab his hand and pull him back down but he was already gone. Before we knew it he was inches away from Sean, glaring daggers.

"If you want to keep playing for this team then you'll shut your fecking face right now."

Sean stared at him, apparently unaffected by Ronan's aggression. "Oh, so now you have a say in who does and doesn't play for the team? I failed to receive the memo regarding your promotion to our manager."

"Leave. Now," said Ronan, his jaw working. If I knew my brother, it was taking a great effort for him not to deck Sean right then. He had a notoriously short fuse, and Sean Cassidy was an expert at knowing how to light it.

Barely a second passed before several of the guys were up from their seats and leading Sean out of the room. He went, but not before flashing Ronan an immense, challenging smile as he left. Ronan sat back down beside Annie, who gave him a soft kiss on the lips and whispered in his ear. I guessed she was telling him not to let Sean get to him.

I knew she meant well, but there was too much animosity between the two men for them to just let it go. Granted, I'd only ever been an outsider looking in, but if I knew anything about rugby, I knew it was chock-full of testosterone and egos, and those two were not a good mix.

After a few minutes, everybody seemed to settle down. Though after

Sean's appearance, our cheerful gathering wasn't quite as jovial as before. Needing to pee, I left the private party and went in search of a bathroom. I was just leaving a stall when I saw Mam standing by the makeup counter, re-applying her lipstick. Her blue eyes caught on me and she gave me her usual expression. It was neither a smile nor a frown, but something in between, a grimace masquerading as a grin.

"Lucy, where have you been all evening? I've wanted to introduce you to the son of a friend of mine. He's a real dish, owns his own company and everything."

"Oh," I said, noncommittally.

I washed and dried my hands, then Mam slipped her arm through mine. "Come on, we can go find him now." Her eyes went to my hair for a second and she sighed regretfully. I knew she was embarrassed by it. In a way, that was one of the main reasons why I did it. In another way, it wasn't. I wanted to be able to express myself in a manner that made me happy. And having hair a color that couldn't be found in nature did exactly that.

We were just leaving the bathroom when I tried to pull my arm from hers. "Maybe later, Mam. I promised Annie I'd be back soon. We've a lot of work stuff to discuss."

"This is a party, Lucy. Work can wait for another day."

I stood my ground, planting my feet firmly on the floor and not allowing her to lead me any farther. I knew my mother had her own issues and insecurities; however, she still stressed me out. I wished things could be different, but it was often hard to be around her.

"No, Mam, I'm going back to Annie. I don't want to meet your friend's son."

She gaped at me, as though surprised by my outburst. I was a little surprised myself. Often I went along with her wishes because I didn't want to upset anyone. A few moments elapsed, and I couldn't tell if she was going to lose it with me or not.

In the end she didn't, probably because there were too many people about. She plastered the fakest smile I'd ever seen on her face and said, "Okay, darling. You go to Annie. Enjoy the party as much as you can. I'll see you back at the house."

And with that she turned and strode off. I knew her last line wasn't as benign as she made it sound. The second I got home tonight I'd be in for it. Yes, she'd hold back all her dissatisfaction until then, when there were no watchful eyes about to witness it. The thought made me start to wish there was something around that I could steal . . . maybe a few champagne glasses. They'd fit in my handbag, right?

God, I was a mess.

Letting out a long sigh, I slumped back against the wall. Pulling my phone from my bag, I checked to see if I had any messages. I had one and it was from Annie. Reading it made me smile and drove away most of my thieving urges.

**Annie:** *If we locked your brother and Sean in a room, what do you think the odds would be on whether they'd murder each other or start crying while having an emotional heart-to-heart?*

I snorted and typed out a quick reply.

**Lucy:** *I'd say that's a ratio of 1,000,000: 0, my friend.*

Although we didn't actually live in the same country, Annie and I had become extremely close over the last few months. I was her sounding board and advice-giver on how to deal with Ronan, and she was my guru and advice-giver on how to survive living in New York. Plus, we worked together to create humorous blog posts about ridiculous celebrities. Tell me two girls who wouldn't bond over that? I swear most of our Skype calls have consisted of ninety-five percent giggling and five percent actual conversation.

Slipping my phone in my bag, I turned to go back to the VIP room and collided with a body. That body was large and male, and appeared to be wearing a very nice suit. It only took a split second for me to recognize the suit. It belonged to Sean Cassidy, who was currently glaring at me.

"Watch where you're going, Mini-Fitzpatrick," he said, hostility in his voice. Clearly, being Ronan's sister meant I was enemy number one to him.

I lifted my hands in the air and replied humorously, "Sorry, Bubs. I'll try to be more careful next time."

One sardonic eyebrow went up. "Bubs?"

I almost laughed when I realized what I'd called him. It was all to do with his glorious bubble butt, of course, but no way was I telling him that. I didn't need to start blushing like a maniac in front of him.

"I've decided to name you after your favorite beverage, Bubbly," I said, trying to lure a smile out of him. Ronan always said I was too nice for my own good and let people take advantage, but maybe Sean wasn't as bad as everyone thought. Maybe he had some good in him somewhere. Or maybe I was just tipsy.

I thought I saw his lips twitch in amusement, but then he grew hostile again. "I thought girls such as yourself limited their repertoires to alco-pops and daiquiris with tacky umbrellas."

His smile was as condescending as his tone and he made a move to walk away. Still, there was something defensive about how he said it that made me think his comment was a pre-emptive strike. He thought that because I was Ronan's sister I automatically hated him, so he'd show he hated me right back. Hmm . . .

"You seem tense, maybe you should try meditation," I suggested.

He stopped and turned back around. "Pardon?"

"Yogi Bhajan meditation is supposed to work wonders. For me, personally, yoga works a treat. I go in all tense and stressed and come out light and airy. Seriously, consider it. You'll be amazed by the results."

This suggestion seemed to both annoy and fluster him. "What are you rambling about?"

I took a few steps forward until I was standing directly in front of him. "You obviously have some unresolved issues and you're using my brother as an outlet for your aggression. I'm trying to suggest some ways to deal with your anger. Oh, and you know what else is great for managing stress? Full immersion relaxation and detox, like going to a yoga retreat. In fact, I'm doing one when I return to the States next week. It's in Squam Lake, gorgeous place. I'm really looking forward to it. You should think about going."

Of course, I wasn't at all serious, but I was tipsy and chatty and felt a bit sorry for him. There was something about Sean Cassidy that reminded me of the dogs that came into the shelter in New York, abused and mistreated, barking at everyone because they didn't know who to trust. Obviously, it was a ridiculous notion. Sean wasn't a rescue dog, he was a primped and pampered thoroughbred.

He listened to me speak, but his eyes weren't on my face. Instead they wandered from my bare arms and shoulders before landing on my chest. I had this small beauty mark close to my collarbone, and he was currently staring at it as though he wanted to get up real close and personal with it.

Whoa, this was not what I'd expected *at all*, but having him look at me the way he was looking at me right then, well, it made my skin tingle.

He took a step forward and into my space, his size and closeness dizzying, and deadpanned, "Aren't those retreats just an excuse for hippies to get together in the middle of nowhere, eat granola, and have group sex?"

The way he spoke made my tingles instantly vanish. Ronan was right. Sean *was* an arsehole. And I was a softhearted fool to think there was something more beneath his sleek and polished surface. We were from two different worlds. He'd grown up in South Dublin, an adopted son in a privileged house. Whereas I'd grown up in North Dublin, in the working class area. My mother had worked two jobs, barely putting food on the table. Everything, from the differences in our accents to our divergent attitudes, put us worlds apart.

"No actually, it's an excuse to go somewhere beautiful, meet amazing people and clear your mind, but I wouldn't expect you to understand that." And with that I turned on my heel and attempted to walk a straight line back to the party.

It could have been my imagination, but I felt his eyes on me the entire time and I may have quickened my unsteady pace until I was safely beyond the privacy door. I hated that he got to me. I was supposed to be the calm one, the enlightened one, and yet with just a few carefully chosen words he'd made me want to throttle him. I now totally understood Ronan's hatred for the guy.

I always tried to believe everybody had the potential to be good, to be redeemed. But this guy might just be the one to prove me wrong.

Yes, as far as I was concerned, Sean Cassidy was completely, irrevocably, and unequivocally irredeemable.

# Chapter Two

*There are three certainties in life, death, taxes, and the cold dread of attending another family gathering.*

-Sean Cassidy.

**\*Sean\***

SOMEBODY NEEDED TO explain to me why mobile phone cameras made that *click* sound whenever a photo was taken. Could you not *see* a photo had been taken? That was like adding sound effects to a salt shaker. Clearly, I saw that my food was being salted. I could taste the salt. I didn't require additional sensory information alerting me that my food had been salted.

I hadn't opened my eyes yet, but I was awake. I could hear her snapping pictures of me, so I decided to wait until she finished. No need to make things uncomfortable.

Hopefully I didn't have drool crusted at the corner of my mouth, and she hadn't drawn on my face. If memory served, she hadn't seemed the sort. Those pictures were trophies for girls like her.

I felt her still-naked body slither along mine, and her hair brushed against my bare shoulder. From the angle of her posturing, I deduced she was now taking selfies with me . . . while I slept.

*No. That's not distressing at all. Perfectly normal behavior. Just pose with the unconscious man, nothing strange about it. I'm sure plenty of people enjoy having their picture taken while they're asleep . . .*

Bloody weirdo.

She leaned away, likely to scroll through her trophy pictures, and I felt her shift on the mattress into a sitting position. Her long fake nails clicked against her phone's touch screen, the sound incredibly irritating.

That was my cue to exit.

I stretched my arms, careful to avoid touching her, and made a big show of arching my back before I opened my eyes. This gave her plenty of time to hide her phone if she felt guilty about being an opportunist. When I opened my eyes, I avoided making contact with hers. I've found it's best to set expectations on a proper course as early as possible in a non-relationship.

"Well, good morning handsome." She slid into the sheets again, her claws coming to my torso.

I glanced at her hands. No sign of the phone. She must've hid it in her bedside table. This was a relief; the less inconspicuous of her kind often requested more pictures over breakfast. The answer was always no. I never ate meals with the help.

I hadn't been drunk last night when I suggested we party. I'd been cold. Ireland is cold year round, even in the summer. And I am likewise cold, unless I can locate a warm body and share her bed.

The woman snuggled against me. Her skin had been soft last night, but now—bathed in daylight—it felt like sandpaper. I peeled her from me, no longer cold, and then sat on the edge of the bed and rubbed sleep from my eyes.

"What time is it?"

"Just past seven," she purred, her nails scratching lightly down my back.

"Stop touching me. Where the feck are my pants?"

She jerked her hand away with a little gasp and was mercifully silent as I scanned the room.

Sex was usually the price I paid for a night of warmth, which made no sense because my nameless partners always faked it, even when I ate them out. They faked it loudly, and with enthusiasm, and sometimes with impressive creativity. But faked nevertheless.

Just once, I wanted to see and hear and feel a woman truly orgasm. Just. Fucking. Once. I'm beginning to doubt women are capable of climaxing. The great female-orgasm myth . . .

"No need to be such an arsehole." She'd recovered the ability to speak. I wished she hadn't.

I was going to be late for Sunday breakfast with *the family* if I didn't get up and out. If I missed breakfast then I'd be subjected to months of passive-aggressive reminders of my tardiness for *that one time,* and be on the hook for a year's worth of favors.

"I need to piss." I stood from the bed and crossed her tiny Dublin flat to the door I assumed was her toilet, finding my pants on the way and pulling them on. I shut and locked the door—just in case she had any ideas about snapping more pictures—and did my business, rinsing off her toothbrush with Listerine before brushing my teeth with it.

I had a ritual when I cleaned up after a night of inane debauchery. Disinfecting the toothbrush, going through the medicine cabinet for aspirin, washing my face with their soap—as long as it didn't smell of flowers or food. One-night stands were worth it just for cosmetic product discoverability.

About six months ago I shagged a woman and used her facial

cleanser. Great stuff, unscented, gentle but left the skin thoroughly cleaned. I couldn't tell you *her* name or what she looked like, but I could tell you she used a cleanser named *Simple* to wash her face. I knew this because on my way home, I'd stopped by Boots and picked it up in bulk.

"What are you doing in there?" Last night's warm body tested the door handle.

I ignored her question and smelled her soap. It smelled like cake. I placed it back on the tray, unused. Why do women want to smell like cake?

If I want cake, I'll eat cake.

If I want a woman, I'll eat a woman.

I heard her huff, it sounded nervous. "How much longer are you going to be?"

I took one more look in her medicine cabinet and found a lotion sample. Unopened. I cracked it open and sniffed . . . *sandalwood.* I squeezed out a dot on the back of my hand, and it went on light and silky. I pocketed it.

"Hey!" She pounded on the door. "What are you doing—"

I yanked it open before she completed the question, causing her to stumble back, startled. I have that effect on people because I'm not small. Truth be told, I'm quite large. I'm larger than was polite or appropriate, as my family frequently reminded me. *Imposing,* my aunt called it.

But I'd like to think I'm also agile, especially for my size.

Tapping into this agility, I maneuvered around the warm body and located my shirt and jacket, pulling them on as she watched. I didn't waste time looking for my tie, instead claiming my shoes and socks, and sitting on a sad little bench by the front door.

Out of the corner of my eye, I saw her take a few timid steps toward me; she was in a bathrobe and her arms were crossed over her chest. "Have you lost your voice? Because you were chatty enough last night."

"No," I said, finished with my right sock and moving to the left.

"Is this a brush-off, then?"

"Yes." I really liked my shoes. I reminded myself to find a pair in brown.

She sniffled. She was crying. I rolled my eyes. Sometimes they cried. Sometimes they cried buckets. I'm never moved by displays of overt mawkishness, especially when I could count on being tagged in a half hour on Twitter when she posted the pictures of me sleeping.

I stood and buttoned my shirt, then checked my back pocket to make sure I still had my wallet and phone. I did.

So I left.

I didn't have time to stop by the shop and search for the mystery sandalwood lotion before breakfast, as I still needed to shower, shave, and dress properly. But I promised myself, if I could make it through the morning without entertaining any games of passive-aggressive superiority, I'd pick up a bottle on my way home.

Who was I kidding? Most of my family detested me. I'd pick up the lotion either way.

\*\*\*

**"DO SIT DOWN**, Sean. You are quite too tall to stand." My aunt waved her napkin at me, then added under her breath, "Excessively imposing." She set the linen in her lap with a graceful movement, the kind that takes years to perfect but appeared effortless.

As she'd told me on numerous occasions, appearance was all that mattered.

Presently, I was standing—which she hated—at the breakfast buffet in her sunroom. The serving spoon I held, suspended in the air between the silver warming dish and my plate. My plate was empty. I hadn't a chance to put any food on it yet as I'd just stood from the table.

"Once I'm finished at the buffet, I will sit down." I was careful not to sound irritated. Any display of emotion was frowned upon and blamed on my regrettable parentage.

"If you must." I wasn't looking at her, but I could see her in my mind's eye, sipping her tea with great effect. My standing was likely the most inconvenienced she'd been all week.

All six cousins were gathered, but Uncle Peter was absent. He'd been increasingly absent over the last few months, though no one had remarked on it. The lack of explanation led me to believe Uncle Peter, my mother's brother, decided to spend more time with his other family in the country.

My uncle's longstanding infidelity was the worst-kept secret in Dublin society, one that gave Aunt Cara the elevated rank of martyred saint amongst the social elite.

"That shindig last night was a complete bore, Sean. Sorry waste of an evening. I don't know why I allowed you to talk me into going." This statement came from my oldest cousin Grady, and my hand tightened on the serving spoon.

Grady was a banker, six inches shorter than me, and a complete eejit. He'd begged me for those tickets last week, then showed up with six friends instead of one, forcing me to pull several strings so they'd all be given admittance.

What I wanted to say: "I'm not surprised. Your staggeringly irrelevant existence meant every night was a bore."

What I actually said: "I found the evening lacking as well."

Both statements were equally true. But just as I finished speaking, the unbidden memory of Ronan Fitzpatrick's sister flashed through my mind giving me pause. *Mini-Fitzpatrick* I'd called her, but she hadn't looked or behaved like her brother.

His manner was that of an ape—reactionary, resorting to violence and threats his only strategy. I, on the other hand, preferred a different approach.

He hadn't done any one thing in specific to earn my hatred. He ignored me mostly. Though it irked, being arguably the best player on the team and having my captain dismiss my efforts as mediocre, I might have overlooked his slights.

But after years of taking a back seat to his popularity and having the first question asked of me during any interview, *What's it like to work with Ronan Fitzpatrick?* I was sick of him. I wanted him gone.

The fact that he was universally liked by everyone else only made me resent him more.

Yes, Ronan was a primate. Sadly, he was a talented primate irritatingly adept at getting people to like him, a skill I'd never mastered.

But his sister was different. She reminded me of a . . . well, of a fairy: cheerful, thoughtful, and adorably curious. I frowned because *adorable* wasn't the right word.

*Seductive.*

Seductively curious.

*Much better.*

A new image, one of Mini-Fitzpatrick lying on her back—shyly covering her sweet curves with a sheet, that delicious beauty mark just visible, her rainbow hair spread over a white pillow—made me wonder why I'd been so belligerent with her last night.

I wondered if she dyed the carpet to match the drapes. It certainly would give a new meaning to the candy slogan, *Taste the Rainbow.*

These were inconvenient thoughts for a Sunday morning breakfast with the Cassidy corpses. I reluctantly pushed the image away, recalling instead her irritated expression just before she'd walked away.

At one point, despite my sordid history with her brother, I suspected she was actually trying to be nice.

This gave me another pause.

I was glaring at the kippers when my cousin Eilish, the only decent one in the lot of us, challenged Grady. "Didn't you beg Sean for those tickets?"

"What? Not at all." He sounded offended by the suggestion.

"Yeah, you did. You were salivating all over him last week."

"Eilish! Do you really have to use such language?" My aunt punctuated her disapproval by sniffing.

"Which word gives offense, Mother? *Salivating*?"

"Can we refrain from discussing such things? Is this another of Sean's influences?"

"No, Mother. I've been home from university for two days and at no point has Sean advocated I discuss saliva."

"Oh! That word." A teacup clattered, highlighting my aunt's distress.

I hadn't realized Eilish would be home from school so early. She'd been sent to boarding schools since she was ten, proving to be too boisterous and unmanageable for my aunt's temperament. But she'd always spent the summers at the tomb in Dublin.

Sorry. Did I say tomb? I meant house.

I was careful to wipe the smirk from my face before I turned to the breakfast table, and was equally careful to avoid Eilish's gaze. If I were caught smiling I'd never hear the end of it.

Meanwhile, Eilish asked the table if anyone had read the latest report on the refugee crisis and was chided for placing her elbows on the table. My aunt made several unflattering comments comparing Eilish to a barnyard animal.

The berating wasn't too scathing and E didn't seem bothered by it. Still, my aunt's comments tend to turn abusive without much warning. I kept an ear in the conversation, just in case I needed to throw myself on the grenade of Aunt Cara's temper.

True to form, none of my other cousins made any outward sign of hearing anything untoward.

Theresa remarked on the weather before she took a bite of her buttered toast.

Brigid sedately asked after Connor's new Bentley.

Liam unobtrusively poured himself another cup of coffee without glancing up from the newspaper.

I followed their example. If I kept quiet, masked all outward expression except boredom, I'd be free of this house within the half hour. And when I left, I knew without a doubt I'd be cold again.

I was always cold when I left the house where I grew up.

\*\*\*

"DID YOU SEE her face? When I said saliva? I thought she might faint." Eilish snickered on a whisper, helping me with my jacket.

"You shouldn't poke the bear," I warned, shaking my head at her, my face drawn with disapproval I tried to feel. Instead I was fighting a smile.

Eilish was perhaps the only person in my life who could make me smile. She was so good.

Well, she had a good heart, but enjoyed testing her mother's patience.

She shrugged. "What can she do? Yell at me? I'm no longer a child."

I smirked at my cousin, saying nothing. I hadn't missed how she still cut the crust off her toast and added too much sugar to her tea during breakfast.

"Be good and I'll take you shopping this week."

We were still whispering because the large marble entryway echoed. I'd offered to let her stay at my flat on more than once occasion. But I think—despite their tenuous relationship—Eilish felt sorry for her mother. She didn't want to leave her completely alone during the summer.

I wanted to tell my cousin her efforts were wasted, but didn't want to be unkind. Nor did I wish to be the source of her eventual and unavoidable disillusionment. I liked Eilish as she was. She was certainly clever, but her spirit was currently unencumbered by the burdens of reality.

If Eilish still held hope for warmth from Aunt Clara, I wasn't going to be the one to burst her bubble. Let her be naïve and hopeful. Yet I dreaded the day she discovered all her efforts were in vain.

She'd learn eventually it's much better to preemptively numb oneself against disappointment.

"You'll take me shopping even if I'm not good." Eilish laughed at me, tilting her head to the side as she studied my face. "You can't help yourself, especially when you see me in mismatched shades of navy."

She was right, of course. But she was also wrong. I couldn't help but take her shopping because seeing her happy inexplicably made me happy. Yet she was also wrong, because I used her mismatched outfits as an excuse. I'd never tell her that. It was part of the game we played.

She pretended she couldn't coordinate her outfits and I pretended it drove me to distraction. I wasn't in so much denial to realize I needed Eilish quite a bit more than she needed me.

"Thursday. Ten o'clock. We'll have tea after, if you're fit to be seen." I kept my tone dry and superior, because doing so made her laugh harder.

"Jesus, Sean. You sound like such a snob."

"Thank you, what a lovely compliment."

This made her snort and smack my shoulder with the flat of her palm. "Get out of here before you're caught making me laugh. They'll never forgive you for being cheerful."

I smiled down at my cousin, wishing again she'd come with me. Having her around during the summer, someone clever to talk to, someone with no expectations, trustworthy—someone good—was the highlight of my year. I knew her reasoning for staying within these cold walls during the summer months, but for her sake, as well as for my own selfish purposes, I wished she'd change her mind.

Before I could suggest—again—that she move in with me for the summer, my aunt called, "Eilish? Come here. It's time to read my letters."

I sighed, watching Eilish's profile as she responded, "Coming, Mother. I'm just seeing Sean off."

"He can find the door on his own. I need you," came her reply.

Eilish smiled a small, pleased smile. And my chest ached at her expression. The words *I need you* still had an effect on my cousin, though they filled me with dread.

Because my aunt needed people until she didn't. Then she'd cast them away. I recognized the manipulation, had hardened myself against it. Eilish had not.

At least, not yet.

# Chapter Three

@**LucyFitz** Always trust in the kindness of strangers…except when it comes in the form of a glass of sauvignon blanc you haven't seen them pour.

@**RonanFitz to** @**LucyFitz** What's going on?! Is some creep offering to buy you drinks?

@**LucyFitz to** @**RonanFitz** Chillax. It's supposed to be humorous.

@**RonanFitz to** @**LucyFitz** Well I don't find the concept of messing with my sister funny.

@**Anniecat to** @**LucyFitz** I apologize for your brother.

### *Lucy*

**"DO YOU WANT** anything from the shop?" definitely ranked as one of my top three favorite sentences of all time. It's right up there with, "School's been cancelled because of the weather" and "Would you like me to go down on you first?"

Admittedly, I'd only been asked the third one twice, and both instances were quite some time ago.

When we were kids, Ronan always used to ask me if I wanted anything from the shop, and my answer was always the same: a can of Coke, a bar of chocolate, and a packet of crisps. We used to call it the

Triple C. Shut up. It wasn't lame.

These days I still wanted things from the shop. Things I hadn't paid for.

Well, perhaps it wasn't so much the things, but the feeling that taking things gave me. I was addicted to that feeling though a large part of me hated it.

It was the evening after the party and my hangover had almost faded. I'd taken the DART into town to meet up with an old friend for coffee. We'd parted ways a half hour ago and I was currently browsing the cosmetics section of Brown Thomas, a glamorous blonde in an all-black ensemble watching me like a hawk.

"Can I help you with anything?" she asked with a smile.

"I'm good, just looking," I answered, returning the friendly gesture.

I couldn't allow myself to be annoyed with her. She was only doing her job. I was the one in the wrong. My fingers itched with the need to *take,* as I remembered Mam berating me when I got home last night. I'd been rude enough to avoid meeting her friend's very eligible son, and behavior like that was sacrilege to Jackie Fitzpatrick.

*Your looks, such as they are, aren't going to last forever, Lucy. Before you know it you'll be forty and still on the shelf.*

I had to bite back the urge to respond with some equally horrible comment, refusing to sink to her level. I was already allowing myself to become a secret thief. I wouldn't lower myself to being mean on top of it.

"Pardon me, but I'm looking for this cream, do you sell it?" a recognizable voice asked, pulling me from my thoughts. Glancing up, I saw Sean Cassidy speaking to the blonde, holding out an opened sample. Of all the gin joints . . .I knew Dublin was small, but it couldn't possibly be this small.

After our encounter last night, I really wasn't in the mood for a second round with Bubs and his abrasive personality, which was saying something. Loud, quiet, sassy, reserved, they were all a part of life's color. But Sean Cassidy, well, he was something else entirely.

Keeping my head down, I swiftly turned to leave.

"Mini-Fitzpatrick, what are the chances?" he said, almost happily, and I exhaled a quick breath. There was something in me that just wasn't rude enough to ignore him, even if he didn't deserve my politeness. I turned back around.

"How's it going, Bubs?"

What? If I couldn't be rude then I could at least amuse myself.

He smiled widely. "Better now that I've bumped into you."

What was with the personality change? He looked genuinely pleased to see me. I glanced around for hidden cameras.

"And if you really want to name me after a drink, then I insist you call me Macallan," he went on. "Because I'm unquestionably both rare and *fine*." His eyes heated and he leveled me with yet another smile, this one smoldering. Was I being hit with the infamous Cassidy charm? I hated to admit that it felt sort of . . . exciting. Letting my eyes travel down his muscular physique, I imagined he'd be an absolute animal in the sack. It was a pity I could never let myself go there.

I mustered a laugh. "Wow, modest."

He grinned.

"Sir, we have 200 milliliter and 500 milliliter bottles, which would you prefer?" the sales assistant interrupted, calling Sean's attention away. While they were both distracted, I took the opportunity to slide a compact of eyeshadow into my handbag.

*Zing, zing, zing* went the familiar rush in my belly. Ah, sweet relief. I missed you, old friend.

"I'll take the 500 milliliter, please," said Sean with disinterest as he handed her a card.

"Well, I'd better get going," I hurried to say. "See you around."

With extra speediness I walked off, and I was just exiting the store when someone clamped their hand around my elbow. I stilled in fear, thinking it was a security guard. But then I looked up into Sean's light blue eyes and my pulse slowed.

"Not so fast, Mini-Fitzpatrick," he said, bending so his mouth brushed my ear. "Don't you know it's rude to just run off on people like that? I wanted to speak with you."

We were out the door and on the street when I pulled my arm from his hold.

"My name's Lucy," I told him.

"Fine then. Are you hungry, *Lucy*?" he asked, emphasizing my name as his eyes flickered between mine.

I wasn't a suspicious person, but Sean's question got me wondering. "What's your game?"

"My game is buying you dinner, and maybe discussing the small matter of the item you just stole. Is Ronan such a tightwad he allows his family to shoplift to get by these days?" he asked with what sounded like amusement.

My heart hammered, wondering how he'd seen. For a moment I was frozen with anxiety, unsure how to respond, but then I grew defensive.

"That's none of your business," I stated, trying to stay calm.

I moved to stride past him but he placed himself in my path, and let's face it, he was more than broad enough to block my passage.

"Now, now, there's no need to be like that," he chided, clicking his tongue and looking down at me. "We'll dine at Marco Pierre's, my treat."

"No, thank you," I stood firm.

"Eat with me or I'll walk right back inside and inform the head of security about your sticky fingers."

This riled me, and I couldn't believe I'd been spotted thieving for the second time in less than two days. My skills were seriously slipping. "Are you so hard up for company that you have to resort to blackmail?"

Sean studied me, his features softening. "I don't want to argue with you, Lucy. What's the harm of one dinner?"

There was something in the way he spoke that drained the fight out of me. "Just let me leave, please," I whispered, staring at the ground now. He was silent for a long moment, long enough that I had to look up. His face was even softer than before and I inhaled sharply.

Reaching out, he slid a hand down my arm, his touch soothing. "Come now, one meal won't kill you," he murmured.

I searched his eyes. "Why?"

He shrugged, then glanced away as he answered, "I'm cold."

I left him waiting a while before I finally replied, with no small amount of wariness, "Okay, but I'm ordering the most expensive thing on the menu."

Now he smiled, like the idea of spending money on me pleased him. "Be my guest."

With that he surprised me by offering his arm, like a gentleman, and we began the short walk to the restaurant. I was struck by the unexpectedness of the situation, but hey, sometimes the best things came from the unexpected.

There was a minute or two of quiet before Sean spoke, "So, is it an adrenaline thing? Or do you really not have enough money for whatever it is you took?" He glanced at me, seeming genuinely interested.

"Can we not talk about this?" Already the buzz of stealing had faded as guilt and shame rose to the fore. Would that shop assistant be punished for what I took? Perhaps I could return tomorrow and buy a bunch of makeup. Those sorts of jobs worked on commission, right? I bit my lip, worrying over it.

Sean shot me a sideways grin, not letting the subject drop. "But the psychology of the whole thing fascinates me. I mean, here you have the sister of a very wealthy rugby star stealing trinkets and baubles for her own entertainment. It'd make one hell of a headline for the red tops."

I stopped walking immediately, threw myself in front of him and placed my hands on his stocky chest. Unable to help the desperation in my voice, I pleaded, "Sean." I paused, making an effort to summon some calm, and failing. "P-please don't sell this story to a newspaper. I know you hate my brother, and he's hardly your biggest fan, but this would humiliate my entire family and I'm already such a disappointment to my mother as it is."

He swallowed, something like understanding in his eyes as he took me in. "I have no plans to do so," he said, appearing uncomfortable for a brief second while he cleared his throat. "Just as long as anything we talk about today stays between us. Agreed?" he continued stiffly. His earnestness took me by surprise.

I nodded, wondering what he might want to talk about. "Okay. I agree."

By the time we reached the restaurant I was well and truly immersed in the bizarreness of the situation. I could just imagine the scene if Ronan and Annie happened to stop by for an impromptu dinner date and discovered me with Sean, slurping oysters like old pals.

Sean spoke with the maître d' and before I knew it we were being ushered to a cozy table for two. I wasn't a large woman, in fact, I'd always been slight. *Waifish*, was what Mam liked to call it. However, I found myself a little pushed for space sitting across from Sean. The toes of his shoes bumped awkwardly into mine and I pulled my feet under my chair to avoid a second encounter.

The table would have been large enough for two if I'd been with anyone other than Sean Cassidy.

Scanning the menu, my mouth practically watered at the options, but unlike I'd threatened, I didn't order the most expensive thing. It was too much of a dick move and Sean was being unexpectedly pleasant. So long as he treated me with respect, I'd treat him with respect in return.

After we'd both placed our orders, Sean leaned in and rested his elbows on the table, clasping his hands beneath his chin. He nodded to my handbag, a multi-colored, handwoven satchel I'd picked up in the East Village in New York.

"So, let's see what you took," he said, his eyes scanning the satchel. "That bag is atrocious, by the way. You should allow me to buy you something less gaudy."

And there he went showing his true colors. I stuck my chin out and smiled, not letting him get to me. "I'm gaudy? Says the man who has poor taste in, well, everything."

His eyebrows, which were several shades darker than his blond hair, shot up in surprise. Normally I lived my life by the mantra, *kill them with kindness*. But it was hard to be kind to Sean Cassidy, especially since he had a knack for offending people before he even opened his mouth.

Remind me again why I agreed to have dinner with him?

Oh yes, because I was a naïve fool, easily charmed by a handsome smile and a few brief minutes of false chivalry.

Now Sean sat back, folding his arms as he met my gaze. "Explain."

Ha! I could win this argument with less than one sentence. "Brona O'Shea."

I swear, if I had a mic I'd drop it. Sean's lips tightened, his eyes narrowed, and I loved his annoyed reaction.

"What? Did I hit a nerve?" I was nearly giggling, enjoying his discomfort far too much.

"If my agreement with Brona proves my poor taste, then your brother also has poor taste by association."

"Ronan doesn't have poor taste, he's just prone to bad judgment. It's a family trait, which explains why I'm sitting here with you right now."

Sean's mouth began to curve in a smile. "If I'd known you were this much fun, I'd have forced you into having dinner with me years ago."

I lifted my glass and took a sip of water before pointing out, "Years ago I was underage."

Sean bit his lip, pulling it slowly between his perfect teeth, and allowed his gaze to wander from my eyes to my collarbone as he murmured, "Yes, you were, weren't you? How old are you?

"Twenty-three."

"You're not *that* young."

I didn't like the husky quality to his voice right then, nor did I like the way his eyelids lowered, making me imagine he was having sexy thoughts. In an effort to distract myself, I picked up the small paper bag he'd placed at the side of the table when we'd arrived and pulled out the cream he'd bought. I didn't ask permission, because that was just my way. Sean didn't utter a word, but simply watched me as I twisted open the lid and took a sniff.

"Smells a bit like a church, but in a nice way," I said.

"It's sandalwood," he replied. "Here, give it to me."

I handed it across the table and he swiped his fingers in, extracting a small blob. Before I could react he took my hand and smoothed the cream into my wrist. His hands were very . . . large. My fingers felt completely encapsulated, minuscule by comparison. A tingling, nervous feeling buzzed in my belly as his fingertips massaged my sensitive skin. When he was done he lifted my wrist to his nose and inhaled deeply.

"Smells good on you," he said. I was momentarily lost for words.

Uh, would it be too overfamiliar to request he do that again, this time all over my body?

The waiter arrived with our food and Sean dropped my hand. I placed it in my lap under the table, like it was now a thing of obscenity too sexual for prying eyes.

Digging into my yellowfin tuna, I tried to push my thoughts to a safer, non-sexually arousing place. Quickly, I imagined Ronan's reaction if he knew I was here right now—his famous temper flaring—and yep, that did the trick.

Sean had ordered the steak, of course he had. The thing was almost as big as my head.

"You rugby boys sure know how to put food away," I commented.

He was currently chewing a cleanly cut slice of meat, and there was something about it that had me squeezing my thighs together. Maybe the way his jaw moved? Not to mention he had the most sensual mouth I'd ever seen.

"Tell me about it," he replied and patted his oh-so-flat stomach.

"This is my second big meal today. Dropped by for a late breakfast with the fam earlier this afternoon."

"Don't call your family 'the fam', Sean. It sounds douchey. Another two syllables won't kill you," I chided playfully.

Sean's smirk indicated he was enjoying my criticism, and I didn't understand that, either. "This coming from the girl with hair like a packet of Skittles."

"My hair isn't douchey," I said, and flicked a few locks over my shoulder. "It brings joy to all those who gaze upon it."

"Is that what those hippies in Vermont tell you? At that Maharishi sanctuary on the mountain?"

"It's not a Maharishi sanctuary, it's a yoga retreat."

"Is there a difference?"

I ignored him because he seemed to be trying to fluster me . . . or flirt . . . or both. "It's a yoga retreat in New Hampshire, on a lake."

"Squaw Lake, yes?"

"Squam Lake. And it's really beautiful, peaceful, calm. Many of the cabins have docks on the water. It's so quiet, especially at night, and the stars are so bright. They fill the sky and feel almost close enough to touch. It's truly a retreat."

He looked reluctantly interested. "That doesn't sound entirely terrible."

I pressed my lips together, trying not to smirk at his less than high praise. "Like I said last night, you should give it a try. Meditation would do you some good."

"Getting in touch with my feminine side?" His eyes twinkled with a devilish glint.

"Oh no. You don't have a feminine side—"

He barked a laugh.

"—but it might get you in touch with the missing syllables in *family*."

Sean's laugh waned, but his smile lingered. His lips really were sinful. I tried not to stare, instead tilting my chin upward in challenge. "I'm serious. Don't underestimate the power of inner peace."

His eyes narrowed on me. "Peace, eh?"

"That's right."

"And who will keep Goldilocks safe from the bears?"

I wrinkled my nose at him. "There are no bears in New Hampshire."

"What about wolves?" he asked, leaning forward, looking wolfish, his eyes on my nose.

I lifted my chin higher, this time with false confidence. "Don't worry about me. I can take care of myself."

For some unknown reason, this statement made him frown. He studied me for a long moment, no longer wolfish but no less intimidating. I endeavored to appear unaffected by his stare by nonchalantly eating the fish on my plate.

Unfortunately, endeavoring to eat nonchalantly wasn't easily done.

Abruptly, his knee nudged mine and his tone grew intent. "What did you steal, Lucy?"

His swift change of subject caused the bite of tuna I'd just swallowed to go down the wrong tube. I coughed fitfully and shifted in my seat, staring at my utensils. "Some eyeshadow."

"I didn't realize eyeshadow was so vital to the survival of pixies it had to be stolen."

"That's not why I took it," I mumbled and shame bit at my gut. Shoplifting was my biggest flaw, the part of myself I saw as the ugliest, but it was also my biggest secret. Which was why I felt terribly uncomfortable discussing it over the dinner table.

"So why then?"

I frowned, still not looking him in the eye. "It's a compulsion. A bad habit. I've been trying to quit, but it's hard when I'm around certain . . . negative influences."

"And those would be?" His knee was full on resting against mine now, but I couldn't tell if he was doing it to comfort me or make me nervous.

"My mother."

"Ah."

"I haven't stolen once since I moved to New York, then I come home for a visit and poof, I'm back to thieving." I slumped in my seat, feeling glum.

Sean's knee knocked mine and I looked up. He stared at me kindly and admitted, "I do it, too."

"Do what, too?"

"Take things that don't belong to me."

"You shoplift?"

"Not exactly. Not from shops at any rate. But I often take things from other people's bathroom cabinets." Very quickly he added as though to defend his habit, "Creams and cosmetics and such. I find it's a good way to discover new products."

"Other people? What other people?"

"Women."

"Women?"

"Yes."

"So . . . who are these *women*?"

Sean rolled his eyes. "Just women."

I scrutinized him and his *just women,* and I knew at once which women he meant. "You mean the women you have sex with? Of the one-night-stand variety?"

He nodded once just before taking a large gulp of his drink, not looking at me.

Huh. That was a very specific habit, and it was still stealing. "Are you sure that's the only reason you do it?"

Sean's eyes cut to mine and he studied me for a long moment; his stare was verging on peculiar when he finally shrugged. "Of course, there's no other reason."

I poked at my food as I thought on it. A few moments passed before I spoke again. "Or maybe, deep down, having these relations with *just women* makes you feel, I don't know, unfulfilled emotionally, since they're essentially strangers and one-night stands are generally all about the sex. So, the next morning, in order to make yourself feel a little bit better, you steal things."

Sean tilted his head. "Are you psychoanalyzing me?"

"I'm attempting to, yes."

He looked away, watching as a few other customers passed by our table. "Well don't. I promise you, I'm not that deep."

He sounded sort of sad.

"We all have depth, Sean. It's a side effect of being human."

He stared at me for so long I began to feel uncomfortable. I had to break the silence, so I stood and gestured to the bathrooms. "I'll be back in a minute."

I tried not to sprint, but it was difficult. I felt his eyes follow me the entire way, causing gooseflesh to rise over my upper arms and heat rise to my neck.

Once I was safe in the ladies' room, I ran some cold water over my hands then held my fingers to my neck, willing my skin to cool down. I suddenly realized that spending time with Sean Cassidy was a lot more dangerous than I thought, because in a strange way I was actually enjoying myself.

In an attempt to lighten the mood, and remembering I'd been neglecting the blog since I'd been home, I pulled out my phone and left the bathroom. Before I reached our table I stood off to the side, snapping a few shots of Sean as he finished his meal.

Almost like he sensed me, he turned his head, catching me in the act. He didn't even have to ask. His arched eyebrow said it all as I hurried over to join him.

"I'm going to feature you on Annie's blog this weekend. I hope you don't mind. I'm kind of stuck for material this week since Dublin's not exactly celeb central."

"Annie's blog?"

"Ronan's Annie. I work for her now, taking pictures, co-writing blog posts, tweeting, Instagramming, Facebooking, the whole nine yards."

"Well," said Sean, carefully setting down his knife and fork, done with his food. "I hadn't pegged you for a paparazzi."

"Really? What *had* you pegged me for?"

"A tarot card reader. Or maybe a yoga instructor," he teased, though his tone was flat. He reached out to take my phone. I watched as he swiped through the pictures.

"These are boring. Come here," he said, grabbing my hand and pulling me up from my seat. A zing of excitement shot through me as he perched me in his lap and raised the phone, snapping a selfie of us together. One of his arms was wrapped around my waist and his body felt warm and solid beneath me. As soon as the picture was taken I shot up, grabbing my phone back and returning to my seat.

"Wow, talk about a sneak attack," I muttered to myself, still feeling tingles from where he'd touched me.

"Now you can write a whole article about the weekend you spent with Sean Cassidy," he preened. "Your views will skyrocket."

I laughed. "I'm pretty sure my brother would blow a gasket if I did that."

"Oh, tell Mother Fitzpatrick to go take a Valium and relax."

My laughter died down as my expression sobered. "He's just protective of his family. Ronan's a good person. You'd know that if you simply took the time to get to know him."

"And why would I do that?"

"Because maybe if you knew him, you'd stop trying to ruin his life."

We stared at each other. Actually, he glared at me while I tried to meet his gaze evenly. It wasn't easy. I could see his mind working, words on the tip of his tongue, and he seemed to be debating whether or not to speak.

"Ruin his life?"

"Brona O'Shea," I repeated. "Ring any bells?"

"I think I did him a favor with that one. His current bird is a definite step up."

"Yes, but the suspension from the team? After he found you two going at it? I don't care much for Brona, but you knew how he was going to react. He almost ruined his career."

"It's not my fault he chose to act with aggression. The man's a chimpanzee, mindlessly flinging excrement at anyone who doesn't worship at his holier-than-thou altar."

My mouth fell open at his audacity and I jabbed my finger toward him. "He's the ape? You're the one who was knocking knickers with his fiancée!"

"No," he responded firmly. "Technically, I wasn't. I never actually tapped that. So, to be fair, going back to your earlier statement, my taste isn't as questionable as your brother's."

"What do you mean you never 'tapped that'?"

"I never fucked Brona O'Shea." His voice was as flat as a deflated tire, and I winced at his vulgarity and tone.

I immediately contradicted him, "Yes, you did." Everyone knew he'd seduced Brona. It's how he'd earned his nickname, Sleazy Sean. "Ronan walked in on you, he saw everything."

"No. He saw what we wanted him to see. And Mother Fitzpatrick, being Mother Fitzpatrick, jumped to all the wrong conclusions. Do you really think Ronan could best me in a fight? Unlikely. I let him win, so I could win." He reached for and gulped his water, watching me.

I studied him, seeing the truth in his eyes. He'd staged the whole thing. How could someone be so despicable? Anger swelled within me, an emotion I didn't often have cause to feel.

"You wanted him to find you. You wanted him suspended."

"No. I wanted him expelled."

Mounting fury had me raising my voice. He wasn't Sleazy Sean, he was Sinister Sean, and I couldn't believe I'd ever agreed to this farce of a dinner date.

"I can't believe you!"

"Shhh." He glanced around the restaurant, presumably to ensure we weren't causing a scene.

Leaning forward, I whispered harshly, "You are such a prick." Then I picked up his water glass and tossed it in his face.

Immediately, I stood, refusing to listen to him any longer. To be perfectly honest, it was a surprise he'd managed to go the whole meal without saying something mean. He'd just reminded me exactly why I shouldn't ever have been gullible enough to give him the time of day.

"Hey," he frowned, mopping the water from his jaw. "What was that for?"

"I'll give you one guess."

"You're leaving?"

I spun on him, so angry I couldn't see straight. "Call me when you get a clue and stop being so jealous of my brother."

He snorted at this and threw the wet napkin to the table. "Jealous. Right. What a joke."

I just shook my head, shot him a final parting grimace, and walked out of the restaurant. He was so oblivious I almost felt sorry for him. *Almost.*

Later, on the train ride home, and after I'd calmed down a bit, I did something that completely contradicted my outburst in the restaurant. I shouldn't have wanted to see Sean's face again for as long as I lived, and yet there I was, pulling my phone from my pocket and searching for the picture he'd taken. I couldn't stop looking at it, studying the curve of his mouth and the intensity of his eyes as he stared directly into the camera. His look made me shiver.

What on earth was wrong with me? Sean was not a nice person. Looking at a photo of him shouldn't be giving me all these . . . feelings. The thing was, for someone who claimed to be without depth, his gaze told a different story. Had I been right last night when I'd thought of him as a rescue dog, behaving badly because he was afraid? Or were those notions complete and utter nonsense?

Either way, Sean Cassidy needed help.

Again, my eyes fastened to the image of his arm, which was wrapped tightly around my waist. The more I looked, the more the picture gave me belly tingles, and despite everything I'd said to him in the restaurant, and all the reasons I told myself he didn't deserve it, there was a small place deep within me that desperately wanted to help him.

And that was the most disconcerting part of all.

# Chapter Four

@**RugbyTart23** to @**SeanCassinova** You are so much bigger than I expected. Loved meeting you XOXO

@**SeanCassinova** to @**RugbyTart23** You are so much more forgettable than I expected. Did we meet? I can't recall.

### *Sean*

I WAS INSUFFERABLY bored.

And cold.

The start of the offseason used to be a relief. It used to be my favorite time of the year. But now the lack of doing something, the being surrounded by hangers-on, and the tedium of their flattery—the monotony quickly grew suffocating.

Clubbing in Monaco was tiresome. I'd hoped to find amusement in Spain on the heels of the one-day mandatory team press junket in Barcelona. A respite was sorely needed after spending a full fourteen hours indoors with Ronan Fitzpatrick and listening to his inane blathering about team cohesion.

Alas, to put it quite bluntly, the nightlife in Spain sucked arse.

I considered traveling farther south, someplace even warmer and sunnier. Instead, and without dwelling too much on my motivations, I booked a flight back to Dublin at the end of June.

Departing the Spanish villa at 6:00 a.m., I abandoned my traveling companions without leaving a note. In truth, I couldn't recall their names. I knew only the basics: they'd been rich and beautiful; I was rich and beautiful; we'd been rich and beautiful together.

And now we were rich and beautiful apart.

First class was the only way to fly when one was six foot six and could bench-press three hundred pounds. Typically, I would book two seats, but the flight was full and relatively short, so I made do with the front row aisle seat. It was snug, but not uncomfortable.

"I'm Dorothy. May I get you something before we take off?" The stewardess inclined her head toward me, an older bird with a grandmotherly air about her.

"Bourbon and 7, please. No ice. Two bottles." I gave her a distracted smile as I'd just spotted a SkyMall magazine. I reached for it, plucking it from the wall pocket in front of me. A new edition? My pulse quickened at the discovery. Brilliant!

The worst thing that happened to air travel in the past ten years was the bankruptcy of Xhibit Corp., the parent company of SkyMall. I recalled with clarity the first time I boarded a flight and it was missing from all usual nooks and crannies.

It had been a dark day.

Dorothy left me and I caressed the crisp edges of the catalog with my thumbs.

Uncle Peter hadn't been much of a father figure, but he had given me my first SkyMall magazine. I'd been instructed to "pick something out for yourself and the maid will order it" after my birthday had gone by unnoticed for the third year—nothing unusual about that occurrence.

Except, as it turned out, it had been a special birthday.

Such oddities. So many bizarre and clever inventions. Who would possibly have thought a large super skateboard parasail would be a good idea? And did men really wear high-waisted control boxer briefs? Of course, I did consider requesting The Human Sling-Shot . . .

Eventually, I settled on a glow-in-the-dark collar and leash for the family dog, first glimpsed on page forty-seven of the catalog. I'd circled it carefully with black marker, prepared to return the catalog to the head housekeeper.

And yet, I couldn't.

In the end, I decided I could live without the leash, but found I couldn't part with the eclectic and wonderful pages upon pages of sundry contraptions. I'd become infatuated with its weirdness.

Presently, I was still debating whether to crack open the unexpected treasure trove of esoteric eccentricity now, or wait until we were airborne, when I was unceremoniously yanked out of my indecision by a familiar voice.

"What the bloody hell are you doing here?"

I was a tad startled, but didn't need to glance up to know which primate had addressed me with such apish manners. Ronan Fitzpatrick.

"I'm sitting on an airplane," I responded evenly, determined to enjoy SkyMall's eclectic offerings despite Ronan's untimely appearance.

"You're sitting in my seat." My teammate's voice dropped an octave.

"Oh," came a feminine squeak from the vicinity behind him, drawing my attention away from the pages of SkyMall.

Ronan's exceptionally pretty, brilliant, and odd girlfriend stood at his shoulder, cheeks rosy and tanned, and with wide eyes peering at me with surprise.

"Ms. Catrel. How pleasant." I grinned at her.

"What are you still doing in Spain? I thought you left weeks ago?" Ronan growled.

I ignored him, addressing my question to Annie as I patted the seat next to me. "Is this your seat?"

Ronan shifted to the side, effectively hiding her from my view. "That is her seat, but you're in mine. So I'll thank you to get your arse up and out."

The grin slid from my face as I pulled my ticket stub from my suit pocket and showed it to my rival. "You're in error. This is my seat. I've just purchased it."

Ronan's Cro-Magnon brow furrowed, meant to display the severity of his disdain; he didn't look at my ticket. "I don't care if you've purchased the whole godforsaken airline. That's my seat, and you're in it. Get. Up."

"Oh dear." The stewardess appeared, holding my cocktail and casting concerned glances between my hulking teammate and me. "Is there a problem?"

"This man is harassing me," I responded flatly.

Mother Fitzpatrick turned an alarming shade of red.

"No," he growled, tossing his thumb in my direction as though the action would smite me where I sat in seat 1B. "This arsehole—"

"Ronan," Annie soothed, placing her hand on his arm.

He began again after taking a breath and holding up his ticket for Dorothy the stewardess. "This *person* is in my seat."

I held my ticket up as well. "That's impossible. I just purchased this seat two hours ago."

Dorothy's eyes moved between our offerings and her forehead

creased with worry. "Oh dear. This is a mess. May I have these tickets? I'll ring the ticket agent."

"Certainly." I relinquished my slip of paper proof and exchanged it for the cocktail she held.

Ronan likewise handed over his and Annie's tickets, sliding into seats 1C and 1D to wait as Dorothy disappeared into the galley.

"The flight is sold out, Mother Fitzpatrick. You can't steal those seats either." I indicated to where he waited, sipping my bourbon and 7. I was glad Dorothy had made it a double.

"I'm not the stealing kind, Cassidy. I've no need," Ronan shot back, his eyes pointedly not meeting mine.

"I suppose you're referring to Brona? Really, isn't that bad form of you? Bringing up your ex in front of pretty Ms. Catrel." I winked at her. She rolled her eyes heavenward.

What Ronan didn't know—what no one but Brona O'Shea and I knew—was that I never touched Brona O'Shea except for publicity purposes.

Actually, that wasn't quite right. Lucy Fitzpatrick knew.

I scowled, recalling how I'd told her the truth. In retrospect, I couldn't fathom why I'd allowed her accusation of bad taste to piss me off so much. I didn't have bad taste. I had impeccable taste. I just didn't act on my impeccable taste because . . . no point.

Regardless, Brona and I had staged the whole scene, our relationship, hoping to enrage Ronan and push him over the edge. Unsurprisingly, it had worked. Ronan was nothing if not predictable, his emotions far too close to the surface.

His loyalty and candid affection for his loved ones would be his downfall.

I couldn't relate. I had no loved ones.

Well, that's not quite right. I had a loved *one*. I had Eilish, but I didn't go blathering on about her.

Presently, to his credit, Ronan managed to sound bored and threatening at the same time when he responded, "Keep pushing, Cassidy, see where it gets you. You and Brona deserved each other seeing as you're both dead inside. Really, it must be nice not to give a shit about anyone but yourself."

Abruptly, the bourbon tasted sour on my tongue. I removed my hand from the cup so as to control my urge to pitch it at him.

"What about your sister?" The words were out of my mouth before I realized I'd said them.

Ronan's glare cut to mine and sharpened. "What about my sister?"

I smirked, though I struggled to form the words as a bizarre sense of loyalty and guilt completely arrested my spitefulness. "Is she the *stealing kind*?"

Panic flickered behind Ronan's glare, heating it to incendiary levels. Ronan knew. He knew all about his sister's sticky fingers. And worried about her.

Christ, I hated myself sometimes.

But not enough to stop baiting Ronan.

My smirk grew into a threatening grin. "I wonder what else little Lucy and I have in common."

"Shut your bloody mouth, Cassidy." Ronan began to stand, murder clearly on his mind, but was stayed by Annie's firm grip on his shoulder and calm reassurances.

"Ronan, he's trying to get a rise out of you. Just let it go. Can't you see how sad he is?"

I felt her last words at the base of my skull, a prickling discomfort, yet managed a slight chuckle. "Sad? Me? Ha. I'm the picture of cheerfulness."

"Yes. You. Sad." Annie's serious brown eyes captured mine across the aisle and her tone was free of malice as she continued, "You are sad and lonely and lost, though you'll never admit it. Instead you pick fights, desperate to feel something."

I swallowed past a cinching bitterness in the back of my throat and drawled, "Oh yes. I'm so desperately sad, and need to be saved. Save me, Ms. Catrel. Save me from my crushing loneliness and despair. All I require is a good woman . . . or two. Or three, at the very most, so do bring some friends along."

Annie shook her head at me, a slight, knowing smile pasted on her lips, but was stopped from responding further by the appearance of the aforementioned gate agent.

"Mr. Cassidy?" She addressed me, her tone painfully conciliatory.

Not a good sign.

"I am Mr. Cassidy," I confirmed flatly.

"I am so sorry," she was tripping over the words, barely able to get them out, "but it appears there has been a mix-up. We never should have released this seat to you. I'll need you to come with me back to the gate."

"You don't say . . ." I gritted my teeth, hating that Ronan would win this round, just like he won everything.

Ronan Fitzpatrick and his apish manners.

Ronan Fitzpatrick and his legion of loyal followers.

Ronan Fitzpatrick and his adoring family.

He didn't deserve to be the team captain. He didn't deserve seat 1B in this airplane. And he definitely didn't deserve the insightful, pretty, and brilliant Ms. Catrel.

I unhurriedly unfolded from the seat, tilting my head to one side so as not to hit it on the roof of the plane. The gate agent backed up two steps, clearly startled by my size. Or perhaps she backed off because I was glaring daggers in her direction.

"Tough luck, Cassidy." Ronan stood as well, grinning triumphantly. "You could always fly coach."

I felt my glower intensify as I volleyed back hatefully. "Perhaps I'll go find your sister in Barcelona and we can chat about all the things we have in common."

Irritatingly, Ronan chuckled and called after me as I walked down the aisle toward the exit. "Not likely. Lucy isn't in Spain, Cassidy. She's in the middle of the woods at some yoga retreat, where you'll never find her."

I turned the corner, now blessedly out of earshot, left the airplane, and straightened to my full height as I strolled up the onramp and back to the gate. Bourbon, 7 Up, and defeat an acrimonious mixture on my tongue.

The gate agent was still apologizing, scurrying in front of me and tossing regretful smiles over her shoulder.

I didn't return her smile, too busy stewing in the simmering heat of failure. Ronan Fitzpatrick lumbered through life, threatening and shouting, getting his own way at every turn. He was a great buffoon, masquerading indulgent, brutish conceit and idiocy as loyalty and dedication.

"We'll get you back to Dublin, Mr. Cassidy. I promise. It might take a few hours, but we'll have it sorted."

He deserved to feel the sting of a true setback. He deserved humiliation. He deserved to suffer.

"I'm not going to Dublin," I said as I thought the words, a plan forming in my mind.

"Oh?" The woman frowned at me, considering and cautious, and her voice held a slight tremor as she offered, "Well, I'm sure we can accommodate you wherever you'd like to go."

I glared at her earnest and solicitous face for several protracted seconds. Holding my gaze, she swallowed as though the action were painful. I dropped my eyes to her hands where they fiddled with the badge around her neck. Her fingers were shaking.

"What's your name?" I demanded, unaccountably irritated by her nerves. I was used to people being intimidated by my presence, yet I rarely enjoyed their discomfort. Just another reminder of how terribly inconvenient I was.

"Marta." She tilted her chin up, looking like a brave little girl.

"Marta." I let her name roll off my tongue, softening my tone, and giving her a smile meant to ease her nerves—a skill I'd perfected over the years out of necessity. "Such a beautiful name."

Her lashes fluttered and pink stained her olive skin. "Th-thank you, Mr. Cassidy." Marta's response was a breathy whisper.

"Now, I need a flight to the United States. Specifically, to someplace called Squam Lake in New Hampshire." I licked my lips and inclined my head toward her, lowering my voice as though I were asking for her secrets. "Can you help me, Marta?"

# Chapter Five

@**LucyFitz** Sometimes I open chocolate bars real slow and imagine what I'd do if there was a golden ticket inside.

@**BroderickAdams to** @**LucyFitz** Okay, first answer that pops into your head. Depp-Wonka or Wilder-Wonka?

@**LucyFitz to** @**BroderickAdams** This is gonna cause controversy but…Depp-Wonka.

@**BroderickAdams to** @**LucyFitz** WHAT!?!


## *Lucy*

I FELT LIKE I'D died and gone to heaven. Here I was, in a place far removed from modern stresses and strains, no Internet, no mobile phone, but most importantly, no Jackie Fitzpatrick. Yes, I was thousands of miles away from my mother and the urge to steal was a long-forgotten, distant memory.

"You look happy," said Broderick as we sat on a patio that faced the lake, drinking our kale smoothies.

"Of course I'm happy, Rick. Look where we are. The people who live here must wake up every morning and feel elated just to be alive."

My friend chuckled. "It's certainly a lot more relaxing than Manhattan."

I nodded. "I mean, don't me wrong, I love New York, but I couldn't spend the rest of my life there. If I ever made enough money I'd build myself a nice little two-bedroom cottage in a place like this, adopt a bunch of dogs, and just forget about the rest of the world."

"But then you wouldn't get to see my handsome face every day," he teased and I grinned at him. I'd had my fair share of platonic male friends in my time, but Rick was by far the prettiest. And don't even get me started on his accent. Gah, I could listen to him speak for hours. I'd quickly come to realize we didn't have chemistry of the romantic variety. In truth, I thought he might be harboring feelings for an ex or hung up on some other girl, and wasn't getting involved in that.

So, we'd become best buds instead and I thoroughly enjoyed his company.

Speaking of harbored feelings, my mind had been a little preoccupied of late, continually wandering to a certain blond-haired rugby player with a bad attitude. Even though our dinner had ended on unfriendly terms, I couldn't help replaying his hands on my wrist, or how naturally his arm had wrapped around my waist, the heat of his body warming me.

But enough about "He Who Must Not Be Named." I needed to start treating him like Voldemort. Don't speak of him, don't even think of him, and certainly don't imagine him tearing my knickers off with his teeth . . .

*Anyway.*

Back to Broderick. Yes, my friend was someone who actually deserved to take up room in my thoughts. He was a small-time music producer who ran his own blog and website. He did album reviews and stuff like that, but really his talent was wasted on writing, because the man had a fantastic set of pipes. Think Al Green meets Nat King Cole.

We finished off our smoothies and headed inside for our mid-morning yoga class. I'd really taken a shine to the instructor. Her name was Maria, an ex-nun from Massachusetts who'd spent a decade of her life volunteering with impoverished communities in Zimbabwe. She was certainly a woman with stories to tell.

The retreat was located in a large wooden house with an interior that consisted almost exclusively of whites and pale blues. There was nothing busy, nothing stressful to the eye, just serene tones and hardwood floors.

Nirvana.

We were a couple minutes early to class, so Rick and I busied ourselves stretching and setting out our mats. We sat close to the front, and it wasn't long before the room started to fill up.

About ten minutes in, as Maria instructed us to turn our heads slowly to the right, I looked across the room only to meet a startlingly familiar pair of blue eyes.

What the fu—

How the bloody hell had Voldemort gotten into the building?

Sean Cassidy sat serenely on a yoga mat, his legs crossed and his hands braced on the floor, grinning widely like he'd just been told Scarlett Johansson wanted to give him a blowie. No longer was I relaxed. My inner peace fled for the hills as my palms grew sweaty and my heart rate sped up. I blinked—like maybe I'd imagined him—but no, when I looked again he was still there, still wearing that same smug grin.

Again I thought of our dinner together, and how I'd so foolishly told him all the details of where I'd be spending my break. It seemed to me that Sean was up to something, something decidedly fishy.

I refused to look at him again for the remainder of the class. The hour was a complete and total write-off though, because my thoughts were a scrambled mess and I couldn't focus. When Maria finished up, wishing us all a good day, I shot out of the room like a rabbit on speed. I didn't even wait around for Rick. No, I took my mat and my water bottle and strode right out of the building, heading for the peaceful waters of the lake.

For a second I considered finding a phone to call Ronan and request he come and extract Sean from my haven of solitude. His very presence turned it into a place of tension and anxiety . . . and yes, unwanted sexual urges.

But no, I couldn't go crying to my brother every time something didn't go my way. I was a confident grown woman, and I could a handle a little problem like Sean Cassidy.

Piece of cake.

With this renewed determination, I took several deep breaths and enjoyed a few more minutes of blessed silence before spinning around toward the house. Unfortunately, as soon as I turned I found Sean standing there with his arms folded, leaning casually against the trunk of a tree.

Startled, I almost tripped over a branch.

"Jesus, what are you doing out here?" I asked, my hand flying to my rapidly beating heart.

"As of the last few minutes I've been watching you have a conversation with yourself. It's a tad worrying, truth be told. I assume you answer your own questions?" He tutted.

I inhaled, my mouth opening to deny his assumption, but nothing came out. *Had* I been talking to myself? I'd been in such a tizzy, I couldn't remember.

I began fidgeting with the hem of my top, staring at the ground as I said, "Look, whatever game you're playing by coming here, I want no part of it. I've been looking forward to this trip for months and I won't have anyone ruin it for me."

When I finally lifted my head to meet his eyes, Sean's masculine brows drew together in a frown. I reluctantly traced the contours of his arms beneath his long-sleeved gray T-shirt, savoring the way his waist tapered into a pair of dark workout pants. God, he was attractive.

"I'm not here to ruin anything. You invited me to come."

"I did not."

"You did."

"I wouldn't."

"You would."

I scowled at him. "Why would I do that?"

"Because, deep down, you like me." He grinned. The grin looked entirely sincere, but also a little dangerous, and a lot sexy.

I crossed my arms over my chest, my water bottle dangling from my fingers, unimpressed with Sean Cassidy's insincere smiles. "I would never—"

"Don't you remember? At the end of season party back in Dublin?"

"I, uh . . ." I blinked, finally remembering. Okay, I had to admit, he had me there. "Look, maybe I did *technically* invite you, but that was before you bad-mouthed my brother over tuna."

"I didn't have tuna," he denied as though tuna were horrifying.

"No, you had steak. I had tuna."

"Oh yeah . . ." He nodded, his eyes shifting to the side, perhaps recalling his steak. Or my tuna. Or both. After a moment he shook himself and refocused on me. "And I'm sorry for that. Truly. I came here to de-stress, hoping to find a modicum of enlightenment and become less of a prick. Let's be friends? Forgiveness is a virtue, Mini-Fitzpatrick."

I pursed my lips and eyed him, trying to decide if he were being genuine. If he were faking the white flag routine then he certainly put on a good show. And really, if he was so determined to stay then there was nothing I could do to stop him.

What would it hurt to call a truce? Peace was the least stressful option available.

Huffing a breath, I replied, "Fine, we can be friends, just try to keep the prick side of your personality to yourself for a few days."

He grinned again. "You're in a lively mood."

"Mmm-hmm, that's what happens when people decide to gatecrash my sanctuary."

I took a few steps forward and passed him by, uncapping my water bottle and taking a small gulp. Sean began to follow me through the trees, his shadow looming as we walked.

"So," he broached, "who's the Mocha Frappuccino back inside? Your boyfriend?"

I stopped immediately and turned to face him, my expression devoid of humor. "Could you be any more racist?"

"I'm not being racist. I'm being descriptive. I'll have you know that some of the warmest nights of my life have been spent with women of color. Lovely, lovely colors."

"If you don't mind, I'd rather not talk about your conquests." I started walking again, faster this time. Sean hurried to catch up.

"Why? Does it make you jealous?"

I laughed, incredulous. "It makes me feel sorry for all the women whose bathroom cabinets you've pilfered."

Sean let out an amused-sounding laugh and brought the conversation back to where it had started. "You still haven't answered my question, Lucy."

I heaved a sigh. "No, Rick—Broderick—is just a friend."

"Just a friend? Are you sure he's not curious about the color of your knickers?"

"No. He's a total lamb. He's my best friend, so I'd appreciate it if you could keep your completely offensive comments to yourself when you meet him."

"I'm not *completely* offensive. If you're allowed to nickname me after a pale fermented-grape drink from France, then I can call—"

"Oh my God! Okay, you're only mildly offensive, now can you please just shut up?"

Sean grinned and made a gesture as though zipping his mouth closed.

We'd reached the entrance to the house and I turned to him once more, emitting a long sigh. I didn't want to be angry with Sean. I just wanted to enjoy the rest of my stay. He watched me as I considered what to say to him. In the end, I didn't mince my words.

"Just . . . don't be mean, okay? Try your hardest."

His expression sobered and he gave me a tiny, almost non-existent nod. Without further ado, I hurried off to my room, needing some time alone to come to terms with the fact I'd be dealing with a daily dose of Sean Cassidy for the foreseeable future.

\*\*\*

I SPENT THE rest of the afternoon hanging out—*not* hiding out—in my room. First I took a nap. Then I got up and opened the windows to let in some fresh air. I ran a bath and put on a chill-out CD. After a long soak in the tub with some soothing essential oils, I felt a hundred times better equipped to face dinner.

We ate all our meals in the spacious communal dining hall, so there was a good likelihood Sean would be there. I blow-dried my hair, put on a cozy, over-sized woolen jumper and some leggings, then headed out to find Broderick. He was in the lounge area chatting with a couple women who were all BFFs and had come for a relaxation weekend. Broderick had a really amiable personality, which meant people tended to naturally gravitate toward him. He was just plain cool, from the way he walked, to the way he spoke, to the effortlessly styled clothes he wore.

"Hey," I said, doing a little wave as I joined the group. The women all chirped their hellos.

"Lucy, where've you been all day?" Rick asked, coming to stand next to me.

"I just felt like taking some time to myself. Can we talk?"

"Sure, I'll catch you all later," he said to the women before standing and offering me his arm. We walked toward the dining hall and I let out a slow breath.

"So, do you remember the guy I was telling you about from back home?"

"The prick who plays rugby with your brother? Yeah."

"He's here right now. At the retreat."

My friend sputtered a laugh. "For real?"

I grimaced. "I might have made the mistake of technically inviting him. It wasn't a genuine invite. If anything, it was a sarcastic invite, but now he's here and I'm kind of freaking out."

"So some dude you've got a crush on is here. Big deal. You're Lucy Fitzpatrick, you don't get fazed by the small stuff."

"I do not have a crush on him," I argued. And little did he know, I *was* fazed by the small stuff. It was the whole reason I was so obsessed with meditation and finding inner peace. Otherwise, I'd probably have a nervous breakdown. Broderick shot me a wry look.

"Man, you want him bad."

"I don't."

"Just let him bone you already."

"Shut up, I mean it," I hissed.

Rick laughed softly. "Be honest, you've been dreaming about weddings and babies for weeks, haven't you?"

"What? No," I scoffed, responding honestly. "Sean Cassidy is the last guy I'd ever want to marry."

"Oh, I see." Rick's eyes narrowed, like he was assessing me. "No weddings and babies. You just want his hands up your skirt."

"I'm not wearing a skirt."

"Sorry. My bad. I shouldn't have been so nebulous. You want to skip the missionary position and do it doggy style."

I scowled, flushing red because he was so right, and my words escaped in a mortified rush, "I kind of hate you right now."

Broderick was still laughing when we reached the dining hall and found a table, but thankfully he let the matter drop. Meanwhile, I was suffering from hot flashes.

For dinner we had the option of quinoa and avocado salad or a superfood soup medley, so I concentrated on making my selection. I opted for the quinoa with a side of hummus and raw veggies. Rick got the same and we chowed down in tense silence.

Well, I was tense. He was smirking.

I was still annoyed with him for teasing me about Sean when a familiar shadow fell over our table.

"Mind if I sit?" he asked and Rick glanced up. I focused intently on my food, ignoring the blooming heat low in my belly.

"Seat's not taken." Rick shrugged, motioning to the chair then holding out his hand when Sean was seated. "I'm Broderick, and you must be Sean."

"That's right. I take it my reputation precedes me."

"Something like that," Rick replied in a friendly manner.

The chair next to mine moved as Sean adjusted himself, his knee knocking mine under the table. Stupid long-legged oaf. I crunched away on my salad, silent as a mouse, while Rick initiated conversation with Sean. He just wasn't the sort of bloke to sit in awkward silences. Broderick could find something to talk about with anyone, from your grandmother to the man who came to clean the windows of your house.

"When did you arrive?"

"Just this morning," Sean answered. "I'm really loving the setting. It's very beautiful."

I glanced at him now, wondering if his statement was true. Sean didn't strike me as the type to appreciate the beauty of nature. Or maybe I was just being cynical, allowing the way he made me feel and how easily he could push my buttons, to cloud my judgment. Maybe my loyalty to my brother was interfering with how I saw him.

"It's definitely pretty. We've been here for almost a week, haven't we, Luce?" Rick kicked my leg under the table. "I don't think either one of us wants to leave."

I glanced between the two of them before realizing I was taking forever to answer. "No, um, no, we don't want to leave."

The sentence came out sounding odd and stilted. Sean smiled like I was cute and something reluctantly warmed within me. He rested his elbow on the back of my chair, his arm touching against my shoulder. I could tell he was looking at me but I concentrated on my food, unable to meet his gaze.

I was relieved when two of Rick's lady friends came to join us, introducing themselves as Cindy and Lisa.

"It's so nice to see another male face around," said Lisa with what I thought might be a hint of flirtation. "You don't get many men coming to places like this."

"I like to think I'm comfortable enough in my masculinity to know when I need to take some time out, get back to basics and all that," said Sean.

"It really is important," Lisa nodded enthusiastically. "We're all so bogged down by obligations and technology these days that we forget to breathe and just . . . be."

"You took the words right out of my mouth," Sean agreed.

God, he was such a schmooze.

Now Cindy joined in. "One of my favorite Deepak Chopra quotes says, 'In the midst of movement and chaos, keep stillness inside of you.' I feel like I can truly be still in a place like this."

"Do you know, I've never heard that one before," said Sean before turning his head to me. "Do you try to keep stillness inside of you, too, Lucy?"

He was trying to embarrass me, but I wouldn't let him succeed. Instead I came up with a subtle put-down. "I'm more of a Gandhi girl myself. I particularly liked it when he said, 'You must not lose faith in humanity. Humanity is an ocean; if a few drops of the ocean are dirty, the ocean does not become dirty.'" I smiled at him while bringing a carrot stick to my mouth and taking a bite.

Sean's eyes gleamed like I'd just baited him to a challenge he was happy to accept. Perhaps I'd bitten off more than I could chew – literally and figuratively.

"Ah, we can all benefit from getting a little dirty every once in a while," he quipped and Lisa chortled. Yes, chortled. I cast my eyes to Rick and his face said it all, *hey, you dug your own hole with that one.*

Sean moved so it wasn't just his elbow resting on the back of my chair now, but the entire length of his arm. His heat sent a bolt of electricity shooting right through me and I shifted in place, unsure how I felt about his closeness. His cologne was nice, that was a positive, but he was starting to make me feel penned in, that was a negative. He hadn't said anything mean yet, that was another positive. Man, were Sean Cassidy's positives actually outweighing his negatives?

"So, what's a fella got to do to get some meat around here?" he asked, not looking too excited about the salad in front of him.

"This is a vegetarian retreat," I answered. "Didn't you read that in the brochure?"

He scratched lightly at the stubble growing on his jaw and frowned. "No, it was more an impulse decision to come here."

"My husband loves his meat, too," said Cindy. "I can take or leave it, but I do like to detox every couple of months. It's highly beneficial for the digestive system."

"You see," I smiled widely at Sean. "A few meat-free days will do you the world of good."

He didn't look like he believed me.

"If we had more time, we could've hit up one of the nearby restaurants, but tomorrow is the last full day," Rick offered. "I've been craving a steak."

"That sounds like a great idea. We should go tomorrow," Sean enthused. "Will you come with us, Lucy?"

"I can't. I'm washing my hair."

"We haven't decided what time we're going yet," said Rick, the Judas.

"And your hair doesn't need to be washed," Sean added, leaning in to take a whiff.

I shot him a startled look. "Did you just smell my hair?"

He stared at me. "Yes."

"Well . . . don't."

"I'd love to come, if you do go," Lisa put in, inviting herself. "We could go for a drive and see some of the sights beforehand."

"Oh, that's a wonderful idea," said Cindy.

"So, are you in?" Sean asked, refusing to drop the subject.

"Like I said, these locks won't wash themselves."

Both Cindy and Lisa were occupied in discussing the idea of venturing outside the grounds of the retreat with Rick, while Sean kept his attention focused on me.

"What will it take to get you to relax and enjoy my company?" he asked. "Do you want me to buy you something?"

"What? No."

"A car, maybe?"

I blinked at him, stunned. I was stunned because he was completely serious.

"Well, that escalated quickly," I mumbled under my breath, still shocked.

"What's your favorite color?"

"You're not buying me a car."

"Why not?"

"Because, why would you?"

"Because I want to."

"It's weird, Sean."

"No, it's not."

I scoffed. "God, you're completely out of touch."

"I agree. It's a terrible problem. I should touch you," he answered low, and there was something about the way he said it that had my mind conjuring up all sorts of unwelcome images.

I surprised even myself when I turned my body so I faced him. My mouth was only inches from his when I replied quietly, "Are you sure you want to do that? Touch me and I'll touch you back."

I watched him swallow and a triumphant rush went through me to know my words had affected him. So he definitely wasn't pretending. Sean Cassidy actually *liked* me. Wow.

"Which cabin is yours?" he asked.

I laughed. "I'm not telling you that."

"Why not? We could be right next door to each other and not even know."

"Rick's cabin is next to mine, so no, we couldn't."

Sean's lips curved into a smile. "Ah, so I'll just ask which one's his to find yours."

"Your skills of deduction truly astound me," I deadpanned.

His tone turned contemplative. "You know, I think you may have offered up the information because you subconsciously *want* me to find you. Shall I sneak in later? Crawl into your bed and wake you up with my head between your thighs?"

I raised both my eyebrows and pointed at him with my fork. "That is quite possibly the creepiest thing I've ever heard. Do women typically enjoy this sort of talk?"

He seemed a touch petulant. "Yes, they do."

His response lacked the usual Cassidy confidence and it made me curious. Perhaps he wasn't the lothario he liked to lead people to believe.

"Are you sure? Because if I ever woke up with a strange man's head between my legs I'd be straight on the phone to the authorities." I tried to keep a sober face but cracked up a second later. Sean shot me a look of annoyance that I'd foiled his attempt at sexy talk.

"What's so funny?" Rick asked, turning his attention away from Lisa and Cindy.

I leaned forward on the table. "So, hypothetical question. If you woke up in the middle of the night and a woman you didn't know, or say you knew in passing, was giving you a blowjob, what would your immediate reaction be?"

Lisa and Cindy wore identical expressions of *WTF* but Rick wasn't even fazed.

See? This was the reason we were friends.

"That depends. How exactly do I know her? Does she work in the local coffee house or is she the mother of a friend of a friend?"

I grinned. "I really want to go with the latter option, because . . . weird, but for simplicity's sake, let's imagine she's the barista at your favorite coffee shop. She's pretty, gives good head, but you know, she's in your house, in your bedroom, and she's taken the liberty of putting your cock in her mouth. What do you do?"

"This is a very strange conversation," said Lisa.

"I don't see the point," added Cindy.

"Humor me," I told the both of them. "There's a point, I promise."

Sean made a sound next to me, kind of a growly sigh.

"And tell me this," Rick went on, seeming to enjoy the imaginary scenario, "when I go in for coffee, me and this chick, do we chit-chat, banter back and forth, or are we all business?"

"Does it have an influence on your answer?" I asked with a wide grin.

"Well, if we have a friendly vibe going on, maybe I mistakenly gave her the impression I wanted her to enter my house uninvited for oral fun. I can't lose my shit if I've led her on."

"Okay. You're friendly to the extent that you say hello and know each other's name, but you don't chit-chat."

"Right," he chewed on his lip. "I think I'd have to respectfully ask her to leave, then report the incident to the cops. I mean, this woman is obviously psychologically unhinged."

I sent a pointed look Sean's way. "You see. It is creepy. I think you need to cut this whole scenario from your dirty-talk repertoire."

My victory didn't last very long because Sean just sat there staring at me, neither a smile nor a frown on his face. He looked like he didn't know what to say, but also a little like he wanted to bend me over his knee and punish me for my behavior.

"Well, this has been real," said Rick, breaking the silence with a wry expression. "But I think I'm going to go hang in my room for a while. Give a knock later if you want to take a walk or something."

"Okay, see you later."

With Rick's departure, Cindy and Lisa quickly made their exits.

"I don't think I've made the best impression with those two," I said, and heard Sean let out a small huff of a laugh.

"And why ever not? It isn't like you scared them off with all that talk of middle-of-the-night blowjob attacks," he surmised.

"It serves them right. Cindy's been all over Rick the last few days, and her with a husband," I declared with feigned haughtiness.

Sean chuckled but it soon petered out, leaving us in silence once more. I wasn't sure how to make an exit, which left me stuck in my chair, no believable excuses springing to mind.

I felt warmth hit the back of my neck when he leaned forward, resting one elbow on the table. "Tell me which room is yours, Lucy," he breathed.

I squeezed my eyes shut for a second, trying not to let his deep, seductive voice affect me. Suddenly, the scenario of him coming to me during the night returned, but this time I wasn't creeped out. No, I was . . . intrigued. What exactly would Sean Cassidy/Lucy Fitzpatrick sex look like?

An acute flash, a quick image of us together, naked, limbs tangled, rough heat, his mouth, his tongue, his fingers, and his electric blue gaze holding mine . . .

Christ, I was sweating and my heart was beating like I'd run a marathon.

. . . *Maybe just once.*

After all, I *was* dying to see that wonderful bubble butt in all its naked glory.

"You never posted the pictures to Annie's website," he said then, breaking me from my thoughts. I flushed, like maybe he could see exactly what I'd been thinking.

I peered at him in question. "Have you been looking?"

He lifted a shoulder. "Maybe."

I exhaled. "Actually, if you must know, I deleted them."

"You deleted them?" He reared back, almost like he was offended.

"Yes." *No.*

He held my gaze for several protracted moments, his stark, summer-sky stare growing increasingly heated, as though incensed, with each passing second. I swallowed mounting unease, uncertain why I'd lied. But before I could come clean, the tense silence was unexpectedly broken.

"Hello, Mr. Cassidy, isn't it? I just wanted to come and quickly introduce myself." This came from Maria, the yoga instructor. He turned with obvious reluctance to face her, giving me a slicing narrowed glare.

As soon as his eyes left me I gathered a deep breath, grateful she'd snagged his attention. Feeling relief, I realized it was now or never. I took the opportunity provided by Sean's distraction to escape.

Rising from my seat, I hurried from the dining hall, figuring that—by the time he looked back—I'd be gone, cocooned safely in the comfort of my room.

# Chapter Six

@**SeanCassinova** If dreams are the subconscious' attempt to live desires, then I need to buy my subconscious a drink. And a house.

## *Sean*

I DIDN'T SNEAK into her cabin that night and wake her up with my head between her thighs. Instead I dreamt of Lucy and her head between my thighs. I woke with a start, sweating, having just climaxed.

Rolling my eyes back into my head, I cursed. The sheets now needed to be washed and, unfortunately, I realized I really wanted to fuck Lucy Fitzpatrick.

Before you clutch your pearls with righteous outrage, or faint under the weight of my uncouth barbarism, allow me to explain why my wanting to fuck Lucy—or any woman specifically—was a thing I dread.

Pragmatic couplings, a means to an end, a way to secure an evening free of constant chill—those I could do with no trouble or effort. A few strategically placed kisses. A whispered assurance of mutual want. Robotic movements meant to expedite the act. She always faked it. Sometimes I faked it . . .

*Huh.*

Lucy's psychoanalyzing words from our truncated dinner back home in Dublin returned to me. Perhaps Lucy was right. Perhaps buried deep, an underlying emptiness possessed me. So I took toiletries from bathroom cabinets. Little forbidden treasures to fill the void.

The thought was sobering.

And depressing.

And far too pitiful, aggrandizing, and introspective.

Therefore, I refused to believe it. I didn't feel empty. I was cold.

Just . . . cold.

Plus, no one was harmed during the exchange. We both got what we wanted, after all. The women I slept with secured their trophy—a picture, a story for her girls—and I secured a night of warmth, of unencumbered sleep. These sorts of currency exchanges were commonplace for me.

Unfortunately, with Lucy, I wanted something altogether different.

She wasn't the first woman to arouse my interest. But after several frustrated efforts in my past, I'd learned to never fuck a woman I truly wanted. Seeing the disappointment or pity in a woman's eyes after a night of clumsy, albeit sincere, attempts at pleasure was an exercise in masochism.

I consider myself more of a sadist.

My want of Lucy made my plan to seduce Lucy a good deal more complicated. But not insurmountable (figuratively or literally). I merely needed to control the event, ensure it would be a hurried, frenzied copulation rather than an encounter of any length.

To that end, armed with a bottle of champagne, sundry food items, and a basket of strawberries, I tracked Lucy down.

Though the retreat grounds were spread over several acres, covered in meandering rocky paths surrounded by tall, unknown trees, Lucy wasn't difficult to find. Most of the large group yoga classes took place in an open-air studio made entirely of a dark wood.

Aesthetically, on the outside, the studio resembled the love child between a barn and a rustic cabin. Inside the floor was glossy and well polished, and with no dividers. It was an expansive, unencumbered space. Folding doors had been pushed aside, leaving structural beams and the roof as the only impediment to the outside, sending a reverberating *Ooohhhhmmmm* through the woods and over the lake.

I mounted the stairs to the studio, leaving my goodies on the porch and approaching the end post with quiet steps. Peeking around the corner as unobtrusively as possible—because, as I learned yesterday when I arrived, these seekers of inner peace grew enraged when their mellow was disturbed—I scanned the studio for Lucy.

I spied her immediately. Surprisingly, it wasn't her rainbow mane that caught my attention. It was her arse. I'd been admiring it yesterday when I arrived, but hadn't realized that I'd memorized it as well. The entire class was bending over, giving me their backsides, so I indulged myself, taking a moment to appreciate it.

Everything about Lucy was small, waiflike, and delicate (in appearance). Everything except her arse. It was perfectly round—almost spherical—and disproportionately big for her small frame. And it made my mouth water.

The class ended far too soon for my taste, driving me away from my hiding spot before I was caught lurking. Leaning against a porch post, I waited for Lucy to emerge.

When she did she was smiling.

But when she caught sight of me, it fell from her face.

"What are you doing here?"

"Waiting for you." I grinned despite her brusque question, my eyes skating over her body. When they again settled on her upturned face I was both pleased and surprised to find her gaze unfocused, perhaps even dazed, as she studied my face.

"What do you want?" Her question held a distracted air to it and I knew she was asking about more than the now. She wanted to know my general intentions.

I don't make a habit of sharing my intentions as they're usually wicked.

Therefore, I answered for the now. "I've come to lure you away for a picnic on a mountain."

"A mountain?"

"That's right."

She crossed her arms, her eyes sharpening. I could see she'd assumed I'd been trying to make her the butt of a joke. "There's no mountain around here."

"There is." Her friend Broderick joined the conversation, stepping next to me as though he'd been asked to validate my claim. I stiffened.

My assessment of Broderick could be summed up in one word: smooth. The last thing I needed was for her smooth friend to invite himself along.

"What?" Lucy frowned at us both.

"Rattlesnake Mountain, though it's more of a hill." He tilted his chin in the direction of the hiking trail. "The views of the lake from the top are awesome."

"Yes. Awesome." I nodded, struggling to find a way to cut him out should he insist on accompanying us.

I was just about to volunteer that I had only two glasses for the champagne when Broderick gripped Lucy by the upper arm and tugged her toward me, basically shoving her into my chest. Automatically, my hands lifted to hold her in place.

"You two go and work off . . . energy," he said, nodding once like all was decided.

"Rick—" Lucy started to protest, but she didn't attempt to break free of my hold. Rather, her hands came to rest on my chest.

"Lucy." His eyes widened meaningfully, though I couldn't interpret his meaning.

She opened her mouth like she was on the edge of launching a complaint.

Broderick interrupted her again, but he addressed me, "Did you know Lucy was thinking about becoming a missionary?"

She snapped her mouth shut.

I cocked an eyebrow at this news. "Really?"

"Yes. But she decided to *skip the missionary position* and instead focus on charity work in the States. With dogs."

"With dogs?" This news struck a chord and my eyes moved over Lucy with new, albeit unwilling, appreciation. I'd had a dog when I was younger. Rather, the family had a dog, though I'd considered him only mine. A pet was everything to an unloved child. I'd mourned his passing alone. At the time it had felt like losing a limb. Or maybe an organ.

As I studied her I supposed it made sense that she was an animal lover. She seemed like that sort, empathetic and compassionate. I felt a niggling thread of guilt and quickly quashed it.

"Yes," he continued, still looking at Lucy, "the position with dogs— "

"Okay, we have to go." Her usually soft voice was shrill as she grabbed my hand and tugged me away from her friend. "That mountain isn't going to hike itself."

I allowed myself to be led, but made her pause so I could collect the basket. She pulled her hand out of mine. I noticed her gaze flicker to Broderick then away to the planks of the porch.

Frowning at her averted gaze, I glanced at Broderick. He watched us with a slight smirk. When I caught his eye his smirk widened into an odd smile, odd, because it was encouraging.

I tried to return it.

I couldn't.

So I turned away.

As we walked off the porch, side by side but not touching, I resolved to follow through with my plan as soon as possible. I already wanted Lucy. Nothing would be more disastrous than actually liking her too.

***

"YOU'RE BEING QUIET. Why are you being so quiet?"

*Because I'm watching your glorious arse as you climb the hill and lamenting that I'll only be allowed to grab it once. If I'm lucky.*

"Uh, was I?" I shook my head, redirecting my attention to her face.

She furrowed her brow at me over her shoulder. We'd been walking single file up the hill with her in front by several paces, her bottom at my eye level.

She was winded. I was not.

"What are you doing?" Her tone was laced with suspicion as she gathered deep, panting breaths. The sound and movement were distracting.

"Admiring the view," I answered immediately because the words were true even if they were misleading.

Her lips flattened, though she was still breathing with difficulty, and she shifted her gaze to the emerging skyline around us. I kept mine fastened on her profile, allowing myself a moment to study the image before me.

Much of her hair had pulled free of her braid and was billowing around her shoulders. I must've done something remarkably good when I was younger, or something remarkably bad, because she was still in her yoga pants and tank top. A sliver of her toned belly and side were visible, as her shirt had lifted during the hike.

I wanted to bite her smooth skin. My teeth ached to sink into her flesh. Lick it. Grab it. However, experience told me women of her kind didn't like large men biting, licking, or grabbing them. They liked soft, coaxing caresses, gentle words, and a soothing hand. They liked dark rooms where they could pretend I wasn't quite the frightening giant I was in reality with all the lights on.

"We're close to the summit." Lucy shaded her eyes and looked at me, her chest rising and falling with gasping breaths. "How can you not be tired? This hill goes straight up."

I shrugged. "I work out sometimes."

She threw her head back and laughed, her open palm falling to her thigh with a smack.

I liked the sound. Without thinking too much about it, I tried to get her to do it again. "Not very often. Just once or twice a day."

"Is that so?" Her lips curved, her smile glorious. "What kind of work outs do you do? Hill climbing?"

"Yes, mostly. I have a hill all my own in Ireland."

"I bet you run to the top of it and yell, 'I'm the king of the world!'"

"I don't."

"Why not?"

"It would frighten the sheep." *And enrage the ape.*

"Oh, you have sheep on your hill?"

Now we were walking side by side. I reached out to help her over a steep spot.

"Yes. The hill is full of sheep, but they're not my sheep."

"You don't like sheep?"

"I prefer dogs."

Lucy stumbled. I caught her before she slipped, bringing her against my side. "Careful, the rocks are loose here."

"Got it." She nodded and set me gently away, reaching for a tree branch to steady her. "So you like dogs?"

"I do, as a matter of fact." I figured there was no harm in discussing my domestic animal preferences. Many people liked dogs. "What's the name of the charity you work with?"

Her eyes darted to mine, then away. "It's not that big of a deal. I don't know why Rick even brought it up."

"What kind of work do they do?"

"It's the Animal Haven Shelter, a no-kill shelter for abandoned animals in New York City. Annie lets me highlight it on the blog and we do a fundraiser. I volunteer sometimes. Like I said, no big deal. So . . ." I heard her sigh, the sound telling me this topic made her uncomfortable. "Look. We're here."

Lucy jogged a few paces ahead and away from me, slowing her steps as she crested the hill. I caught up quickly, but my steps faltered when I reached the top, the full view finally coming into focus.

Silence fell between us. Separately, yet together, we absorbed the splendor of the valley. Broderick had been right, but he'd also been wrong. The view was a lot more than merely awesome. It was extraordinarily magnificent.

The lakes glittered beneath us, dotted with pinpricks of light from the mid-afternoon sun, sapphire blue, serene, and calm. Lush, green trees lined the bank, intensifying the colors of the cloudless sky and tranquil water. The beauty was both at hand and at a distance, and it was breathtaking.

I became aware that Lucy's fingers were threaded with mine when she squeezed and pulled me some steps closer to the edge of the bluff. I had no idea who had reached for the other, only that we were now touching and her hand was cool and soft.

"See?" I whispered. "I told you it was nice."

Lucy turned a disbelieving face toward me. Though she smiled, the way her nose wrinkled told me she thought I was mad. "Nice? This isn't nice. This is fucking gorgeous."

I chuckled at the dichotomy of her exuberance. "You're right, Lucy. Please forgive me. It's fucking gorgeous. Well said."

She nodded, her smile wide and impish. "I never get tired of hearing those words."

"It's fucking gorgeous?"

"No. You're right, Lucy."

Now I did laugh. She joined me as she released my hand, making a grab for the basket. "I'm starving. What's in here? Steak? Beef jerky? Veal?"

"No. No meat." I shook my head, watching her as she pulled out the blanket, let it fall to the ground, and rummaged through the basket. The truth was, I couldn't find any meat at the retreat, so I had to settle for strawberries, kale salad, and feta bites . . . whatever the hell those were.

Lucy extracted the champagne and examined the label, then gave a low whistle. "Cripes, Sean. This is no way to detox."

"If detoxing doesn't include a steady diet of alcohol and steak, then I guess I'll always be somewhat toxic."

"Hmm," she replied noncommittally, not looking up from the bottle. Placing the basket on the ground next to the blanket, she peeled the foil away from the cork. "So why do you like dogs?"

I grabbed the champagne from her. "Give me that. That's my job."

She lifted an eyebrow at me. "Why is that your job? I'm quite good at opening champagne bottles. I used to wait tables at a posh restaurant."

"It's my job because I'm rubbish at everything else."

This statement earned me a smile. "Okay, fine then. I'll spread the blanket and set the food out. Let me know if you need help popping it open or if you'd like a lesson in picnicking from a professional."

I untwisted the wire holding the cork in place. "You're a picnicking professional?"

"Yes. I'm quite accomplished at eating outdoors."

"Really?" I was curious.

"In New York, in the spring, everyone picnics in Central Park. It's gorgeous and green and patchworks of blankets cover the ground. I love going just to people watch, but I also feel like food tastes better outside." Lucy talked as she worked, her movements relaxed and unhurried. I stepped away from the blanket she'd just spread and watched her, fascinated by her easy chatter.

"Do you go by yourself?" I didn't know what compelled me to ask the question, but I suddenly needed to know.

"Sometimes." She shrugged, then laughed lightly. "Actually, most of the time. But I don't mind."

Relief. I was relieved. But I said nothing, happy to have her continue speaking of her picnics, finding I was greedy for the details.

"And there's every kind of food you could want in the city. I have a special picnicking blanket, a thrift store find, a quilt of metallic-colored fabric—silver, gold, and copper. Basically, it's outrageous, but I love it. I love spreading it on the ground and sitting on it, like it's a throne and I'm the queen, a five-by-five porthole to an alternate dimension."

Finished setting out the cups, plates, and napkins, Lucy glanced up at me. Her eyes were bright and undesigning, as was her smile. She reached out to me with one hand.

I stared at her dumbly, uncertain what to do.

Her smile slipped as she lifted her eyebrows. "Sean?"

"Yes?"

"Do you want to sit?"

I glanced at her, then the blanket, then the food, then back to her. "Yes. Of course."

I sat.

"Sean?"

"Yes?" I looked to her again.

"Do you want me to finish up with the champagne?"

I examined the bottle in my hands, discovered it was still corked. "Ah, no. I can finish."

"Okay." She gave me a smile, it looked a bit nervous.

I gave her a smile, feeling a bit nervous.

I filled the glasses to the brim, offered one to her first, then gulped mine. We sat in a silence that was both tense and sacred while I had the distinct impression of being lost.

Born out of a desire to break the thickening tension, I announced, "I've brought strawberries."

"Oh," she said, the soft exclamation tinged with regret.

"What?"

"I'm allergic to strawberries," Lucy confessed, her expression apologetic as she finished her first glass of champagne. "I take one bite and I swell up into a red mess."

"So, you become that which you fear." I refilled her glass.

"What?"

"You turn into a strawberry."

She choked on a surprised laugh mid-sip, but recovered with adorable self-deprecation. "Exactly, but not nearly as tasty."

I tilted my head to the side and scrutinized her, mumbling under my breath before I could catch the words, "That's debatable."

She must've heard my comment because she squirmed and averted her eyes, casting them to the sky while she took another sip of her champagne and changed the subject. "This is good stuff, Sean. If I'd known you had champagne in your cabin I would have been nicer to you."

"Ah, so champagne is the way to your heart?"

"That's right, Bubs. Give me a good bubbly and I'm a happy woman." She appeared to be on the verge of laughing.

"And you've nicknamed me after champagne? I guess I'm flattered."

"You should be." Lucy gulped the rest of her glass, then added as though it were an afterthought, "I only nickname people I like."

I'd been reaching for the bottle to refill her glass when she said the words, halting my movements.

*I only nickname people I like.*

Strangely, inexplicably, the air was too thin and I couldn't quite gather enough into my lungs. I sensed her eyes on me so I forced a smile.

"But we both know you don't like me," I said.

"Of course." Her voice held a slight tremble and she held her glass out to be refilled. "Of course I don't like you."

"Good." Oddly, her words didn't make me feel good.

She gulped half of her third glass, then added with a tad of belligerence, "What do you mean, *good*? Don't you want me to like you?"

"Not particularly."

She stared at me, her eyes the color of the morning sky, and her pretty mouth curved into a sharp frown. "Well, why not?"

"Because it wouldn't be good for you."

"How so?" She looked and sounded offended. Her words slurred just a smidge. I glanced between her and the half-empty glass.

Lucy Fitzpatrick was a lightweight. It made sense, though at five foot seven or thereabouts, she wasn't particularly short, but she was still very slight. Well, aside from her gloriously well-endowed bottom.

Without forethought to my desire for vengeance against her undeserving yet exalted brother, I responded honestly. "Because I'm not good for you."

"Because you want to have sex with me?" Lucy jutted out her pointed chin with champagne-fueled bravery, her words and the darkening of her eyes catching me off guard.

Lucy Fitzpatrick was full of surprises.

"That's it, right? You think I'll grow attached and moon over you like you're God's gift?"

I blinked at her, unsure how to respond to this onslaught of brutal honesty. Usually, women weren't honest with me until the morning after I disappointed them. Sometimes they weren't honest even then.

Turns out I didn't need to say anything because Lucy cut me off with a loud, derisive snort.

"As if." She tossed her hand not holding the champagne into the air as though throwing away the idea of her ever growing attached to me. "I've got some news for you, Sean Cassidy. I know I'd be just one of the notches in your bedpost. I have no delusions about meaning something to you. You may be a hot piece of arse, but you're not the kind women want for anything long-term, not if they're smart."

I slid my teeth to the side, was forced to narrow my eyes so I didn't betray the effect of her words. Lucy's sloppily tossed gauntlet hit a target she doubtless didn't realize existed, sending a jarring shock of swelling unpleasantness to the back of my throat, jaw, and the tips of my fingers.

I was a hot piece of arse. This was true. That's all I was.

Smart women didn't want anything long-term, not with me. This was also true.

"How observant you are," I said mechanically, swallowing the rising bitterness. "How very clever."

Lucy's frown intensified until I thought she appeared regretful for what she'd said, guilty even. Perhaps alcohol made her mean, or perhaps it simply made her speak the truth.

"Sean," she began, reaching out to touch my arm, as though to apologize, but I quickly cut her off.

"You're right, of course." I gave her a smile I was sure didn't reach my eyes. "About everything."

Her chest rose and fell with rapid breaths and she stared at me for a long moment before asking, "Why are you this way?"

"You may as well ask, why does a bird fly? It's in my nature, of course." I studied the writing on the outside of the champagne bottle, similar sentiments from my childhood playing on repeat between my ears.

*You were born this way, Sean.*

*It's your parents.*

*Look at you. You can't help your nature.*

*You'll never be better than the people you came from.*

Lucy shook her head slowly as she studied me and parted her lips to speak. But I'd had enough of her mouth for the day, no matter how alluring it was.

"The forecast said there would be rain. We should head back." I stood, piling the picnic items back into the bag, mentally calculating how quickly I could get back to the beautiful, rich, indolent people I'd abandoned in Spain.

That's where I belonged.

I did not belong on a sunny hillside in New Hampshire. I did not belong with a tart, odd-haired, magnificently arsed pixie who wore her heart on her sleeve.

My distain for Ronan Fitzpatrick hadn't waned, but my interest in using or abusing his sister to exact my revenge had entirely fled. And I was abruptly tired.

Tired and cold.

While I packed up, Lucy had stood from the blanket and was hovering at its perimeter, watching me. I bent to retrieve it. She bent in unison, tugging it toward her.

"Let me help," she said.

"No need." Distractedly, I surveyed the ground, ensuring I would leave nothing behind.

She tugged harder. "I can fold it."

"I've got it." I noted the ground was free of debris.

"Let go of the blanket, Sean."

With what can only be described as an angry yank, Lucy wrenched the blanket from my grip and began to fold it with brutal violence.

I studied her and her vicious blanket folding for two seconds, then hazarded to ask, "Are you quite all right?"

"This was a stupid idea."

"The picnic?"

"All of it." She sliced a hand through the air, gesturing to the world, then added, "And talking to you, specifically."

Her movements were still forceful and jerky. I took a step closer, intent on grabbing the blanket before she ripped it.

I kept my tone purposefully soft, hoping to disarm her before she detonated. "Don't worry, I won't bother you again."

Her hands stilled, the blanket now a tight, twisted ball nowhere near folded, and her pale eyes cut to mine.

Something decidedly female was going on in her head, something of the mystery-to-men variety. I had no idea what she was thinking, but she looked both aggrieved and remorseful. I held very still because it seemed like the safest thing to do.

We stared at each other. She dropped the blanket. She took a step away and pushed her wild hair from her face.

She charged, closing the distance between us, her hands reaching for and fisting in the neck of my shirt.

Then she kissed me.

# Chapter Seven

@**LucyFitz** Life is like a bottle of champers: expensive, bitter and often gives you indigestion.

@**Anniecat to @LucyFitz** Agree. When given the choice between champagne and cake, it's cake every time.

@**LucyFitz to @Anniecat** This is why I love you.


### *Lucy*

SEAN CASSIDY HAD his tongue down my throat.

Or maybe it was me who had my tongue down his. I knew I'd been the one to initiate the kiss, but I couldn't remember who started the tongue action. Sean was kissing me in a way that made my toes curl, my skin prickle, and my ladies parts clench with need.

His big, warm hands travelled slowly from the back of my neck, down my spine, before unceremoniously cupping my arse. He squeezed hard and I whimpered against his lips.

"I want you," he breathed and his mouth moved to my neck, planting wet kisses along my sensitive skin. A rumbly groan escaped him as my hands went to his muscular shoulders, gripping tightly. His fingertips dug into my flesh with need, and unexpectedly, I discovered I liked how rough he was.

Nipping lightly at the underside of my jaw, he murmured, "Are you wet?"

As I fuzzy-headedly prepared to answer, his phone began ringing loudly, the melodic tone disrupting the quiet. I broke away from him, my breathing heavy because, well, I was aroused.

"Um," I said, trying to catch my breath while proper brain function continued to evade me.

"Lucy," he groaned and reached for me, completely ignoring the call as he tried to pull my mouth back to his. I placed my hands on his chest to keep him at bay.

"You should answer that," I told him in a shaky voice. It was still ringing inside his pocket, and he sighed irritably as he pulled it out as though to press ignore. When he glanced at the screen he did a double take, and I followed his gaze to find the caller ID displaying the name Mother Fitzpatrick, my brother's reluctant nickname. Why on earth was Ronan calling him?

I almost felt like laughing. Was this some sort of spooky brotherly sixth sense on his part? Like Sean would answer and Ronan would start barking down the line, *"Get your hands off my sister!"*

Sean appeared just as curious to know why Ronan was calling him as I was. He hit accept and answered, "Hello?"

"Hey, is this Sean?" a female voice replied. It was so quiet out here that I could hear her clear as day. It was Annie. What the hell?

"It is, and who may I ask is speaking?" he queried, like he didn't already know. He sounded calm and at ease, not half as frazzled as I was.

"This is Annie. Ronan Fitzpatrick's fiancée. We've met on a number of occasions," she explained.

"Yes, I remember," Sean purred. "I never forget a face as pretty as yours."

I frowned, annoyed at how he flirted with her – and disturbed by the fact that I was annoyed. I folded my arms.

"Hang up that phone right now!" I heard Ronan growl angrily in the background. There were a few loud footsteps, as though Annie was running to get away from him. I heard the click of a lock, like she'd just shut herself inside the bathroom. Sean and I shared identical expressions of confusion. When Annie spoke again, she sounded breathless as she shouted to Ronan. "Let me talk to him. You're too stubborn for your own good sometimes."

"Unlock the door, Annie, I mean it," Ronan demanded.

"Hi, uh, sorry about this," said Annie, speaking to Sean again and letting out a nervous laugh. "My fiancé is being difficult."

"What else is new?" Sean chuckled, like he was thoroughly enjoying this unexpected interaction. Anything to get one over on my brother. I sighed and moved closer to him, resting my head next to the other side of the phone so I could hear better.

"Yes, well." Annie cleared her throat. "I've called because I need your help and Ronan is too proud to ask you himself. He, William Moore, and Bryan Leech have been contracted for a sportswear photo shoot with Adidas in New York this weekend. Unfortunately, William's fallen ill and won't be able to attend, so I was wondering if you'd be interested in replacing him?"

"I already have a deal with Puma. I'm not sure my contract will allow it."

Annie heaved an audible sigh. "You rugby players and your sponsorship deals."

Sean grinned. "I take it I'm not the first person you called."

"No," she answered sheepishly. "Ronan isn't exactly your biggest fan. I actually called your agent first. She said she was under strict instructions not to schedule any promo work during your break, but I thought I'd call to see if you'd be interested in doing us a favor. I know you probably don't want to come all the way to the U.S., but I think this would be a great way for you and Ronan to mend some bridges."

I heard my brother let out a loud, derisive laugh in the background. Clearly, he had his ear to the door, listening in just like I was. Annie had no clue Sean was already stateside.

"Your husband-to-be doesn't sound very convinced," said Sean with a smile in his voice.

"Let me deal with Ronan," Annie stated firmly.

He cast his gaze on me mischievously. "You know what? New York is sounding a lot more appealing these days."

My heart pounded at the prospect of yet more time in the same general area as Sean Cassidy.

"So you'll do it?" Annie asked, a hint of relief in her voice.

"I'll have my lawyer look through the Puma contract and get back to you. If he says it's okay to be affiliated with another brand, then yes, I'll do it."

"Thank you."

"It's my pleasure."

The moment he hung up he came at me. "Now, where were we?"

When he began sliding his arms around my waist I pulled away, my heart racing. "We shouldn't have kissed."

His hooded, aroused expression morphed into a frown. "I see . . ."

"I don't mess around with rugby players, and being with you is a really bad idea for a number of reasons."

"Such as?"

"Sean," I narrowed my eyes at him, "just moments ago you told me I shouldn't like you."

"Humor me. Tell me why it's a bad idea." He was entirely too close, but he made no move to touch me with anything but his gaze.

I angled my chin. "Well, for one I'm not your type."

Sean lifted an eyebrow and wrapped his arm around my waist. He brought me flush against him, pressing my belly against his dick, which was hard as steel beneath the fabric of his jeans. "Obviously, you're wrong."

I swallowed and tried not to think about the size of him, because God, the *size* of him. I also wondered if he'd maintained his erection all through the phone call with Annie, or was he just that quick to get it up again?

That thought was both intoxicating and sobering.

I had no words, especially considering the sexy *I want to devour you* look on his face. The universe must have heard my plea, because right at that moment the heavens opened and rain began pouring down.

"It's raining. We should go." I hurriedly pushed him away and turned to start the hike back down. I almost expected him to argue, but he didn't.

Silently, he picked up the picnic basket and followed my lead. Neither of us spoke the whole way down, and by the time we reached the retreat the tension between us was unwieldy. Also, I was soaked to the skin.

When I realized my nipples were peeking through my wet clothes, I folded my arms across my chest as I turned back to Sean, unable to meet his eyes. "I'll, uh, I'll see you later."

Before he could reply I was gone, already halfway to my cabin.

Once there, I stripped off my soaking clothes and started the shower. When the water heated, I stepped under the spray, my kiss with Sean playing on repeat in my head.

I remembered the way he'd grabbed my arse, like a man possessed, and disappointedly realized I'd never taken the opportunity to cop a feel of his.

How ridiculously poetic had it been that a call from Ronan (well, technically it was Annie, but it was Ronan's phone) was the thing to interrupt our moment.

I knew exactly why I'd kissed him, too. I'd seen more of Sean's human side today, and combined with how physically attracted I was to him, it was almost impossible not to kiss him. He liked dogs, and when I'd told him of my volunteer work at the shelter, his expression told me he thought it was a worthwhile pursuit.

But most importantly, deep down, I didn't think he liked himself very much.

It made me sad. It also made me want to make him happy.

I turned off the water and stepped out to find someone had shoved a small note under my door. My heart sped up, wondering if it was from Sean. But sure enough, this had become Broderick's and my way of communicating the last week or two, and the note was from him.

*I can't find Sean anywhere, so I guess that means no steak.*
*Meet me in the dining hall for dinner?*
*I hope you enjoyed your hike ;-)*
*Rick.*

I wrapped a towel around my body and scribbled a quick response on the other side of the note. It was the last night of the retreat, but I wasn't in any frame of mind to be good company.

*Not feeling well.*

*Breakfast instead?*

*Lucy.*

As I went to quickly shove the note under Rick's door, I stepped outside and came face to face with Sean. His fist was raised mid-air, as though he'd been about to knock. I looked him over, noticing he still hadn't changed out of his wet clothes.

"Um," I said, biting on my lower lip as his hot gaze swept across my toweled form.

He didn't reply, but simply stepped forward, entering my cabin as I instinctively stepped back, dropping the note. Slamming the door shut behind him with a foot, he kept coming at me until the backs of my knees hit the sofa. I think I may have let out a tiny squeak but really couldn't be sure.

"Let's try this again. I want you," he said as his hands clasped my neck and he pulled my mouth to his.

His kiss was hard and unrelenting, and I felt my legs grow weak. As though sensing this too, he slid a hand around my waist, holding me tight against him. Before I could stop him, he broke our kiss and released my towel. It fell away, exposing my entire body, and I trembled under his astute attention.

Sean's molten-hot stare devoured me, tracing the dips and curves of my form before swearing and bending to suck one of my nipples into his mouth. I yelped in surprise because his teeth smashed against my skin.

Perhaps he was just eager.

This definitely seemed to be the case when he swiftly lowered me onto the sofa. My head knocked against the armrest and my breath whooshed out of me.

*Well, that hurt a little . . .*

Sean began sucking at my breasts in a hot frenzy as his hand went between my legs. I was so aroused by the fact that I was naked and he was touching me intimately that it took me a moment to realize he was doing everything wrong.

And I mean, seriously wrong.

His hand was on my vagina, but he was just rubbing away with no rhythm or technique. He might as well have been trying to get a persistent stain off the carpet. I mean, his fingers were nowhere near the vicinity of my clit, and *that* was the most important part.

*The* most important part, people.

His other hand squeezed my breast harshly and rotated it back and forth in a wax-on, wax-off movement, like he was disconnected from the ramifications of his touch. Plus, his tongue was playing no part in the action, only his mouth. I frowned but he didn't see, because he was too busy giving me the worst foreplay of my life.

How could he be such an amazing kisser but such an unskilled lover?

Bracing my hands on his shoulders, I awkwardly pushed him away and he groaned like I was ruining a perfectly good time.

"Wait, wait a minute. Stop," I said, wincing because I felt terrible. I mean, how do you tell one of the most attractive men you've ever met that he sucks at foreplay?

You don't.

You don't tell him. You beg off and pretend to have a headache, which was a crying shame. Really, Sean's inability to put his body to good use was a crime against all womankind.

"Ronan will never find out," he assured me and moved to get right back to business.

I stopped him again, wincing. "That's not why it's a bad idea."

He stared at me, his eyebrows suspended between panic and frustration. "What's going on, Lucy?"

His low, gravelly voice almost undid me. Almost. But then I remembered his clumsy, uncomfortable, decidedly unsexy maneuverings. I was never good at faking, and I wasn't going to start now.

"I'm, well, I'm not really feeling it, Sean."

He stared at me for several protracted moments. I was certain no woman had ever pressed pause on him before. Christ, most of the women he slept with were probably so elated to be doing it with Sean Cassidy that they didn't even care if the sex was crap.

Well, not this woman.

If sex didn't feel good, then there wasn't really a point for me. I didn't shag for status.

"You're not feeling it." The statement of acceptance rang with a note of hallow self-contempt, surprising me, forcing me to take a closer look at Sleazy Sean Cassidy.

Resentment hardened his features, but his bitterness was turned decidedly inward. He wasn't angry with me. He was upset with himself.

And that's when I realized the truth.

Sean *knew* he was rubbish at foreplay. Something in my expression must've registered my discovery because he flinched and sat back away from me. He ran a hand through his hair, looking humiliated.

Sean Cassidy was blushing.

"You're right," he said through gritted teeth. "This was a bad idea."

Rising from the sofa he brushed off his shirt and without another word, turned to leave.

A brick dropped to the pit of my stomach, my gut twisted and I suddenly felt terrible. He was so big, so powerful, cocky, and yet in that moment appeared terribly inconsequential, defenseless, and humiliated. *Alone.*

Without thinking, I stood, grabbing the towel and quickly covering myself before going after him.

"Wait," I called.

He turned around stiffly, hands on his hips as he stared at the floor. "What?"

Jeez, he sounded angry. "I'm sorry."

Now he looked up, his stare glacial. "Don't apologize. Never apologize for not wanting to have sex. You were just being honest."

"Yes, true. But, here's the thing, I do want to have sex, with you. I do."

He barked a bitter laugh. "A pity fuck? Don't do me any favors."

"No," I replied firmly. Now I frowned at him. "That's not what this is. I like you. You turn me on and I want to have sex with you, but I just think we're playing from two different songbooks. Like, I'm performing Mozart but you're rocking out to Led Zeppelin. We both need to be playing the same tune."

The reluctant glimmer of hope behind his gaze made me want to hug him. I could see he was more than tempted and his vulnerability boosted my confidence.

I added for good measure, "If not the same tune, then at least the same genre."

Sean rubbed his jaw, his mouth tugging to the side with an adorably shy smirk, and he took a step forward. "So what are you suggesting?"

I swallowed, remembering our wonderful kiss on the hill. If he could kiss like that then surely the rest was just a matter of . . .

A matter of . . .

*Hmm* . . .

"I'm suggesting we go inside my room and give this another try."

His jaw worked as he considered my suggestion. After a long moment he finally replied, "Okay, then."

I nodded and gestured for him to follow me into the bedroom. Once there I sat on the edge of the bed and looked up at him. "Right so, first things first. Take off your clothes."

His smirk widened—less adorably shy and more adorably cocky—but he didn't make a move. I threw up my hands.

"Oh, come on. I'm not being a pervert. I'm practically naked and you're fully clothed. We need to even the playing field a little."

"Okay," he responded softly and proceeded to pull his shirt off over his head. My mouth fell open as he revealed inch after inch of abs and perfectly toned muscle.

Perhaps I should just get him to stand there so I could look at him naked while I got myself off?

Nah, too weird.

Maybe next time.

Off went his jeans and then he was lowering his boxers to the floor. My eyes snagged on his dick, which *was* in proportion to the rest of his physique.

Okay, I could work with this. I could *definitely* work with this. His eyes heated and my breathing deepened as our gazes locked. He seemed preoccupied with the dip and curve of my collarbone, and I felt oddly exposed with his eyes there.

"Tell me what to do," he said in a low, husky voice, and I watched as his cock began to harden with alarming speed.

I didn't say anything for so long that he started to approach the bed. I found myself shifting up as far as the pillows, pulling my knees to my chest as I contemplated the gorgeous hulk of a man who wanted to have his wicked way with me.

I just had to tell him what to do.

Right.

*Think, Lucy. Think!*

He was already kneeling on the bed, completely naked, and gripping my calves to pull my legs apart. The movement caused my towel to fall free once more, and his attention wandered to my breasts. He took his time admiring them before lifting his gaze to my face.

He must have found something funny in my expression because he chuckled in amusement. "I'm waiting, Lucy."

I exhaled heavily and cleared my throat. "K-kiss me."

My head lay against the pillows as he braced himself above me and lowered his mouth to mine. His lips moved slowly, almost hesitant, but when I slid my tongue against his he groaned and deepened the kiss. I felt myself heating up, a slickness forming between my thighs, and in no time at all I was panting, my clit swollen and aching for pressure.

"What do you want now?" Sean whispered and my arousal heightened.

"Kiss me," I repeated the same command as before.

His mouth curved in a smile. "I am kissing you."

"Somewhere else," I said shyly and his eyes darkened. I quickly added, "But no teeth. Not yet. Just your lips."

"As you wish," he murmured and began planting soft, barely there kisses down my body. Once his head was between my legs he paused, like he was wary of getting things wrong again.

"B-blow on me, gently," I said, throat catching.

His lips formed an O as he softly blew and I moaned so loudly I'd be surprised if Broderick didn't hear it next door.

"Lick my clit," I went on, my entire body flushing with embarrassment. It felt strange to be instructing him, but at the same time it was a massive turn-on. He was like an obedient servant, waiting on my every command.

Sean Cassidy as my own personal sexual servant . . . I wondered if I could get him to peel me some grapes afterward.

Bringing his mouth closer, his tongue snaked out and he licked me. My body bucked, my clit pulsing at the contact, and his hand went to my hipbone to hold me in place. My eyes met his and I realized he was waiting for further instructions.

My voice was throaty and strained. "Now use your tongue to draw circles around it."

"Gently?"

"Yes."

He did as I asked and I moaned again. A low, gravelly hum emanated from the back of his throat as he continued to lick circles around my clit.

"Oh God," I breathed. "Now a little faster."

My thighs clenched tight and I knew if he kept this up it wouldn't take long for me to come.

"Look at you," Sean whispered, eyes blazing.

"Put your fingers inside me," I said and he complied.

"Like this?" he asked, moving two fingers slowly in and out, *gently.*

"Yes," I answered, my voice suddenly high-pitched.

I closed my eyes, feeling an orgasm building. Sean's fingers were hitting just the right spot, and combined with his circles on my clit, I found myself panting and shaking as I came violently on his tongue. I let out a long, satiated sigh, then opened my eyes to find him watching me intently.

I collapsed into the pillows and threw an arm over my face, slightly embarrassed by his close inspection. He climbed up the bed and pulled my arm back so he could look at my face.

He seemed fascinated. I stared back at him, unsure why he was looking at me like he was.

"What?" I whispered, self-conscious.

"You came," he said, his voice awed.

I couldn't help letting out a small laugh. "Yes, that's generally what happens when you go down on a woman as fantastically as you just did, Sean."

He huffed a gruff breath and grabbed my face, kissing me again. I tasted myself on his tongue. "I could get addicted that."

"To what?"

"To giving you orgasms."

I laughed. "Well, who am I to deny you?"

He smiled, wide and bright, and kissed me some more before murmuring against my mouth, "I want to fuck you now."

I hummed my agreement, my body a pliant mass beneath him. His cock nudged at my opening and it felt amazing, but then I started, realizing he wasn't wearing any protection.

"Sean, wait. We need to get a condom."

"Christ," he swore and held himself up. "Are they in your bag?"

I instantly deflated. "No. I didn't bring any. I hadn't planned for . . .

this."

He studied me, brows drawing together. "No, I don't suppose you did." A pause and then a spark lit behind his eyes. "Actually, I think I have one in the back pocket of my jeans."

"Oh?" I said questioningly.

He grinned. "You can never be too prepared."

"You were planning on getting laid during the hike, weren't you?"

Pulling the small foil packet from his jeans, he returned to the bed. His grin didn't falter. "Well, you are a picnic professional. Why not add another skill to your belt?"

"I don't aspire to gain skills that could get me arrested," I answered, flirtation in my voice.

"No, I imagine your thievery gets you into enough trouble as it is," he shot back.

My smile fell, and a sharp stab of pain sliced through me. I wasn't sure why, perhaps because we'd just been intimate, but the careless way he made fun of an addiction I truly struggled with had me feeling less than enthusiastic to continue.

I sat up on the bed, pulling the covers around myself to hide my nudity.

"That's not a very kind thing to say," I told him in a quiet voice.

His lips formed a frown, confusion diminishing gradually into understanding and concern as he threw down the condom and climbed back onto the bed.

"No, it wasn't. I'm sorry," he murmured in apology as he tried to pull the covers away.

I held them tighter and gave him my profile. "You know, maybe we should call it a night."

"Lucy," he reached for my hand and, after a bit, I allowed him to take it. He kissed me on the back of my knuckles. "Please look at me."

I moved just my eyes to his, found him staring at me with a mixture of alarm and sincere regret.

"I am sorry. I think by now you know me well enough to realize I'm terrible at more than just foreplay."

This earned him a reluctant and suspicious smile. "You're just trying to get in my pants."

"Technically, you're not wearing any, but that's not why I apologized." His eyebrows knit in consternation above his cobalt eyes. "It was a completely insensitive thing to say. I *am* insensitive. But I'd like to be otherwise, with you, if you'll give me the chance."

I felt myself melting. He was either a world champion at faking sincerity, or his candor might be the sexiest thing about him, and consequently my ruin.

"I'm sorry," he whispered, and then again, "I'm sorry."

He lowered his mouth to mine and kissed me once, twice. Before I knew it I forgot my worries as I lost myself in Sean Cassidy again. His hands lowered the covers and roamed my body, resolutely gentle, as though all his movements were mindful. He pulled my thighs around his waist as he picked up the condom and tore the foil with his teeth.

I watched with rapt interest as he rolled it down his shaft then peered at me in question. "How can I make this good for you, Lucy?"

Oh, wow, he really was beautiful. I found myself adrift in his gaze for a second before I came to my senses. "Just . . . don't hold back."

He seemed surprised by this and swallowed thickly. The muscles in his arms tensed as he positioned himself and I lost my breath when he pushed into me.

"Oh," I cried out.

"Should I move?" Sean groaned and began to move before I could answer. His hips thrust back and forth, and he didn't hold back, just like I'd asked. I felt so small, almost fragile, in comparison to his sheer size and virility.

"You feel incredible," he said, looking into my eyes. I felt a connection to him, like we truly saw each other in that moment. But then, as though somebody had cut the electricity too soon, he came.

*What the hell?*

Don't get me wrong, watching a man as attractive as Sean orgasm was an experience in itself. It was just that things had only gotten started and then they were over.

"Fucking hell," he swore, burying his face in my neck and shifting to remove the condom, still breathing hard. "Fuck."

I didn't know what to say. I'd never had a man finish so quickly before.

"Sorry," he said, his voice sleepy as he trapped me with his arms and snuggled against me.

I couldn't speak. I was still too astonished. I mean, we're talking less than a minute here. I brushed my teeth longer than he'd lasted. And I wasn't sure whether I should be embarrassed or flattered.

At length, I finally whispered, "Sorry for what?"

Sean remained quiet, and I thought maybe he was too abashed to answer, but then I started to notice his breathing evening out.

He was asleep.

Wow.

*Wow!*

I chuckled my astonishment, but then frowned and shook my head.

Now I didn't know whether to laugh or feel hard done by. Then again, he had made me come quite spectacularly with his fingers and tongue, so it wasn't like he'd left me hanging. And I *had* told him not to hold back. I just didn't think he'd take the request quite so literally.

His arms held me to him, his massive body warm and encapsulating me entirely. I lay awake for a few minutes and briefly considered waking him, but in spite of everything, I didn't want him to leave. It had been a long time since I'd spent the night with a man and I just wanted to enjoy being held, feeling safe and warm. It was nice.

Closing my eyes, I snuggled close to him, and before long I fell asleep, too.

When I woke up Sean was still there, sound asleep, and I was roasting. The heat from his body was lovely but a little overwhelming. As carefully as I could, I extracted myself from his hold without waking him. After paying a quick visit to the bathroom, I threw on some clothes and stepped outside to take a walk. I covered almost the entire grounds of the retreat and then made my way to the dining hall for breakfast.

Armed with a bowl of porridge and some fresh fruit, I went to join Broderick where he sat with Cindy and Lisa.

"Sorry I missed dinner," I told him. "I wasn't feeling well."

He shrugged. "No biggie."

I ate in silence while they chatted around me, my mind elsewhere. I couldn't help thinking of Sean and the contradiction of how much he turned me on, but how clueless he was when it came to sex.

Wasn't his nickname Sleazy Sean?

How could somebody be so renowned for conquests yet never learn anything from the experience?

Was it all so drunken and fumbling that neither party ever bothered to figure out what made the other feel good?

And he seemed to know he was bad at it. So why hadn't he ever consulted the Internet? Why hadn't he tried to learn how to do things right prior to now? He seemed eager enough to learn last night . . .

I was adrift in these thoughts when the noise of a chair scraping back grabbed my attention. Glancing up, I found Sean joining us at the table. His hair was wet and he'd changed his clothes. For a moment, I felt bad for leaving him to wake up in my cabin all alone.

His gaze held mine for a beat, his expression somber. I tore my eyes away from his, fighting a fierce surge of heat threatening to overtake my neck and cheeks.

*I will not blush. I am not shy. I am an adult woman who likes having sex. So what if I had to teach him how and it was sexy as hell?*

I lifted my gaze to Sean once more. He was still looking at me and the heat behind his gaze, the intensity and vulnerability of it, obliterated all my reasoning and good sense. He looked at me like I was the center of something important. Like I was important to him.

*Fuck, fuck, fuck!*

I blushed.

Then I cursed under my breath and stabbed my porridge with my spoon, resolved not to make eye contact again. This was all in my head—it had to be. I couldn't go imagining last night meant something to Sean Cassidy.

Sleazy Sean, I reminded myself of his nickname again. This did not make me feel better.

He ate and chatted with the others for a few minutes while I regulated my breathing, then his thigh moved against mine as he leaned in close and murmured in my ear, "We should talk."

I raised a brow at him speculatively, ignoring the goosebumps caused by his hot breath against my neck. "About what?"

He leaned back, studying me, and pressed his lips together. "Things."

"Oh." I exhaled the word.

Smiling, he shook his head. "No need to look so frightened."

"I'm not frightened." I was a little frightened.

He pondered me a moment, his voice holding a hint of self-deprecation. "Perhaps that wasn't the correct choice of word. Traumatized is probably more fitting."

"I'm really not following you."

He sighed, his smile growing brittle, his words halting and tinged with apology. "Last night, I didn't exactly live up to what you expected."

"I didn't have any expectations, Sean," I lied, stunned by his self-effacement.

He scrutinized me for several moments, like I was an unsolvable equation, then pressed, "Be that as it may, I want to make it up to you."

"Make it up to me?" I squeaked, imagining all the things that statement could mean.

"Yes, but first . . ." He frowned, still examining my face, and turned in his chair, his arm coming to rest along the back of mine. With a painfully sincere expression—one that made my heart both flutter and squeeze—he whispered, "I want you to teach me."

## Chapter Eight

@**SeanCassinova** How is sex like a party?

@**THEBryanLeech to** @**SeanCassinova** Ok I'll bite. How is sex like a party?

@**SeanCassinova to** @**THEBryanLeech** It's more fun when everybody comes.

@**THEBryanLeech to** @**SeanCassinova** You're only figuring this out now?

### *Sean*

THERE'S THIS IDIOM I'd never fully appreciated until I sat across from lovely Lucy Fitzpatrick and asked her to teach me how to fuck, good and proper.

*Go for broke.*

Last night had been a nightmare. Then it had been a dream. And she'd been an angel.

*My* angel.

I wasn't quite sure what to think about that.

But waking up this morning, the bed still warm from her body—our bodies together—and heavy with her scent, my first conscious thought was of her face as she'd hit her orgasm. I closed my eyes and relived the pulsing of her reflexive response, the aftershocks of her pleasure, the way her skin flushed pink, and the beads of her rose-colored nipples drawing firm and tight.

And, fuck me, lying in her bed, remembering her, smelling her, I was hard. I was needy for her raw arousal. I couldn't wait to have her again.

And though I probably should have been, I wasn't embarrassed or emasculated by the memory of my blunders. For once. No. Something about this girl, this *woman*, gave me the distinct impression of acceptance. It was as odd and disorienting as it was invigorating.

With these thoughts spurring me awake, I'd left, showered, and dressed in a rush. I quickly called my lawyer about the Adidas shoot, demanding he find a way to make it work with my Puma contract. I jogged to the communal dining hall intent on being with Lucy in New York for a week at least, longer if she were agreeable to an extended arrangement.

I didn't realize until I caught sight of her halo of hair that I'd neglected to rifle through her toiletries before leaving her cabin.

*Curious, that.*

I pushed the thought away, unwilling to be distracted from my present course. Time was of the essence. Today marked the end of the retreat. She was bound for New York this afternoon and therefore, so was I. I needed her to agree to my hastily conjured proposition.

Last night she could have laughed at me, but she didn't.

She could have faked it, but she didn't do that either.

I was coming to believe there wasn't anything fake about Lucy other than her hair color. Yet the swirling rainbow framing her gorgeous face—like sunlight through a prism—suited her perfectly.

Yes. I was *going for broke* with Lucy Fitzpatrick. As such, I was sweating and jittery. And nervous in a new and completely terrifying way.

"You want me to teach you?" Her dark eyebrows winged above surprised, pale blue eyes.

I nodded. "Yes."

She leaned an inch closer, her voice dropping to a whisper. "You want me to teach you what exactly?"

"Everything."

"You have to be more specific." Her words were choked.

"Fine. I want you to teach me the art of foreplay and sex. I want you to teach me where to touch, how to touch, how long. I want you to teach me about pressure, licking, and sucking, and—"

"Stop. Please stop talking." She covered my mouth with her hand, her eyes sharpening. "You can't be serious."

I gently gripped her wrist and coaxed her fingers away, kissing the tips before setting her palm on my leg. "I'm very, very serious."

"Sean." Her whisper adopted an urgent edge. She snatched her hand away and her eyes did a quick sweep of the table, as though to make sure no one was listening. "You don't need me for that. You can watch YouTube videos, or do a Google search, or buy a book. I hear there's this one called the Kamasutra that's supposed to cover the basics."

The urge to touch her again amplified, but I didn't want to scare her off. I allowed my thumb to trace a circle on her shoulder. She didn't pull away.

"I've watched videos, Lucy. I've read books. But . . ." My eyes cut away to the freckle on her collarbone. In my haste I'd forgotten to taste it last night, and she might not give me another chance.

I didn't think she'd laugh in my face, but my gut tightened at the possibility she might say no.

"But you want a test subject?" Her whisper was accusatory.

*No.*

*I want you.*

Unable to catch my breath, I licked my lips, remembering the taste of her, the feel of her coming against my tongue. Her gaze dropped to my mouth and I heard her breath hitch, followed by a strangled whimper. "That's not nice. Don't do that."

"Don't do what?"

"You know what."

I frowned, shook my head, searching her eyes. "I honestly don't."

A low frustrated growl sounded from the back of her throat. "You're unbelievable. It's as though you're a toddler who paints like Rembrandt."

I lifted an eyebrow at this. "Did you just compare me to a toddler?"

"Yes. Because you are completely oblivious to—" She huffed, looking away and crossing her arms. "Never mind. My point is . . . I don't even know what my point is."

I studied her profile, noting her neck had turned pink and the stain was creeping over her cheeks. I wanted to touch them. Her hair was a disordered mass around her shoulders. I wanted to wrap it around my fingers and pull her head back. Her lips were pursed in thought, or a pout, or something else irresistible. I wanted to kiss them and bite them.

Christ, this was torture.

Having nothing to lose, I leaned forward and whispered in her ear, "Please, Lucy. Just give me a week."

She shivered and swayed toward me, her chest rising and falling with measured breaths.

"Please teach me how to make you feel good. Teach me how to make you come."

Her shoulder leaned heavily against my chest, as though the indecision were too heavy a burden to carry alone, so I waited. I wanted to smell her hair, but I didn't. I didn't move.

Finally, *finally,* she nodded, straightening away, her eyes flickering to mine. "Fine."

The impulse to stand from my seat and toss her over my shoulder— so we could get started immediately—was strong. Strong, sudden, and completely out of character.

I nodded tightly, trying not to smile too widely. "Good."

"Okay."

"Well, then . . ."

She glanced at me once more, her eyes narrowed with suspicion. She lifted an index finger and jabbed me in my chest. "But this is between us, Sean. Do you understand? No one—and I mean no one—is ever to hear about it. If you tell anyone I'll put your balls in a blender."

Her phrasing choked a laugh out of me, but I quickly capitulated. "Yes. Of course." I hadn't thought through the particulars any further than the next week, but I'd agree to just about anything at this point.

She issued me one more searching glare, then stood abruptly. Her chair scraped, drawing the attention of the entire table.

Lucy looked around at our tablemates, twisting her fingers, then announced a little too loudly, "I have to go pack."

She left. I watched her go. And I grinned.

There was something inextricably enticing about the dichotomy of her. For a softly spoken fairy princess with a rainbow mane, she had a remarkably tart mouth.

When I realized I was staring after her like a fool, and grinning at nothing specifically, I promptly stopped. I cleared my throat, replacing the smile with a frown, and searching my surroundings to ensure I hadn't been caught.

I stiffened when my eyes connected with Broderick's. We were alone at the table, the women having left without my realizing. He was observing me. His usually, as far as I knew, impassive features were etched with the barest hint of a smirk.

I'd been caught.

"You have something to say?" I leaned back in my chair, crossing my arms. The chair protested, groaning under my weight.

"No."

My frowned deepened. He was an odd sort. And he definitely wasn't a lamb.

"Then do you mind if I ask you a question?"

"Depends on the question." Broderick, still smirking, sipped his coffee.

"Would you consider it racist for me to call you a Mocha Frappuccino?"

Broderick coughed his surprise. Coffee sprayed on the table and he covered his mouth with a napkin, his eyes widening as he glared at me.

I waited for him to collect himself, offering no assistance.

"You must have taken Lucy at her word," he rasped, wiping his mouth.

"About what?"

"That I'm a lamb."

"Does she call you that often?"

"Often enough."

I narrowed my eyes on him. "You're no lamb. You're a black wolf in black sheep's clothing."

"And you're a white sheep."

"In white wolf's clothing?"

"No. Just a plain, everyday white sheep."

My frown intensified into a scowl. "You think I'm so ordinary?"

"Ordinary?" He shrugged, as though considering the word, then added, "Average is the word I'd use."

"Really?" I drawled, his assessment extraordinarily irritating for some unknown reason. I questioned sarcastically, "What makes me average? Is it my height?"

"It's because you think you want to be average." He lifted his eyebrows, indicating to my brain. "Wanting to be average makes you average."

I stared at him for a beat. "I think I want to be average?"

"Yes," he said, blowing on his coffee, and taking another sip. Disturbed steam traveled upward, disappearing into the atmosphere above his eyebrows.

"Lucy attempts to psychoanalyze me as well." I rolled my eyes away from him, though I recognized he wasn't trying to insult me. His words held no malice. "Is that what you two do all day? Analyze each other?"

Broderick wasn't . . . well, he wasn't at all apish. Nor was he mean. He was quiet—like a lamb, yes—but also clever. He was surprising.

"I was in the Navy. We don't analyze people. We label them, easier that way, more efficient. Everyone has a role, it's defined for them so they can fill it."

"And what is Lucy's role?" I asked, humoring him.

I was not at all curious about his response.

And I was definitely not impressed or uncomfortable with his succinct assessment of what I wanted.

"She's not average."

Despite myself, I fought a smile. "You certainly have a way with words."

"I know." Broderick's features rearranged themselves, settling back into impassive neutrality. "Everything out of my mouth is goddamn poetry."

I surrendered to the smile and fought a laugh. "Loveliness, the incarnation of beauty in spoken form."

"Like a fucking butterfly, but with sounds."

And now I surrendered to the laugh. He laughed as well. We laughed together in a way two people cannot and do not laugh alone.

It was a novel experience, not laughing at another's expense, but rather together. It was something I'd only ever done with my Eilish. Lucy had been right. Where she was concerned, Broderick was a lamb. And I liked him the better for it.

\*\*\*

**BRODERICK DROVE.**

I sat in the front by default because my legs were far too long for the backseat of his BMW. In truth, my legs were too long for the back seat of almost any vehicle.

Lucy sat behind Broderick. In order to catch a glimpse of her, I had to turn completely around. I found this to be most irritating. I'd offered to call a car service, have a limo pick us up for the hours-long journey to New York City.

She'd flushed a delectable shade of pink and declined with a prim, "No, thank you."

Unfortunately, she said very little during the drive, leaving Broderick and me to converse without her. Though I did catch her staring at me from time to time. I ignored her lingering stares, not wanting to give her any reason to be self-conscious. She could look her fill. I rather liked it. In fact, she could do whatever she pleased just as long as our agreement held.

Broderick carried most of the conversation. Typically, I cared very little about a person's past. Most people were boring. They'd led insignificant little lives doing insignificant little things.

As an example, I consider myself boring.

Broderick was not boring.

"You were stationed in Guantanamo? At the naval base?"

He shrugged, turning on the street and maneuvering around two yellow taxis parked outside the hotel. "Just for three years."

"What did you do there? Did you guard the detainees?"

"I was the triage officer for the base. We're here." He gestured to the Ritz Carlton with his chin, placing the automobile in park.

I made no move to exit. "What does the triage officer do?"

We'd been talking—or he'd been talking—for the last several hours, though it felt like hardly any time had passed. I could see why Lucy liked spending time with him.

"I'll save that story for another day. I need to get back to the studio." Broderick lifted an eyebrow at me, then his attention caught on the rearview mirror. "Lucy, mind if I drop you off here? Heading uptown is crazy during rush hour and I'm running late."

"Uh, no problem. Thanks for driving."

We piled out of the car and a bellman jogged over with a cart. A spur-of-the-moment idea had me requesting he load Lucy's bags next to mine while she and Broderick exchanged goodbyes.

To my surprise, before turning to go, Broderick stepped forward and shook my hand. "Nice to meet you, man."

"Yes. You as well." And I meant it.

"Get my number from Lucy. I'll take you to my favorite pub in the city. We'll have steak."

Astonished by the offer, it took me a moment to respond. "I will."

He nodded once, then left. I watched him pull into traffic, a curious, hollow sensation in the middle of my chest.

"I think he likes you." Lucy nudged my arm with hers, drawing my attention to her. Her gaze teasing and smiling as she added in a sing-song voice, "And I think you like him."

I frowned and responded automatically, "Nobody likes me."

The smile fell away from her eyes and was replaced with surprise, then determination. "Well, I like you. And so does Broderick. So, once again, you are wrong."

I studied her open features, the fullness of her bottom lip, the point of her chin. "Do you like me enough to have dinner with me?"

Her lashes fluttered. "S-sure. When? Tomorrow?"

I stepped into her space and wove our fingers together. "Tonight. Now."

"Oh." Obviously caught unaware, Lucy blinked at our surroundings, perhaps searching for her bag. "I, uh. Well, I need to go home and change."

"We'll order room service." I tugged her toward the hotel entrance and held the door as I ushered her in. "No need to change. I had the bellhop take your bags up to my room."

She glanced at me from the corner of her eyes. "Presumptuous much?"

"I'm a problem solver."

"I'd like some clean clothes."

I shrugged, leading her to the VIP check-in desk. "We'll send your laundry out for washing."

"Sean . . ."

"Or I can buy you something new. The hotel has a shop."

"No." Her tone was flat and dismissive.

I wrapped my arm around her waist, drew her to my side, and whispered in her ear, "Or we could be naked."

She stiffened, her breath hitched, but she didn't pull out of my grip. I leaned just slightly away so I could see her profile. She kept her eyes diligently forward.

While I checked in, she remained silent, making no move to separate our bodies. And when I added her to the room and presented her with a key, she accepted it, slipping the rectangle into her handbag without a word.

# Chapter Nine

@**SeanCassinova** Where might one procure a shoe horn in NYC?

@**RugbyFan101 to** @**SeanCassinova** I'll loan you my horn any day of the week, baby ;-)

@**SeanCassinova to** @**RugbyFan101** Who is this and where did you get my number?

@**RugbyFan101 to** @**SeanCassinova** Uh, this is Twitter.

@**SeanCassinova to** @**RugbyFan101** That's a very strange name. What were your parents thinking?

@**EilishCassidy** @**SeanCassinova** Stop being an arse.

### *Sean*

"**WHAT DO YOU** want to do?"

"I'd like to lick your pussy."

Lucy choked on her water. She'd been mid-sip from an Evian bottle when I responded. I listened, perusing the room service menu, as she continued to cough and sputter.

"Sean—"

"Then I think I'd like a steak." The restaurant had several nice cuts of meat; I decided on the prime rib.

"Sean—"

"Wine with the meal. After dinner, perhaps drinks? Then sex?"

"Sean."

I lifted my eyes from the menu, found her scowling at me from across the room. "What?"

She huffed. "Foreplay is more than just the physical."

I considered her statement for several protracted seconds, unsure as to what she was trying to say or how it related to my ordering of steak.

Finally, I admitted, "I don't follow."

She placed the cap back on the water bottle. "Part of being intimate with a person is how you speak to her."

"Ah. You want me to butter you up."

"Yes." She nodded, but then frowned. "No." She shook her head. "I mean, yes. If you want me to teach you how to . . . do all the things, then it starts with how you speak to me."

I set the menu aside, considering her. "And you don't like it when I tell you how I'd like to lick your—"

"I'm just saying . . ." She held her hands up and spoke over me. She was now a brighter shade of red. I rather liked it. "I'm just saying, I want to be a good teacher. The first step in foreplay is how you speak."

"Flirting," I said as I surmised her meaning. "I can do that."

She lifted a disbelieving eyebrow. "You can do that sometimes, and usually by accident."

"I'm a good flirt," I said, unable to keep the defensiveness from my claim.

Her expression flattened and she lowered her voice to that of a mock-tenor, quoting me, "Shall I sneak in later? Crawl into your bed and wake you up with my head between your thighs?"

I won against my urge to smile, dipping my chin so she wouldn't see it, but kept my eyes on her. "So, too subtle?"

She grinned, then laughed, pointing at me. "See? You just did it, you just flirted with me accidently."

"I did?"

"Yes. You did. And you did a good job, too."

I frowned. "What did I do?"

"That thing with your eyes, and the chin." Lucy deposited her bag on the sofa and crossed to stand in front of me. "And the small smile, and the cheeky remark. All good things. Much better than dragging me back to your lair and clubbing me over the head with your big cock."

I barked a laugh at the image her words conjured and was pleased by the sound of her rejoining laughter.

"You're cute sometimes."

"And you're beautiful," I said, because it was true.

"Oh. Good job."

"Good job?"

"Yes. Another good example of flirting. Good job." Lucy grinned at me encouragingly, patting my shoulder, and turned away. "Where is the bathroom? I need a shower."

I stared at her back as she walked to and disappeared into the bedroom, realizing she thought I was trying to flirt rather than merely speaking my mind.

Perhaps all I had to do in order to flirt with Lucy—and therefore initiate quality foreplay—was tell her the truth.

A short while later, I heard the shower. I didn't dwell on it, because if I thought about a wet Lucy I'd want to join her. Shower sex felt like an advanced-level technique, something to work up to.

Instead, I called for room service. Since I didn't know what she wanted, I ordered one of every vegetarian item on the menu. Finished with my task, I flipped on the television. Nothing was on. I turned it off.

She was still in the shower.

Now my mind did wander to an image of her. Wet. Soapy. I chewed on my lip, staring at the bedroom door, which was ajar.

Maybe she needed help washing her back . . .?

Restless—and by restless, I mean growing forcefully and painfully hard—I kicked off my shoes, dropped to the floor, and did pushups. When I heard the door to the bathroom open, I did clapping pushups. They helped dispel the "restlessness."

Well, they helped until I heard her ask from the doorway, "What are you doing? Are you clapping? While doing *pushups?*"

I paused, glanced up just long enough to see she was dressed in a bathrobe. Which meant she was basically naked.

*Bloody brilliant.*

"Yes." I pushed up, clapped, returned my hands to the floor, pressed down, repeat. I should have gone on a run. Even with the pushups I was entirely too worked up. It was embarrassing. Perhaps I should move on to burpees . . .

"Huh."

I watched her approach in my peripheral vision. Her feet were bare.

*Push up, clap, press down, repeat.*

"That's really impressive."

I chuckled at the admiration in her voice, then asked, "You want to see something even more impressive?"

"Sure . . ." Once again she sounded suspicious.

Planking, I braced my hands just a half-inch farther apart then pushed up with more force, clapped my hands behind my back, caught myself, and pressed down. Repeat.

"Christ on a bike. That's ridiculous." Lucy scrambled to kneel next to me and assumed a plank position, yanking up the bathrobe in her haste. "Teach me."

I rolled to my side and faced her. She was grinning, clearly excited. Her hair was wet and braided over her shoulder. It looked like rope.

"Sean?"

My eyes cut to her face. Her smile wavered when I stared for too long without speaking.

"Uh, yes. Okay." I nodded, turning back to the carpet and gripping it instead of her. "We'll start with the basic pushup."

Lucy snorted. "I know how to do a pushup."

"I need to watch your form."

"I have a great form."

"Yes. You do."

She snorted again, this time paired with a laugh. "Now the flirting is getting out of hand. Turn it down."

I smiled at her in response. Her lips were curved into an alluring smirk and one dark eyebrow was raised in accusation. Lucy's eyes shone like sapphires as she looked at me.

*Lovely.*

"Earth to Sean. Can you stop practicing your come-hither look for ten seconds?"

I blinked at her, reentering the present. "Yes. Fine."

Clearing my throat, I gave her instruction on how to do a single-clap pushup. She bit her bottom lip in concentration, listening intently to every word. Eventually, I had to stand over her, my hands on her hips, my feet on either side of her legs, and hold some of her weight until she mastered the movement.

She was a fast learner and was surprisingly strong. But not long after mastering the single-clap, her arms began to shake. Also surprising, teaching her had taken the edge off my impassioned frame of mind. I was no longer uncomfortably primed.

"I think that's enough for now." I picked her up by her hips and placed her back on her feet.

"Eee-gah!" She waved her arms in front of her, trying to recapture her balance, clearly not expecting me to pluck her from the floor. When she found her center of gravity, she turned toward me. My attention strayed to the nearly open front of her bathrobe.

"Wait, I want to do the back-clap one." She was out of breath.

"No. We'll try tomorrow. Your arms are tired."

Heaving a sigh, Lucy relented. "You're right. They are tired."

I eyed her speculatively. "Are you too tired?"

"For what?" She rubbed her biceps through the terrycloth robe.

"For my lesson."

Her hands stilled. All earlier amusement faded from her eyes, replaced with heat and awareness. I took that as a good sign.

She shook her head and responded softly, "No. Not too tired."

My pulse quickened, I made a fist with my hand so as not to draw her toward me. "Good."

She swallowed. Reaching for and uncurling my tight fist, Lucy led me into the bedroom without another word.

The bed was king-sized. Releasing me, she crossed to the head of it and selected a pillow. Turning, not looking at me, Lucy walked to the end of the bed and sat.

She placed the pillow on the carpet in front of her feet and gestured to it, finally meeting my gaze again.

"Kneel down," she said.

I frowned, hesitating, unsure. Her tone was demanding and impersonal. I didn't like that.

Lucy tilted her head to the side and repeated, "Kneel down."

"Lucy." I crossed my arms over my chest, allowing her to see and hear my displeasure. "I don't like being ordered about, and I don't *kneel down.*"

Her expression softened and a small smile danced over her lips. "Sorry. I didn't mean to order you about. I'm a little nervous."

I narrowed my eyes at her and saw the truth behind her words. "Don't be nervous."

Her shoulders lifted then lowered with a deep breath. "Okay. I'll try. But sometimes nerves are a good thing."

I snorted derisively. "Not in my experience. When I'm nervous is when I'm worst at this."

She gifted me another smile and her words adopted an instructional air. "Kneeling at the end of the bed is much more comfortable than craning your neck and supporting your weight while on the bed. It's a better position for me, too."

"Why? Why is it better for you?"

"Because it's easier for us to make eye contact if you're not hovering over me on the mattress. Plus, you'll be able to, uh," she swallowed, cleared her throat, "you'll be able to see more as well. Of me. Down there." I didn't miss the encroaching heat staining her cheeks.

I mulled this over, liking the idea of seeing more of her, *down there.* And I liked the idea of being able to watch her face again.

Decision made, I cast pride aside—for the moment—and slowly lowered myself to the pillow, holding her gaze the entire time and pushing her knees apart.

"Fine. I'm kneeling." I flexed my fingers on her legs.

"Okay. What do you want to do now?"

"Everything."

She released a light, melodic laugh that I felt at the base of my spine. My erection pressed against my jeans uncomfortably.

So much for taking the edge off.

"Specifically, what is the very next thing you want to do? What do you want to move and where?"

I licked my lips. "My first instinct is to spread your legs and dive in."

She nodded thoughtfully. "How about, instead, sliding your fingertips lightly up my thighs? Or tracing them in circles behind my knees?"

"Why would I do that?"

"Because it feels good and builds tension. It prolongs the act."

"Prolongs the act," I repeated, turning this concept around in my mind and considering it from all angles.

"Yes. For a woman, if you want her to come before you do, you need to find that delicate balance between prolonging the act and providing fulfillment. You can't provide fulfillment if you haven't built tension. It would be like trying to force-feed me before I'm hungry."

"Hmm . . . you want me to make you hungry."

"Exactly."

My eyes drifted to where her bathrobe opened. I stared at the creamy expanse of skin. An idea gripped me.

I lifted my fingers from her legs and untied the robe. I slid my hands inside, finding her body hot and smooth. She shivered.

"Are you cold?"

"No." The word was hushed.

I traced a single finger from her bellybutton, between the valley of her breasts to her collarbone. I hooked it around the robe's lapel and peeled it away, finding the distracting freckle on her collarbone.

Grasping her arm, I gently tugged her forward and licked the spot. She shivered again.

"What are you doing?" she whispered.

"I've wanted to do that for quite some time."

"What?"

"This freckle. It taunts me." I used my teeth, careful to nip instead of bite.

I placed my other hand on her knee. Then, as per her suggestion, lightly skimmed my fingertips higher, opening her legs, and drawing barely there circles on the interior skin of her thighs.

Her hips shifted. I moved my hand away. She whimpered.

"Tell me how to touch you, lovely Lucy." I lowered my mouth to her pink nipple and licked it.

She gasped. "Don't stop."

Her little noises drove me mad. I pressed my hips against the mattress, trying to find relief for the stiffy in my pants.

"Don't stop what?"

She hesitated, then said softly, "Don't stop touching me."

"Where?"

"Your fingers, on my . . . rub your thumb over my clit."

Despite the pain in my groin I grinned, enjoying how shy she sounded as she coached me. "Gladly. Gently?"

"Yes. At first."

I did as instructed, parting her and rubbing the pad of my thumb over the fleshy bud between her legs, and an odd thing happened.

Her sounds changed. And I listened to them.

I tried biting her breast and she grunted. So I tried swirling my tongue around her nipple and was rewarded with a breathy groan.

Trailing my mouth down her body, placing the light kisses she'd enjoyed during our first time together over her ribs, I pushed her back to the bed and spread her legs farther apart.

I blew on her.

She panted, moaning tightly, and I nearly came in my pants.

*Fuck.*

Wanting to improvise and improve rather than just replicate last night, I swirled my tongue around her clit in much the same way I'd just done to her nipple.

"Oh God." Her hands lifted and threaded into my hair, holding me in place.

I backed off, using just the tip of my tongue and spreading her with my thumbs. I waited to see how she would respond, remembering her words about building the hunger.

She seemed to enjoy it at first, sighing lightly and moving her hips. After a time she grunted restlessly. So I sucked her, because I could tell she wanted more. And also because I wanted to. Because *I* loved the feel of her flesh against my tongue and lips, the taste of her arousal, the slick sweetness of her. Yet I kept the pressure gentle, because Lucy seemed to need gentle.

"Oh God, oh God, oh God—fuck!"

I lifted my eyes to hers, found her watching me, felt the first tremors of her release against my tongue as she threw her head back and moaned. Actually, it was more of a howl, and it was sexy as fuck.

Her nails were painful as they dug into my scalp, but fuck. It felt so fucking good because I recognized it as a mindless response. She was beyond thought. Because of me. Of what I was doing. Before her tremors subsided, I realized I hadn't placed any fingers inside her. I slipped two into her perfect warmth and was immediately rewarded with a strangled cry, her thighs tightening as her hips bucked off the bed.

"Sean! Oh fuck! Sean . . ." Thinking she liked that.

Her pulsing quickened, renewed, intensified, and I groaned against her delicious suppleness. Because she was coming again. And it was perfect.

# Chapter Ten

**@LucyFitz** Would you rather live the rest of your life with a human head and a horse's body, or a horse's head and a human body?

**@BroderickAdams to @LucyFitz** Human head + horse body = centaur. Horse head + human body = WTF. So, the first one, obvs.

**@RonanFitz to @BroderickAdams @LucyFitz** No more acid tabs for either of you.

### *Lucy*

OH, MAN. OH, *wow*.

I couldn't tell if it was down to me being such a good teacher or Sean having so much untapped potential, but our first sex lesson was going swimmingly. I lay back on the mattress, completely spent as I tried to catch my breath. Then a light, disbelieving chuckle escaped me. This situation was just beyond weird. Anyone might think I was getting far more out of the arrangement than him. I mean, he had given me two pretty fantastic oral sessions, even if he'd come prematurely during sex . . .

He was currently sprawled out beside me on the bed, his head turned to the side as he surveyed my post-orgasmic bliss with barely concealed fascination. He'd laid a claiming hand on my stomach; it was so large it splayed from my ribs to my hipbone.

"What's so funny?" he murmured tenderly.

I shook my head, unable to answer, words catching in my throat.

Looking at him now, his eyelids lowered and his voice heavy with wonder and longing, a force of uncomfortable and unanticipated emotion gripped me. Maybe it was the stellar and surprising double orgasm, or perhaps I was just tired from the trip, but seeing him now, how he watched me made me feel greedy for him. And the greed felt foolish and unsafe.

I sat up and pulled the bathrobe closed, turning away and swinging my legs over the edge of the bed. Taking several deep breaths, my gaze then snagged on my suitcase.

"Lucy?" His hand was on my back, rubbing a circle at the base of my spine.

I closed my eyes, needing to swallow before I could respond. "You're a very fast learner."

Now he chuckled, a sexy, low rumble. It hit me like a wave crashing over my skin.

"Thank you. You're an exceptional teacher." He sounded pleased.

"Ah, well . . ." I forced amusement into my voice and stood, moving purposefully away from him and his warmth. I crouched in front of my bag and pulled out a pair of clean yoga pants, underwear, and a baggy T-shirt.

"You're getting dressed?" By the distance and direction of his voice, I could tell he was still on the bed.

"Yes." I plastered a carefree smile on my face and, gripping my clothes to my chest, turned to face him as I walked backward into the bathroom. "Unfortunately, I will not be able to stay for steak and sex. I have places to be and pictures to take."

His scowl was immediate. His eyes sharpened and felt like piercing icicles as he studied me. I held my breath. I thought he was going to argue.

Scratch that.

Idiot me *hoped* he would argue. I hoped he would ask me to stay, or flex his newly found flirting muscle and coax me into staying. I didn't understand this desire, but there it was: weird and alarming and completely unwelcomed.

For a split second, I thought I would get my wish because he opened his mouth as though to contradict me.

But he didn't.

"Fine," he said, his lips curving into a quick grimace of a smile, his expression growing distant. Sean lay back on the bed, moving his hands behind his head and stared at the ceiling. "But I'll see you tomorrow, right?"

Crappers! I felt like a total bitch. He'd just given me the elusive double orgasm and I was leaving him hanging.

"Yes. Absolutely." I tried for cheerful, but didn't quite manage it. "And tomorrow we'll focus on you. Sorry to leave you hard up."

Sean shook his head, his voice sounding distant in a way that made my heart ache. "I've told you before, you should never apologize for not wanting to have sex with someone."

My steps faltered on the threshold to the bathroom and I hesitated, wanting to correct him. I *did* want to have sex with him. I wanted to have *more* than sex with him. And that was the problem.

Instead I said, "Tomorrow afternoon should be fine, but I'll only be able to stay for an hour." I didn't have to leave after an hour, but I needed to set some boundaries for myself.

"Fine." He nodded, then grabbed a pillow, pulled it to his chest and turned his back to me. "Turn off the lights, would you? I think I'll take a nap."

*** 

NOTHING LIKE A long bath, an hour of quiet yoga alone in my apartment, and marathon episodes of Blackadder to pull me out of my weird sentimental funk. Well, that and a good, stern self-talking-to.

Also a big help, doing a Google Image search for "Sean Cassidy Girlfriend" and being positively dumbfounded by the sheer number of Sean +1 bimbo images. The most recent one was from a few weeks ago and the woman had taken a selfie with Sean while he slept . . .

While. He. Slept.

*Bloody weirdo.*

But I couldn't help but notice that the only woman he'd appeared with more than once was Brona O'Shea. Now I knew his involvement with Brona had been a deception, I was no longer surprised that Sean was so terrible between the sheets.

No woman had stuck around long enough to tell him he was rubbish, or that premature ejaculation was the sex equivalent to jumping the shark.

Feeling considerably more centered, this last thought gave me an idea.

I could repay Sean for his oral kindness while at the same time teaching him some self-restraint. And I could provide instruction without allowing myself to get tangled up in fanciful ideas again.

Therefore, armed with a plan, I knocked on his suite door exactly five minutes after noon.

"Lucy," he said, both frowning and smiling at me, his eyes alight with confusion. "Why didn't you use your key?"

Instead of answering, I stepped into the suite, dropped my bag by the front door, and lightly pushed him backward with a hand on his chest.

"You need to lay on the bed and take your pants off."

Sean's eyebrows jumped, but he moved where I led him and his hands were already unfastening his belt. "Why?"

"So I can give you a blow job," I answered simply.

He let out a choked laugh, his gorgeous blues darting over my face, a warm, interested smile on his. "Far be it from me to be uncooperative."

Toeing off his shoes as we entered the bedroom, Sean dropped his pants along with his red—yes, red—boxer briefs, and stepped out of them. I stood in front of him with my hands on my hips as though surveying his progress, though I itched to tug his shirt over his head.

Thankfully, he removed his shirt all on his own. I had to close my mouth before I drooled on the plush carpet. Obligingly, he lay back on the bed, his eyes never leaving my face.

"Don't get excited just yet," I tut-tutted, my eyes trailing down his body to find his erection already at full mast.

Crickets! Was this guy ever *not* hard?

My thighs clenched instinctively at the idea of putting his beautiful, perfect cock in my mouth . . . um, what was I saying again? Oh right, I was about to tell him about the catch. "You're not allowed to come for ten whole minutes."

The room grew very quiet. All warmth and amusement fled his expression.

Finally, he asked, "Pardon?"

I ignored his incredulous expression, which really just said it all. Ten minutes was nothing. Still, I kept my voice soft and sultry when I asked, "Tell me something. When you have sex with a woman, how long do you usually last?"

He looked toward the window and shrugged. "I don't know. Am I supposed to time that shit with a stopwatch or something?"

"Don't be clever. You know what I mean. In general, how long, Sean?"

He wouldn't look at me as he answered, "A few minutes, maybe."

I raised my eyebrows as his attention refocused on me. His expression was irritated, though you'd never know it to look at his cock.

His cock looked happy.

"Oh, come on, it's not my fault. I'm usually drunk. Drunk sex is quick and sloppy."

"Well, you're not drunk now."

"You're being unreasonable," he huffed.

I climbed on top of him and his hands gripped my thighs. I was wearing leggings and a shift dress. I pulled off the dress, leaving me in a black lace bra. His eyes went instinctively to my breasts.

"The next time you're inside me, don't you want it to last a little longer? Don't you want to savor it with me, Sean?" I whispered huskily, and all he could do was nod and swallow. He seemed almost entranced by my body. "Good, then let's try this. When I put you in my mouth, I want you to close your eyes and think of something bland. Something that doesn't excite you in any way."

Leaning forward, I planted a quick kiss to his chest and he sucked in a harsh breath.

"Like what?" he rasped.

"Like doing your taxes."

"My accountant does those for me."

"Vacuuming your living room, then."

"I have a cleaning lady for that," he said disdainfully, like the very idea was insulting. I tried not to judge him for it, because I knew the kind of family he came from, and talk like that was par for the course, learned from childhood. He didn't realize how spoiled he sounded.

"Isn't there any menial task you don't enjoy doing?"

He thought on it for a moment. "I'm not the biggest fan of leg day."

Of course it would be something to do with sport. "Okay, well, imagine you've just been told to do two hundred squats."

He scoffed. "You don't just do two hundred squats, Lucy. You do sets."

I cocked an eyebrow and pointed a finger into his chest. "Do you want this blow job or not?"

"Fine," he replied huskily and it really was quite sexy. Goosebumps danced along my skin. "I'm doing two hundred squats. Preposterous, but I'm doing them. Now what?"

"Close your eyes and really visualize it," I whispered, leaning back down to press my mouth to the defined V at his hipbone. His stomach muscles jumped at the touch and I smiled, enjoying how reactive he was.

Continuing to kiss my way down his body, I paused when I reached his cock. He groaned when I kissed it, featherlight. Then I licked him, this time with more force, before taking him fully into my mouth. He swore profusely.

"Really hard to keep thinking about those squats right now," he grunted, hands fisting the sheets.

I moved down the entire length of him and back up, and a spurt of salty pre-cum filled my mouth. Man, he was never going to last ten minutes. I glanced at the clock.

12:07.

Sean reached down and pulled the tie from the end of my braid. He ran his fingers through my hair, freeing all the strands as I sucked him off. His warm palms cupped my face for a second, almost reverently, before clutching my hair in a tight fist. I looked up and our gazes locked. He cursed. My attention flicked to the clock again for the barest second.

12.09

"Jesus," Sean grunt-gasped, his brow furrowing like he was concentrating really hard. I wanted to tell him to close his eyes like I'd instructed, but I was too foggy-headed with arousal and I couldn't seem to manage it.

I let his cock fall from my mouth then licked up its length, cupping his balls. He groaned, the sensation rumbling up out of his chest.

"I can't do this, Lucy. Fuck, you're so beautiful."

"Close your eyes. Think about those two hundred squats," I told him shakily, because hearing him call me beautiful in that sexy gravelly voice had my knees going a little weak.

"I don't want to close my eyes when I could be looking at you," he whispered.

I took him in my mouth again, this time moving faster. His thighs tensed and his eyes flared, owning me with a single look.

God, I was done for. So completely done for.

He was beautiful. Despite all my plans and boundaries, my heart was clenching again with feelings I was too afraid to explore.

This was madness. I was mad. I tried remembering the face of that woman who'd taken a picture of herself with Sean while he slept. I reminded myself that he'd never had a girlfriend.

Sean Cassidy didn't do relationships.

And even if he did, even if he wanted something more than lessons with me, there would never be an *us*. I was being ridiculous.

I blamed his body. His body made me want the impossible.

It was definitely his body and not the haunting vulnerability of him. It wasn't his quick, witty rejoinders, or the way he'd discovered my darkest secret and hadn't responded with judgment, but instead understanding, comradery, and concern.

Definitely not any of that.

A second later he came, filling my mouth as he held my cheeks in his palms again, his expression fierce as he drank me in. Sean's head fell back into the pillows and I discreetly wiped my mouth with the back of my hand.

I sat there for a moment, trying to gather my senses. Something was happening. Something I'd thought was a fluke yesterday. Something unplanned and inconvenient.

His hand felt hot when it stroked along my back, lazily seeking my attention. I turned to face him and mustered a small smile. The clock read 12:13. He'd lasted almost six minutes.

"Come here," he whispered and my insides melted. I hesitated, wanting to go to him but afraid, too.

I was saved from having to make a decision when my phone rang loudly in my bag. Jumping away, I went to get it.

It was my friend, Mackenzie. Her name flashing on the screen pulled me back to reality.

"Hey girl," she chirped as soon as I answered, her voice a welcome relief. "Facebook's 'not creepy at all' location tracker was kind enough to inform me that you're back in the city. How was New Hampshire?"

I forced a snicker at her trademark snarky attitude. "It was wonderful. Rick and I had a great time," I replied as I felt two strong arms coil around my waist. Sean's nose nuzzled into my neck before he sucked my earlobe into his mouth. It took every ounce of willpower I possessed not to moan. He was already hard again. I could feel his erection pressing into my backside.

"So, I know you probably don't want to dive straight back into work, but if what I've heard on the grapevine is true, Carly Stevens and Dean Newman are going to be dining at Le Cirque in an hour. It could make for some great pics for the blo-og," she said, finishing in a singsong voice.

I batted away the encroaching fog of lust inspired by Sean's seductive movements and focused on my excitement at the opportunity for some new content. The Socialmedialite site had been wanting for articles in the last few weeks since I'd been home visiting and then at the retreat. Mackenzie was a photographer for *Cosmopolitan*, which, if you knew her, was just hilarious. She was the least Cosmo girl I'd ever met.

Sean continued to lavish my earlobe with attention as I considered my options. Stay here for the next forty-five minutes and enjoy fleeting but sweaty hotel sex with Adonis himself—falling deeper into this pit of irrational whatever it was—or venture out into the stress of the city and get some work done.

I encouraged myself to embrace my guilt. Annie would be really disappointed if she knew I'd turned down the chance to picture Carly and Dean, so, with this thought in mind I knew what I had to do.

"Sounds great. I'll see you there," I told Mackenzie before hanging up.

Sean let out a slow breath. "You're leaving, aren't you?" he said as I turned in his arms to look up at him.

"I'm sorry, duty calls," I answered regretfully. The obvious disappointment on his face had me blurting, "Do you want to come?"

His brow arched. "To photograph celebrities?"

I felt suddenly unsure, probably because the idea of Sean Cassidy crossing over into my everyday life felt way too relationship-y. "Uh, yeah."

He shrugged. "Okay, well, just let me grab a quick shower first."

He went into the bathroom and I put on my dress. My hair was a mess so I threw it up into a haphazard bun. Unfortunately, my camera was back at Annie's apartment, where I'd been living for the last few months, and we wouldn't have time to go there and get it. The one on my iPhone would just have to do.

About five minutes later, Sean emerged completely naked, droplets of water coating his fine, fine skin. I swallowed, feeling suddenly shy, and busied myself with checking my Twitter notifications. Meanwhile, he seemed oblivious to my ogling, which was so entirely frustrating. When I looked up again he was dressed.

"You ready?" he asked. I nodded and before I knew it we were outside the hotel, flagging down a yellow taxi.

"East 58th Street, please," I told the driver as I pulled up the restaurant's address on Google.

Sean sat next to me, his legs spaced in what was the quintessential definition of man-spreading. Though being as large as he was, I imagined he couldn't really help it. He stared out the window, watching the city go by (albeit slowly since it was rush hour in Manhattan). My eyes traced the strong, masculine line of his jaw and how his dark blond hair was sexily tousled on top but shaved tight at the back.

I noticed his mouth start to curve in a smile before his eyes flicked down and to the side.

"Enjoying the view?" he asked, his voice quiet, intimate, and edged with a deeper question.

"You must know how beautiful you are," I murmured.

His lips firmed and it took a second for him to reply. When he did he cast his hooded gaze on me, taking my hand and smoothing his fingers over my knuckles. "I'm too big and imposing to be beautiful."

"That's ridiculous."

"Is it?" His eyes searched mine. "Most beautiful things are delicate, so fragile that even to look at them feels like they might break." He whispered this last part and I found myself catching my breath. It felt like he was trying to tell me something; that I was the delicate, fragile thing he described. My heart beat fast like the wings of a butterfly.

"That's not true. Beauty comes in many forms, and the strong, powerful kind is the most admirable. It's easy to be weak; you simply do nothing, but strength takes courage and effort."

His eyes blazed as he lifted my hand, bringing it to his mouth and pressing his lips to the inside of my wrist. I shivered. "You have this incredible way of showing me new ways to look at things, do you know that, Lucy Fitzpatrick?" he asked, and my tummy flipped over on itself.

"You shouldn't say things like that," I blurted.

"Why not?"

"Because they mix me up."

His attention dropped to my lips. "Would that be so bad?"

"Yes." I nodded once, very emphatically, and paired it with a strained laugh, speaking louder than was strictly necessary. "It would be the worst."

He narrowed his eyes as though to protest, but I scrunched up my face at him, forcing playfulness. Pulling my hand out of his, I pointed a teasing finger of accusation in his face. I needed to break the tension.

"And you know why it would be the worst. So keep your compliments and hands to yourself while I'm trying to work."

*Because I'm weak when you're kind to me, and I need to be strong.* These were the words I left unsaid.

He didn't respond. Instead, he just stared at me like he wanted to argue.

The taxi pulled to a stop and I dragged my attention away from Sean to see we'd arrived just down the street from Le Cirque. I made myself focus on work, in truth happy to have an excuse to change the subject, and craned my neck. I soon spotted a gaggle of photographers already gathered outside. They were hanging back, chatting amongst themselves, so I knew the happy couple weren't there yet.

Sean's hand went to my lower back as he ushered me out and I realized he'd already paid the driver. When we were on the street his hand still remained in place, and something fizzled in my tummy at the idea of us being together like this in public. In a way, I adored the anonymity. Nobody knew us here, who our families were, or where we came from, nor did they know all the reasons why we shouldn't be together.

Catching sight of Mackenzie's jet-black ponytail and red-tartan bomber jacket, I led Sean over before tapping her on the shoulder, trying to shake off the residual feelings of unrest caused by his closeness, and words, and . . . everything.

She turned and broke into a wide smile when she saw me, her expressive green eyes framed by thick tortoiseshell glasses.

"Lucy! I missed you," she exclaimed, pulling me into a hug.

"Missed you, too. Any sign of Carly and Dean yet?" I asked and she shook her head.

"No sightings of Carl-D so far. I'm trying to make Carl-D a thing, do you think it will take?" She grinned impishly but then her mouth fell open when her eyes landed on Sean. She peered up at his face, her attention traveling slowly down his body before she let out a choked cough.

"Uh," she croaked. I thought she might be a little tongue-tied.

"This is Sean. He's my, um, my friend from back home," I said, still feeling a bit muddled myself as I introduced him.

"Hi," said Mackenzie, her voice going all weird and breathy. She'd always told me she became a stuttering mess around attractive men, but I'd never seen it in action until now.

"And this my friend Mackenzie," I went on. "Sean, Mackenzie, Mackenzie, Sean."

"It's a pleasure," Sean purred, taking her hand and lifting it to his mouth for a brief kiss. I narrowed my eyes at him, wondering if he did it on purpose just to fluster her.

"Oh my God, your accent," Mackenzie blurted and then turned bright fuchsia. She glanced at me and not so discreetly mouthed *wow*.

Out of the corner of my eye I noticed two black SUVs arrive and hurried to pull out my phone. Mackenzie flew into action too, grabbing her camera that had been hanging around her neck, lifting it to eye level.

I held up my phone, frustrated by how far back we were. There were too many people in front of me and I couldn't seem to get a decent shot. Since Mackenzie was a good few inches taller, she didn't have the same problem.

"What's wrong?" Sean asked, his arm brushing against mine as he drew close.

I huffed. "My vantage point is too low. I can't get any good pictures."

"Well, that's easily remedied," he said, and without another word he lifted me. I squealed in surprise as he hoisted me up onto his shoulders. Apparently I weighed absolutely nothing.

"Sean," I yelped on a small, startled gasp.

"I'm just trying to help you," he said, gripping my thighs, which were currently straddling the back of his neck. "Now quick, get your pictures before they go inside."

I swallowed and turned my attention to the A-list couple who were now being ushered into the restaurant by their security team. The camera on my phone was decent, but the flashes from the photographers all around me were blurring my shots. I managed to get a decent one of Dean with his hand on Carly's lower back, and I knew our female readers would either love or loathe the affectionate gesture, depending on what sort of fans they were.

Sean had done the exact same thing to me as we got out of the taxi. The thought caused a flutter of girlish exhilaration to rush through my belly. I needed to get a handle on this girlish exhilaration. This girlish exhilaration needed a reality check. Maybe even a bitch-slap.

One of his hands lightly squeezed my thigh and I yelped again. "Hey, behave," I warned, glancing down at him. He shot me a smirk and then a flash blinded me. Turning my head, I saw Mackenzie facing us, snapping a picture.

I shot her a look. "What are you doing?"

She shrugged and glanced down, lowering her camera. "Sorry. You two are just adorable together."

"Delete the picture, please," I said, a spike of panic causing my back to straighten.

"Why?" she asked, not understanding.

"Just please delete it, Mack," I said and she nodded. There couldn't be any photographic evidence out there of our relationship—no, not relationship, *agreement*— because if it ever fell into the wrong hands, my brother would have my guts for garters.

Just like that, I emerged from the Sean Cassidy spell, because Ronan really would have my guts for garters. Being with Sean wouldn't just anger Ronan, it would hurt him. He would feel betrayed.

And I'd rather chew on glass than hurt my brother.

Sean let out a sigh, like he was frustrated by something, then began lowering me down his body. Once my feet hit the ground, I tried to ignore the frown marring his features and clung to the sobering thought of Ronan.

"I need to eat. Let's go." Sean grabbed my hand somewhat gruffly. "Again, it was a pleasure to meet you, Mackenzie."

I gave her an apologetic smile, told her I'd call her tomorrow, and then let Sean drag me away. We walked for a while in heavy silence, me fixating on Ronan's reaction if he were to find out, Sean growing visibly more aggravated with each step.

Soon the roaring sound of his silence eclipsed my concern over Ronan discovering my disloyalty, and I pulled us to a halt. "You know, it's a little weird to be holding someone's hand when they're angry with you."

He arched a brow and glanced down at me. "I'm not angry with you. I'm . . . disappointed in you. There's a difference."

"You're disappointed in me?" I asked, a pang of guilt seizing my chest. This day had gone from simple to complicated at an alarming rate.

I'd woken up with a sturdy sense of self and a plan to give Sean a blow job. *Just* a blow job. An exercise in delayed gratification. A simple, impersonal lesson.

Now look where we were.

So much for well-laid plans.

Sean turned to face me. "Yes, Lucy, I am. Tell me, how is it that a girl with wild rainbow hair and such a fun, carefree spirit could care so much about what other people think?"

"You know why." I stared at the ground because his gaze was too heavy for me to hold.

I felt him studying me as his hand came up to cup one of my cheeks. Finally, he let out a long sigh and said, "I'll let you have it your way this time."

His words multiplied my confusion, because as far we'd agreed, no one was ever supposed to find out about us. He told me himself he'd make sure Ronan never discovered what was happening.

The scary, inconvenient feelings that I didn't want to think about flared more powerful than before.

I liked Sean Cassidy. I liked him with something more than just my vagina.

Giving him a barely there nod, I suggested, "There's a really good hot dog kiosk nearby, if you're still hungry, that is."

His brow furrowed. "I thought you were a vegetarian?"

Thankful for the change in subject, I decided to run with it. "Only when I'm detoxing, the rest of the time I eat meat. Do you know how much we could reduce environmental damage if we all had one vegetarian day per week?"

"I didn't, but thank you for informing me," he said. I couldn't tell if he was being sarcastic.

"You should consider taking part in World Meat Free Day this year." I nudged him encouragingly with my elbow. "I'm doing it, and so is Rick."

"You can't maintain a physique like mine by surviving on chickpeas," Sean replied. "Now come on, let's go get some street meat for dinner. You really do know how to treat a man."

"Oh, don't be such a snob," I chided, laughing, and led him in the direction of the kiosk.

Along the way I spotted a guy playing Frisbee with his dog in the park. Pulling out my phone, I snapped a few shots. Sean arched a questioning brow in my direction, so I explained, "Taking pictures of animals is a hobby of mine. I've been collecting them for a while now. I'm actually hoping to set up a blog. Instead of Humans of New York, it could be Animals of New York. Or something like that. I don't know. Maybe it's silly."

"I don't think it's silly," said Sean warmly. "I think it's a great idea. Plus, if the millions of views videos of kittens get on YouTube is anything to go by, there's certainly a market for it."

I shrugged, bashful but pleased he hadn't thought it a stupid idea. When I'd told Mam about it she'd laughed and said I was just trying to find another way not to have a real job.

"I thought I could pair stories with the pictures, too," I went on. "At the animal shelter we always get dogs coming in with tales of abandonment or how they've been left to fend for themselves. I feel like people need to hear their stories."

Sean nodded enthusiastically. "And if these dogs get adopted into homes, you know, rehabilitated, you could add that, too. Give the story a happy ending."

I smiled widely, taken aback by his suggestion. "That's a lovely idea. Anyone might think you have a soft heart under all that muscle and brawn, Sean Cassidy," I teased.

He lifted a shoulder. "I just like a good underdog story, that's all. Every stray deserves a chance at love." He stared at me a moment, and I was captured by the sincerity in his gaze. After a second, he grew self-conscious. "And you know, a home, a warm bed to sleep in at night."

"You're right. No dog, or person for that matter, should ever be left out in the cold."

Right after I said it, Sean seemed to still, like I'd just said something that resonated with him. The intensity coming from him was almost too much, so I decided to move the conversation along.

"Anyway, if you're interested, you should come along with me to the shelter some time. They always need the extra help, and I'm sure they'd be more than happy to welcome a big strong guy like you. There's this gigantic malamute named Stan, and I swear he's so powerful he almost pulls my arm from the socket when I take him for walks."

Sean chuckled loudly. "When I was a kid I had an Irish wolfhound. His name was Wolfie, original, I know. The dog was huge. Up until I had my growth spurt at fourteen he'd run circles around me."

I could tell by the way he spoke about the pet that he'd loved him, and something in my heart warmed to think of Sean loving something other than himself. It was a dangerous sort of warmth, one that could transform into true feelings if left unattended.

"I wish I could have met him."

"He was . . . a good friend. I had him for ten years. He died when I was twenty-one and I never quite had it in me to get another. This is

THE PIXIE AND THE PLAYER L.H. Cosway & Penny Reid –151

going to sound ridiculous, but it was like losing a person," he said, laughing tenderly as I heard something catch in his voice.

I grabbed his arm and squeezed it. "It's not ridiculous, far from it. You loved him. And," I went on, grinning now, "as far as I'm concerned, dogs are people, so never let anyone tell you otherwise."

Sean smiled back at me, and in that moment it felt like we truly "got" each other.

We walked a bit farther in comfortable silence, the type of pleasant limbo one shares with a friend, until we reached the hot dog kiosk. Once there, I ordered for him, and then we sat on a nearby park bench to eat. Sean took several giant bites out of his hot dog and it was already gone. I was a little bit stunned by how fast he ate.

"Wow, do you rush through everything the same way you rush through sex?" I asked honestly, truly wanting to know. Meanwhile, my entire hot dog sat untouched in my lap.

He considered me as he chewed the final bite. "That's a low blow, but yes, I just don't see the point in waiting around. If you want something, go for it."

"Well," I said, lowering my voice, "you don't know what you're missing. There's a lot to be said for savoring things."

"Are we talking about hot dogs now, or sex? Because I'm a little confused."

I lifted my shoulders then let them fall. "We're talking everything. Sex, art, books, movies. Would you put on a DVD and fast-forward right to the end? No, because then you can't enjoy the progression of the story."

"So this is like the foreplay thing again, right? You want me to tease it out, take my time, tantalize you." His grin was devilish.

"Exactly," I said, finally lifting my hotdog and taking a bite. I chewed slowly, then swallowed before turning back to him. "If you just shove food down your throat you're going to miss out on all the wonderful flavors."

He was focused on me now, his eyes growing hooded and sexy. "Speaking of, when do I get to taste your flavors again, Lucy?"

I cleared my throat, unable to meet his gaze but still trying for sassy. "No one's stopping you, Bubs."

He let out a deep, hearty laugh and draped an arm around my shoulders. "I'm not sure that nickname suits me anymore. Think of another one," he said in a husky tone.

"Bubs suits you perfectly," I threw back. "Besides, you don't even know what it really means yet."

Now he angled his body toward me, closing the distance between us. "You lied?"

"Maybe."

His expression showed intrigue. "Tell me."

I grimaced slightly, because let's face it, the true meaning of his nickname was kind of embarrassing. "That night we first spoke, I named you Bubs in my head because of your bubble butt."

"My . . . bubble butt?" He looked genuinely perplexed.

"Oh, don't give me that. You know your arse is fantastic."

He laughed softly and leaned down to brush his lips over the underside of my jaw. "So is yours, as it happens." A pause. "How far are we from your place?"

"Not far."

"Let's go, then," he urged. "All this talk of backsides has me wanting to take you from behind."

I gasped a surprised laugh, because he really did just say whatever the hell he wanted sometimes. When our eyes met, his had darkened, and I swallowed amid the rush of arousal I felt.

My hunger suddenly forgotten and replaced with a different kind, I wrapped up my hot dog and stowed it in my bag. Not allowing myself to think too much about my actions, we caught another taxi to Annie's apartment and before I knew it, I was leading Sean up the stairs, a ball of anticipation forming in my belly.

I was a pile of jittery nerves and horniness. Sean ran a hand up and down my back while I searched for my keys. Then, to my horror, I heard movement come from inside.

Realization dawned on me, and I had just enough time to shove Sean away and out of sight before Annie opened the door.

"Lucy," she exclaimed, pulling me into a hug. "I'm glad you're back. We just arrived at the airport an hour ago."

"Hey Annie, I didn't realize you were coming to visit," I said, turning her just slightly so I could cast my panicked gaze briefly to Sean over her shoulder. *Go*, I mouthed at him and he seemed to get the message. Quickly turning and striding back down the hallway, I could finally breathe when he disappeared out of sight. He didn't seem happy though, not one bit.

For a second I wished I could call him back, say to hell with all the secrecy and just tell my brother that Sean and I were friends . . . with some sort of benefits. Unfortunately, I wasn't quite equipped to deal with WW3 just yet.

My heart continued to pitter-patter in my chest, still in panic mode.

"I know," said Annie, ushering me into the apartment. "Ronan has a photo shoot with Adidas this week, so I thought I'd come along. We're only back for a few nights. There's so much to be done for the wedding so we can't be gone long. A flying visit, really."

"Oh well, I'm happy you're here, even if it's only for a little while," I said.

I heard a cupboard slam and then my brother emerged from the kitchen. "There's nothing to eat," he grumbled before he saw me.

"Lucy, when did you get back from New Hampshire?" he asked as he came to give me a hug. I was stiff and awkward considering the fact I'd almost tumbled into the apartment, ready to do very naughty things with his archnemesis.

"Just yesterday morning," I answered. "Broderick drove us back."

My brother's attention was quickly drawn to other matters. "What's that smell? Did you bring food home? Please say yes."

"Oh, yes, I did actually," I answered and fumbled in my bag for the hot dog. Ronan yanked it straight out of my hand and dug right in.

"I shouldn't be eating this."

"It's the offseason. You can have one hot dog." Annie laughed, shaking her head at my brother.

"Man, why does fast food always taste so good?" he groaned.

"Because we all love the things that are bad for us," Annie chimed in as she sorted through a folder full of travel documents.

Ronan winked and gave her a simmering look that I tried wholeheartedly to ignore. I loved my brother and all, but I didn't want to know about his sex life, thank you very much.

"Where've you been, Lucy?" Annie asked as I went to sit down on the couch. "You look a little flushed."

"I just came from Le Cirque," I hurried to answer, wishing my pulse would slow down already. "I only had my phone with me, but I managed to get some decent pictures of Carly Stevens and Dean Newman heading inside for dinner."

"Oh great, let me see," she said, coming to plop down beside me.

I handed her the phone, pulling up the photo gallery and she began to scroll through. "These are good. We can definitely use them," she said enthusiastically.

I was glad she hadn't noticed the unusually high angle, but was prepared to tell her I'd stepped up onto a wall or something if she did. Yes, that was right, a big, manly wall made from pure muscle.

Glancing back down, I saw that she was almost to the end of the pictures I'd taken today, and if she scrolled any farther she'd come to the ones of Sean. The ones I couldn't bring myself to delete for some strange reason. I swiped the phone from her hand more forcefully than necessary and jumped up from the couch.

"Well, I think I'll go lie down in my room for a while," I said, my voice jittery. "I'll send these to your email if you want to write an article to go with them tonight."

Annie frowned. "Are you feeling okay? You seem a bit off."

I mustered a weak smile and joked. "Is that your way of telling me I look tired? I'm okay, just a little exhausted from all the traveling yesterday. We'll hang out tomorrow."

"I've got a stupid bloody strategy session with my publicity team early tomorrow, bunch of fuckwits. And then meetings with the Union managers for the rest of the day," Ronan grumped.

Addressing me, Annie gestured to her laptop. "If you don't have plans, I was thinking we could go over the schedule for the blog tomorrow? Readers responded well to your last article and if you're interested, you could take on more of the posts."

"Oh! Really?" This was huge, as Annie's blog had thousands of followers, and it meant more responsibility. I was suddenly very glad I'd nixed sex with Sean-Adonis earlier in favor of following up on the Carl-D tip.

*Jobs before Bobs!*

"Yes, really. But you'll have to develop your own pseudonym, online personality, the works. I have a meeting at my old offices, but we can start after lunch. It'll take all day."

"That works. I have to be at the animal shelter early tomorrow to help out for my shift, but I'm completely yours after that." I nodded vigorously, then tried to play it cool by adding, "I mean, sounds good. Whatever you think is best."

Annie was laughing again. "You Fitzpatricks are too cute."

"Soon you'll be a Fitzpatrick, too." Ronan stepped behind Annie, sliding his arms around her waist.

"That's my cue to exit." I tossed my thumb over my shoulder and began walking backward toward my room.

"Okay, go hide." Ronan waved me off. "But after the photo shoot on Friday, we're going for dinner at Tom's if you want to join us."

"Yeah sure, sounds great," I called back and closed my door.

Once I was alone inside my room, I exhaled heavily. I was still clutching my phone so tightly I was in danger of cracking the screen. That had been such a close call.

Unable to resist, I flopped down onto my bed and pulled up the pictures of Sean and me, admiring them like a twelve-year-old pulling petals off a flower and chanting, *he loves me, he loves me not.*

This wasn't good. Not good at all.

# Chapter Eleven

**@SeanCassinova** I much prefer the company of dogs to people. Dogs don't get mad when you forget to do the dishes. Dogs > Humans

**@EilishCassidy to @SeanCassinova** Nope. They just lick your face and love you anyway. Remember Wolfie? I miss him.

**@SeanCassinova to @EilishCassidy** Me too :-(

## *Sean*

AFTER LEAVING LUCY, I walked around the streets of New York with no destination in mind.

I did some shopping. I grabbed a cappuccino from a favorite bakery in Little Italy. But the city, oppressively hot and oddly empty, felt lonely in a way I hadn't experienced or noticed during my previous visits.

I thought about calling one or two acquaintances, shallow people who would appreciate being seen with me. I decided against it. I didn't particularly want that kind of company. Being alone struck me as infinitely more alluring than saddling myself with insincerity.

So I went to evening mass at St. Patrick's and returned to the hotel early. Having nothing else to do, I went down to the gym and worked out, hoping Lucy would call, but not terribly surprised when she didn't.

After a few hours, when I'd reached exhaustion, I showered and fell asleep, trying very hard to think of trivial things rather than the growing and uncomfortable tightness in my chest.

Eventually I slept. But I dreamt of Lucy.

In truth, I woke up in the middle of the night, my massive erection frustrating and persistent. Having no other choice, I took the matter in hand, thinking of her and our next lesson.

What would she teach me next? Would we move on to master's courses now that I was rapidly conquering the basics? Would she let me take her in the shower? The fantasy turned infinitely dirtier as I imagined her in the locker room back at the Union field in Dublin.

She was waiting for me after a match, everyone else having left. I imagined her sitting on the plush bench in front of my locker, spreading her legs and hiking her skirt to coyly show me she'd been wearing no knickers while she'd watched me play from the stands.

Oddly, in this fantasy, I was only able to reach climax after she'd come. Multiple times. On every surface of the team room. And in the showers. And in the sauna. Then I passed out again, surrounded by the darkness of the hotel room, needing a shower but too exhausted to move from the bed.

When I awoke the next morning, I searched my sheets for her, confused at first by her absence. Then I remembered it had been a fantasy, a half-waking wishful dream that could never be.

I groaned, miserable and irritated. What was happening to me?

The chiming of my phone cut through my wretched thoughts and I hastily reached for it, wanting it to be her. I didn't allow myself to dwell on the way my heart jumped when I saw she'd texted.

**Lucy:** *I hope this doesn't wake you, but I wanted to give you a heads-up: I can't meet today. I'm at the animal shelter for a shift this* *morning and working this afternoon until late. Enjoy your day off!*

A twinge of disappointment twisted between my shoulder blades, or perhaps it was lingering tightness from my workout the night before. I reread her message again, an idea forming. Without allowing myself to debate the intelligence of my suggestion, I quickly tapped out a response.

**Sean:** *Where is the shelter? I'll bring you coffee.*

She answered straightaway.

**Lucy:** *I already have coffee, but if you want to come down here and help, I won't turn you away.*

**Sean:** *What will I be doing?*

**Lucy:** *Today is grooming day, so everyone gets a bath. Wear casual clothes.*

**Lucy:** *That means no fru-fru designer sports coats.*

**Sean:** *What about my diamond-encrusted shampoo bottle?*

**Lucy:** *That's fine. I have mine here as well, along with my ruby-and-emerald soap dispenser. I'll text you the address.*

I grinned at our easy exchange, my disappointment forgotten. I quickly showered and changed into a pair of running shorts and a microfiber shirt. Both were breathable and quick drying.

Needing to work off some energy before I came face-to-face with the object of my nightly fantasies, I decided to run the three miles to the shelter. It wasn't as oppressively sweltering in the early morning as it had been in the late afternoon.

I managed to work off the worst of my edginess by the time I made it to the address Lucy had texted. However, and again, my heart jumped around my chest when I opened the door to the shelter and strolled inside.

At once I was hit with the familiar smell of flea powder and dog. A wave of unexpected nostalgia swept up and over me as I thought of weekday afternoons, training on the fields behind my aunt and uncle's sprawling country estate, and taking breaks to play fetch with Wolfie.

Before I was pulled too deep in to the undertow of memories, Lucy's voice cut through my brief reminiscence.

"Hey. It's you."

I turned and found her walking toward me clothed in torn, baggy jeans and a plain white T-shirt. She wore a wide, friendly smile. She sounded surprised to see me.

"Did you not think I'd come?"

Lucy stuffed her hands in the back pockets of her pants and shrugged, the grin lingering over her lips. "I didn't know if you were serious about helping. But I'm glad you're here."

We surveyed each other for a long moment. I discovered I was smiling as well, but too late to hide it.

Made bizarrely uncomfortable by my discovery, I decided to change the subject. "Have I dressed appropriately?" I gestured to my shirt.

"Yes. You're perfect," she said brightly, then turned and motioned for me to follow her. "You can towel dry and brush in the pen while I wash."

She led me through a short hallway. The sound of barking dogs grew more distinct. We entered the room where I assumed we'd be working and I swallowed past my nostalgia, schooling my expression.

Cages lined the walls. Some dogs were alone. Some dogs were partnered. Most barked as soon as I entered. A big metal basin sat off to one side, positioned under a faucet. I strolled past Lucy and walked to the first cage, offering the back of my hand to the pit bull mix who was barking the loudest. He immediately sniffed, grew quiet and wagged his tail as I crouched in front of him.

I hadn't expected being in such close proximity to canines to be so disorienting.

Certainly, I'd been around dogs before. But here I was surrounded on all sides. My desire to play with and pet them all was overwhelming. As was the sadness they didn't have homes. They lived in a shelter, a temporary place where they didn't belong. In a cage.

I knew what that was like.

"Meet Hampton." Lucy placed her hand on my shoulder, grinned down at me, and motioned over to a huge black dog pacing the length of a large pen at the end of the room. "He's a newfie and he needs his coat brushed."

"Putting me to work right away?" I straightened, narrowing my eyes at her with mock distrust. "No hello kiss?"

She shook her head and turned my shoulders, pushing me toward Hampton's pen. "You don't need lessons in kissing, you do that just fine. And you said you wanted to help."

I sighed mournfully and opened the chain-link door to the newfie's cage, closing it behind me. "Slave-driver."

Lucy laughed lightly. "Call me what you will, but we need to wash all these dogs before noon. Annie is in town and I have to work this afternoon."

"Fine." I held my hand out to Hampton the newfie and allowed him to sniff before approaching.

"He's already mostly dry." She handed a brush through the cage. Presumably, she expected me to use it on the great brute in front of me, tail wagging, and tongue lolling at the side of his mouth.

Apparently, Hampton liked how I smelled and we were best of friends. I grinned at him, careful not to show my teeth.

"What did you do last night?" Lucy asked, walking to one of the other cages and retrieving a short black and white terrier.

"I went to mass at St. Patrick's." Unable to stop myself, I patted his head and knelt at Hampton's side, brushing the thick hair at his neck, just behind his ears. His tail wagged faster.

Lucy gave me a small, quizzical smile over her shoulder. "Are you practicing?"

By practicing, she meant, *Are you a practicing Catholic?*

"No. I actually haven't been to church in years. Not since I'd started playing rugby at secondary school."

"You didn't go with your parents? My mam always made us go every Sunday and, since we went to private school, we went every morning during the week. Those nuns used to scare the crap out of me."

I cleared my throat before responding, keeping my eyes fastened to the panting dog. "No. I didn't really know my parents. My mother gave me to her brother when I was very young."

In my peripheral vision I saw Lucy cock her head to the side, her eyebrows pulling low. "What do you mean? She gave you to your uncle?"

"Just that. My mother . . . didn't make good choices." A polite way of saying she'd left me abandoned at her flat for days at a time. "My uncle Peter and his wife, my aunt Clara, saw I had athletic potential. So they offered to take me off her hands."

Though my irresponsible mother had foisted me upon my aunt and uncle, they'd accepted me as their own.

But with a condition.

"As you know, the best families had one or more rugby players in their lineage. Take your own family as an example." My gaze flickered to hers.

Lucy shook her head, issuing me an odd look. "I don't consider myself a Fitzpatrick. They want nothing to do with me. If you asked my grandparents, they'd tell you they've never heard of either Ronan or me."

"That's because they already have the proverbial feather in their cap. Your father was a rugby player, and your great-uncle Brian. I was the first Cassidy to demonstrate any aptitude for it."

Lucy was staring at me now, her face carefully devoid of expression. She was wise, my Lucy. Because if she'd been looking at me with pity, I wouldn't have continued. But as it was, her accepting silence spurred my words.

"My aunt and uncle agreed rugby needed to be my priority. So while their family went to mass, I trained with the private coaches they'd hired. I was an opportunity."

"An opportunity," she echoed, an edge of irritation in her voice. "You were a kid."

"Yes, but I was eager for their praise. I trained. All day, every Saturday and Sunday. When I wasn't in school or sleeping, I trained."

"What about friends? Mates? Girlfriends? What did you do for fun?"

I shrugged, bobbing to the side just as the great beast I was grooming tried to lick me. "I had no friends, other than my dog, because friendships were distractions. I've never had teammates, not really. I was frequently reminded that all the blokes I'd ever played alongside were a means to an end."

*"I need you to train, Sean. I need you to make the team,"* my aunt had said, making me believe my success was paramount to *her* happiness.

In the end, rugby had been my saving grace. I was large, strong, and athletic.

"My aunt has never liked my size," I continued, unprompted. "But she did like the idea of a professional Union player in the family. When I made the team it elevated her social status."

The box had been checked.

I'd fulfilled my role.

My usefulness was at an end.

I was no longer needed.

Now merely tolerated.

"That's appalling, Sean. No one deserves to be used like that, least of all a little boy."

I gave Lucy an empty smile. "No matter. It's in the past."

She exhaled, it sounded pained, like she wanted to argue.

I waved her concern away. "I lived the first part of my life wanting to please my aunt and uncle. And now I live my life to please myself. So, in the end, it all worked out," I lied. Because to have no purpose was a terrible thing.

"Do you at least like it?" she pressed, her voice tight.

I thought about the question, moving to Hampton's lower back and using long, smooth strokes with the brush.

"I'm quite good at it."

Lucy huffed impatiently and turned the water off, her hands were now covered in soap as she lathered the small Boston terrier in the tub. "Being good at something is not the same as liking something."

I shook my head, grinning at her. "And the opposite is also true. Liking something is not the same as being good at something, which is why excellent teachers are so essential."

It took her a moment, but she eventually understood my meaning. When she did, two slashes of color glowed over her cheeks.

"Be serious. If you could do anything in the world, other than play rugby, what would you do?"

I stood from my crouching position, patting Hampton on the head.

As much as I admired her attempt to keep the conversation on track, I couldn't help but try to derail her efforts. "Oh, come now, Lucy. I think you know what I'd like to do with my time, if given the opportunity."

Hampton scratched at my leg. When I didn't pay him any mind, he jumped up, his paws landing on my hip.

She gritted her teeth, but ultimately failed to hide her embarrassed smile, unable to meet my gaze. "I've created a monster," she muttered.

"No, you've merely roused—and aroused—a dormant hunger." The newfie pushed at me. Had I been smaller in stature, he would have succeeded in pushing me over. As it was, I braced my feet apart and kept my eyes fastened to the lovely, blooming, blush heating Lucy's neck.

"You're a sex fiend," she said teasingly, her lips twisted to the side, compressing as she tried again—and failed again—to mask her smile. Lucy lifted her gaze and I warmed as it drifted over me.

But then her eyes widened and she gasped, "Oh my God, Sean." She pointed at me. "Sean, the dog!"

I lifted an eyebrow at her, then glanced down at Hampton and I choked on my shock.

The great beast was humping my leg.

I pushed him off at once, but he must've thought it was a good game. He landed on his feet and came charging back, his tongue still lolling from his mouth, jumping at me once more. I held the brush up to ward him off. Unsurprisingly, it proved to be a woefully inadequate deterrent.

Lucy was holding her stomach, laughing so hard she didn't seem to care that she'd gotten soap all over the front of her shirt.

"Looks like you've *aroused* a dormant hunger in Hampton," she managed to say, then doubled over laughing at her own joke.

"Christ! He won't take no for an answer." Despite the circumstance, and much to my surprise, I found I was laughing too as I attempted to evade the newfie's persistent advances.

"Just . . . let him . . . finish, he won't . . . take long," she gasped, wiping at her eyes with the back of her hands as Hampton chased me around the dog pen.

This was half horrifying, half hilarious. I couldn't stand still long enough to open the door, because every time I stood still, Hampton was on me.

"What? No! I don't want him to finish. Go find another leg, Hampton." I tried to gently kick him away, but he barked happily.

"He thinks you're being coy."

"I swear, this dog would make an excellent tighthead prop, he'd be unbeatable in a ruck."

"Or a scrum," Lucy squealed.

"You're hilarious, Lucy. But you're not the one being mauled by a giant Newfoundland."

"Ha! Mauled." She pointed at me acknowledging my inadvertent rugby pun. "Come now, Sean. He just needs some lo— Oh my God!" Lucy yelled and fell back on her bottom as Hampton tried to mount me once again, this time jumping higher and licking my face.

"*Now* you're trying foreplay?" I asked dryly, though I was laughing as well. "Too late, Hampton. Maybe if you'd bought me a drink first."

Jumping to the side to avoid his maneuvers, I finally managed to open the gate. I quickly stepped through, closing the chain-link door before he could follow. He jumped at it, banging the metal, then bounced away, pacing the length of the pen.

I glanced at Lucy, saw she hadn't recovered. Her shoulders shook and she looked as though she couldn't catch her breath. Her head was thrown back and tears of hilarity were leaking from her eyes.

Christ, she was beautiful.

Meanwhile, Hampton barked at me. He sounded frustrated. Let down. Put out. I almost felt sorry for him . . . but not really.

No one likes being the leg that's humped. No one.

# Chapter Twelve

@**LucyFitz** Topic of the day: Celebs who look like other celebs.

@**BroderickAdams to** @**LucyFitz** Julia Roberts = Steven Tyler.

@**LucyFitz to** @**BroderickAdams** #mindblown

**\*Lucy\***

SEAN HAD BEEN an excellent helper.

Despite Hampton's attempts at seduction, Sean's mood had been cheerful and obliging. I'd never seen him so relaxed. And when it was time for me to go, he'd stayed behind and helped the second shift groom the rest of the dogs.

Whereas I jumped in a taxi and sped home, making it back just before Annie walked in the door. We immediately set to work, though I was having some trouble concentrating. If I wasn't thinking about Sean's terrible childhood and growing angry on his behalf, I was distracted by how gentle he'd been with the dogs at the shelter.

What was it about men who were animal lovers? He'd been such a good sport about everything, working hard, wanting to help. It made my heart go pitter-pat.

The next morning, after sleeping fitfully because my dreams were plagued with ridiculous images of Sean, me, and our future pet—a lovely chocolate Labrador mix with big brown eyes—Annie was up before me.

Not surprising given she was on Dublin time, which was five hours ahead.

When I moseyed out to the kitchen I saw she'd laid out a delectable assortment of pastries. This was one of the things I loved most about Annie; the woman had a robust appreciation for pastries.

"Grab an eclair and some coffee," she called from the living room. "Then we'll get back to work on your new online persona."

"Sounds fun." I grabbed the eclair as instructed. Who was I to argue with chocolate ganache at 8:30 a.m.?

Just as I took my first bite, I heard my phone chime from my room, alerting me to a new text message.

"Be right back." I spoke around the eclair I was chewing and shuffled back to my room, eyeing the carafe of coffee longingly as I went.

Pulling the cell from my bag, my heart skipped as I read the new message.

**Sean:** *What time are you coming over?*

For some unknown reason, I shut my door before I responded.

**Lucy:** *Sorry. I meant to tell you yesterday. Teacher needs a day off to catch up on work stuff. How about tomorrow?*

**Sean:** *Where are you? Are you at your apartment? Should I bring you sustenance? Street meat perhaps?*

**Lucy:** *Don't bring food. I'm at my apartment working all day with Annie. She gave me a promotion.*

**Sean:** *That's great. Let me take you out tonight to celebrate. I'll pick* *you up at 6.*

    **Lucy:** *Very funny.*

    **Sean:** *I wasn't being funny. Let me take you out.*

I frowned at Sean's latest text message.

    **Lucy:** *Bad idea.*

    **Sean:** *Why?*

Was he trying to be cute? Or was he just completely obtuse. I responded on a gust of irritation before thinking through my words.

    **Lucy:** *Because I'd rather not have my brother know I'm teaching his archnemesis how to give women orgasms.*

He didn't respond for over a minute. Just as I was about to toss it to the bed, the phone vibrated with a new text.

    **Sean:** *Technically you're only teaching me how to give you orgasms. How do I know if this information is generalizable to all women?*

    **Lucy:** *Trust me, it is.*

    **Sean:** *If you're busy today, perhaps I should conduct a test.*

I stared at the last six words he'd just typed, my heart beating in my throat, my face flushing with uncomfortable heat, my chest hurting every time I tried to breathe. I didn't know why I felt so blindsided. Wasn't that the point of our lessons? I looked into my bedroom mirror, studied my reflection.

"You're okay with this," I said to myself, then cleared my voice when I noted the slight tremor in it. "He's not meant for you. He's a rugby player. He's Ronan's nemesis. And he's an arsehole, except when he's helping groom rescued stray dogs. Don't be so surprised."

I thought about adding, *You're good enough, you're smart enough, and doggone it, other men want to fuck you,* but felt like that would be self-affirmation overkill.

I took several deep breaths until my mind calmed and the pain in my chest became a dull ache before responding.

**Lucy:** *Sure! Feel free to try out your new techniques on the women of New York. They can send their notes and gifts of gratitude to my PO box. Have fun!*

With that I turned off my phone.

I turned it completely off.

And I buried it under three pairs of jeans in my drawer.

**\*\*\***

WE WORKED ALL day and into the night, going to bed well after midnight.

I spent the following morning finalizing my new social media accounts and finishing up research for Annie. She and Ronan had already gone to the photo shoot.

I also busied myself trying not to think about what (or who) Sean may or may not have done the night before. Not helping matters, I was reminded of him every time I moved my upper body. I was trying not to feel regretful about doing all those clapping pushups with him three days ago. My arms and abs were bloody killing me.

When lunchtime rolled around I was still in my pajamas. Such was life when you worked from home, and were in denial about being depressed because the guy you're crushing on was out giving other women orgasms.

I was in desperate need of a shower, so I ventured into the bathroom.

Once out, I blow-dried my hair and put on some tight pale jeans and a floaty tie-dye top. For makeup, I gave myself kitten flicks and painted on some clear lip gloss. I wasn't going to allow myself to moon over Sean Cassidy.

When I'd finally finished beautifying myself, it was almost time to go meet Annie and Ronan for dinner. They'd left me the address of the studio, telling me to go there and then we'd all catch a cab to the restaurant. I was both excited about and terrified of seeing Sean.

Partially because Ronan would be there with his eagle, cranky brother eyes. And partially because I dreaded learning that Sean had taken his new skills for a test drive last night. But I reasoned it would be just as well. No need to prolong this arrangement, especially since I seemed to be the only one feeling more than I should.

When I arrived, a personal assistant checked to make sure my name was on the approved list and then I was ushered through. There was music on when I stepped inside the spacious, airy studio, busy-looking people milling all about. I caught sight of Annie as she sat on a chair by one of the windows sipping on peppermint tea.

"Hey," she greeted me. "Did you find the place okay?"

"Yep. How's the shoot going?"

She grimaced. "Your brother and Sean Cassidy have been fighting like cats and dogs all morning. Sean is being extra douchey, acting like he's got one over on Ronan. I told him it was all an act but you know your brother, he just can't let things go."

My stomach tightened at her words, because technically Sean did have something over on Ronan. *Me.* God, I was going to have serious words with that man the next time I got him alone.

The click of a camera caught my attention and I turned to see Ronan, Sean, and their other teammate, Bryan Leech, standing in front of a white background. All of them were wearing athletic pants but no tops. Sean captured my gaze and it was hard to do anything but stare at him.

His body was almost too perfect to be real: toned abs, defined obliques, totally lickable pecs.

His smile was a slow curve, his eyes heating as they traced my form. Suddenly, my skinny jeans felt way too tight and it was difficult to swallow. Perhaps it had been a bad idea coming here.

"Did you get some rest last night?" Annie enquired.

I tore my eyes from Sean and gathered a bracing inhale before answering my brother's fiancée. "I did. I feel much better."

"Well, you look much more refreshed." She gave me a warm smile. "I wish we lived closer, and not just because I love hanging out with someone who enjoys drinking tea and eating pastries."

"Me too." I returned her smile, my heart swelling a bit with how happy I felt to have Annie in my life. She was perfect for Ronan, but she was also starting to feel like a true sister to me. "I wish I could help you more with the wedding."

Annie's grin widened and she glanced at the ceiling. "I think we both know it's best just to let your mother have charge of it."

"I hope she's not driving you too crazy."

Annie had been an absolute saint with my mother. They'd had a rocky start, but my mam had quickly changed her tune when it became widely known that Annie was a super-famous and universally adored celebrity blogger.

"No. She's fine. We've been getting on pretty well, especially since I make sure Ronan calls her and takes her out for lunch once a week."

I snorted. "She stopped making me go out to lunch with her when I started dying my hair."

"I love your hair. And it's so pretty down like that." She ran her fingers through the ends in admiration and I shifted in my seat, feeling uncomfortable by Annie's praise.

I decided to change the subject. "Did you get a chance to finish that article to go with the Carl-D pictures?"

"Carl-D?"

"Carly and Dean. My friend, Mackenzie, made up a nickname for them. You know, like Kimye or Brangelina."

"Oh right." She laughed and stroked her chin. "What do you think Ronan's and my couple nickname would be? Ronnie?"

I chuckled loudly. "As in Corbett? No way. Annan sounds better. It's sophisticated, like a brand of French perfume."

She smiled wide. "Annan. I like it."

"What are you two grinning about?" came Ronan's voice as he approached. I glanced across the room to find the photographer had called for a break. Sean was standing just a few yards away, sipping an energy drink. I was suddenly reminded of those sexy Diet Coke ads . . .

"Celebrity nicknames," Annie answered as Ronan bent down to kiss her on the cheek.

"Hey Lucy," Sean called over, interrupting us. I looked at him again to see his body was twisted so both his head and his arse were facing me.

"How does my butt look in these pants?"

I swear, in that moment every ounce of embarrassment I was capable of feeling hit me full force. Still, I managed to muster a snappy comeback. "A bit flat, actually." It wasn't flat. It was round and muscular and completely bite-worthy.

His eyes flared in challenge as he cocked his head to the side. "You think so? Why don't you come over here and give it a squeeze? Maybe you'll reconsider."

Oh, he was going to die when I got my hands on him. He was seriously going to die.

I was lost for words when Ronan butted in. "Don't talk to my sister, Cassidy. She's far too intelligent to fall for your bullshit charm."

*Oh, Ronan, you have no idea.*

Sean smiled with teeth, his eyes falling on me, then returning to Ronan. "You'd think that, wouldn't you?"

Ronan stepped toward him. "Excuse me?"

I jumped up from my seat, grabbing Ronan's arm and pulling him back. "When do you think the shoot will wrap up? I'm starving."

My brother frowned down at me, not speaking for a moment.

"Oh God, me too," Annie added. "I need a mountain of creamy mashed potatoes and gravy, stat." She paused and then glanced between Ronan and Sean, an idea sparking behind her eyes. "Why don't you join us, Sean?"

Ronan cast his fiancée a look of disbelief and both men spoke at the same time.

"He's not joining us."

"It would be my pleasure."

"Good, it's settled then," said Annie, walking to Ronan and pulling him into a hug. He was tense, his posture strained, but then she began whispering something in his ear and the tension fell away.

Huh.

I glanced at Sean, who was wearing a giant shit-eating grin. Flaring my eyes meaningfully, I tried to communicate the order, *make up an excuse not to come.* Unfortunately, his returning expression said, *Oh, I'm coming.*

When Annie finally let go of Ronan. he turned to address Sean one last time. "You can come to dinner, but if I get even a hint of your usual bullshit I'll kick you out of the restaurant so fast your head will spin."

Sean only smiled. "I'll be on my best behavior."

Why didn't I believe that?

Ronan frowned at him as though trying to figure out his game. In the end he let out a low, irritable grunt and stalked off to use the bathroom.

An hour later, I sat in the back of a taxi with Ronan and Annie while Sean and Bryan shared one that followed behind us. I really wished I'd gotten the chance to pull Sean aside and warn him of all the things he wasn't to do at dinner, but the shoot had been a crazy rush and there had been no way of cornering him. As well, I didn't want to listen to him detail his exploits from the previous night.

Irrationally, I felt like any orgasms he'd dished out belonged to me. He was giving away *my* orgasms. Some strange, possessive part of me felt ownership of him and his new abilities.

In other words, I was completely loony.

When we arrived at Tom's, I saw him emerging from his cab with Bryan just a little distance away. He caught me staring and his expression turned intense. I closed my eyes, remembering his mouth on me, how good it felt when we touched, and a shiver of longing pulsed through me.

I wanted him again.

The realization had my skin prickling and my belly coiling tight with need.

But how stupid was I? He'd likely spent last night testing out his skills on someone else. Perhaps even several . . .

Opening my eyes, I steeled my reserve and determined to get through dinner without any mortifying revelations coming to light. Then I'd say goodbye and never have to speak to him again.

Good plan.

The second we stepped through the door, Tom was there to greet us. He was tall, auburn-haired, and stocky in a way that said he worked out but still ate his fill. Basically, he looked a bit like Josh Homme. He was also my brother's best friend from school, who had since become one of New York's most successful head chefs. He pulled Ronan into a man hug, then turned to embrace Annie, placing a soft kiss on her cheek. Smiling wide when he saw me, he stepped forward and hugged me, too.

"Little Lucy Fitzpatrick. Look how big you've gotten," he exclaimed. "I hear you've been living in New York for six months and have never taken the time to grace my doors." Tut-tutting.

I laughed. "Hey, I'm here now, aren't I?"

"Yes, and I insist you come again soon. Take advantage of my kindness," he said, kissing me on the cheek the same as he'd done to Annie.

Suddenly, I felt a cool gust of air sweep in as the door opened behind me, and I knew it was Sean and Bryan without even having to look. Chancing a quick glance over my shoulder, I found Sean glaring daggers at Tom while Bryan stood beside him, smiling obliviously.

"Bryan," said Tom. "Long time no see, mate."

The men exchanged pleasantries while Sean came to stand by me, his silence disconcerting.

"And you must be Mr. Cassidy," Tom went on somewhat dubiously.

"It's a pleasure," said Sean in his usual refined manner. They briefly shook hands, but needless to say, Tom knew exactly who Sean was and there was certainly no love lost between them.

A few minutes later, all six of us were seated at a table. Ronan, Annie and Bryan sat on one side, while I was sandwiched between Tom and Sean on the other. I also didn't fail to notice how Sean quickly took the seat on the other side of me when he saw Tom politely pulling out my chair. I cast him a searching look, trying to ask what he was up to, but he only stared back with no answers. Maybe he didn't even know himself.

Tom had arranged for his best sous chef to cook for us, and for a starter we were served the most delicious catfish cakes with a tangy lemon dipping sauce. Sean was being decidedly quiet as the men chatted about the upcoming rugby season. Thankfully, Annie was directly across from me, so we could chat about plans for the blog.

"Does all this sport talk bore you as much as it bores me?" Tom leaned in to ask, somewhere in between the starter and the main course.

I chuckled and gave him a friendly smile. "Pretty much. I'm far more interested in the food we're eating."

Tom grinned widely, his hand going to his chest. "Ah, a woman after my own heart."

Right at that moment, I froze as I felt a warm hand grip my thigh beneath the table. I'd just lifted my glass of white wine to take a sip and almost spat it out. My heart raced as Sean's thumb drew circles on my knee before his palm slid slowly upward.

Lifting a foot, I made sure no one was paying attention when I stamped it down hard on his. He only smiled in return, like my attempt to hurt him was adorable. While Annie was momentarily distracted talking to Ronan, and Tom was focused on Bryan, I turned my head discreetly to Sean and whispered, "Stop it."

His knuckles brushed lightly over my crotch and I trembled as he lifted his wine glass to his mouth to disguise his response. "No."

Why was he being like this?

I frowned, both angry and aroused, and decided I'd had enough when his thumb dipped beneath the hem of my top and smoothed over the lower part of my belly.

Swiftly rising from my seat, I told Annie I was going to use the bathroom before the main course was served. Once I'd flicked the lock over and was cocooned safely in the privacy of a cubicle, I felt like I could breathe again. My hands were shaking, and for the first time in my life I felt like stealing for a reason completely unconnected to my mother. The little complementary hand towels and soaps by the sink were in serious danger of being shoved inside my handbag.

I closed my eyes and worked to calm myself.

*Be content with what you have; rejoice in the way things are.*

*When you realize there is nothing lacking, the whole world belongs to you.*

Ah, that was better. I didn't need those hand towels, and I certainly didn't need the fancy little eucalyptus-scented soaps wrapped in pretty purple wax paper. I just needed to relax and accept what was really happening here.

Sean's beef with Ronan, and my inconvenient feelings for a man my brother disliked immensely were giving me a severe case of anxiety. That was a fact. I needed to simply accept it and get through the evening. That was all.

I sat down on the closed lid of the toilet just as I heard the door open and someone step inside. There was a long, masculine sounding exhalation before Sean said, "Lucy, let me in."

And just like that, I was on edge again. My eyes flared in disbelief that he'd followed me into the bathroom. There were only six people at our table, and the absence of two wouldn't go unnoticed. Jumping up swiftly, I threw open the door.

"Get out of here now," I hissed, my hands going to his chest and pushing him toward the exit. He gripped them in his own and held them there, his eyes meeting mine.

"Relax, no one's going to catch us," he said in a low voice. "I just need to make you come. I promise I'll be quick."

I stared at him and his audacity for a full three seconds before I shrieked on a whisper, "Are you out of your mind?"

"Lucy, please," he whispered. "I can't get you out of my head."

"Puh-lease! I'm sure you were thinking about me all last night when you were out with other women, 'testing your new evil orgasm powers.'" I added air quotes to the last part, wanting to be as obnoxious as possible.

"No," he ground out. "There were no women."

I gasped, then sputtered in surprise. No women? Why did that make my heart soften so instantaneously? Crap!

He took advantage of my stunned state to march me back into the cubicle, releasing one of my hands just long enough to close and lock the stall door. "But I did think about you all last night when I was alone and I touched myself, imagined you coming on my tongue," he kissed my jaw, "and fingers," he kissed my neck, "and cock," he kissed my lips.

Something like aroused hope and dread had my neck burning and my voice shaking as I pulled away from his intoxicating kiss. "I thought you were going out last night to find somebody else?"

"I don't want anyone else."

*I . . . who . . . when . . . WHAT?*

I needed to think.

I needed a minute.

I needed an ice-bath.

"This is neither the time nor the place, Sean," I said weakly, right before he smashed his mouth to mine, his tongue sliding past the seam of my lips to taste me. He groaned and the noise did something, turned me into a pliant pile of mush rather than an anxious kleptomaniac mess.

His hands cupped my cheeks as he turned us and my back hit the wall. He ground his erection into my hip, then lifted one of my legs to wrap around his waist so he could press into my softness.

A second later he was fiddling with the button on my jeans and sliding his hand inside my knickers. I moaned when he moved two fingers along my slickness, finding me ready.

I almost let him do it, but the knowledge of Ronan and Annie and everyone else waiting at the table had me channeling all my strength and pushing him away.

"No," I told him breathlessly. "We can't do this here."

Sean exhaled heavily, his breathing agitated. "Is this because of that Tom prick? Because he clearly wants to fuck you."

"What?" I exclaimed. "No. *God, no.* Tom is like a cousin to me. You're being a lunatic."

The way he lifted one eyebrow said he didn't believe me.

I laughed my frustration at the ridiculousness of the situation. "What's going on with you? What are we doing here?"

"Have I been too subtle?" He pressed his erection against me again. "Fine. Let me be clear: Lucy Fitzpatrick, lovely Lucy, I want you."

I let my head hit the wall behind me as I evaded his kiss, needing him to see he was acting crazy. We absolutely could not have sex in the bathroom. If we had sex in the bathroom, Ronan would find out and the shit would hit the fan.

My voice was unsteady as I tried to think and speak at the same time. "I thought things were clear between us. You said Ronan would never find out. But then I arrive at the photo shoot and you start acting up, trying to rile my brother. It's so stupid and pointless when you both could easily just get along."

Sean's tone was disdainful. "Ronan and I will never get along."

I held him away, wanting to see his face as I challenged, "Why not?"

Now his brow scrunched up and he seemed conflicted. "Because . . ." he started, then paused as though trying to find the right words. "Because everything he wants just falls right into his lap. He never even has to try and people think the sun shines out of his arse. Maybe he deserves a little animosity every once in a while."

"And you're the one to provide it, are you?"

Sean released me and, as much as was possible in the confined space, took a step back. "I don't see why not."

I frowned. "Everything doesn't just fall into his lap. He gets things because he works hard for them. And people think highly of him because he's a good person and treats them with respect. Why do you have such a problem with that?"

Sean raked his hands through his hair in agitation, ruffling the short blond strands. "Because I work just as hard, but nobody ever pats me on the back or tells me how bloody wonderful I am."

I stared at him, suddenly seeing something I hadn't before. I tried to gentle my voice. "Hard work is one thing, Sean, but you have to be kind to people, too. You could work your fingers to the bone, but if you go around flipping everybody off while you're doing it they're never going to respect you."

His glare turned into a tired frown and he turned his head to the side as he muttered, "God, what am I even doing here?"

I let out a breath and took his hand, sliding my fingers between his. "You're having dinner with a bunch of cool people. Why not try enjoying their company?" He grimaced at me and I stopped for a second as an idea formed, adding, "Why not try enjoying my company?"

"I always enjoy your company," Sean muttered automatically, his eyes softening as they skated over my face.

I swallowed a building lump in my throat and suggested, "How about we go back outside and try something?"

His look was cautious. "Like what?"

"When we rejoin the others, you have to chat with Ronan in a polite and friendly manner and you have to give him at least one compliment."

Sean stared at me as though I'd turned into a raving lunatic and eventually shook his head. "I don't think so."

"What have you got to lose?"

"My self-respect," he scoffed.

"Oh, come on. Now you're just being melodramatic." I paused and squeezed his hand. "Please? Do it for me, and I promise you'll feel better for it. Be kind to my brother and watch the difference in how he treats you, how everyone treats you."

Sean grunted and asked, "What if I don't know how to be kind?"

"You're kind to me. And you were kind to those dogs, even Hampton, who basically sexually harassed your leg only seconds after meeting you."

His eyes flickered between mine and I saw he was fighting a smile. Then his gaze lowered to my lips. "Fine," he conceded. "But if this turns out to be a disaster it's on your head, little pixie."

I smiled at the reluctant affection in his voice. "Everything will be better. I promise you."

I ignored the small voice that told me making peace between Sean and Ronan wasn't just for altruistic reasons. If Sean and Ronan didn't hate each other, then perhaps . . .

His eyes narrowed on me as he continued staring at my mouth. "I want something in return."

From the way he was looking at my mouth I wouldn't need three guesses. "A blow job?"

"No. I want you to come over tonight."

"For a blow job?" I teased.

"No." His gaze lifted to mine, the earnest intensity made my breath catch. He shook his head slowly. "No expectations. No lessons. Just . . . come over and spend the night. Be with me." And then he quietly added, almost like an afterthought, "Let me feel your warmth."

# Chapter Thirteen

**@THEBryanLeech** ABCDS

**@SeanCassinova to @THEBryanLeech** ABCDS?

**@THEBryanLeech to @SeanCassinova** Always Be Calmly Drinking Scotch #WordsToLiveBy

**@SeanCassinova to @THEBryanLeech** UYCBIAW… TDB

**@THEBryanLeech to @SeanCassinova** UYCBIAW TDB?

**@SeanCassinova to @THEBryanLeech** Unless You Can Be Inside A Woman… Then Do Both #WordsILiveBy

### *Sean*

I DIDN'T KNOW what I was doing.

Requests, things I wanted, words I would never speak or allow myself to think were now uncontainable.

*It's the sex*, I reiterated. Again. I'd used this explanation, now on repeat, as a simple justification for the complex cacophony of my mind.

"Be with you?" Her long, dark lashes fluttered, beating like distressed butterfly wings against warming pink cheeks.

I licked my lips, tasting her there. "Yes."

She stared at me, confused. I was also confused. And oddly frightened.

Because it wasn't the sex.

Several seconds ticked on as we studied each other in breathless silence. She found her voice before I did. "What does that—"

"Lucy?" Annie's voice was paired with a soft knock on the bathroom door. "Are you okay?"

I opened my mouth to whisper a clarification to the question Lucy hadn't quite posed, because I was compelled to tell her it wasn't the sex. We didn't have to have sex. We could just . . . talk. Or play cards. Or touch. Or look at each other from across the room.

We could merely be together.

But she covered my mouth with her hand. Her features arrested with unmistakable panic.

"Yes. I'm fine! I just . . . started my period is all. Made a mess in my jeans, like a crime scene." Lucy hollered in response then grimaced. She immediately mouthed *I'm sorry* to me. Her cheeks flushed red.

I lifted an eyebrow. She rolled her eyes, ducking her head with obvious embarrassment. I pressed my lips together so I wouldn't laugh.

Issuing me a quelling look, Lucy released me and skittered out of the stall, whispering, "Stay here and count to three hundred."

"Oh! Do you need anything?" Annie's voice was less muffled and I surmised she'd opened the bathroom door.

"Ah, no. Have it all sorted now. Thank God Tom has these nice absorbent napkins instead of those troublesome hand driers. Although I feel like I'm wearing a nappy. They're bad for the environment, so I should talk to him about replacing the napkins. Maybe make a few available for emergencies . . ."

Lucy's anxiety-riddled chatter faded as the bathroom door clicked shut.

I released an audible exhale. My heart was beating as though it might leap from my chest. I needed to catch my breath. Neither had anything to do with being caught.

*What the fuck were you doing?*

*It was the sex. She's phenomenal in bed. You've never had that before. It was just sex.*

I nodded, reiterating the logic of my justification for the uncharacteristic behavior. If I repeated it enough, perhaps I would believe it.

I didn't count to three hundred as instructed. I counted to one hundred and twenty-three, then realized what I was doing.

"You're mad, Sean," I muttered, shaking myself and promptly leaving the ladies' room. I checked the cufflinks on my dress shirt—a nervous habit—and strolled back to the table, eyeing the assortment of eejits gathered.

Tom, as an example, was a complete eejit. I hated the way he looked at Lucy, like she might be delicious. I no more believed he saw her as a cousin than I did.

Of course, Ronan was an ape.

Bryan Leech, however, was something else. Unfortunately, he'd drunk the Ronan Fitzpatrick Kool-Aid, but he was far too subversive to be a total moron. He was the only man in Union history to be suspended three times in a season and still retain his contract for the next year. He was a sneak, but not quite an eejit.

Annie, Ronan's fiancée, must've been an eejit on some level. Why else would she sacrifice all that brilliance and lusciousness to an ape?

And then there was Lucy . . .

I reclaimed my seat next to her. She was in the middle of a conversation with fuckwit Tom. He was talking, likely about himself or his little restaurant.

"Sean." Bryan tapped on the table, drawing my attention to him. "Are you headed back to Barcelona after this?"

I shook my head, but before I could answer, Ronan cut in, "Nah, he was in Dublin before this. He tried to take my seat out of Spain."

I shifted in my chair, clenching my jaw to keep my acerbic remark to myself. I had to swallow a gulp of water before I could respond. "Was it a pleasant flight?"

Ronan narrowed his eyes on me, clearly distrustful of the benign direction of my comment.

Our team captain leaned back from the table and scratched his jaw, examining me. "Once you were booted, it was pleasant."

I nodded, having nothing else to say since I couldn't say anything nasty. I felt Lucy's eyes on me as I cut into my steak, chewed it, swallowed, and drank another gulp of water.

"Thank you for that, by the way." Annie joined the conversation. "Thank you for giving up your seat."

"He didn't give it up." Ronan scowled at his fiancée. "They made him leave."

"Ronan," the pretty brunette warned.

"What? It's the truth." The ape shrugged.

Annie sighed.

Lucy cleared her throat.

Bryan smirked. "I've been tossed off a flight or two myself over the years. Worth it, though. There's a lot to be said for joining the mile-high club."

"Bryan." Ronan frowned, eyes going pointedly to his sister like he didn't want Bryan defiling her innocent ears. I resisted the urge to snicker. She'd already been thoroughly defiled, and would continue to be if I had my way.

I took another bite of my steak, chewed, swallowed, and wracked my brain for a serviceable compliment so I could cross it off my list and end this farce of a dinner. Perhaps something like:

*Your enunciation is exceptional for a primate.*

*Kudos to you for not flinging your excrement at the dinner table.*

*You smell not terrible.*

Instead, I glanced at Lucy and said, "You have an excellent memory, Ronan."

"What is that supposed to mean?" he challenged, eyes narrowing further.

"Just that." I shrugged. "Your recollection of our flight seating mishap is impeccable."

"Well, it was just a week ago," came his flat reply. "I might be older than you by two months, but I'm not long in the tooth just yet."

"A week ago?" Lucy held my gaze for two beats, a whisper of a smile curving her sweet lips. I lifted my eyebrows subtly, hoping she'd interpret the meaning of the small gesture.

She squinted at me, admirably suppressing her grin, then turned her attention to Annie. "Why were you in Spain?"

I released a silent, relieved exhale, and did not follow the ensuing conversation.

The compliment had been paid. Now it was her turn.

***

I LEFT FIRST, begging off after the main course. Neither Tom nor Ronan protested my departure, but Annie and Lucy encouraged me to stay, likely because I was playing so nicely.

Playing nice only required that I say nothing, but was essential if I didn't want to give Lucy any excuse to miss our rendezvous. I'd also been playing nice because, much to my delighted surprise, it aggravated Ronan to no end.

The hotel wasn't too far from the restaurant. I walked, checking my phone at every corner for a message from Lucy. It didn't buzz with a text until I'd walked into the hotel lobby.

**Lucy**: *A great memory? Really?*

**Sean**: *Yes. Really. His memory is faultless. Pristine. Immaculate.*

**Lucy**: *That's a shitty compliment. That's like telling a person they don't smell.*

Is it odd that this made me laugh? I took gleeful satisfaction in the book-report nature of my compliment.

*Ronan is a man. He has very brown hair, and very brown eyes, and a very good memory.*

**Sean:** *No specification was made as to the quality of the compliment, only that one was required.*

**Lucy**: *You're a filthy cheat. Dinner is over. I'll be there in an hour.*

**Sean**: *Why an hour? Come over now.*

**Lucy**: *I need to pick up a change of clothes if I'll be out all night.*

I frowned at my screen, then at the surrounding opulence of the lobby. I hadn't been at liberty to touch her as I'd wanted in over two days. I had plans that couldn't wait an hour. They involved her bending over the lounge chair in my suite and me grabbing handfuls of her arse as

I slid into her hot, wet pussy.

She would cry out in ecstasy, of course. And come several times. And beg for the repeated pleasure. And spend the night. And we would talk. And I would hold her while we slept. And she'd stay for breakfast.

A shop front in the lobby caught my eye, just closing for the evening. Rather, a nightgown in the window caught my eye. I crossed to the shop as I tapped out my next message.

**Sean**: *I have a change of clothes for you. Don't go home first.*
**Lucy**: *Please do not tell me you bought me clothes.*
**Sean**: *I didn't buy you clothes.*

Technically, this was true. I hadn't yet purchased her clothes.

Issuing instructions to the first salesperson I encountered, I picked out three sets of lingerie, a ridiculous nightgown—more a suggestion of a nightgown than anything else as it was see-through and silk—and I allowed the clerk to select proper clothes. I had no interest in those. While she did so, I eyed the jewelry case.

And here's where I ran into a predicament. I saw a necklace and it reminded me of Lucy. A yin and yang pendant on a long platinum chain, set with black diamonds for the yin and white diamonds for the yang. I walked away from it, perplexed by the impulse to buy it for her.

The clothes made sense. She obviously needed clothes, so I could remove them from her body.

The stunning necklace did not make sense. Frivolous, an item for her with no benefit whatsoever for me.

*And yet . . .*

I imagined her opening it. I imagined how pleased she'd be, how she'd want to wear it straight away, how it might remind her of me in the future.

"Sir? Will there be anything else?"

The clerk's soft voice came from just behind me. Meanwhile, my phone continued to vibrate in my hand. Scanning the screen, I read Lucy's most recent messages.

**Lucy:** *If you didn't buy me clothes then how do you have a change of clothes for me?*

**Lucy:** *What are you doing?*

**Lucy:** *EARTH TO SEAN!*

**Lucy:** *You're buying the clothes right now, aren't you?*

**Lucy:** *If you buy me clothes to wear tomorrow then you have to let me buy you clothes, and I'll bring over an orange Speedo and Birkenstocks.*

My sudden burst of laughter surprised me. I loved her humor.

"Sir?" the saleswoman prompted again.

"The black and white diamond pendant," I said, smiling as I reread Lucy's messages; I glanced over my shoulder at the woman. "I'll take it as well."

\*\*\*

ONCE UPSTAIRS, I ordered champagne from room service and had a shower to wash off the day. I also beat off, needing some release from the perpetual case of Lucy Fitzpatrick-inspired blue balls. It didn't help much.

But she would be here soon.

My attention caught on the small box I'd placed on the nightstand next to the bed. Originally, I'd left it on the bar. Then I'd moved it to the table in the sitting area. After trying out the desk in the bedroom, the counter in the bathroom, and the center of the bed, I'd settled on the nightstand.

I was just about to relocate it back to the table in the sitting area when I heard her knock sound from the hallway. Smirking at her refusal to use the key, I jogged to the door and opened it.

"You didn't answer my text messages," she accused, leaning against the doorframe, still dressed in the clothes she'd worn at dinner. These were the same clothes I'd almost successfully breached in the loo at Tom's little restaurant. I might not have liked Tom, but I would always have fond memories of a certain bathroom stall on the premises.

"I was busy," I said, sounding oddly out of breath to my own ears.

Her attention lowered to my chest, eyebrows lifting. "And you're in a towel."

"Yes. Let's fix that." I reached for her without further preamble. She came to me willingly, didn't protest when I brought my mouth to hers, pressed the length of her against me, and kicked the door shut.

Lucy was pliant and tasted sweet, so unbelievably delicious. I groaned when her tongue slid along mine, an acute hunger I'd been endeavoring to discount raged unchecked. The flimsy top she wore frustrated my need for her skin. I reached under the hem and smoothed my hands up her sides to her ribs. Satisfaction came in the form of her whimpers when I lifted her bra, bent my head to her nipple, and sucked on her through the fabric of her shirt.

"Sean . . ." she panted, her nails digging into the back of my head, holding me to her chest. "Ah, wait. Wait a minute."

She was here, beneath my fingers, mine for the night. All my earlier plans were eclipsed by the reality of her and my ferocious need to make her feel good.

"Would you like me to go down on you first?" I blew on the wet patch of her shirt, an instinctive growl reverberating through my chest as I watched the nipple strain and pebble.

I wanted to devour her.

"Oh, well, if you insist . . ." she squeaked, her pelvis tilting against my leg even as we stumbled backward toward the living room.

I popped open her jeans button, savoring the succulent sweetness of her mouth, pushing my hand into her knickers, greedy to feel the wet slickness between her thighs, and growling once more when I found her ready.

She sighed, rolling her hips as I stroked her with my middle finger. So luscious. So soft. So hot.

"Or do you want my cock first?" I whispered. "Should I make love to you from behind? Shall I bend you over? Do you want to kneel as I enter you? Would that make you feel good?"

"Christ, Sean," she gasped against my mouth, holding my wrist in place as I slid my finger around her clit, keeping my touch teasing and gentle. "Have you been taking lessons from someone else?"

She meant it as a joke, I was certain.

But it angered me.

Tension pulsed through my veins and my arm constricted around her waist. The movements of my fingers ceased. I waited until she opened her eyes, at first foggy with lust, then focused on me, before responding.

"No, Lucy. There is only you." My anger seeped through the words. I watched as she swallowed and blinked.

"Sean, I—"

"Only you. Only me." I didn't comprehend the impulse, but I needed her to understand, to know. I thought of no one else.

Lucy swallowed. Her eyes were wide and rimmed with determination, an acceptance that heightened, rather than eased, my frustration.

"Only tonight," she whispered, making me frown even as her hand came to my jaw and guided my mouth to hers. She brushed a soft kiss over my lips.

Not enough.

I deepened it, chasing her mouth as she smoothed her hand over my shoulder, scratching her nails down my chest and stomach, dipping her fingertips into the towel wrapped at my waist.

I needed more of her skin, so I allowed our bodies to separate just long enough to discard her shirt and bra, for her to step out of her jeans and sandals and lacy knickers. Sampling bites, savoring her neck, the side of her breast, I maneuvered her against the wall as I lowered to my knees on the plush carpet. I held her body in place and my mouth watered at the promise of her taste.

"You're kneeling, Sean," she whispered, her voice unsteady yet laced with teasing; a playful reminder of the last time I made her come.

I lifted my eyes to hers, skimming my fingers up the back of her legs and drawing circles on the backs of her knees.

"I'll beg," I said, clearly senseless with my need to make her come, though I meant it.

I would beg if she required it.

My frankness was rewarded straightaway. "What are you doing to me?" she asked, dazed. Her stare moved over my face, helpless hunger making her eyes glow. Her legs trembled beneath my fingertips.

"Please, Lucy . . ." Holding her gaze, I separated her with my thumbs and deliberately leaned forward, gently traced the warm flesh of her slit with my tongue. Always gently. "Please let me taste you. Please let me make you feel good."

"Damn, damn, damn . . ." She pushed her hips forward, widening her stance, her head falling back against the wall.

Her legs flexed as I devoured her, and I followed the indentations and curves of her muscles with my fingertips to the silky smoothness between her thighs. As I traced, I catalogued her skin, discovering and memorizing her most sensitive places.

I knew when she grew restless, tired of my teasing touches and the light flicks of my tongue. I fed her hunger, easing two fingers into her body and licking a path from the apex of her thighs to her clit, sucking the bead between my lips.

She came with an abrupt, sharp cry, her body clenching, her hips rocking over my mouth, her fingers twisting in my short hair.

I needed this. I needed the sounds of her pleasure, the artless spontaneity of her release.

And I needed her to do it again.

# Chapter Fourteen

**@EilishCassidy to @SeanCassinova** Where are you?
#CrankyAuntWantsToKnow

**@SeanCassinova to @EilishCassidy** Someplace I never want to leave.
#Heaven

### *Sean*

**I TUGGED LIGHTLY** and she tumbled forward, unable to support her own weight. I captured her, gathered her close in my arms. She grasped me weakly, her head resting against my shoulder as I listened to her shuddering breaths, felt her body trembling.

Accomplishment. And . . . pride. A deep, thorough satisfaction spread like wildfire through my veins, warming me from the inside as she snuggled closer, gripped me tighter, sighed the sigh of replete contentment.

"A plus plus," she murmured against my neck, placing a kiss there.

I lifted an eyebrow, loving the friction of her soft skin as she moved. "Pardon?"

"You get an *A* double plus in cunnilingus, Sean. You've graduated."

I smiled to myself, because though I didn't require additional verbal verification beyond her panting groans and cries of pleasure, I enjoyed her candor.

"Good." I kissed her temple and sought her hand. I kissed her knuckles one at a time. Then I searched for something else to kiss and decided on her neck since it was closest.

Her head lolled to the side, allowing me greater access. "Seriously. Gold star. Your parents will be so proud at the end of term."

I chuckled, understanding and appreciating the joke even though my familial history made it more perverse than funny. Pushing thoughts of my parentage away, I fondled her breast, massaging it, loving the weight and feel of it beneath my palm.

"Oh, Christ. You're not done, are you?" She groaned, though it was a happy groan, spiced with excitement.

"Not by half." I tasted the skin of her neck, looking for a spot that made her squirm, and found it just below her ear.

Her breath hitched. "Is this where I'm supposed to kneel for you?"

*Yes.*

I concentrated my efforts on the spot I'd discovered because the thought of her kneeling for me sent all my blood racing southward. I nipped at her earlobe, brushing my thumb back and forth over her nipple, forcing myself to go slow.

I needed to be mindful, especially when she made me mindless.

"That depends," I whispered. "Do you want to kneel?"

She nodded lazily. Her nails carved half-moons into my shoulders as she arched against me, offering more of her neck.

"Will you beg?"

She nodded more vehemently, rubbing her thighs together restlessly. I slid my hand down her ribs—counting them on the way—and grabbed a handful of her gorgeous, round arse.

"Will you say please?" I swirled my tongue into her earlobe and she shivered. I made note of the reaction.

My Lucy had sensitive ears. Good to know.

"Please." The single word was choked, pitched high, and pleading.

I grinned. If this exchange were any indication, being mindful was its own reward.

"Please what, lovely Lucy?" Bringing her clawing hand to the towel over my cock, I encouraged her to stroke me through the cloth.

Just *there*.

"Please fuck me, Sean."

"How?"

"Please take me from behind."

I stopped kissing her and stilled her hand. Gritting my teeth, I thought about doing two hundred squats. I wanted her to beg—because the dirty words from her sweet mouth, in her sweet voice were maddening and sexy as fuck—but I was quickly losing control.

When I was certain crisis had been averted, I cleared my throat and straightened from the floor, on my knees before her, discarding my towel as I moved. Her fingers immediately encircled my length and she knelt as well.

"Please." She stretched to place a hungry, biting kiss on my neck, her breasts brushing my chest.

I bowed away from her touch and turned her around, thoughts of two hundred squats not far from my mind as I cupped her bottom and whispered in her ear, "And?"

She faltered, glancing over her shoulder at me with wide eyes. "A-and?"

I smoothed my fingers from her hip to her pussy and stroked, growling when I found her still wet from my earlier efforts and her arousal. Her breath hitched and she pressed her back against my chest, widened her legs. My touch was a light caress on the sensitive flesh. I savored the slick, swollen feel of her. When I licked my lips I tasted her there.

"Tell me what you want me to do." I whispered rather than spoke, for no reason I could discern. "And beg me to do it."

"Please," she panted, chasing my mouth.

I leaned away, placing my hand on her back and guiding her forward until she was on her hands and knees.

"Please what?"

Her body tense, a straining, beautiful, aching thing. She pressed back, rubbing her bottom against my groin.

"Please fuck me already."

Reaching for the condom on the side table, I fisted myself as I rolled it on, barely resisting the urge to thrust forward, and placed my other hand on her hip, holding her in place.

*Fuck. Lucy wet. Hot. Wanting me. Wait. Control yourself. Control.*

And I did. I controlled my body and my voice, asking, "Shall I take you now?"

"God, yes." Lucy arched her back and spread her legs wider, offering herself and shooting daggers at me over her shoulder. "You're dirty talk is great, Sean. But seriously, can you just get a move on?"

I grinned at her, my fingers flexing on her hip. "You're hungry?"

"Starving." Her eyes narrowed.

"You're sure?" I teased her entrance with the head of my cock.

"Stop the chit-chat, Cassidy. Put the penis in the vagina and let's get this dinner train rolling."

I barked a laugh and without further discussion, I gripped her hips and thrust forward, sliding into her slick warmth. She gasped, pushing backward, tossing her rainbow hair to one side.

I rocked within her, keeping my movements slow and deliberate, partly to prolong the moment and partly because I suspected Lucy preferred a soft touch.

However, to my surprise, after several moments, her hips rocked restlessly, as though searching. A grunt of dissatisfaction met my ears just before she ordered, "Harder. Faster. Dirtier."

"Pardon?"

She wiggled her bottom. "I said harder. Fuck me harder. Pull my hair. Slap my arse. Touch my clit. Do something."

Sparks fired at the base of my spine at her words. I reached around, finding her clit and traced it. Bending forward, I bit her back and side, thrusting faster.

Soon the sounds of sex, primitive mating, the rough slapping of skin, paired with her whimpering moans, filled the room. We were both covered in a sheen of sweat. I was mesmerized by the sight of her: the expanse of soft, damp skin, the round curve of her perfect backside.

"Say something now," she begged, pulling me from my meditation on her body. "Tell me I've been bad."

"You've been very bad." I tapped her clit, keeping the touch there light while I pounded into her. "I'll have to punish you."

She moaned. "What will you do?"

I hesitated, having not thought that far ahead and not feeling particularly creative, trying to keep my orgasm at bay while feeding hers.

"I'll make you strip for me," I blurted a secret desire, and was rewarded with another moan.

"Yes . . ."

"And I'll touch you, however I please."

"Fuck, yesss . . ."

"Then you'll kneel in front of me, and suck my cock."

"Oh God."

"And touch yourself."

Lucy pushed back, her toes pointing, legs flexing, hips rolling with jerky movements. "Fuck, fuck, fuck!"

And I felt it. I felt her come while buried inside her sweet, perfect body. Elation was eclipsed only by the wildness of my own need. Three more quick thrusts had me seeing stars and calling her name and making all nature of promises as her body clenched in spasm around me.

It was an unreal, potent pleasure. As I came down from the high, my face pressed to her back between her shoulder blades, I couldn't help thinking about the next time I would get my fix.

Lucy Fitzpatrick was my drug of choice, and has quickly become a necessity. I had no desire to contemplate rehab.

***

"YOU SMELL GOOD," she said, gifting me a warm, lazy smile.

She was warm—or was I warm?—and we were laying together on the bed, liberally touching each other's bodies.

"So do you," I said, stroking her bottom before I squeezed it.

Her arse drove me crazy. How could I want to brutally bite it and reverently caress it all at once?

"But you smell like sandalwood. I just smell like my shampoo." She leaned forward and sniffed me, her hand smoothing over my bicep, lingering there. "Even after sweaty sex, you still smell fantastic. It's witchcraft."

"Not witchcraft. Merely the power of sandalwood essential oil in cosmetic-grade jojoba."

Lucy snorted. "Did you just say jojoba?"

"That's right."

She lifted a sardonic eyebrow. "You are a cosmetics snob, but I kind of love how you speak sometimes. You're very…wordy."

"I am a cosmetics snob. And I speak as I think. I was raised in South Dublin. I'm an everything snob and my vocabulary is a result of the most expensive education money can buy," I sighed, shrugging, sliding my hand up to her breast. Christ, I loved her body.

"Why are you such a snob?"

"I was raised to be a snob."

"Were you?"

"Yes. I was allowed to do anything I wanted, so long as I was a snob."

Lucy studied me, her mouth tugging to the side with a sad smile. "What about being a good person?"

"Frowned upon."

"That sounds bloody awful."

I chuckled. "It was. It was awful."

"Why are you laughing then?"

"Because that's how snobs deal with uncomfortable subjects. We belittle their importance, laugh at them, and change the subject to weather or sport."

Lucy murmured, "You make me glad I don't know my grandparents."

I thought for a moment, then realized who she meant. "The Fitzpatricks?"

My attention caught on a thick bundle of Lucy's magnificently colored hair lying across her neck. I shuddered to think how different she might be had she been embraced by that cold family. She might have grown up like me.

*They would have ruined you.*

The idea of a cold, haughty snobbish Lucy Fitzpatrick was as unnatural to me as it was abhorrent.

"What?" she asked, pulling me from my thoughts.

"What?"

Lucy was giving me a hesitant grin. "You said something like, 'They would have ruined you.'"

"Oh." I blinked at her. "Did I say that out loud?"

Her grin blossomed into a gigantic smile. "You're too cute sometimes. I mean, *seriously* too cute."

"I'm not cute. I'm aloof and manly." I lifted a disdainful eyebrow at the idea of me as cute. Ridiculous.

"You are cute. You can't change what you are," she teased, her voice adopting a melodic sing-song quality as she touched my nose with her index finger, her attention snagging on my mouth.

I caught her hand, held it on the bed between us. "You said earlier that I'm a snob."

"But you're not a snob with me."

"That's because I like you."

Her eyes widened, refocusing on mine, and she gave me an impish smile. "You like me?"

"You know I do." I rubbed my thumb over the back of her knuckles, enjoying the exquisite softness of her skin.

Lucy's gaze sharpened, this time with obvious suspicion. "Is this you trying to flirt? Practicing your new skills?"

"No, lovely Lucy." I kissed her palm, sighed against her wrist when I detected a delicious hint of her perfume. "This is me being honest."

We watched each other, residual traces of our earlier smiles fading with each passing second. Her breathing had changed, and something about her eyes was different. They'd grown a darker shade of blue.

"What are you doing, Sean?" Her voice held an edge of anxiety. I didn't like it.

I brought her hand to my chest, cradled it there as a hostage. I didn't want her leaving, not yet. Maybe never.

I responded honestly, because with her, honesty was a compulsion. "I don't know, Lucy."

Two wrinkles of worry appeared between her eyebrows. I wanted to kiss them away. Instead I held her gaze because the moment was an important one.

"You're mad," she whispered. "You've known me for a week."

"I've known you much longer than that."

"Fine, a few weeks. It's the sex."

"It's not the sex. You know it's not." My hand reflexively tightened on hers, pressing her palm over my heart.

She shook her head, rejecting my words. "It is. You said yourself. You've only been with women when you're drunk. Sloppy and quick. I'm just the first girl you've taken your time with, sober, mindful of what you're doing."

"We're not having sex now," I said through clenched teeth. Her words stung despite—or perhaps because of—their veracity.

"No. But don't mistake deeper feelings for a good time in the sack."

"Lucy—"

"No." She wrested her hand away, squaring her jaw with resolve.

She rose to a sitting position on the bed and wrapped her arms around her legs, a physical manifestation of the wall between us. "I like you. I do. You're witty and funny when you allow yourself to be. You're fun to be with. You have depth even if you won't admit it. But I'm not fooling myself here. You hate my brother and we both know the feeling is mutual. These things you think you're feeling? They'll pass. Give it a week, a month at maximum. You'll forget my name."

Anger and its partner frustration had me growling before she'd finished. "You underestimate yourself if you think you're so forgettable."

"You know what I mean." She waved her hand in the air. "I'm sure you'll always think of me fondly—me and my blow jobs. But what are you giving up? Nothing, that's what. And when you grow tired of the novelty, you'll just move on. Meanwhile, I'd be giving up my brother, and that's like asking me to give up my arms and legs. He's the only one, the *only one*, who has ever been there for me. My whole life, he was the only person who cared about me. He loves me. And I love him. And I couldn't . . . I couldn't . . ."

She didn't finish because her features crumpled with sorrow and tears strangled the words. My anger immediately deflated in the face of her distress and I reached for her, not allowing her to push me away.

Some instinctual need to calm her, ease her fears, take away her burdens had me holding her tightly and rubbing her back, had me promising to do whatever she needed, be whatever she needed.

"Okay. Okay. It's fine. Please, stop crying." I didn't know what I was saying; really, I would have said anything to put an end to her sorrow. It panicked me.

Lying against my side, I felt her chest rise and fall with several bracing inhales, as though she were doing breathing exercises to stem the tears.

"I'm not crying," she said defiantly, her voice still watery.

"Oh?" I squeezed her, needing her to be happy. "I apologize for my hasty assumption. Clearly you're not crying."

Lucy huffed an unsteady laugh. "Clearly." She sniffled.

We lay together for a time, surrounded on all sides by brooding silence and a fate-ish sort of finality.

I couldn't stay in New York.

We'd been in each other's orbit for a week, so why did it feel like the end of something vital? Why did my bones ache at the thought of not being able to speak with her, touch her, or see her? Why did I become absurdly furious whenever I thought of her with someone else?

This would be our last night together. It had to be. I didn't want any additional lessons with a disinterested teacher.

I wanted more.

I wanted a shot with Lucy.

I wanted to *go for broke*.

But she didn't want that with me, not enough to make a mess of her life. I was too risky.

I couldn't fault her logic, but I gave myself permission to hate it.

# Chapter Fifteen

**@LucyFitz** A man wearing a red evening gown just came on the subway and started singing Sir Mix-A-Lot to the beat of two empty Coke cans #NYC #neveradullday

**@Anniecat to @LucyFitz** I kinda miss the crazy #feelinnostalgic

**\*Lucy\***

I WOKE UP alone and naked.

When I glanced around the room, I saw that Sean's suitcase was gone. The door to the closet was open and only sunlight on empty hangers greeted me.

Sunlight on those empty hangers was maybe the saddest thing I'd ever seen. My heart sank. My limbs felt too heavy to move.

I didn't cry. Not immediately, at any rate. Instead, I lay back in the bed and did breathing exercises, attempting to clear my mind. It didn't work. So I reminded myself that I'd been the one to say no. I'd pushed him away. My reasons were valid. I was being intelligent and realistic.

And then I cried.

I curled up into a ball and cried like an infant until a knock sounded at the door. My heart leapt, because my heart wasn't thinking clearly. I jumped from the bed, pulling the sheet around me as I raced to the door.

Yanking it open without looking through the peephole, my silly heart took a nosedive when I found a man in a suit standing outside the door. Behind him was a room service tray and another man, dressed in a waiter's uniform.

"Ms. Fitzpatrick?" the man in the suit asked, showing no sign of being surprised by my appearance.

I gripped the sheet tighter to my chest. "Uh, yes?"

"I'm Davies, your concierge. And I have an item for you from your Mr. Cassidy. He's also sent up a tray. May we bring it in?"

I blinked at this Davies chap for several seconds before his words arranged themselves in my brain. They didn't make sense, not precisely, but I realized I was gaping at him like a mental patient.

"Oh, yes. Please bring in the tray." I stood back from the door, allowing the waiter to push it into the room.

Davies didn't cross the threshold. Instead, as the waiter set up the service, he handed me a note and several boxes, all embossed with the hotel insignia.

"He left specific instructions that the room be kept for you as long as you like—a day, a week, a month—so please know we are at your service."

These words were also gibberish, so I accepted the packages and note, nodded politely, and searched for my bag so I could give these fellas a tip. "Ah, okay. Thanks."

Davies held up his hands as the server rolled the cart out of the room. "That won't be necessary. Mr. Cassidy already took care of everything."

"Um—"

"We were also careful to ensure none of your food came in contact with strawberries, as Mr. Cassidy explained you are allergic."

"Oh." My heart fluttered. He remembered.

"Enjoy your breakfast." Davies reached forward and shut the door as I stumbled to the side, clutching the boxes and note to my chest.

I frowned at the items, the room eerily bright and quiet.

*What just happened?*

Blinking my eyes, finding them dry and crusty, I brought the card and boxes into focus.

Juggling the items, I ripped into the card first, devouring his script.

*My lovely Lucy,*

*Thank you. For everything.*

*You are magnificent.*

*Now you have two people in all the world who will always be there for you.*

*Yours,*

*Sean*

I read it maybe ten times, traced the neat, efficient letters with my fingertip. Raw, unmanageable emotion brought new tears to my eyes.

He was such a dunderhead; such a wonderful, sweet, funny, impossible, thoughtful, sexy eejit. I sniffled and opened the largest package first. It was full of clothes. Beneath were several pairs of sexy bras and knickers.

*Didn't buy me clothes my arse.*

I set the large package aside and opened the next box with shaking fingers, gasping when I saw the item inside.

It was a pendant with white and black crystals against a silver-toned metal. Included was a silver-colored chain. A yin and yang pendant.

It was perfect and it would always remind me of him, of us.

I drifted over to the food and lifted the metal cover, finding a vegan feast of almond yogurt, fresh granola and fruit, three kinds of nuts, sprouted grain bread, and blackberry preserves.

Usually I'd devour this type of spread.

But today I put the cover back in place and claimed a chair in living room, right next to the spot where we'd had sex the night before. I closed my eyes at the memory, gathering several bracing breaths.

We.

Us.

Sean and I.

I hated that our lives existed in two very different worlds.

And I hated that he had to leave. Hate was a strong emotion, one I often tried to avoid, but there it was in all its ugly glory. Sean Cassidy had made me feel things, intense things, and far too many of them for that matter.

I thought about dressing quickly and going to the airport, just to see him off, just to say goodbye in person. But I cared too much. If I started getting all weepy and teary-eyed at the departure gate, then he'd know the growing depth of my feelings for him.

That couldn't happen. It would be a big, fat mixed message, which wouldn't be fair to either of us.

There was no Sean and me. No us. There never had been. Not really.

Yet for a moment last night—not while we were going at it against the wall or on the rug, but while we were lying in bed, touching, speaking of ourselves, sharing each other—it had felt possible.

\*\*\*

**MY MANTRA OVER** the next few weeks was *distance was good.*

Although it seemed like a small part of me was being torn away, distance was what we needed. It was for the best. Distance would make my heart grow less fond—I hoped.

Had he forgotten about me already? Moved on? Realized I wasn't worth the effort? Found a new . . . teacher?

The questions had me feeling positively morose and it was so unlike me to get worked up over a man.

It was a full two weeks after he'd left that I received the first text message, the first morsel of communication between us after an endless sea of uncertain silence. I was waiting in line with some friends at a food truck event in Central Park when my phone buzzed.

**Sean**: *Is it strange that every time I see a gay pride flag I think of you?*

I snorted a laugh at the question, giddy as a school girl that he'd decided to make contact, my insides all aflutter. I excused myself, stepped out of the line, and immediately responded. Obviously, the distance hadn't worked. Plus, I'd been wearing the yin and yang pendant. I'd been wearing it every day, touched that he'd gone to the trouble of buying me such a thoughtful gift.

**Lucy**: *Not at all. Every time I see two spherical objects side by side I think of you.*

**Sean**: *???*

**Lucy**: *Begins with a B, ends with an utt.*

**Sean**: *How obsessed we are with one another's rear ends…*

**Lucy**: *I like to think it's a healthy level of interest ;-)*

Several minutes passed before I received anything else. When I did I chuckled, rolling my eyes at his brazenness.

**Sean:** *If you send me a picture of yours, I'll send you a picture of mine.*

**Lucy:** *Wow, you don't care about the cloud at all, do you?*

**Sean:** *Nope, not when there are dozens of photos of me already floating around the Internet.*

I frowned, recalling the images I'd seen of him online, taken by women he'd had one-night stands with. They'd posted them like they were trophies, something to be proud of, when really they should have been ashamed of themselves.

Sean wasn't just some hot piece of arse to be shagged and then bragged about. He was a person with feelings. And yes, I never thought I'd see the day that I defended Sean Cassidy and his feelings, but here we were. Those women were as bad as all the men who went around treating women like sex objects. My next text was fueled by this anger and therefore startlingly honest.

**Lucy:** *I'm having some really violent feelings toward the women who did that to you right now.*

**Sean:** *Don't be angry. I'm not.*

**Lucy:** *You should be. You're worth more than that.*

**Lucy:** *Thank you for the pendant, btw. I love it.*

Another full minute passed and then came his response.

**Sean:** *I miss you.*

I inhaled, the three simple words taking the wind out of my sails and causing a sharp pang of emotion to cut through my chest. I didn't even hesitate to respond.

**Lucy:** *I miss you, too.*

He didn't respond after several minutes, so I tucked my phone back in my pocket and rejoined the line and my friends. But when it came time to order, my stomach was a swirling mess. I couldn't eat. I could barely draw a full breath.

\*\*\*

**AFTER THAT WE** messaged almost every day, chatting about all manner of things, and I found myself looking forward to our interactions, a smile on my face every time my phone pinged with a new alert.

**Sean:** -unicorn vomiting rainbow emoticon- *Another thing that reminds me of you.*

**Lucy:** *Not sure what to think of that.*

**Sean:** *I'm going to have it put on a T-shirt as a Valentine's Day gift.*

**Lucy:** *How romantic.*

**Sean:** *Terribly so. How are you?*

**Sean:** *I still miss you.*

I didn't contradict him, but rather just accepted the affectionate way he often spoke when we texted. However, I was also becoming uneasy, because the nicer he was the bigger my feelings grew.

*God, what was I doing?*

This couldn't continue, eventually we'd have to move into the friend-zone or end our text messaging.

Simply put, if I valued my relationship with my brother at all then I couldn't be with Sean. It was reality and it made me sad, which was why I found myself continuously trying to figure out ways to make Ronan accept us. If I told Ronan that Sean had never actually slept with Brona, then maybe he'd change his mind. Or perhaps if I found something they could both bond over they'd finally put all the bickering aside and become friends.

I know. I was living in a dream world.


**Lucy:** *I'm great. Work is keeping me busy. You?*

**Sean:** *Exhausted. Just finished training. Eating dinner now.*

**Lucy:** *Oooh, what are you having?*


He responded with a picture of a plate containing two steamed breasts of chicken, broccoli, aubergine, and a gigantic glass of some thick, beige smoothie.


**Lucy:** *Ouch.*

**Sean:** *Yep. And when Coach McLaughlin told us to start doing running squats I nearly got hard. I think you've ruined me ;-)*

**Lucy:** *Omg, lol! Sorry.*

**Sean:** *Don't be. Memories of us together are keeping me warm at night. I have this particular favorite of kneeling behind you on the carpet while you're on all fours...*

**Lucy:** *Sean!*

**Sean:** *Lucy.*

I put the phone down, fanning myself with the collar of my T-shirt, a tad overwhelmed by the imagery. I saw his hands gripping my waist, his head between my legs, tongue licking . . .

Focusing back on my work, I replied to a few comments on the blog and began answering a couple of emails, but my head wasn't in the game. Sean was invading my every thought and it was driving me crazy. The frustration of being an ocean away—far beyond touching distance—was a new form of torture.

My phone buzzed again. I glanced at it, biting my thumbnail.

**Sean:** *Are you still there?*
**Sean:** *I'll be good. I promise.*

Unable to help myself, I tapped out a quick reply.

**Lucy:** *Are you capable of being good?*
**Sean:** *Yes. I'm always good.*
**Sean:** *You're coming home next week for the wedding, aren't you?*
**Lucy:** *Yes. I'm flying in on Tuesday.*
**Sean:** *We should meet up.*

I closed my eyes for a second, swallowing as my tummy churned with anticipation. I knew I shouldn't, but I really wanted to see him. Even so, I didn't want to send mixed signals . . . well, I didn't want to send any additional mixed signals.

**Lucy:** *It'll be a busy time. Got to plan Annie's hen party and I'm also maid of honor.*

**Sean:** *I'm sure you can fit me in somewhere* :-D

**Lucy:** *Is that an innuendo?*

**Sean:** *Of course.*

**Lucy:** *Leave me alone, pervert. I've got work to do and you've got a whole lot of beige to drink* :-P

**Sean**: *Okay, but we should get together while you're here. I'll take you out to dinner and you can toss your drink in my face again, mock me for how I say "fam."*

Placing my phone down on the desk, I didn't respond. He made me feel too many conflicting emotions and my confusion was exhausting. Instead, I opened up the folder on my laptop containing the itinerary for Annie's hen night, happy for the distraction and smiling as I perused it.

I'd purchased a bunch of Where's Wally jumpers and hats for us to wear, though Broderick was keen to inform me that he was known as Waldo in the States. I also booked an hour on a Pedibus around the city. It was going to be hilarious. After that we'd have dinner and karaoke at one of my favorite Japanese restaurants before heading out to Temple Bar for more drinks.

I chuckled because Mam was insisting on coming and I knew she'd hate every moment of it. Everything about the night was going to be ridiculous and sloppy, my favorite kind of fun, and her most hated.

Noticing the time, I let out a few choice swearwords as I realized I was late to meet Broderick for lunch at our usual spot. Throwing my hair up in a ponytail, I grabbed my coat and handbag before heading out.

I saw him as soon as I stepped inside, sitting at our favorite spot by the window, headphones on, a coffee and pastry in front of him. Shooting him a quick wave, I went to order some food while surreptitiously sliding a raisin and oat cookie into my pocket.

It was a common tactic: buy something to cover up that you've stolen another. I'd been doing the exact same thing for five afternoons in a row and I didn't understand why. I knew it didn't make things any better, but I'd even been giving the cookie to a homeless man who sat begging outside the café as I left. I thought I had a handle on my compulsion but it was coming back for some reason, even though I'd barely spoken to my mother in weeks.

The barista smiled at me, completely oblivious, as I dropped a ridiculous amount of coins in the tip jar, took my things and headed over to join my friend. Broderick pulled off his headphones as I sat, a heavy baseline blasting from the speakers.

"You'll make yourself deaf listening to music so loud," I said, picking up a knife and cutting into my scone.

"And you'll get arrested if you keep stealing baked goods," Rick answered back casually. "What's the deal with that anyway?"

My eyes widened, my mouth opening slightly as I stared at him in disbelief.

"I . . . I, uh . . ."

He quirked an eyebrow. "Cat got your tongue?"

I leaned closer, whispering, "How did you see?"

"You're not exactly the artful dodger, babe. Every time we come here you take the same damn cookie. At first I thought I was imagining things, but then you kept doing it over and over again."

Letting out a sigh, I sat back, a terribly guilty look on my face. "It's just this thing I do sometimes. It's not a big deal."

"Stealing is a big deal, Lucy. You're not in Ireland now. New York is a whole other ball game, and if you get arrested here you'll be facing a lot worse than a slap on the wrist and a call home to Mommy."

I frowned, muttering under my breath, "No need to be an arsehole about it," but then immediately regretted my words. I was the one being an arsehole. God, I hated myself for how I was acting.

"I'm only being an asshole because I care. So tell me? How long have you been doing this shit?"

Letting out a long sigh, I told him all about the beginnings of my strange habit, how it related back to my anxiety and pressure from my mother. She'd never been a particularly loving parent, but her belittling behavior only really started in full-force after I turned eighteen. I was an adult by then, starting to follow my own path in life, a path that didn't reflect the one she foresaw. I ended my story by telling him how I'd been successful in quitting shoplifting until recently.

"Huh," said Broderick, a thoughtful look on his face.

"That's all you're going to say?"

"No, that's not all. What's changed in the last couple of weeks?"

"I don't understand." I folded my arms defensively.

"Of course you do. What's changed that's caused you to slip back into old habits? There has to be something."

I scrunched up my brow, wracking my brain until it finally hit me.

It was so bloody obvious.

Sean had gone home. I'd had amazing sex and a scarily intense connection with this big, handsome, incredible man with the word "forbidden" stamped on his forehead and then poof, he left, leaving my life feeling empty without him.

"I know that look," said Rick. "You've figured it out, haven't you?"

"Maybe."

"And . . ."

"And it's none of your business," I snapped, surprising even myself with how snippy I was. I'd never spoken to him like that before. Never. How on earth had the loss of Sean Cassidy turned me into such a sour old shrew?

Rick gave me a look that was all, *fine, have it your way*, and I sighed, feeling guilty yet again.

"I'm sorry. I'm being horrible."

"You don't want to talk about it, believe me, I understand. But think about seeing someone, a therapist or a counselor who can talk things through with you. It'll do you the world of good, I promise."

I sighed and fiddled with a sugar packet. "Actually, I tried that once. It didn't end so well."

"No?"

Shaking my head, I answered, "Nah. Mam found out about it and kicked up a fuss, thinking people would discover I was a klepto and it'd tarnish Ronan's reputation. She forbade me from going to any more sessions after that."

Broderick frowned like he thought my mother was a mental case, which she wasn't. She was just overly concerned about what the neighbors would think, concerned in the extreme.

"I don't know what to say, Luce. That's fucked up, and I'm certain Ronan wouldn't give a damn about his rep if he knew his sister was getting the help she needed."

"Yeah well, that's my mother for you, always worrying about Ronan. He's the one who keeps her in designer handbags and weekly blow-dries after all," I said, my intended humor falling flat.

A small trace of his frown remained as he reached over to squeeze my hand. "If you ever need someone to talk to, I'm right here, okay?"

I gave him a wide smile. "You're my best friend, have I told you that lately?"

He grinned and winked. "No need. I'm entirely aware of my brilliance."

## Chapter Sixteen

**@BroderickAdams** $350 for a Guns N' Roses ticket? I think not, Saul Hudson, I think not.

**@LucyFitz to @BroderickAdams** Whaaa? Does it come with a striptease from a 1988 Axl Rose?

**@BroderickAdams to @LucyFitz** LMAO.

### *Lucy*

IT WAS EXACTLY three weeks to the day after my last cookie thievery that Broderick and I arrived at JFK for our flight to Dublin. Being such a good friend of Annie's, he was coming to the wedding, too, and I was looking forward to forcing him into joining us girls for the hen night.

Sean and I had continued to swap text messages. With each exchange I grew increasingly confused and . . . involved. Two weeks ago I'd taken a picture of my cup and sent it to him because the person had spelled my name *Loosey* instead of *Lucy.*

**Lucy:** *I demand you change my contact information to Loosey on your phone. It is now my name.*

**Sean:** *If you want me to, I'll fly over to NYC and beat the shit out of the guy who wrote that on your cup.*

**Lucy:** *You don't think it's funny?*

**Sean:** *No one calls my girl loose.*

The next day he sent me a picture of his coffee cup; the barista had written a phone number on the side. I felt a pang of jealousy until he texted.

**Sean:** *At least you get a word. They've assigned me a number. Just call me Jean Valjean.*

**Sean:** *And yours is "loosely" based on your name.*

**Sean:** *See what I did there?* ;-)

**Lucy:** *I can't even with you. How do you know who Jean Valjean is?*

**Sean:** *Everyone knows 24601.* ;-)

**Lucy:** *Random thought. If everyone winked as much in real life as they do on social media and in text messages, the world would be a much creepier place.*

**Sean:** *I'd send you a "I'd love to lick your pussy" emoticon, but my iPhone doesn't have one.*

**Lucy:** *Those Apple engineers have seriously been sleeping on the job*

**Lucy:** ;-)

**Sean:** *Ah yes, embrace the creepy winking.* ;-)

Those everyday—because now we were messaging every day, all day—conversations were confusing because they were friendly, but they were often much more than friendly. Yet neither of us made any attempt to call the other. And the lack of resolution had me feeling like a mixed-up basket case.

Hence my current airport crime spree.

"You got something up your sleeve?" Broderick asked several seconds after I'd slipped a tube of lipstick up there.

*How the hell had he seen?*

"What?" I asked, frazzled.

Rick smirked. "You've got this mischievous expression going on. Tell me what you're up to."

I exhaled heavily in relief and lifted a shoulder. "Just looking forward to introducing you to all my girlfriends in Dublin. They're going to absolutely adore your accent."

He didn't react how I expected him to, instead he frowned and perused a bottle of men's cologne. "Oh, right."

I chuckled. "Don't get too excited or anything."

"I'm excited," he said in the least excited voice ever.

"Oh my God! Broderick Thelonious Adams, you're seeing someone, aren't you?"

He shrugged and attempted to look unconcerned. "I knew I'd regret telling you my middle name. And no, I'm not seeing anyone."

"Your dad named you after Thelonious Monk, that's a bloody cool middle name. But seriously, you're not hiding a girl somewhere?"

"You got me. Smuggled her in my suitcase. Don't tell airport security."

I gave him a narrowed-eyed grin just before my phone started ringing. My heart pounded for a second, like it always did as I wondered if it might be Sean. But no, I pulled it out to see my mam's number flashing on the screen.

Taking a few steps outside the cosmetics section of the duty free, I lifted the phone to my ear and answered.

"Hi Mam. I'm just at the airport now. We'll be boarding our flight soon."

"Lucy, what's all this I'm hearing about you staying at Ronan's house?" she asked in a shrill voice.

I sighed and closed my eyes for a second, wishing away this entire conversation. "It's just easier since I'm Annie's maid of honor and everything. There's going to be a ton of last-minute stuff to organize. And we'll be staying at the K Club from Thursday onward, so it's not like it matters much either way."

"Yes, well, you could've at least let me know. I had Bernie make up the spare bedroom and everything, thinking you'd be staying with me, then I have to hear from your brother that you're not. Nobody tells me anything these days," she said, a note of disdain to her words as she tried to affect a hurt tone. Bernie was her housekeeper, though she called him her manservant. You'd swear she'd been born with a silver spoon in her mouth and not to the humble beginnings she'd actually had.

"I'm sorry. I would have told you but it completely slipped my mind. Things have been crazy busy over here."

"Of course they have. I suppose you've been spending every waking minute working in front of a computer, not giving a thought to your poor, neglected social life. If you stay indoors all day you'll get a terrible, pasty complexion, Lucy."

Good Lord, she had no idea what I did all day, nor how half my work involved chasing after celebrities with a camera in hand.

"I'm sure I'll be doing enough socializing at the wedding to make up for it," I said in an effort to placate her.

Now her voice grew animated. "Speaking of which, there's someone

I've just been dying for you to meet—"

"Oh, they're calling for my flight to board," I said, interrupting her. "I've got to go but I'll call you as soon as we land."

Hanging up, I exhaled a breath, anxiety building at the idea of being forced to meet a bunch of "suitors" at the wedding that my mother happened to approve of. The funny thing was, she'd probably be head over heels for Sean, even though his past history with Ronan was a mess.

Speak of the devil, the moment I ended the call my phone buzzed with an incoming text.

**Sean:** *I'll meet you at the airport and take you for breakfast?*

My heart thudded at his suggestion, and I hated how text messages never conveyed the tone in which things were said. Like, was it a casual, *can I meet you at the airport?* Or an urgent, *I will meet you at the airport!*

Was he asking because he was desperate to see me as soon as I stepped foot on Irish soil, or was he simply trying to be helpful?

Gah! I hated the uncertainty of this feelings business. Hated it. I suddenly understood why Buddhist monks were celibate. You couldn't find Zen when you were all muddled up in the head. Sex just complicated everything.

**Lucy:** *Annie and Ronan are meeting us. But thanks for offering. It was very kind.*

Directly after I sent the text I regretted everything about it, because reading it back, I sounded cold and detached. I should have tacked a bloody smiley face on the end or something, a few kisses maybe.

Sean didn't respond, and by the time I was sitting on the plane I had a brand new toothbrush, eye cream, a hair clip, and a packet of chewing gum in my carry-on bag—not a single one of them paid for.

My guilt was the cherry on top. I wished I could go back and return everything, tell the shop workers I was sorry. But no, life didn't give you second chances like that, and if I went back I'd be arrested. I was a bloody mess.

As soon as we landed in Dublin, I checked my phone to see Sean had left me a new text.

**Sean:** *I don't want to make things hard for you with your brother.*

I frowned at the message, trying to decipher the deeper meaning—if there was a deeper meaning. My concentration, however, was fractured when we stepped through the arrivals gate and were met with a dour-faced Ronan and an unusually quiet Annie.

They each hugged me and Broderick before we walked to the car park, but I sensed something was up. When we were finally buckled into the car, I couldn't take it anymore.

"Okay, spill the beans. What's going on with you two?"

My brother's hands fisted the steering wheel and Annie shifted uncomfortably in her seat. Ronan met my gaze through the rear-view mirror.

"Your future sister-in-law took it upon herself to invite Sean Cassidy to both my stag party and the wedding," he said. *And* my heart stilled.

"You've invited every other member of the team, Ronan. Think of how poor Sean would feel being left out," Annie put in, a pleading tone to her voice.

Ronan snickered. "This is assuming the bloke actually has feelings, which he doesn't, so it's a non-issue."

Frowning slightly, I leaned forward in my seat to give Annie's shoulder a small squeeze. "If it's any consolation, I think Annie's right. You can't just invite everyone and not him, Ronan."

He shook his head. "Am I the only one who remembers how much of an arsehole he was last year? That he tried to get me booted from the Union?"

"Sean Cassidy?" Broderick sent me a searching glance and I gave my head a quick shake, my heart thundering with panic lest Broderick say something to my brother about Sean being in New Hampshire. Thankfully, my friend seemed to get the message.

"You should be thanking him," Annie chimed in. "Look how well everything turned out, and he was the catalyst."

My brother scowled at his fiancée but it soon turned into a smile. "You have a point there . . ."

Seeing Ronan's shift in mood, I pressed, "Plus, maybe he's sorry. Maybe he wants to mend fences. You should give him a chance. I don't think he's as bad as everyone makes out."

Ronan locked eyes with me in the rear-view mirror. "Oh, believe me, he is. You're too soft-hearted with people, Luce. You're always giving them the benefit of the doubt, but you don't know Sean Cassidy as well as I do."

"What if I do?" I blurted without thinking. Broderick widened his eyes at me all, *you're going to tell him here?* Ronan narrowed his gaze.

"What do you mean?" he said slowly, suspiciously, and I wished I could take it back.

I scratched feverishly at my wrist. "Well . . . I sort of do know him.

We went out for dinner once." Technically, it was the truth. The first time I'd had a proper conversation with Sean was when he took me out for dinner at Marco Pierre's.

Ronan abruptly pulled the car over onto the hard shoulder as Annie put her hand to her chest at the suddenness. "Ronan, what are you doing?"

He completely ignored her as he twisted in his seat, his expression a mixture of anger and disbelief. "You, my sister, Lucy Fitzpatrick, went out for dinner with Sean Cassidy? Is this an April Fool?"

I couldn't meet his eyes. "It isn't April."

"Stop avoiding the question."

"It was ages ago," I shrugged.

"That doesn't make it any better," Ronan barked and every single person in the car jumped in fright. He looked at Annie. "First you and now my sister. Is everyone blind to Cassidy's true nature but me?"

"You're not my keeper. I can have dinner with whoever I like," I whispered.

He shook his head, his thoughts obviously a churning mess. "I can't believe what I'm hearing. Have you no loyalty?"

His question made me feel awful, and my eyes grew watery as I folded my arms across my chest. Maybe Ronan was right. Maybe I was a horrible sister with no loyalty. And maybe it was for the best that I never told him all that had transpired, all that was *still* transpiring between Sean and me, because I was certain it would irrevocably change our relationship. And I needed my brother. He and Annie were the only real family I had.

Annie took Ronan's hand in hers in an effort to calm him. "You heard her, Ronan. It was ages ago. There's no sense getting all worked up about it. You're being a bully."

"I'm not . . . " He paused and rubbed at his jaw. "I'm not a bully. I'm just angry."

"Yes, and we've talked about this before. Anger is counter-productive. If you're upset with Lucy, tell her, but don't yell at her like she's a misbehaving child."

And just like that, the sweet and shy Annie had gotten through to him. His anger deflated and he cast me a guilty look.

"I'm sorry for shouting at you."

I only nodded, my voice failing me for a moment. I sat in my seat, quiet as a mouse, with Broderick shooting me concerned looks. He was the only one who knew it wasn't *just ages ago*, and that things between Sean and me were far from over.

But how could I tell my brother that after how he reacted to us having one dinner together? He'd probably disown me. Fear had me wrapping the secret up tighter than ever before, determined for him never to find out.

Ronan exhaled and gave me one final glance, before putting the car in gear. I swallowed what felt like a lump in my throat, my mind a whirl of worries. Annie muttered something in Ronan's ear that seemed to calm him further, and I saw the tension leave his body.

Watching them together, I was struck by how grateful I was for Annie, for how happy she made my brother, and how she could ground him with nothing but a few softly spoken words. Ronan had found someone who understood him, who cherished him, who wanted him just as he was. A foreign sensation struck me and I rubbed at my chest. It took me a minute to recognize what it was—longing.

\*\*\*

WHEN WE ARRIVED at the house, I swiftly made my way to my room to do some much-needed yoga. Calm was vital to me right then. I needed to sort out my feelings before I came face-to-face with Sean, which I now knew was inevitable since he'd been invited to the wedding.

Broderick had never been to Ireland before, so I promised to give him the grand tour that afternoon. Unfortunately, my mam showed up and insisted we all go out—meaning, we all be seen—for lunch at her super swanky club. Afterward she wanted Annie and me to go lingerie shopping with her.

The horror!

I was able to beg off by claiming plans with Broderick. As such, we spent that evening and the next morning wandering about the city, checking the sights and whatnot. To his credit, he didn't bring up Sean at all. Broderick was both wonderful and infuriating in that he never pushed me for more than I was willing to share.

Time flew by and soon it was time to head back and get ready for the evening ahead, i.e. Annie's hen party.

A couple of the rugby WAGS (wives and girlfriends) whom Annie had befriended over the last few months were already there, alongside my mother, who was happily chatting amongst them. I'd invited a few friends, too, mostly to make sure the whole thing wouldn't be a massive rugby fest.

When everyone had arrived, it was a little funny to see my kooky gaggle of girlfriends mixed in with the uber-stylish fashionista WAGS. Cara was a Goth lesbian with a mohawk and undercut, Hannah a hipster librarian with ironic '80s glasses, and Veronica an ethereal hippie with hair down to her backside, who only bought her clothes from charity shops.

When I came downstairs carrying the Where's Wally costumes, several of the WAGS immediately turned their noses up, my mother included. Not all the WAGS were intolerable, but one in particular, Orla Flanagan, wife to the fullback Gary Flanagan, couldn't help voicing her opinion.

"Didn't you get my email about having some figure-hugging jerseys made with our other half's names on the back? I thought that would've been really cute."

Making brief eye contact with Cara, we each exchanged cynical expressions. "I'm sorry, but tonight is a man-free zone. Besides, not all of us are lucky enough to have a rugby-playing beau in our lives," I said, trying to keep my tone friendly.

Orla shot another of the WAGS a smug smile as she brought the champagne flute to her mouth. "Yes, I suppose you're right."

When I glanced at Annie sitting on the other side of the kitchen, she sent me a look of apology, but I shrugged it off. Being Ronan's sister, I'd gotten used to women like these years ago. They weren't all bad; some were rather nice, actually. But the ones who embraced the stereotype weren't exactly my favorite people.

"Did you all bring a pair of comfortable shoes?" I asked, glancing around the room and spotting a few too many Louboutins. "You know we're going on a Pedibus, right?"

"Yes, we all brought flats in our bags," said Orla. "Though I don't know why you insist on us going on that bicycle thing. We'll be horrible and sweaty by the time we're done."

"That's the whole point. A hen party is about having a laugh, not strutting about looking like you just stepped off the pages of a fashion magazine."

Orla arched a brow as she looked me up and down. "Maybe not for you."

I bit my tongue as I turned away from her, knowing later on I'd be grateful for the simple jeans, T-shirt, and Converse I'd decided to wear. Placing my hand momentarily to my chest, I felt a strange sort of comfort as I felt Sean's pendent resting beneath my top.

I handed out the stripy jumpers, hats, and fake glasses, and after Annie exclaimed her delight at the silly costumes, the rest of the ladies soon put their prejudices aside and joined in on the fun.

The Pedibus was sort of like a tandem bike, except it was more of an open-air tram with a table in the middle. We all had to cycle to keep the thing moving, with a driver at the front to steer us in the right direction around the city. We got a ton of honks and shouts of approval and I was delighted to see Annie was having a blast.

Broderick was wedged in between two WAGS, but he seemed happy enough to chat with them. That was kind of what I loved about him, no matter the environment, he'd always find some way to ingratiate himself.

I almost lost my footing on the pedals for a second when I felt my phone vibrate inside my jeans. Pulling it out to check the message, I found it was from Sean.

**Sean:** *Half the boys are already loaded and it's only six. Although there's supposed to be a stripper arriving soon so things could be looking up. Literally ;-) How's your evening going?*

This was the first time he'd texted me since his odd message about Ronan yesterday. I felt an unexpected pang of annoyance and jealousy at the idea of him ogling some booblicious stripper, but was happy to hear from him no matter the context.

**Lucy:** *Great, aside from Orla Flanagan kicking up a fuss about my plans for the night. She wanted the girls to wear jerseys with their other half's names on the back. Kill me now.*

**Sean:** *Well, you could've worn mine ;-)*

**Lucy:** *Ha! That wouldn't create a shitstorm of unnecessary drama at all.*

**Sean:** *I dunno. I kinda like the idea of you wearing my jersey...and nothing else.*

**Lucy:** *Why am I not surprised?*

**Sean:** *Because you like the idea, too.*

**Sean:** *Come to my place later.*

I inhaled, momentarily flustered as to how to respond. In the end I went with an easy excuse to be noncommittal.

**Lucy:** *I don't know your address.*

**Sean:** *I'll text it to you.*

**Lucy:** *Let me think about it. I'm not sure what time we're finishing up. It could be really late.*

**Sean:** *I don't care how late it is.*

Annie elbowed me in the side, distracting me from the message. I startled slightly before tucking the phone back in my pocket.

"Everything all right?" she asked.

"Fine and dandy. You enjoying yourself?"

"I'm having a great time. Plus, I'll feel so much better about gorging on sushi later since I've earned it with all this exercise." She paused to lower her voice. "Your mom has already been warning me about the dangers of not fitting into my dress on the day of the wedding."

I leveled her with a serious look, making sure to lower my voice as well since Mam was sitting just a few seats away. "Never listen to my mother. If she had her way we'd all be going around looking emaciated."

Annie barked a laugh. "Don't worry, I have no intention of giving up my beloved pastime of eating. It's a good thing your brother likes the curvy gals." Now she gave me a sassy wink.

"Please, no talk of Ronan's sexual preferences in front of me. I don't want to vomit up the champagne I drank back at the house."

"Believe me, there's absolutely nothing barf-worthy about your brother and sex, absolutely nothing."

She was doing it on purpose now. I held my hands over my ears. "Yes, yes, we all know how happy you are in the bedroom. Just keep the details to yourself, please."

Annie laughed loudly. "You're too easy sometimes."

When we arrived at the restaurant, I was delighted that the cycling had made the WAGS hungry for carbs, so I wouldn't have to sit through them all ordering salad with no dressing. Mam had wrangled her way into a chair beside Rick and was being a little too flirtatious for my liking. My friend seemed vaguely bewildered by her attention, and since I knew (but wished I didn't) that my mother had developed a taste for boy toys in recent years, I cast her a sharp, disapproving glance that said, *please don't.*

She pretended she hadn't seen, the wagon.

A waiter went around the table, pouring glasses of sake as we all perused the menu. After we'd eaten our fill it was time for karaoke, which I adored even though I didn't have a note in my head. I managed to lure Annie up onto the stage so we could sing "Talk Dirty" by Jason Derulo, which was just hilarious since she blushed through the whole thing.

Rick shook his head at my corny choice of song but I just stuck my tongue out at him, the big music snob. Besides, I knew he found it funny because I could see him trying not to laugh.

Orla, drunk on sake, stood on her chair and filmed us on her phone. I knew the video would probably find its way onto Facebook but I was having too much fun to care.

When it was time to pay the bill, I had Ronan's credit card at the ready while the ladies put on their coats to move on to the next venue in Temple Bar. I slid my arm through Annie's and we chatted about her jitters for the big day. It was as we were wandering down the cobbled streets that I heard a few recognizable hoots and laughter.

We'd crossed paths with the stag party.

Tom, having come home to be Ronan's best man, had been the one to organize it, but I thought they'd go someplace boring, like the rugby clubhouse or an old codger's pub. Before I knew what to think about this unexpected turn of events, the hens had mixed in with the stags, everybody drunk as a skunk, and I knew there'd be no separating them.

"Annie dearest," came Ronan's voice as he extracted Annie's arm from mine and folded her into his embrace. She protested at first but then started giggling, and before long, the two were canoodling like a pair of lovesick teenagers.

I would have been grossed out if I hadn't been a mess of anticipation and nerves, unconsciously searching the horde of muscular rugby players for one in particular.

In the end, I felt him before I saw him. I felt his familiar presence and when I looked up I found Sean standing a couple feet away, leaning against the outside wall of the pub, his gaze on me.

I shivered, unable to tear my eyes away, hungry for the sight of him.

He smirked, his eyes traveling over my silly outfit.

I scowled—mostly for self-preservation, because God forbid I be caught dreamily staring at my brother's nemesis—and glanced around to make sure nobody was looking as I mouthed, *what?*

He just kept on grinning like he couldn't get enough of the sight of me. My chest felt airy with anticipation and I was barely able to meet his gaze as it transformed from amused to intense.

With that single look I knew, regardless of my best intentions and weeks of espousing the benefits of distance, Sean and I were far from over.

# Chapter Seventeen

@**SeanCassinova** Throw me a goddamn parade.

@**THEBryanLeech to** @**SeanCassinova** You mean a pity party?

@**SeanCassinova to** @**THEBryanLeech** Go fuck yourself.

@**THEBryanLeech to** @**SeanCassinova** Too late :-D

### *Sean*

"THAT'S A BAD idea," Bryan said, standing next to me, a lurking pariah. Clearly, he'd noticed the mutual eye ogling between Lucy and me.

I responded without sparing my teammate a glance. "If I wanted your opinion, I would have asked for it." I hadn't seen Lucy in weeks, and was hungry for the sight of her. I wasn't craving goody-goody censure from our team's bad egg.

Well . . . the *other* bad egg.

"First his girlfriend, now his sister? *Tsk*," Bryan tut-tutted, though his tut-tutting was slurred and sloppy. "Why don't you lay off, eh? It's his feckin' wedding. Give him a bloody break, ferchissakes."

Most of our teammates were pissed—some more than others—yet I wasn't even buzzed. I'd made a conscious decision to maintain my sobriety. I'd meant it when I'd texted Lucy that I didn't want to make things hard for her with her brother. If I'd drunk to excess then I was liable to do just that.

I'd lost count of the number of times I'd nearly announced my intentions to claim Lucy as my own. But I hadn't, not yet. Instead, I'd bitten my tongue or excused myself.

Basically, I'd been a saint.

"Not everything is about Mother Fitzpatrick," I mumbled, though I hadn't yet looked away from Lucy. But then she hadn't yet looked away from me. An enchanting smile still lingered on her lips and behind her eyes.

Christ, I'd missed her. The last month had been the longest of my life.

Aside from the first two weeks after my departure, we'd texted every day but she'd never sent a picture of herself, always memes or shots of arseholes coming on to her, purposefully misspelling her name on coffee cups. I'd missed seeing her. I'd almost asked her to send a picture, but she'd drawn a line before I left. A line I didn't know how to cross without storming over it and begging her on my hands and knees to give this—us—a chance.

In other words, I didn't know how not to be a fool with Lucy Fitzpatrick. And oddly, I didn't care.

Nevertheless, I had no pictures of her or of us together, a sad fact I planned on remedying as soon as possible.

"You're a fecking eejit." Bryan chuckled, forcefully pushing my shoulder.

"Am I?"

He didn't respond at once and I sensed his inebriated attention shift away from me, several seconds passing before he admitted, "She's hot."

"She's beautiful." My declaration a pointed contradiction to his underwhelming assessment.

Bryan nodded, presumably now inspecting Lucy with a critical eye. "Pretty in an odd, freaky sort of way."

My frown was immediate, hating his description, but I maintained my hold on Lucy's gaze.

She wasn't odd. She was unique.

She wasn't freaky. She was free-spirited.

She was enchanting.

Breathtaking.

Wonderful.

Perfect.

And if we didn't stop staring at each other we would soon be drawing more attention than just Bryan Leech's inebriated opinions.

But Lucy was no longer smiling at me. Her gaze had intensified, grown solemn, almost tortured. She felt the pull—of that I was certain. Now, if only I could arrange for a well-timed push . . .

Bryan snorted inelegantly, interrupting my thoughts. "It doesn't matter if she looks like Helen of bleedin' Troy. That bird is off limits— off limits to me, to all these other arsehole wankers here, and most especially off limits to you."

Bryan's giant hand circled the air around us then landed on my shoulder—a heavy, meaningful weight. He gave me a little shake to emphasize his point.

Of course, *arsehole wankers* was both an accurate description of our teammates and a term of endearment. And the rest of his words were true as well. Lucy Fitzpatrick was off limits in the same way Eilish was off limits to those barbarians.

You don't fuck with family, literally or figuratively. It was against the rules of decent behavior. Then again, I'd purposefully set out to break the rules with Lucy—which, by the way, had backfired quite spectacularly. And I'd never been a poster boy for decency.

I'd always maintained that decency was entirely overrated.

Now frowning and looking decidedly affected, Lucy tore her eyes from mine, her gaze falling to the street. She appeared to be confused, if not overwhelmed by her thoughts. I wanted to go to her.

I straightened from the wall and almost did, but Bryan's hand held me in place. "No, no, no." He shook his head, stepping in front of me and pointing a finger in my face. He was one of the few members of our team nearly my size. "No fecking way."

"Move."

His grip tightened. "Nope. It's for your own good, mate. You're a bloody fuckwit, but you're a great flanker."

"Am I to call you Mother Leech now?" I taunted, knowing he of all people would despise the moniker. Tracking Lucy's movements over Bryan's head, I watched as she rejoined the wives and girlfriends. I noticed a man in their company. Broderick.

I liked Broderick.

More importantly, Broderick seemed to like me. He harbored no ridiculous prejudices against me, such as my well-deserved title of grand manipulator and malefactor.

"You can call me whatever you like, Cassidy. Just as long as you continue playing nice with Ronan and keep your hands off his sister."

I wondered how many more pints were required to render Bryan Leech unconscious. I suspected more than several. We rugby players, as a rule, were infuriatingly capable while in our cups.

Lucy was now splitting furtively anxious glances between her brother and me. My gut tightened. Seeing true distress in her expression and how she held herself rigid. Misery—at causing her a moment of anguish—deflated any design I had on a stolen shag.

Two months ago, I might have relished causing anyone associated with Ronan Fitzpatrick any level of discomfort. But now . . .

My attention moved back to Bryan's grim expression. "I don't know what you're talking about," I said, removing his hand from my shoulder. "It's getting late. I'd better be off."

He blinked at me. Confusion and suspicion wrinkled his forehead. "What's your game, Cassidy? You can't be giving up so easily, it's not in your nature."

"Exactly," I agreed, though not just with the last statement. I wasn't giving up, and giving up wasn't in my nature. Rather, for once, I wanted to be decent, or at least give the appearance of it.

For Lucy.

Allowing myself one final, lingering look of her, I stuffed my hands in my pockets and turned my back on the revelry, slipping away without offering words of congratulations or parting well wishes. I didn't quite have it in me to be insincere. Insincerity was taxing once you'd breathed the refreshing air of artless candor.

It was a cold night and I zipped my jacket against it. The memory of my week with Lucy had kept me warm for nearly a month. I doubted my actions this evening, no matter how noble, would achieve a similar effect.

\*\*\*

**I DON'T UNDERSTAND** why you can't get one of your women to accompany you to this wedding." Eilish peered at me through the reflection of the shop mirror. "Don't you have throngs? I believe I read one article that claimed they fling themselves at you by the dozen."

"I can't recall anyone ever flinging themselves—as it were—in my general direction, let alone twelve women at once." I scratched my chin, examining my cousin's choice of dress and deciding it was too short.

"That seems like something one would remember with some clarity."

I ignored her teasing. "Although once, I did have a lady fall down a flight of stairs and land at my feet."

"But did she *fling* herself?"

"No. It was more of a stumble. And an ambulance was called. But I did visit her to sign the cast. By the way, that dress is too short."

Eilish lifted a red eyebrow at me and glanced down at herself. "Sean, you're being ridiculous. It's past my knees."

We were at the back of a fancy women's boutique on Clarendon Street, in an area meant for trying on clothes. Several curtained stalls lined the back wall and a couch was placed to one side. It was the only place to sit, so it was where I waited, scrolling through the website Lucy took pictures for on my phone. I wasn't even sure why, because clearly there weren't going to be any photos of her, or me for that matter, but somehow the practice calmed me, made me feel like I was with her even though I wasn't. Go psychoanalyze that.

Lucy had sent me several texts since our wordless encounter the night before. I hadn't answered any of them. Their lack of sentiment irritated me.

**Lucy:** *Did you leave?*
**Lucy:** *Thanks for being so nice to Ronan.*
**Lucy:** *Finally home, exhausted. Going to sleep.*

And that was all she'd sent.

See? Irritating.

Good sense told me nothing had changed. Lucy had offered me nothing. Her behavior had been consistent from our first encounter to our last, and all the text messages in between. I had nothing with which to reproach her.

Still . . . No mention of missing me, wanting to see me. Was a simple *I can't live without you* too much to ask?

And yet, though we hadn't spoken nor had she given voice to the want so evident in her eyes, seeing Lucy last night had cemented something. We weren't over. Far from it. Our inability to go a day without making contact meant the thing between us wasn't going away.

Those were my ruminations while Eilish tried on dresses behind her curtain. Every so often, if she liked a frock, she'd emerge and show it to me while she assessed her reflection.

"Then it's too tight," I argued. I liked that dress the least so far.

She smirked. "It's not too tight. It's just fine."

I frowned at her smirk and her pacifying tone.

"Wouldn't you prefer something less revealing?" I asked.

My cousin's mouth dropped open and her eyes went wide just before she tossed her head back and laughed with gusto, turning around to face me and placing her hands on her hips.

I usually liked shopping, both with my cousin and in general. Most men don't like to shop. I was not most men. In fact, the only thing I didn't hate about the farce of a relationship with Brona O'Shea was taking her shopping and dressing her in smart clothes.

Some would call me superficial. I considered myself merely keen on aesthetics.

Of course, I never actually enjoyed shopping with Brona or buying her things. She'd been grateful, but I'd discovered it wasn't gratitude I wanted.

In fact, I wasn't sure what I wanted or why buying things for Eilish gave me such a deep sense of satisfaction.

Since I'd left New York, I'd taken Eilish out no less than seven times and bought her all manner of clothes and accessories. I liked spending money on her, and she didn't argue, just accepted the lavishing like a good girl.

But there were so many things wrong with the current dress, I was having trouble ordering its defects in their entirety.

First of all, it was black, with a bit of lace along the V of the neck. And though it reached past her knees, it was entirely too tight for a girl her age. She'd paired it with spiked heels—which couldn't have been good for her feet. I worried for her ankles.

Overall, it looked . . . sexy. Wrong. I hated it.

I grimaced at her good cheer and brightened gaze, which only made her laugh harder.

"Ah, Sean," she wiped at her eyes, "your expression right now is adorable."

"You can't wear that." I sniffed, checking my cufflinks. "You're too young."

"I'm nineteen."

I scowled, with both irritation and confusion.

Was that true? When had Eilish turned nineteen? Wasn't she fifteen? Sixteen at the oldest . . .. I counted backward. She'd been sent to a boarding school in the States when she turned ten. Had it already been nine years since I'd consoled her the night before her departure?

My gaze flickered over her body once more and annoyance reignited as I realized she did, in fact, look like a woman. When I met her eyes again, her wide smile was still in place.

"You're not allowed to be nineteen."

Her answering chuckle was melodic and tinged with an unmistakable air of affection. "Nevertheless, I am nineteen. I'm in my second year of university at Brown, or had you forgotten?"

"No." Come to think of it, I did recall something about her going to school in Massachusetts. "I haven't forgotten . . . precisely."

"Don't feel badly about it." She waved away my regretful expression and something like practiced apathy affixed to her features. "I don't think my father or my siblings know where I go to school, or my major for that matter. Your disinterest doesn't bother me."

Par for the course: pretending little things like life goals and ambitions were unimportant. I didn't like how easily Eilish was able to pretend. Though, with her family, pretending was far safer than the alternative.

Suddenly, it felt very important that she know I was, and always had been, interested in her wellbeing.

"Get off it, E. I know where you go to school. And I seem to remember your major is something boring—like journalism or some such to do with the letter J."

Her lips twitched as she met my eyes in the mirror. "Computational Biology."

"Yes. Exactly." I nodded, trying valiantly to keep my smile hidden. "That's what I said."

She shook her head at me, but I was pleased to see her grin, however small it might be.

I picked up the purple frock I'd favored earlier. It had pink flowers and a turtleneck, and the skirt would entirely hide her legs. "What about this one? Isn't purple your favorite color?"

She rolled her eyes, huffing, and turned back to her reflection. "I'm not ten, I don't have a favorite color. And I'm not wearing that."

"Look, the flowers almost look like little mitochondria. Right up your alley."

"What do you know about mitochondria?"

"I read. The powerhouse of the cell, correct?" Truth be told, I'd spotted a shower curtain with a model of an animal cell on the pages of SkyMall magazine and ordered it for myself. I liked studying it while I showered. Plus, it looked like abstract art.

Her mouth flattened while she fought her grin. "Correct."

"So . . . this one? With the pink flowers?" I tried again.

"No. I quite like this one." She turned to the side, her grin breaking free as she inspected herself.

Ugh.

Disaster.

I'd asked Eilish two weeks ago, as soon as I'd been invited, as I had no desire to pretend with someone else. Any other date would require feigned interest and attention. But my cousin, whose company I honestly enjoyed, would be easy.

Plus, no matter my level of disinterest, the idea of arriving with a date when Lucy would be in attendance made my stomach tighten uncomfortably and my head felt too small for my brain. I rather hoped she and I would be able to steal a few moments at least. Eilish would be a valuable ally, covering for us if need be.

But now I suspected I'd be spending the evening warning away horny rugby players from my too-beautiful and unworldly cousin.

Bested by an impish redhead well under a foot shorter than me, I reluctantly presented my credit card to the salesperson who'd been standing at attention, watching our exchange with practiced indifference. "Anything she wants, even that ghastly dress."

Eilish laughed again, tossing a curtain of glossy, perfect hair over her shoulder. She resembled my aunt in appearance and gracefulness of her movements, but their manner couldn't have been more different.

"Do I really look ghastly?"

"No. You're gorgeous, but that dress is ghastly. I'll be fending off lascivious rugby-playing perverts all night with you dressed like that."

Stepping away from the mirror, Eilish crossed to me. I stood and allowed her to place a light kiss on my cheek. Though she rose on her tiptoes, I still had to bend down in order for her to reach my face.

"You're quite nice, Sean," she whispered conspiratorially. "Don't worry, I won't tell anyone your secret."

"I'm not really." I wasn't, not usually, at any rate.

"Yes, you are. You've always been nice." She squeezed my arm. "Remember when mother sent me away? I was terrified, and you made me feel better. You helped me be brave."

"You were only ten, and she was being a bear."

"You were very kind."

I shrugged, growing increasingly uncomfortable with the picture Eilish was painting of me. "All I did was hug you."

"For an hour at least. And then you promised to punch anyone who was mean to me."

I shrugged again, glancing over her head at nothing in particular. "I didn't like it when you cried. Plus punching nasty little girls sounded like fun."

"It worked out though, didn't it? I was the lucky one." Her tone had grown introspective and I shifted my attention back to her, found Eilish considering me with a meditative look. "Too bad they didn't send you away as well."

The bell to the shop chimed, announcing a new customer. But E and I continued swapping commiserating stares, paragraphs and pages of understanding shared with a single look.

"Have you tried contacting your father?" she whispered, her brow furrowed with concern.

I'd learned the identity of my father after my mother passed some six years ago; he was a German sportsman of some fame. A mountain climber, and more than twenty years older than my mother. Eilish knew because I'd called and told her at the time. Yet I'd taken no action.

I shook my head, deciding I was bored of the subject. "I'm starving, and it looks like rain."

Food and weather, wonderfully benign as neither required an opinion.

She crossed her arms and glared at me. I could see she wanted to press the issue, but would bide her time. She was devious in that way.

"You just ate an hour ago."

"I know. I ate a whole hour ago." I glanced at my watch and gave her a slightly panicked look. "I might die for lack of sustenance. I'm wasting away."

E took a step away and smiled again, then turned, pulling her hair over her shoulder. "Here, unzip this and I'll change. I'll take you to an all-you-can eat buffet. That should tide you over for a bit."

"I've been tossed out of most of those places at least once." I unhooked the top of the frock and searched for the tiny zipper pull, my large fingers not quite nimble enough. "All you can eat never really means *All Sean Can Eat.*"

Eilish snorted an inelegant laugh just as someone said, "Oh! Pardon me."

The exclamation and apology pulled my attention from the elusive zipper tab. Both Eilish and I glanced at the woman hovering at the entrance to the dressing area. I blinked at her, finding her familiar but not quite able to place her.

"Hello, Mrs. Fitzpatrick." Eilish nodded politely, doffing her very best South Dublin air of superiority.

Ah, mystery solved.

The older woman inclined her head, now fully composed, in such a way that made me want to give her a recommendation for a good chiropractor, or perhaps someone who could help her remove the rod from her arse.

Lucy's grandmother.

"Good afternoon, Eilish," then to me, "Mr. Cassidy," then back to Eilish, "How is your mother?"

I studied this woman as Eilish and she exchanged meaningless pleasantries. Truth be told, she looked a great deal like Lucy. Their eyes were the same shape and color. Lucy had inherited her grandmother's ethereal grace and delicate pixie-ish features. Her appearance of fragility.

But this woman was not beautiful. She was cold and aloof. Controlled. Predictable.

Whereas Lucy was unequivocally stunning, warm, and engaging. Carefree. Impulsive.

Lucy was everything gorgeous and good. She may have looked delicate, but she wasn't. She was steadfast, and loyal, and resilient.

And this woman refused to know her.

"Shopping I take it?" Mrs. Fitzpatrick asked benignly.

"No," I said, just to be contrary. A ferocious unpleasantness caught me unexpectedly. As such, all my remarks henceforth would be acerbic at best, belligerent at worst.

Eilish gave me an odd look and forced a laugh. "Of course. We're dress shopping for a wedding this weekend."

Belligerently, I added, "For your grandson's wedding, as a matter of fact."

Mrs. Fitzpatrick blinked, but the empty curve of her lips, meant to be a smile, didn't waver. "Quite."

"Yes. Did you know Ronan is getting married?" I pressed. "And to a lovely girl, too. Brilliant, actually."

Eilish's odd look became something altogether different, because she knew how I disliked Ronan. To her ear, it must've sounded like I was taking up for him.

And perhaps I was.

*Troubling thought, that.*

"Mr. Cassidy, we don't speak of those people. They're hardly—"

"What? Hardly what?" I didn't raise my voice. Rather I lowered it, softened it,

Yet something in my tone must've communicated my ire because the senior Fitzpatrick lifted her chin and sniffed before responding with a dismissive flick of her wrist, "Hardly anyone of import. We all, as I'm sure you can appreciate, have unfortunate relations we'd rather not discuss."

I ignored her slight against me and pushed the issue. "And what of your granddaughter?"

"I don't know the girl, nor do I wish to."

I flinched, not certain why I'd expected a different answer. How the woman could speak of Lucy as if she were unfortunate was beyond me. Was violence against women permitted when the woman in question was as warm as a can of piss?

My features likely betrayed my thoughts as Eilish felt it necessary to insinuate herself between me and the high and mighty Mrs. Fitzpatrick. "Let me take you to the front, Theresa is ringing our purchases, but I think Bridget should be free to lend a hand if you're looking for something . . ."

Eilish's voice faded, gently leading the other woman into the main shop and away from me.

My cousin's interference was a good thing as my thoughts were still violent.

Lucy's grandmother was the matriarch of nothing in particular since she'd refused to accept the children of her only son as family. My aunt and uncle wouldn't win any parent of the year awards, but they had taken me in when my mother fobbed me off. Aunt Cara was unpleasant and unfeeling, but at least she'd gone through the motions.

But the elder Mrs. Fitzpatrick . . . I surmised her pride was the only source of warmth in her house. It was a big house, so her pride must've been substantial. Colossal even.

"What was that about?" Eilish reappeared, her green eyes wide and rimmed with astonishment.

"She's an unfeeling old shrew."

"*Shhh!*" Eilish rushed over, flapping her hands frantically, and whispered harshly, "She'll hear you."

"I don't care if she does. Nor do I imagine she cares what I say."

I recalled Lucy's words from so many weeks ago, when we were in the taxi, just before I'd hoisted her to my shoulders and she'd subjected me to street meat. It was something about finding beauty in strength. A sentiment I'd rejected at the time, but which made a great deal more sense now, faced with her weak relation.

My cousin surveyed me for a moment, confusion etched in the way her forehead wrinkled. "What has gotten into you? I thought you despised Ronan?"

"He's not so bad." I glanced at the ceiling, deciding and saying the words at the same time.

If Ronan had been the one responsible—as Lucy had claimed—for keeping her protected from the influence of those awful people, giving her a loving home, support, keeping her safe, then I supposed I could do better than my constant badgering.

"I never thought I'd hear you say those words." She was all astonishment. "You've always called him an ape."

"Apes aren't all bad." I shrugged. "They're loyal and strong, they take care of their own. He acts without thinking, takes risks, wears his heart on his sleeve, allows his emotions to overtake good sense. But perhaps . . ." I stared over her shoulder, my attention caught on a shiny, rainbow sequin dress, hanging on a return rack.

"Perhaps what?" Eilish prompted, trying to follow my line of sight.

I felt my mouth curve with an unbidden smile, because I was going to buy the dress for Lucy. Rules and decency be damned. Somehow I was going to convince Ronan Ape Fitzpatrick I was worthy of his sister.

"Perhaps, my dear cousin, good sense is overrated."

# Chapter Eighteen

@**LucyFitz** Simon Cowell is my weird celeb crush. There, I said it.

@**Anniecat to** @**LucyFitz** I always suspected high-waisted slacks put the float in your boat ;-)

@**LucyFitz to** @**Anniecat** It's actually the twinkle in his eye. Makes me wonder what he's thinking...

### *Lucy*

"I SUPPOSE IT won't be long before we hear the pitter-patter of little feet," Mam said to Annie as we sat in the sauna in our swimming costumes—sweating—because apparently it was good for the skin.

It was the day before the wedding and we were at the K Club, a gigantic period hotel and golf course in Kildare, where both the ceremony and reception were being held.

Annie cast Mam a smile and responded, "Maybe give me a couple years to enjoy being a newlywed first, Jackie."

I grinned, so proud of my soon-to-be sister-in-law. She'd been so meek and shy when she first began seeing Ronan, but now she'd really come into her own, and she had absolutely no reservations about trying to put my mother in her place.

"Oh, just you wait. You'll be pregnant before the honeymoon is through," Mam went on, refusing to give up the subject.

"Mam!" I hissed. "For God's sake, leave it out. She still needs to get through the wedding day first."

I might have overreacted. I'd been tense for nearly a month. Seeing Sean two nights ago and being unable to even speak to him had made everything exponentially worse. I couldn't stop thinking about him.

Annie shrugged and gestured to Orla and Marie, who had also joined us for our spa day. "It's fine. These two have already been on my case about babies for months now, so I'm used to it."

Marie, the long-term girlfriend of one of Ronan's teammates, smiled kindly. "We're trying to give you some friendly encouragement, that's all."

"Exactly," said Orla. "And think how beautiful your kids will be. I can just imagine those big gorgeous Bambi eyes on a little girl."

"Too true," Mam chirped happily.

Staring at my toes through the steam, I huffed a breath, rubbing a tight spot between my shoulders. "Man, I kind of feel sorry for this kid. She hasn't even been conceived yet and the expectation of beauty is already being saddled on her."

Okay, so I was being a bit of a sour chops. I wasn't normally such a grump, but the lack of resolution with Sean was wearing me down. I was straddling the line of being loyal to my brother (which I wasn't) and being more than friends with Sean (which I wasn't, not really). I wanted both, but couldn't have either. My brain felt like it was being torn in two.

I hadn't heard from Sean since the night of the hen party. I'd texted him three times and he hadn't answered. I told myself it was for the best. Because it *was* for the best.

Too bad my heart didn't agree.

Also, and just keeping it real here, I needed bedroom action, some kind of a release, but it had to be from Sean. The thought of allowing anyone else to touch me sent my stomach rolling with revulsion.

It had to be Sean.

I needed him to touch me.

"There's no questioning that any child of my *son's* will be beautiful as can be," Mam put in, her narrowed eyes leveled on me. "You've always been jealous of Ronan, Lucy."

"I'm not jealous of anyone. I love my brother. All I'm saying is, a baby shouldn't be measured in terms of physical attractiveness. It's a bloody baby, for Christ's sake."

"Please, don't start with another of your politically correct rants. Just because you chose to hide your only good features doesn't mean you have to make those who are attractive feel like less."

There was something in her tone that made me lose my rag. "Christ, you're condescending."

"I'm speaking the truth. Now hush, you're embarrassing us and making a scene," she said, casting her eyes down to a group of women at the other end of the steamy room.

"Well, God forbid I do that."

"Lucy," she said in warning, her eyes demanding I shut the hell up.

"Do you know what, Mam? Sometimes it feels like my very existence is an embarrassment to you, so I think I'll just do you a favor and get out of your hair for the rest of the day. And don't worry, I'll be returning to New York after the wedding, so you won't have to put up with me at all for much longer."

Having said my piece, I stood and shot Annie a look of apology before walking out of the sauna. Yes, I was being a tad hysterical and overly contrary, but my mother was a trigger and it was just one of those days.

"Lucy, come back here," Mam called, her aggravation barely concealed. I ignored her.

I was completely anxious and tense as I walked to the showers. The warm water and lemon-cucumber-scented soap did little to ease my discomfort.

Once I was clean and dressed, I checked my phone for messages. I'd been checking it constantly, like an addict looking for her next fix.

I didn't expect anything, but I hoped. And when I saw there were several spanning over the past hour and they were all from Sean, my heart pounded. A rush of hot nerves flooded my system as I hit the button to read them, remembering our loaded, needful glances from two nights ago, when the stags and hens had collided.

We hadn't exchanged a single word, yet the look he'd given me had expressed his want more than a thousand sonnets could have. I was certain my own looks had reflected that want right back at him.

**Sean:** *Just checked in to the hotel a day early. I'm in room 206 if you find yourself at a loose end...and I've got a jersey in my suitcase with your name on it ;-)*

**Sean:** *Actually, it has my name on it, but you know what I mean. I'd really like to see you, Lucy.*

**Sean:** *You looked beautiful the other night, even in that God-awful costume. I hated that we couldn't speak or touch. It was the worst kind of torture...*

I swiped my thumb over the screen, biting my lower lip as I considered how to reply, my heart still thundering and my chest tight and achy. I wanted to see him, God how I wanted to, but I was here for my brother's wedding. Having any kind of intimate encounter with Sean right now would be completely disrespectful.

And by intimate encounter I meant lots and lots of hot, satisfying, sweaty sex.

Ronan didn't deserve my disloyalty. With that in mind, I decided to ignore the text messages even though they had me all aflutter with nervous excitement and unbearable longing.

*On the other hand . . .*

Sean was going to keep asking to see me.

Going to his room to clear the air would be good.

I needed to set him straight, let him know he wasn't to try anything this weekend.

No more longing looks.

No more suggestive texts.

I didn't want to ruin a single moment for Ronan and Annie.

*Yes. Smart plan. I must see him to tell him I can't . . . see . . . him . . . Right?*

With new determination, I shot off a text.

**Lucy:** *Be there in 5. We need to talk – Just talk.*

I went to the suite I was sharing with Annie and dropped off my things before heading to room 206. The entire way there my heart was in my throat, as I prepared a speech in my head. Lifting my hand, I knocked on the door, and seconds later Sean opened it.

I caught my breath slightly at the sight of him. Seeing him the other night had been nothing compared to this. Here we were alone, with nothing to stop us from touching, just like Sean claimed he'd been dying to.

"Lucy," he said, like my name was an answer. He smiled and his expression was open and hopeful, excited and pleased.

And, *crap, crap, crap, crap!* My heart leapt. A wistful kind of warmth traveled up my spine, down my limbs, and curled around my brain, making me forget the speech I'd been practicing.

"Sean," I said, and it was the sound of my voice—all dreamy and full of anticipation—that snapped me out of my stupor.

"Been out on the yacht with the *fam*, have we?" I asked with shaky confidence. He wore a navy long-sleeved rugby shirt with a white collar, beige chinos, and boat shoes. I smirked at the outfit, wanting to disarm the moment with humor.

He grinned, as though he thoroughly enjoyed my teasing, but said nothing. Just continued to stare at me.

I cleared my throat, my attention snagging on the phone he held in his hand. A video played on his screen. It only took me a second to recognize it was footage from the karaoke session the other night and I winced.

"Is that on YouTube?" I asked, my cheeks heating in embarrassment.

Sean smiled at me so warmly, with such fond affection, that I thought my heart might explode. "It is. You never told me you had aspirations for a hip hop career."

"Turn it off, please. I'm going to murder Orla. I was so drunk during that."

"I'm quite enjoying it, actually," said Sean as I stepped into the room and he returned his attention to the video. "Did you just sing the words 'your booty don't need explaining'? Oh my God, Lucy, I'm making this my ringtone."

I swiped for the phone "Shut up. Maybe your bubble butt inspired my song choice. Ever think of that?"

"Well, we did suffer quite a few weeks apart. I suppose your daydreams of my rear were working their way into strange areas of your life." He paused, watching the video in quiet for a moment before lowering his voice to a sexy rumble. "You've got some very intriguing dance moves. Perhaps you should give me a private show."

"Oh sure, I'll just go put your jersey on for it too, shall I?" I deadpanned, a whisper of panic making my spine stiffen.

His grin was wide. "That would be much appreciated, yes."

I just shook my head at him, swallowing my anxiety. I knew he'd be all too happy to sit and watch while I pranced around in nothing but his team jersey. A moment of quiet ensued as I sat at the end of the large bed that took up a good portion of the room.

This was fun. I was having fun with Sean and our clothes were on, hence the panic.

The easy rapport we'd developed felt comfortable and therefore dangerous. This wasn't friendly banter. This was conversing like two people in a *relationship*. Two people who liked and had committed to each other.

He seemed to circle me like a predator circles its prey, and prickles beaded my skin. I could feel his attention but was too afraid to look, so I stared at the carpet. If I looked at him I knew I'd forever forget every word of my speech and let him have his way with me.

Or rather, let us have our way with each other.

Staring directly ahead, I asked, "Could you sit?"

"Why?"

I finally looked up at him, my voice unsteady. "Because you're making me nervous standing over me like that."

His lips curved slightly. "I quite enjoy making you nervous."

My gaze turned pleading. "Sean."

He swallowed, nodded once, eyes growing intense as he walked to the armchair across from me and took a seat. "In your text you said you wanted to talk."

I gripped the edge of the bed, my palms sweaty. "Yes, I just wanted to clear a few things up."

"How very formal of you. I have to admit, Lucy, this isn't exactly how I expected you to greet me after all these weeks apart." He sounded put out.

Unconsciously, I toyed with the pendant around my neck—Sean's pendant. His eyes went to the movement and they seemed to heat when he saw what I was wearing. "You're wearing the necklace."

"I love it," I said without thinking.

"I can buy you another."

"That's not necessary."

"I rather like seeing you in diamonds. You should have more of them."

I choked, my eyes bulging. "Diamonds?"

"Yes. Diamonds."

I glanced at the pendant, seeing it anew. *Diamonds.* What I'd assumed was a beautiful silver and crystal necklace was in fact something altogether different.

Staring at it, I realized its value changed its meaning. It felt heavier around my neck and in my fingers. Yet I didn't love it more because it was expensive. I loved it just the same.

I let it drop to my chest over my clothes, gripping the bed again. "You shouldn't have bought it for me."

"Why not?"

"Because it's too expensive."

He shrugged, picking a piece of lint from his pants. "I actually enjoy buying things for the women in my life, taking an interest in their attire and purchases. Just ask my cousin Eilish, she'll attest to it."

Now I frowned. "You take your cousin shopping for clothes?"

"Not like that. Eilish is just nineteen. She's like a younger sister to me."

"Oh."

"You might actually get to meet her tomorrow. I'm bringing her as my date to the wedding."

This piece of information surprised me. In fact, it warmed my heart to think of Sean taking a little sister-type as his date.

It also relieved me. I wasn't sure I could stand him showing up with some vajazzled, fame-obsessed parasite that cared nothing about Sean other than his celebrity status.

"That's very sweet of you," I said, my voice a little unsure.

"I can be incredibly sweet."

I looked at the plush carpeted floor. "Can you?"

"You know I can, when I want to be." A moment passed and Sean sighed. "What did you want to discuss, Lucy?"

"Stop that."

"Stop what?"

"Stop saying my name in that voice."

"It's the only voice I have."

"You know what I mean. The sexy voice. Stop it."

"I can't help it if you find my voice sexy, or my arse, my mouth, teeth, tongue . . ."

I stood abruptly from the bed, squeezing my eyes shut and trying to count to ten to calm my racing pulse. Being this close to him and seeing all the vulnerability and longing and sex in his eyes was making me break out in a cold sweat.

Rubbing at my temples, I pleaded, "Don't do this, Sean."

My eyes were still closed when I felt a familiar heat close in around me. Sean had folded me into his arms, my face resting at his sternum. God, he was tall. And built. And warm. The unexpected relief of being this close to him was overwhelming. My throat grew tight and dry, while butterflies flitted around inside my stomach with wild abandon.

His hand massaged my shoulder before cascading down my back to the base of my spine. There he applied a slight pressure and I let out the tiniest moan. His arm that was still around me pulled tighter, and I felt a hardness start to grow at his mid-section. I trembled.

"I think of you all the time," he said, mouth muffled where it rested against my hair. "You're my first thought when I wake. During training, when I'm having dinner, driving home at the end of the day, every single time I get off."

"Sean . . ."

"You, occupying all my thoughts, that's not normal, Lucy. You said I'd forget. I haven't. I can't. And I don't want to."

I shivered again as he wielded my name like a nuclear weapon. "It's the distance. You think about me all the time because you know you can't have me."

"There were so many weekends when I was just one click away

from booking a flight to New York to see you. Just to *see* you. To talk, as we've been doing now. I want to be with you all the time."

I couldn't catch my breath, acute pain and longing piercing my heart.

"What would you have done?" he continued. "Would you have turned me away?"

His words made me melt and his hand at the base my spine lowered, cupping my arse and causing a breath to whoosh out of me. His fingers curled between my legs, brushing tantalizingly close to a spot that ached for him. I whimpered and he answered it with a rumbling growl.

"I love watching you come, the way you look. It's branded into my mind. Please, let me make you come now." His growl turned to a whisper.

"No," I said, so quietly I wasn't sure he heard.

He groaned. "Why not?"

"Because we still need to talk."

"We have been talking."

This was crazy. Because it wasn't the promise of sex. It wasn't even really his words. It was how he said them. The adoration. The unmistakable vulnerability. Pining. Pleading. Promise.

Inhaling a deep breath for courage, I pushed away from him with shaking hands and went to sit on the bed again. When I looked at him his gaze was on fire, and I knew sitting here had been a bad choice. He was undressing me, stripping me with his eyes, and the intensity was jarring. Standing again, I walked over to the armchair he'd previously occupied and crossed my legs.

"I just don't want to jeopardize anything about this wedding," I began, hands fiddling with the hem of my top. "I'm . . ." I thought about confessing to my shoplifting crime spree but decided against it. "I'm on edge."

"If you're on edge, I know something that will relax you," he said seductively. I felt his words penetrate deep in my bones as my libido screamed, *yes, yes, let him help you relax!*

I shook my head. "I mean it, I need to keep out of trouble, Sean. I'm already the black sheep of the family, and I just flipped out on my mother for no real reason. That's not a good start to the most important few days of my brother's life."

Sean tilted his head. "You're far too colorful to ever be the black sheep."

"Can you be serious with me for a minute?"

"I am being serious," he said, before striding forward to kneel in front of me. He took my hands in his, rubbing his thumbs over the insides of my wrists. I tried to ignore how wonderful it felt. "If your mother thinks you're something to be ashamed of, then it's her loss, because I've experienced how amazing you are. The moment you walk into a room you brighten it, Lucy Fitzpatrick, and I for one feel like the luckiest bastard in the world for having known you."

"You . . ." I started but my voice failed me. "You can't say stuff like that when I'm trying to tell you we can't be together. It isn't fair."

His thumbs stilled, and when he spoke his voice was frosty. It was a stark contrast to his previously heated tone. "Wait a minute. Answer me honestly. Did you come here to tell me we couldn't be together until after the wedding, or did you come to tell me we can't be together at all?"

"I...I don't know."

He stared at me for a beat, the astonished hurt in his eyes making my stomach drop. Standing from his kneeling position, he walked to the other side of the room as he ran a hand through his blond locks. I watched as the muscles in his shoulders bunched with tension. He let out an irritable breath before resting his hands on his hips.

"You're making something that could be so simple into something really complicated here, Lucy," he said in frustration, still not facing me.

"There's never been anything simple about you and me," I returned. "We both knew it could go no further than the physical from the very start. I told you—"

"Yes, but that was before. Things are different now. I'm different."

I couldn't help giving him a skeptical look. "Are you? The last I knew you were keen to go out and start practicing your newly gained 'skills' on other women."

Okay, so that was a low blow, but I was feeling desperate and defensive.

His icy blues turned dark as they surveyed me, his jaw working. When he spoke he crossed to me; his voice rose with every word until he was near shouting. "That was me talking shit and you know it. I wasn't keen to go out and find other women. I was keen to stay in bed with you. Or grab coffee with you. Or chase celebrities with you. Anything, as long as we were together." His gaze was erratic now, wandering over my features like he didn't know whether to kiss me or strangle me.

I could barely speak, so enthralled by the look in his eyes. My next words were a weak whisper. "That's bullshit."

"Does this feel like bullshit to you?" he growled before yanking me from my seat, cupping both my cheeks, and pulling my mouth to his.

Jesus, Mary, and Joseph, I'd forgotten how utterly devastating his kiss could be.

As soon as his lips met mine, I lost the battle with myself. His tongue swept into my mouth and I knew I was helpless to stop. I didn't want to stop. I wanted this—him—more than words could say, and when he lifted me, I locked my legs around his waist, holding on for dear life like I never wanted to let go.

My back hit the soft, plush mattress and he climbed atop me, my thighs on either side of his waist. His tongue slid against mine in a seductive dance and the vague thought hit me of how he'd always been an amazing kisser, despite everything else. A second later he broke the kiss, swearing profusely as he lowered his head, pressing his face into my chest.

"Jesus fucking Christ," he ground out, fingertips pushing into my back as he held me. I tried to catch my breath while I ran my hands through his hair.

"Sean, are you all right?"

"Yes, I just . . . I'm trying really hard not to come and embarrass myself right now, but I haven't touched you in weeks."

His unexpectedly candid statement took the wind out of my sails and I almost laughed. He'd been the one to grab me and toss me on the bed, after all.

"Then come," I said.

He arched a brow.

I lifted a shoulder, too exhausted to fight off my overwhelming need for him any longer. "Maybe having sex now will make things easier at the ceremony tomorrow," I said, like I was trying to convince myself of the idea's merits, rationalizing like a true addict.

Sean frowned. "What about after the ceremony?"

I shifted, rubbing myself against him, feeling him tense. His gaze grew darker.

I rushed to say, "Let's just . . . Listen, let's just get through the ceremony tomorrow without tearing each other's clothes off. Then we'll talk about what comes after."

He chuckled, some of his previous tension slipping away as he placed a soft, worshipful kiss on my lips. "That would make for some very interesting wedding photographs."

I couldn't help it. I smiled at him, struck by the light, airy feeling of joy it gave me to share a moment of humor with him. "Indeed."

But then his humor tapered the longer he stared at me. An unusual and unmistakable worry creased his forehead. "I'm not going to be satisfied with just one more time, Lucy. This isn't goodbye."

I swallowed, nodding somberly, and pressed my palm to his strong jaw, needing to touch him. I whispered, "I know."

Heat and promise filled his gaze, his attention traced the line of my eyebrows, nose, lips, and strayed to my neck and chest. He began unbuttoning the shirt I wore and pressed hot, hungry kisses to my breasts. Taking my lace-clad, pebbled nipple between his lips, he gave it a sharp bite, and I gasped. My thoughts turned to mush as soon as he started moving down my body until his face was between my thighs. He nuzzled me there, and I let out a sharp yelp at the sensation before he flicked open the buttons and pulled off my jeans.

"What do you want?" he asked, staring up at me as he slid a finger beneath the hem of my knickers, finding me wet.

"You know how I like it," I answered, my voice more air than sound.

"Yeah," he said, his brows drawing together in an attractively masculine and thoughtful expression. "I do, don't I?"

At this he pulled my underwear to the side, exposing me to his intense stare. Bending his head, he licked lightly at my clit and my entire body bucked.

"Oh God."

Sean reached up, deftly unclipping my bra and pushing my shirt away from my shoulders until I was completed naked before him. With his eyes on my breasts, he began lapping at me in earnest and I closed my eyes, my head falling back into the pillows as I savored the sensation. He moved two fingers inside me and I moaned loudly at the feeling of fullness.

Only about a minute went by before I was coming on his mouth. He sucked my clit between his lips, holding it there as the waves of my orgasm consumed me—the relief and torture of it. I noticed he was making a lot of noise, like he was enjoying making me come just as much as I enjoyed coming. But then, when he rose up on his knees, staring down at me with such dark possession, I noticed the wet patch at his crotch.

He'd come, too.

I couldn't believe he'd come just from doing that to me. I knew he was a quick finisher, but I had a feeling there was more to it. Us together was so much more intense.

Sean + Lucy = Spectacular.

With both hands he toyed with my breasts, brushing his knuckles along the sensitive sides and making me shiver. He leaned down to kiss me softly. I tasted myself on his lips.

"I'll be right back," he murmured before climbing off the bed and going to the bathroom.

I lay there, sated and foggy-headed, as I listened to the water come on in the next room. When Sean returned he was naked, and my eyes did a leisurely sweep of his perfectly formed physique. I didn't even try to hide my ogling.

He smiled warmly. It was a private smile, a smile for lovers, and it made my heart clench.

"I love when you look at me like that," he said huskily as he came and lifted me by the hips. A second later he'd flipped us with a fluid movement so I lay on top of him.

"Why?" I asked, still all mushy-headed.

"It's territorial. A look that makes me feel like I'm your man. I like the idea of being yours."

His words knocked me for six, and all I could do was stare at him, open-mouthed, as I wrapped my head around the fact Sean Cassidy wanted to be mine.

What the hell?

And why the hell did the concept sound so bloody appealing?

"That's . . . that's . . . um," I rambled, unable to think of a proper response.

Sean chuckled. "You don't have to say it back. I know I'm more into this than you are and that's okay."

"Are you serious?" I squeaked. "All I can think about is you, Sean. I'm into this. Believe me. If it weren't for certain circumstances, I'd be wooing you like a motherfucker right now."

He laughed harder, his voice full of affection. "I believe I'm the one who's supposed to woo you."

"Hey, I'm a modern gal. I'm all for girls wooing boys, and vice versa. Whatever works."

I was vaguely aware that Sean had started rocking our bodies together. He was hard already, now there was a surprise . . . not.

The head of his cock brushed against my clit and I shivered. It felt amazing.

"You like that?" he whispered, staring up at me with hooded eyes as he continued to rock us.

I bit my lip. "Mmm-hmm."

"Do you want me inside you?"

"Yes, please." I added the please because I knew he liked it when I said it; and, oddly enough, I liked saying it to him.

His cock nudged at my entrance and I closed my eyes. He wasn't wearing a condom and the feel of us skin on skin was too good. I'd tell him to put one on . . . in a minute. I just needed to feel this for one . . . more . . . minute.

I was still slick and wet from when he'd gone down on me, and before I knew it he'd ever-so-easily slipped inside me.

He was mind-blowing. His hands were on my hips, almost going the entire way around my waist.

"Fuck, you feel incredible," he groaned, pumping up into me.

"Sean," I breathed. "We didn't . . . you forgot the condom."

His eyes flared in mild panic as soon as I said the words. "Shit," he swore loudly. "If you're not on the pill I can—"

"No, I'm on it, it's just . . ." I sliced my teeth across my lips, very much doubting he had the self-restraint to pull out even if he wanted to. This was the same man who complained about lasting ten whole minutes for a blow job, after all.

Understanding seemed to dawn in his eyes, "I'm clean. I get tested all the time for work. My last one was just three weeks ago."

"Three weeks?"

He frowned, his expression turning fierce. "You must know, there's been no one but you."

I nodded and added my own blurted confession. "I'm clean. And there's been no one but you either."

"I don't want anyone but you," he said, like a chant, like he was so focused on the feel of me, he hadn't heard my words.

"Oh," I said, because it was all I could manage, closing my eyes again. He was still moving inside me. It was instinctual, like he couldn't stop now that he'd started.

"Does this feel good to you?" he asked, still so concerned about my pleasure. I couldn't believe he'd gone from a serial one-night-stander who didn't care at all about the satisfaction of his lovers, to a man who savored every moment of *my* enjoyment. Had I done this to him? The thought was both exhilarating and sobering.

"God, yes, do you even have to ask?" I answered, my words coming out in a rush.

"I want to be sure. It's important to me to make you feel good."

"You're thinking too much. Get out of your head and just do what your body tells you."

I started to ride him and he groaned, his head falling into the pillows. I opened my eyes and he was watching me. His gaze never left mine, his hands still held me tight, as we both pushed our bodies to the brink of ecstasy. A moment later he began moving his flattened out palms up and over my hips. Instinctually, I took his hands and raised them to my breasts. They covered them completely and I loved how it felt, loved feeling him on every inch of me.

"Keep touching me," I urged as I felt a sharp, keening pleasure formulate from the pit of my stomach and all the way down to my clit.

He pinched my nipples and I gasped. "Yes, that feels amazing."

Growling, he rose up to take one nipple in his mouth, his other hand pressing into my lower back. My moans filled the room as he continued to fuck me, his other hand going down between us to find my clit.

"Sean," I cried out as he rubbed me, too many sensations hitting me all at once.

"Come," he demanded on a growl, the sound vibrating from his mouth still on my nipple right through me. His fingers kept circling my clit, and I felt the wetness between us coating him. "Come with me," he urged again right before his mouth left my breast and sought my lips. His kiss was wet and desperate, and when his tongue plunged inside I came violently right there with him still inside. I filled with warmth as his movements slowed and his mouth fell from mine to bite possessively at my jaw. He kept moving until he'd drained every last moment of his orgasm.

"Jesus Christ, Lucy," he rasped, holding me tight.

"Sean," I panted, wrapping my arms around his neck as we both fell back into the bed, savoring the after-effects of what was possibly the most amazing sex either one of us had ever experienced.

I was certain of it.

Because it wasn't just sex . . .

Turning us, he spooned me from behind. I loved how big and warm his body was. I loved how he nuzzled my neck. I loved how his hands were caressing and reverent.

"Stay with me," he said, more a soft rumble than spoken words.

I nodded, giving myself over to it—to him—pushing away encroaching fretfulness for just a little bit longer.

Because this was nice. It was more than nice. It was spectacular. It felt necessary.

I liked—no, I loved—being in his arms. I loved the after just as much as I loved the during.

At my nod, he relaxed. And after a while his breathing evened out and I realized he'd fallen asleep. A moment later my phone lit up with a call.

*Ronan.*

My heart lurched. Since it was on silent, I let the call ring out, and a minute later I saw he'd left a voicemail. Picking up the phone and rising carefully from the bed, I held it to my ear and listened.

*Hey Luce,*

*Look, I know things have been hectic the past few days and we haven't really had the chance to talk, but I wanted to apologize for how I spoke to you in the car. Annie's right, I was being a bully. I just care about you so much and I don't want you getting hurt by bad people. You're your own person and I understand that you get to make your own decisions, so I'm going to try to be less of a protective oaf from now on. Well, as much as I can be. Just know I'm sorry and I'll always be there to look out for you. Anyway, call me when you get this.*

As soon as the call clicked off, I looked back at Sean, indecision churning in my gut. My brother wasn't the kind of guy to often admit when he was wrong, so that message was a big deal. And as much as he didn't want to upset me, I didn't want to hurt him.

But I didn't want to upset Sean, either.

I didn't know what to do.

What Sean and I had just shared had been monumental, life altering, and as much as I loved Ronan, I wasn't sure I could give up what I had with Sean just to keep Ronan happy.

And I couldn't bring myself to feel regret. If I'd had the chance, I knew I'd do everything exactly the same. I'd make the same choices. I wouldn't give up my time with Sean for a mountain of inner peace. Still, I needed time to think, to figure out a plan to tell Ronan about Sean and get him to accept him in my life without summoning the apocalypse.

By the time I was dressed he was snoring lightly, and I hated myself for leaving him, but there was nothing else for it. Finding a pad of paper and a pen, I scribbled down a quick note and left it on the end of the bed.

*Tonight was everything. I'm sorry I left when I promised I'd stay, but I just need some time to think. We'll talk after the wedding.*

*Yours,*

*Lucy.*

*xoxo.*

With one last look at his handsome profile in slumber, I slipped out of the room without making a single sound.

# Chapter Nineteen

@**SeanCassinova** When you forget to pack gym socks and all you want to do is run until you're numb.

**\*Sean\***

I'D BEEN ACCUSED of being heartless. Frequently. By everyone.

Well, everyone but Eilish. She was delusional.

Regardless, the accusation never bothered me much because I considered it entirely possible. I liked Eilish, I liked her a lot. I liked my shoes. I liked my fame. I liked having an effective moisturizer. I liked power and money and a good steak.

I almost loved SkyMall magazine.

The last and only thing I knew without a shadow of a doubt I'd loved had been my childhood dog.

But when I woke up and Lucy was gone, such a depth of sorrow and anger and fear flooded my chest that I felt as though I would drown in it.

At first, I tried to explain her absence. Call it self-preservation. Call it wishful thinking. Call it the power of Lucy Fitzpatrick's messy influence.

However, I'd never been good at lying to myself. When I confirmed she was nowhere in the suite, I knew with absolute certainty I was not heartless. I pressed my hand to the ribs on my left side. A violent, stabbing sensation wrest a grimace from me, which made each inhale uncomfortable and shallow.

I was not without a heart. Because, and I admitted this fully aware of how completely pathetic I sounded, there was a good chance my heart had just been broken.

Really, until that moment, I'd been in denial. I'd thought the weekend was the beginning of something new and solid for us. I'd told her I hadn't forgotten her like she'd insisted would happen. For some bizarre reason, I thought my devotion would make a difference. I thought she'd see my constancy and . . .

I don't know.

See that I was right?

Give us a real chance?

Choose me?

Present a united front to her brother?

I was a fool.

Her absence could mean only one thing.

And because the acute pain in my chest had only grown more unmanageable within the span of five minutes, I picked up the lamp by the bed and threw it against the wall, shattered pieces of porcelain flying in all directions. I cast my gaze about the room, searching for something else to destroy, still unable to draw a full breath, and caught my reflection in the mirror.

I appeared dazed, incensed, and wholly uncivilized. I'd officially become a melodramatic, sentimental arsehole.

I was an ape.

Disgusted, I turned from the mirror. I stormed to my suitcase and dressed in my workout clothes. I let fly a string of curses when I realized I'd forgotten gym socks.

*When the hell had I ever forgotten gym socks?*

I'd been eager to see her and rushed through packing. All I had were gray argyles for my suit. I might have been mentally unhinged and enraged, but I was not without sensibility for fashion decorum. I wasn't completely insensible. Not yet at any rate.

I wore my shoes without socks—which I abhorred—and slammed the door after me, not caring if I woke or offended any of the hotel's prissily stoic inhabitants. I needed to use my body, run until I was numb, or else I would decimate the interior of my hotel room.

Perhaps I would do both.

Anger pumped through my heart, stitching together the broken pieces, hardening and cooling the blood in my veins. Too impatient to wait for the lift, I took the stairs, deciding as I descended that I was going to hate her. I needed to loathe her.

I'd already begged. Leaving after promising to stay meant she'd refused me. I would not pine.

Bursting into the lobby just minutes later, I made a beeline for the west corner of the hotel, irritated by the plaster pattern on the crown molding. Were those fish? Flowers? I hated it. Garish and appalling.

Since the K Club had an extensive world-class golf course, they also had a pro shop with a small collection of clothing. The hour was late, but not too late. The shop was still open.

A man lifted his head as I entered, his greeting dying on his lips at my glare.

"Socks," I demanded.

His eyebrows jumped, his eyes widening in alarm. Swallowing nervously, he lifted his chin to the back wall. "Yes, sir. In a basket, just there."

I grunted my non-response and marched to where he'd indicated. I glowered at the basket. It was full of the most ridiculous and tasteless patterned socks I'd ever seen. Golf balls on cartoonish smiling tees, golf clubs arranged in a heart, little golfing men swinging a club.

Atrocious.

I lifted my head to shout at the man, demand he bring me socks for actual athletes, when a streak of color caught my eye. More precisely, many colors. All the colors of the rainbow.

Lucy.

Heart and lungs seizing, I stumbled a half step back, blinking at the sight of her entering the shop, not trusting my eyes. Yet, there she was. Shopping.

She'd left—ended us—no more than an hour ago. Apparently that's what one does after breaking someone's heart. They browse the goods at a pro shop within a gaudy golfing hotel in Kildare.

Obviously.

My original errand completely forgotten, I stalked over to her. Because I had to. It wasn't a conscious decision and I had no idea what I was going to say or do.

I just . . .

*Christ.*

I just wanted to see her.

The last month had been torture without her easy smile and teasing laugh. My only reprieve had been the daily text messages.

I sought to hold fast to my anger, yet I couldn't manage it. Raw, swelling sorrow choked me as I halted my approach and studied her profile.

Fuck.

I hated this.

She'd been crying. Her eyes were puffy, her lips swollen and abused, the tip of her nose red. The rest of her typically glowing skin was white and drawn. Observing her misery didn't help. Rather, it fueled a sudden desperation to ease her discomfort. Unthinkingly, I began closing the remainder of the distance between us, intent on taking some action.

But then she did something rather unexpected and it brought me to a full stop. She picked up a three-pack of expensive golf balls and slipped them into her handbag. Afterward, she stood frozen for several seconds. She then proceeded to pick up four more three-packs—the obnoxious neon yellow kind—and placed those in her bag as well.

Then she darted for the exit.

I gaped at her, unable to fathom what I'd just witnessed.

Unless she'd developed an insatiable penchant for expensive golf balls in the last forty-five minutes, Lucy was shoplifting to soothe acute emotional distress. I'd only witnessed her habit once—months ago now—and I'd brushed it off as a harmless, meaningless diversion.

Two hundred euros in golf balls was not a diversion. It was a compulsion.

She'd nearly made it to the perimeter of the shop when I shook myself from the grip of stupor and charged after her, not wanting to lose her in the lobby of the hotel. But then my stomach dropped, because the shop alarm gave a loud *whoop whoop*. A previously unseen detector flashed red and white, alerting all within that someone was trying to escape with fancy golf balls.

I quickly glanced around, horrified to see the man I'd interrogated about socks just minutes prior jogging toward a paralyzed Lucy, his expression thunderous.

"You there! Empty your bag."

She mouthed the words, *Oh shite*. Her eyes closed as a scarlet flush of mortification spread up her neck and cheeks. He reached Lucy before I did and yanked her bag away, the same bag I'd mocked at the restaurant after I'd spotted her shoplifting the first time. He then unceremoniously turned it upside down and shook it.

*Rescue her*, an impulsive voice insisted in the recesses of my mind. *Rescue her as she'd rescued you.*

Possessions rained from her purse, clattering on the shop's marble slab floor. Four containers of golf balls fell along with her phone, purse, and other sundry items.

When her phone collided with the marble, an unmistakable cracking sound of the screen shattering reverberated like a gunshot between my ears. It was the final straw that spurred me into action.

"You've broken her phone," I said, charging forward, drawing both Lucy's and the store clerk's attention to me. I felt her eyes like a physical touch. I didn't need to see her face to know I'd shocked the hell out of her.

He backed up a step at my approach, lifting his chin to meet my glare, and responding with haughty impatience, "Sorry for the inconvenience, sir. But I've just caught a thief." He gestured to Lucy, either misunderstanding or mishearing my complaint.

"No you haven't," I insisted, stepping in front of her protectively and crossing my arms.

*Delay*, my mind insisted. *Bluff. Threaten. Improvise. Fix this.*

The man's mouth opened and closed, working to sort through my words.

"Do you know who she is?" I gained another step forward, towering over him and glaring menacingly.

"Sean," her soft voice pleaded. "Don't."

The man's eyes narrowed and he set his jaw. "I don't care if she's the Queen's sister, she's a thief and I'm calling the police."

"You'll lose your job," I threatened, pleased to see his eyes widen with a moment of hesitation. "She's Ronan Fitzpatrick's sister, captain of the Irish rugby squad."

"I don't care for rugby," he said, sniffing self-importantly. "I prefer golf."

"Well, you ought," I growled, both irritated and perversely pleased he wasn't a rugby fan. "He's getting married here tomorrow. What do you think management will say if you call the police on his little sister after he'd spent thousands of euros on his special day?"

He frowned, a deep V of consternation forming between his eyebrows. A sound to my right caught his attention and I allowed my gaze to stray for a brief moment. We'd drawn a crowd. Gawking passers-by had stopped to watch the exchange.

Unfortunately, their presence seemed have the effect of reinforcing his resolve. He puffed out his chest and lifted his chin higher. "As I said, I don't care who she is. Nothing negates the fact that she's attempted to steal several hundred euros of valuable merchandise from my store. Now if you'll excuse me, I have a call to the authorities to make."

Unthinkingly, I placed a hand on his arm to stay his movements, "Wait—"

"Unhand me, sir!"

"You have the wrong person."

He wrestled his arm from my grip. "I certainly do not."

"You do," I seethed, seeing intimidation of the normal kind would get me nowhere and, scrambling for a solution that would see her free and safe, I announced, "I put the balls in her bag."

"Sean!" Lucy was at my side, her hands wrapping around my wrist. "Stop this."

I threaded my fingers through hers to still her movements. "While she wasn't looking, I put them in her bag, thought it would be a good joke. She had no idea."

"You did no such thing," the man huffed, clearly seeing through my lie.

"I did, and you can't prove the contrary."

Lucy tried to bypass me, so I wrapped my arm around her, covering her mouth just as she said, "No he—"

"I did."

She strained against my grip, her hands coming to mine in an effort to pull my fingers away so she could speak.

"I did it. It was me. Call the garda. I don't care."

The clerk looked between the two of us like we were crazy. Lucy growled, now trying to elbow me in the stomach.

"What's going on here?" a new voice asked, one I immediately recognized. "Let go of my sister, Cassidy."

I didn't. I held her tighter for fear she would blurt her guilt. Lucy had stiffened, having abandoned her struggle as soon as her brother appeared.

I shot Ronan a look, hoping I could take advantage of his typical reactionary behaviors for the next few moments.

"Ah. Ronan. May I introduce the man who is trying to arrest your sister?"

"Arrest Lucy?" he asked dumbly, his eyes moving over the three of us. Behind him, I spotted several of our teammates, all watching the scene with a hushed readiness. Prepared to jump into action should their captain require assistance.

For once their blind loyalty didn't aggravate me.

"That's right. This man is determined to call the Garda even after I explained it had been a joke."

"It was not a joke," the clerk raged. A vein stood out in relief on his red forehead. "That girl," he pointed to Lucy with obvious spite and contempt, and I saw Ronan tense at the movement, "tried to steal from my shop, and this odious man is trying to take the blame for it."

I shifted my eyes to Ronan's, finding his wide with dawning comprehension.

"And if *he*," the clerk gestured to me, "would unhand the thief, she'd confess everything herself."

"Don't unhand her," Ronan ordered, giving me a stark look. Then addressing the clerk, shouted, "If he said he did it, then he did it. Stop badgering my sister and go call the Garda. Have them come and sort it out. Go."

The man stiffened in surprise, gaped, then opened his mouth like he was ready to argue. But he didn't. Instead, he gave a belligerent, prideful sniff and spun on his heel, marching to the shop desk and grabbing the phone behind the counter.

Lucy huffed through her nose, drawing my attention back to her. I relaxed my hold slightly and tried to look down, examine her expression. She stared forward, looking mortified and angry.

I bent to whisper something in her ear, a plea for her to stay quiet, but was interrupted from doing so by Ronan.

"I don't know what happened," he'd lowered his voice so only we three were privy to his threatening words, "but whatever you're trying to do to my sister—"

"Just listen for one fucking second, okay?" I growled, leaning closer. "I'm trying to keep her from getting into trouble. Just let me take the blame and get her out of here."

Lucy's garbled protest was lost to my hand while Ronan reeled back, frowning and blinking at me. His attention seemed to settle on my palm over his sister's mouth, touching her with obvious familiarity.

"And why would you do that?" he demanded on a harsh whisper, after adequately recovering from my words and the blatant truth of what he was seeing. He might have been a bullheaded oaf, but he was a perceptive bullheaded oaf. Something in his gaze told me he was quickly adding things up, painting a picture, and coming to some kind of conclusion.

Lucy squeaked and tensed.

Ignoring her, I stared at him, flexing my jaw, undecided as to what course to take.

The moment of truth.

Would Ronan ever accept me for his sister? Probably not.

Would Lucy ever choose me over her brother? Most assuredly no.

Therefore, what did I have to lose?

Nothing . . .

Everything.

I'd already lost Lucy. She'd already made her decision by leaving my room. But the lovesick fool in me couldn't bear to see her unhappy. Telling her brother about us, tearing apart her world, wasn't my decision to make.

I swallowed the sentiment that, likely due to self-preservation, hadn't quite formed in my mind.

Instead, I answered unsteadily, "To have one over on you. Why else?"

Ronan lifted a disbelieving eyebrow, his eyes moving between mine, searching. Then his gaze dropped to that of his sister's. To my surprise, something like shrewd understanding knitted his eyebrows. And the longer he studied Lucy the more incredulous his gaze grew, as though he were reaching into her mind and forcefully extracting the truth.

"Well fuck me," he breathed, blinking once at his sister. Ronan lifted his glare to mine again, his expression one of both anger and shock. "You're in love with him."

***

I WASN'T ARRESTED.

Nor was Lucy.

The hotel manager arrived to intercept the Garda and reprimand the clerk.

I didn't feel sorry for the man. He was old enough to know better. The world revolves around money and power and those who wield both. He'd been a fool to press the issue.

Ronan did most of the talking and the team stuck around to sign autographs for the cops, myself included. Though I couldn't escape Ronan's seething glares. In fact, I welcomed them.

With all his ire focused on me, perhaps he'd take things easy on Lucy.

Meanwhile, after I helped her collect the contents of her bag, Lucy had been unceremoniously ushered upstairs by Bryan Leech and William Moore, the Oklahoman. She'd been quiet in her wretchedness, and it was clear she was tearing herself apart, guilt warring with shame.

The shame felt like a sucker punch in my stomach. But I was a big boy. I'd persevere. In fact, as I stood next to Ronan, signing autographs for both the Garda and the hotel guests, an unfurling rage took hold.

Lucy had a problem. Not a little problem. A big problem.

And what had her brother done? Carted her off, sent her to New York as though she were an embarrassment. No wonder she'd developed an insatiable penchant for fancy golf balls, and eyeshadow, and whatever else.

Ronan sent me a dirty look that promised a world of hurt, and I volleyed one right back at him. I itched to get my hands on the bastard. The last time we'd fought, I'd pulled my punches, as pummeling him had been counterproductive to my goal of seeing him expelled from the team for misconduct.

But this time . . .

He clapped a hand on my shoulder, murder in his eyes, and flexed his beefy fingers into the joint. "Time for us to have a chat, arsehole."

I shook him off and gestured to the door leading outside. "Ladies first."

He smirked humorlessly, shaking his head, but preceded me out the door. I strolled behind him at a safe distance. I had no plans to attack him from behind. As well, our teammates had fallen in line behind me. Even if I wanted to tackle him, I had nine of his biggest fans watching my every move.

Once outside, he paused until I drew even with him, then we walked side by side down the lawn, toward the fountain at the center of the drive.

He spoke first. "Explain to me how this happened."

I chuckled grimly. "I don't owe you shite, Fitzpatrick."

He continued as though I hadn't spoken. "First Brona. Now Lucy? Is my mam next?"

I shuddered inwardly, grimacing, but catching the insult about his mother just before it left my tongue.

"Are you going to mess around with all the women in my life? I'd just like to know what to expect." His tone was deceptively light. I knew once we reached the grounds beyond the fountain, where the light tapered to darkness, he would make his move.

"For the record, I never fucked Brona." I stuffed my hands in my shorts pockets as I taunted him with a forced air of boredom. I couldn't wait to drive my fists into his pretty face.

"That's bullshit."

"Nope. I never touched her beyond what was required to color your perception of the situation. You did all the heavy lifting with that one, Mother Fitzpatrick."

Ronan's steps slowed and he was quiet for several beats. "You never fucked Brona?"

"I did not."

"And did you . . ." He cleared his throat and I turned my head to watch his profile. His throat worked and I saw true anguish pass over his features.

Clearing his throat a second time, he called to the guys behind us. "Back off, would you?"

They stopped at his command and we continued toward the fountain.

"What about Lucy?" he finally managed gruffly once we'd gained some distance from the others.

I frowned at him.

I noted he couldn't bring himself to ask, *Did you fuck Lucy?*

Furthermore, some of the air left my balloon of fury at the hint of vulnerability coloring his words.

I sighed, shaking my head and looking away. "I wouldn't call it that."

"What would you call it?"

"None of your goddamn business."

Ronan choked a harsh laugh, his tone incredulous. "None of my business?"

"That's right. What goes on between me and Lucy—"

He jerked to a stop, grabbing my shirtfront. "Don't you fecking say her name."

I pushed him off, aware of the others hovering several yards away. My earlier anger had been eclipsed by a remarkable exhaustion. Maybe since the first time I'd laid eyes on the man, I didn't want to fight Ronan.

"What happens with us is between us."

"Like hell it is," he charged at me, "not when you're trying to—"

"I love her," I admitted, to him and to myself.

He stopped, brown eyes flashing dangerously. "That's bullshit."

I laughed—again humorlessly—shaking my head at the irony of his statement. "That's what she said when I told her I wanted her to be mine. When she rejected me."

Why I was opening that wound in front of Ronan Fitzpatrick, I had no idea. Perhaps that was what people in love do. They become morose Byron-esque caricatures of self-loathing. They become masochists.

Fuck, I hated myself.

Ugh.

I was quite suddenly everything I couldn't stand about the man in front of me.

And furthermore, I couldn't bring myself to care.

"She rejected you?"

That stopped him, and he stood a little straighter, his expression telling me he was proud of his sister. Obviously, he'd misinterpreted my meaning. He likely thought she'd rejected my untoward sexual advances. Little did he know . . .

I thought about correcting his assumption but decided to let him swim around in his dream world. As I'd said, it wasn't any of his business.

Now to the other matter.

"What I want to know," I started, waiting until he met my glare before continuing, "is why, if you knew Lucy had a thieving problem, did you never insist she seek psychological help?"

Ronan flinched. Clearly my words had caught him completely off guard. He opened his mouth to respond. I cut him off, renewed irritation flaring at his apathy and inaction.

"She needs help, Ronan. She's not something to be ashamed of, sent away."

He sputtered for a moment before lamely explaining, "I didn't send her away. I thought that it had stopped— I thought she wasn't—"

"Well, clearly tonight's events prove that you're wrong," I reprimanded. "And this isn't the first time I've come across her flexing this compulsion. Your mother is obviously a bad influence, so I blame her. You know Lucy doesn't steal unless that blasted woman is around, driving her to do it."

Ronan continued looking at me as though I'd grown a rugby ball for a head until I glowered at him and added, "And I blame you, too."

"You blame me?" he asked stupidly, eyes wide.

"Yes. You're her brother. You should be watching out for her, not ignoring her cries for help."

"Her cries for help?" he parroted, looking even more stunned.

"Yes," I ground out through clenched teeth, losing my patience. A growl rumbled from my chest. "Oh, for Christ's sake, Ronan. Could you spare a moment in your self-absorbed little bubble to think of your lovely sister? She's . . . magnificent and wonderful and selfless and needs you. And where are you?"

"Where am I?" That question he asked with a slight grin.

It infuriated me.

"I don't know. But you're not taking care of her, are you?" I challenged, daring him to contradict.

He studied me, his gaze coolly assessing. It took me several moments to see through my own irritation before I realized he was no longer angry. Or, at least, he didn't appear to be.

"Hmm."

Then he nodded, turned, and walked away.

And I watched him go, a frown of stunned confusion on my face. Finally finding my voice, I called after him, "Where are you going?"

"To talk to Lucy," he called back over his shoulder, almost cheerfully. Then added, "And, for Christ's sake, Sean. Go put some socks on. You can't run in bare feet."

# Chapter Twenty

@**LucyFitz** Up, down, up, down… I AM SO READY FOR SOME
CALM F%$&ING WATERS!

### *Lucy*

AFTER BRYAN AND William escorted me to the suite, I found
Annie and Broderick sharing a late night cup of cocoa in the lounge area.
Honestly, I would've found the sight adorable if I hadn't been so
distressed. Annie saw the look on my face and quickly stood, coming to
wrap her arms around me.

"What happened?" she asked with concern.

I bit my bottom lip to keep from crying and shook my head. "I'm the
worst sister in the world."

Annie placed her hands on my arms just above the elbows and gave
me a reassuring squeeze. "Surely, whatever it is, it can't be that bad."

My non-response was a tangle of self-recrimination. "Annie, your
wedding is tomorrow. Yours and Ronan's. And I'm a selfish harpy. What
the hell is wrong with me?"

"Lucy, calm down. Just tell us what happened."

My panicked eyes met Broderick's over her shoulder and he gave
me a flat, mollifying smile. "Did the shit hit the fan?"

I nodded, covering my face with my hands. "Why am I this way?

Why can't I just be normal?"

"No one wants you normal." Annie wrapped her arm around my shoulders.

"But you and Ronan—"

"We're not talking about Ronan and me. We're talking about you."

"So Ronan found out? How did he take it?" Broderick cut in, sounding sympathetic. I didn't deserve sympathy.

"Okay, someone fill me in here." Annie tugged my hands away from my face. "What is going on?"

"I have . . ." I started, stopped, took a deep breath, and started again. "I have a problem, Annie. I've been keeping a secret."

"Secret? Don't you mean *secrets*?" How Broderick managed to say that and still sound sympathetic was beyond me. He was a Jedi master of being likable.

"Broderick . . ."

"Someone fill me in before I explode with curiosity. What could possibly have you this upset?" Annie lifted her voice, glancing between the two of us.

I opened my mouth to confess, but Broderick beat me to it. "Lucy is a compulsive shoplifter and she slept with Sean Cassidy."

Annie gasped.

I glowered.

Broderick shrugged.

"You were beating around the bush. Now it's out there and you didn't have to say it. You're welcome."

"Is this true?" Annie asked, her eyes wide with concern.

Concern.

Not judgment.

I sighed dejectedly and flung myself into one of the suite's club chairs, again burying my face in my hands. "I just tried to steal two hundred euros of golf balls."

"Holy shit. That's a lot of golf balls." Broderick gave a low whistle.

Now I was crying. Not big, gusty sobs crying. Just quiet, *I-am-the-worst-person-in-the-world-lament* crying. "It's not really. It's only about twelve balls. They're just really expensive here."

"Okay, wait." Annie pulled her chair close to mine and gently pulled my hands from my face. She gave me a coaxing smile. "Start from the beginning."

I gave her a shaky nod then proceeded to spill my guts. I told both her and Broderick everything, the entire saga of Sean Cassidy and Lucy Fitzpatrick, sans the Sean being rubbish in the sack part.

They listened, and Annie wore a thoughtful expression completely free of judgment. It was a world away from how Ronan had stared at me with stunned disbelief, as he somehow came to the conclusion I was in love with Sean.

Was I in love with him?

I rubbed at my chest, where a swelling ache had lingered ever since I left that note for him to find. How could I end things when all I wanted to do was curl myself around him and never let go?

Trying to ignore these perturbing thoughts, I turned back to Annie. "I'm so sorry I made a scene on the eve of your wedding."

She waved away my apology. "Please. I don't care about that. I care about you."

"I have no idea what to do." I shook my head, new tears leaking from the corners of my eyes.

She pursed her lips, opened her mouth, closed it, then opened it again. "Well, I think you should be with Sean, Lucy."

I opened my mouth to object and she lifted a hand to stop me.

"I understand your reservations. You're going to have a hell of a time talking Ronan around. He almost burst a blood vessel when I told him I'd invited Sean to the wedding. But, honey, it's your life. Not Ronan's. You need to live it and stop worrying so much about what he— or your mother for that matter—thinks about your decisions. You have to trust that Ronan is going to love you no matter what."

Her response both gave me hope and deflated me. I was happy she thought I should be with him, but depressed she'd echoed my worries over Ronan.

Annie opened her mouth to speak again when an insistent knock sounded at the door. "Lucy, open up," came Ronan's stern voice. Annie froze in place.

"The wedding's tomorrow. You can't see me, go away," she called to him, frazzled.

Ronan's tone softened a little. "I'm sorry, love. Could you go into the other room for a little while? I need to talk to my sister."

Annie glanced at me in question but I fervently shook my head, sniffing and wiping my nose with the back of my hand. I needed a tissue and a hiding place.

"You're going to have to talk to him eventually," she whispered, and I grimaced.

"She's right. Go talk to your bro," Rick added, whispering too.

"What are you all whispering about in there? I can hear whispering," Ronan grumped.

I sighed and said, "Fine, I'll talk to him. Now you and Rick go hide in the other room."

They each gave me sympathetic looks before walking through the doorway leading to one of the bedrooms. Once the door was shut, I released a shaky exhale and went to let my brother in. Ronan strode inside with purpose, a foreign restlessness about him as if he didn't know where to begin.

He shot me a deeply concerned look as he paced.

Unable to take his anxious silence, I blurted, "I'm so sorry."

He stopped pacing, his eyes narrowed on me as he questioned, "For what?"

I gathered another large inhale and responded on a rush, "I am so sorry for causing the scene downstairs. It's your wedding tomorrow and I know that was selfish and destructive. I promise, I was so much better. I hadn't stolen anything in almost six months before the summer. But then I—"

Ronan waved his hands through the air and spoke over me. "Lucy, you have a compulsion. I'm not saying stealing is fine and dandy. I'm saying it's a problem and it needs to be fixed. Once and for all."

I nodded contritely and repeated, "I'm so sorry."

My brother's eyes softened and he gave me a small smile. "Stop being sorry. You're not a bad person. I'm just worried about you."

I nodded, pressing my lips together and firming my chin to keep it from wobbling. We stood apart from each other, my big brother—my hero—and me.

The disappointment.

The embarrassment.

I was so tired of being the embarrassment.

*Speaking of . . .*

"Is Sean okay?" I asked hesitantly.

Ronan let out a mirthless laugh, his gaze losing some of its softness as he began pacing again. "Yes, he's fine."

"He wasn't arrested?"

"No."

"Oh, good. That's good," I said, relief setting in. I'd been so worried.

On one hand, I was amazed by the way he'd stepped in and tried to divert the blame away from me. On the other hand, I was irritated with how he'd stepped in and diverted the blame away from me.

I'd stolen the overpriced balls. The blame rested on my shoulders. I needed to take responsibility for my actions. So, yes, I was glad he hadn't been arrested for my fecking everything up.

When Ronan finally stopped stomping around like an angry bull, he asked, "Start from the beginning, tell me how all this . . . business between you and Cassidy . . . Tell me how it came about."

I shrugged, unable to maintain eye contact for very long. My attention kept flittering about the room like a manic wasp.

"I'm waiting, Lucy," Ronan lifted his voice.

I wiped at my eyes, glancing at the carpet. "We first met at a party for the rugby team. I thought he was awful," I told him honestly.

"Right. So how do you go from thinking he's awful to looking at him with big googly eyes?" he asked with a wild hand gesture.

I scowled a little. "I don't look at him with googly eyes. I look at him with normal eyes."

Ronan gave me an arched brow and that big-brother stare that said I was stalling. I sighed and shifted in place.

"Fine. I guess it started properly when we bumped into each other in town one day. He asked me to dinner. I thought he was taking the piss.

He wasn't. I said yes. Things progressed from there."

"So this is the dinner you told me about? Why did you say yes?"

"Fine. Okay, he kind of blackmailed me into it. He saw me take some eyeshadow, shoplift, and used it as leverage. But, honestly? I would have gone either way."

Ronan's eyes widened as though I'd just told him Santa Claus and Genghis Khan had been having a torrid love affair since the twelfth century.

"Oh God, Ronan, come on." I rolled my eyes, feeling marginally better now we were engaging in normal brother and sister bickering. "Even you must see how gorgeous he is. It was going out to dinner once. At least, that's what I thought. And then he said something rude and I threw my drink in his face and left."

This news seemed to settle him somewhat.

"Good." He nodded once. "That's good. So how do you go from throwing your drink in his face to googly eyes?"

I released a giant exhale and sat heavily on the couch, studying my fingers as I answered. "It's complicated. I knew going out with him was wrong and that it would anger you. I told him we could be friends and nothing more. He never told anyone about my shoplifting problem. And at first I thought he and I *were* friends, or becoming friends. I was doing him a favor, helping him out. But we just have this thing between us that's hard to ignore. A draw."

"You were *drawn* to him?"

"Yes," I answered simply. "Didn't you feel the same way when you first met Annie? Like even though you knew pursuing her was going to be whole lot of trouble you could do without, you couldn't help doing it anyway?"

Now he only looked at me, his expression inscrutable. He folded his arms, and his lips pulled into a firm line as he admitted grudgingly, "I might have."

A few moments of silence elapsed before Ronan spoke again. "The thing you have to understand here, Lucy, is that Annie and Sean are two very different people. Annie is lovely and fundamentally kind. Whereas Sean is a selfish, spoiled brat. Sure, he might toy with the idea of caring for your safety, but when it comes down to it, the thrill of a new relationship is going to fade and he's going to realize how much hard work it is. I don't want to see you invest in a man who's going to flake out on you in the long run."

"You know he never actually slept with Brona, right?"

Ronan exhaled heavily. "He said something to that effect downstairs, yes."

"So you should also know he's not the spoiled brat he likes to lead everybody to believe. It's like a defense mechanism. If he pushes people away from the start, he doesn't have to worry about being rejected later."

Ronan was already shaking his head before I'd finished. "Luce, even if that's true, don't you think it's a little fucked up? Yeah, he might have never slept with Brona, but he still fabricated a relationship with her. That isn't the behavior of a well-adjusted individual."

"Listen, I'm not defending Sean or what he did to you, I'm just trying to explain a person who is a lot more complicated than one action. He is more than a spoiled brat." I stood from the couch, no longer in danger of crying, feeling the rightness of my words as I said them. "If someone looked at me tonight, the mess I made downstairs, stealing fecking golf balls of all things, they might call me a spoiled brat and leave it at that. Yes, I'm messed up. What I did was messed up. But I'd like to think I'm not defined by—"

"No, Luce. That argument doesn't work because you have a compulsive problem. You don't steal because you want revenge on the K Club Golf Shop. Sean Cassidy does shite to be a mean arsehole. That's the difference."

"But don't you see? Pushing people away is Sean's compulsion. He's been rejected his whole life. He did what he did to you because he's jealous. He thinks you have everything handed to you on a silver platter and everybody loves you without question. It's basic juvenile jealousy, Ronan. And I bet if you'd been friendly to him from the first time you met, things would've been a whole lot different."

Ronan lifted his voice with frustration. "I wasn't unfriendly to him. I barely even spoke to him."

I gesticulated with my hands. "Exactly. Don't you see? You ignored him, so he built this ridiculous, nonsensical jealousy thing. For God's sake, you big burly men are all little boys when it comes down to it."

"I'm not a little boy."

"In regards to Sean you are. You both need to let this absurd feud go already. Sure, I'll be the first person to admit he's not perfect, that he has issues he needs to work on, but so do I, and so do you, Ronan."

"You're comparing me to Sean Cassidy?"

I ignored this outraged question and pressed on. "We all have issues. Human beings are flawed, and all we can hope for is to work toward making ourselves better. Not perfect, just better."

Ronan began pacing again, his hands on his hips, his jaw set. "Bloody hell," he growled, then a full minute later, "I hate how you make so much sense sometimes."

I gave him a small smile, realizing the admission cost him

something.

"You'd make sense too if you just took a second and thought things through before barging in full steam ahead and throwing all your toys out of the pram."

My brother narrowed his gaze at my phrasing but didn't deny it. "I still think it's going to end badly. Can't you just stop this thing before it goes any further? You think you love him but how can you? It's not possible."

I bristled as I shot back defensively. "I never said I loved him."

"You forget I've spent a lifetime learning your ticks, Lucy. I saw you with him downstairs. I saw it written all over your face, but it's just lust. I'm sure it's the same on his end. He thinks he's in love with you, too."

It took me a good twenty seconds to recover from Ronan's statement before I managed, "He told you that?" The question was a weak whisper, my heart clenching. I wasn't sure why, but the idea of Sean confessing his love for me to my brother, the one person who might beat the living shit out of him for it, made me feel all warm and mushy inside.

Ronan huffed. "Yes, he did."

I let that sink in for a moment, savoring the loveliness of it all before I circled back to the other thing he'd said. "Why do you think it's so impossible for us to be in love?"

"Isn't it obvious? You haven't even slept together yet. For all you know, he could be terrible in bed."

At this I burst out laughing, a full-on belly laugh, my hands going to my middle to hold my stomach. One, because Ronan didn't know how apt his comment was, and two, because he thought we hadn't slept together. I almost wanted to roll my eyes at how he still saw me as his chaste, quirky little sister.

"What are you laughing at?"

"Who gave you the idea we hadn't slept together?"

Ronan's distinctive eyebrows drew closer and closer until they formed one dark line of disapproval. "Sean told me downstairs."

I found that hard to believe. "He actually said it, word for word? *Lucy and I haven't slept together?*"

Ronan frowned so hard I thought his face was going to break. "Well, maybe not word for word. He said you rejected him, I thought . . ." Now his expression turned to disbelief, then to anger, then to brotherly disappointment. I felt it cut through me like a knife.

"I did reject him," I said softly. "I rejected him quite a few times . . . until I didn't anymore."

Now he stared at me like I was a stranger, and that hurt most of all. He raked his hands through his hair and swore. "Fuck."

But Annie was right.

Her words from earlier came back to me. I needed to be living my own life. Ronan might not like my choices, but that was okay.

"Ronan," I continued, my voice still soft. "I never did any of it to hurt you. You of all people should know we can't control how our feelings develop, how sometimes they latch on to the least likely and most inconvenient person. I love you. I would never intentionally disrespect you. I didn't set out to be anything more than Sean's friend. You're my hero, and you always have been. I've looked up to you since I was little, thought the sun rose and set on your shoulders, and I still do. But at some point, and quite against my will, I fell for Sean Cassidy."

I shrugged, because I felt a little helpless. I had no control over whether or not Ronan ultimately forgave Sean. But then, Ronan had no control over the depth of my feelings for Sean, either.

"If you couldn't accept Sean and me, it'd break my heart. But I would understand. I will love you, no matter what you decide."

At that moment, I realized just how much bullshit that note I'd left Sean had been. I didn't want to stop being with him. I'd read enough books about happiness and self-fulfillment to know that denying yourself the very thing that brings you joy will only create a hole inside you. And that hole will fester until it becomes black and toxic.

The more I thought of Sean, the more a new, unexplored feeling began to suffuse my chest. I couldn't believe how differently I felt for him now, as compared to how I'd felt about him when we first met. And if he hadn't been there in that shop tonight, if he hadn't been there to step in and sacrifice himself for me, I would've been arrested. I would've spent the night before my brother's wedding in a jail cell.

I would have deserved it.

But Annie and Ronan didn't deserve such a scene, nor me being an embarrassment on the eve of their wedding. For that I was truly sorry and I was determined to make it up to them, just not in a way that was unhealthy or had me sacrificing happiness for my brother's peace of mind.

It was also ironic. I'd thought my secret relationship with Sean would ruin Ronan's wedding, when in reality it had been the thing to save it. Sean tried his hardest to act like he was a vacuous, careless snob, but deep down he was so good. And I loved him.

I loved him so much it terrified me.

I loved that he'd been terrible in bed. I loved that he hadn't wanted to be terrible in bed. I loved that I'd had to teach him how to make me come. I loved that he was vain and materialistic. I loved that he loved dogs. I loved that he stole things from random women's bathroom cabinets, and that he was completely out of touch with reality. I loved how he told me my style was awful even though I knew he secretly adored it. I loved how much he enjoyed giving me pleasure even more than he enjoyed his own. And I loved that he wanted to protect me so much he'd risk being arrested if it meant I'd get to walk free.

Ronan and I had been quiet for so long that a small knock came from the room where Annie and Broderick had shut themselves away. My friend poked his head out.

"You two all right?" Rick asked, stepping into the lounge and glancing carefully between Ronan and me. Annie remained hidden in the bedroom.

I looked at my brother. "I'm not sure."

Ronan heaved a heavy breath and laid his cards on the table. "Right, so here's how we're going to do this. I'll not . . . get in the way of you seeing Sean."

I gaped at him. "Has hell frozen over?"

He glowered. "Don't be a smart-arse and just listen. I'm not saying I'm going to give you my blessing to run off to Vegas and get hitched, but we can see where things go between you two. Baby steps. But before I start playing nice with Sean, and you're not going to like this part, Luce, I need you to start seeing a therapist."

Again, it took me at least ten full seconds to process his words, and when I did they left me completely confused. "But Mam said it was embarrassing and could hurt your career, me seeing a—"

"I don't care what Mam says. Let me deal with her. In fact, I'm going to make her go with you. You steal when you're anxious, and our mother is a major source of anxiety in your life. And she is your mother,

Lucy, the only one you're ever going to have. So even though it might be easier to stick your head in the sand, you can't just cut her out. You both need to deal with the issues between you if you're ever going to get better."

"But I live in New York. How are we going to have therapy sessions if we're living in two different countries?"

"You can do it over Skype. Or I'll even fly her over once a fortnight if need be. Either way, we're doing this. I'll try to get over my issues with Cassidy, but you have to work towards getting over your issues, too."

I stared at him as I chewed on my lip, flabbergasted he was considering mending his bridges with Sean, even if there was a catch. I'd been all but ready to never see Mam again after my outburst in the sauna, but I knew that wasn't fair. Ronan was right. She was the only mother I would ever have, and we needed to sort our shit out. If she was prepared to accept me as I was, then I was prepared to accept her as she was . . . even if she made me want to tear my own hair out sometimes.

"Okay, I'll do it," I told him as I shakily held out my hand.

He took it and we shook before Ronan pulled me into a massive bear hug, knocking the wind right out of me. I felt him hold me tight as he said with regret, "I'm sorry if I haven't been there for you lately. It won't happen again. And I'm sorry if I've been a brute. I just want you to be happy and safe. That's all I've ever wanted."

I didn't say anything, just accepted the hug and the warm feeling of brotherly comfort. We only broke apart when Broderick said, "Aw, aren't you two just adorable?"

I scowled playfully at my friend, at the same time feeling like a weight had been lifted. I hadn't even realized it, but for a long time it had been hard to breathe. This heart-to-heart with Ronan had injected air back into my lungs.

He was watching me then, smiling and shaking his head. "Sean bloody Cassidy. You couldn't have chosen an unlikelier candidate if you'd come home and told me you were in love with Donald Trump."

I laughed loudly as Broderick shuddered.

"I'm sorry," said Ronan, laughing softly as he cast his eyes in the direction of the bedroom where Annie was hiding. With a deep exhale, he walked to the door, knocked lightly and called in a gentle voice, "Sleep well, Annie dearest, because tomorrow I'm going to marry you."

I could tell she was smiling when she responded in the tiniest voice, her face probably pressed to the door. "I love you, Ronan."

He placed his palm against the wood. "I love you, too."

And then, after bidding Broderick and me good night, he left.

I swear my heart glittered inside my chest at their tenderly whispered words. My brother could be a bullheaded oaf at times, but other times I thought he just might be the most romantic man in the world.

# Chapter Twenty-One

**@LucyFitz** Judge Judy's hair is the same color as her face is the same color as her table is the same color as her chair #randomthoughts

**@BroderickAdams to @LucyFitz** Hey, that rhymed :-)

**@RonanFitz to @LucyFitz** Do I need to repeat myself re: the acid tabs?

### *Lucy*

**I TRIED TO** track down Sean, to clear the air, to apologize, to throw myself at him, but he'd disappeared. Or—and perhaps more likely—he didn't want to speak to me.

My phone was shattered, so I tried using Broderick's to send him a text message. He didn't respond.

I stopped by his room and loitered outside for twenty or so minutes, finally slipping a note under his door.

*Sean,*

*I'm so sorry, about everything. My phone is wrecked, so you can reach me by dialing Broderick. We need to talk. I'm sorry.*

*-Lucy*

*PS I'm so sorry.*

I think I finally lay down around 2:30 a.m., a chaotic bundle of nerves, and fell asleep closer to 4:00 a.m. When I woke the next morning, the suite was a riot of activity.

Out in the lounge, Annie and the other bridesmaids were having their hair and makeup done. She'd been entirely too nice and hadn't woken me up. Having overslept, I was running late, and had just enough time to grab a shower before it was my turn with the hairdresser.

Broderick, the lucky bastard, was already suited, booted, and ready to rock. It really was annoying how much easier men had it on occasions like these. A shower and a shave and they were done.

It was as the hairdresser was almost done with me that my nerves from the night before started to settle in. I told myself to stop thinking about Sean, to just enjoy my brother's big day without any additional drama. I owed it to Ronan and Annie. Today was their day.

After the ceremony and reception, Sean and I could talk. Kiss. Make up. Shag each other's brains out for days on end. The usual.

Unfortunately, that things had been silent on his end worried me. I hadn't received a single phone call or text, and I didn't know what it meant. Did he get my messages? Or did he just not care? Was he still mad at me for the note? Or was he simply giving me space to work things out with Ronan?

When Annie came out in her dress, I momentarily forgot my worries about Sean, because I was suddenly welling up. She looked beautiful. Stunning. Like a flipping fairy princess. I sniffled and tried my hardest not to cry so I wouldn't ruin my makeup. Her white dress had short lace sleeves, a sweetheart neckline, and a floor-length skirt that flowed gorgeously over her curvy hips. Her hair was in an elegant updo, with lots of intricate twists and curls.

The bridesmaids all wore calf-length, champagne-colored dresses, with lacy sleeves and matching champagne heels. Our hair was styled into sophisticated, loosely-curled chignons. I couldn't remember the last time I'd looked so hot.

Mam sat in a corner seat, all dolled up in her pale-blue tulip dress. I could tell from the look she was giving me that my hair was bothering her, mainly because it was so mismatched against the blondes and browns of the other bridesmaids.

Remembering my promise to Ronan last night, I sucked it up and prepared to ignore her disapproval until we could have a serious talk. I knew I needed therapy, but I thought maybe my mother needed it even more than I did.

Somebody handed me a mimosa, and before I knew it we were heading downstairs for the ceremony. Since Annie's parents were deceased, Broderick was going to give her away. As usual, he didn't seem at all nervous, and in typical Rick style, took on the role with effortless confidence. Annie, on the other hand, looked a little bit peaky.

I was supposed to be heading up the bridesmaids, but instead I ran quickly back to her, took her clammy hands in mine and told her earnestly, "Ronan is the luckiest man alive to be marrying you. And I'm the luckiest girl to be gaining you as a sister. Don't be nervous. You're going to rock this."

She swallowed and looked up at me with wide brown eyes. "Thank you. I needed to hear that. There are going to be so many people down there. It's a little scary."

"Just do what I do," I told her with a grin.

"What?" she asked. "Imagine them all naked?"

"Nah. Too obvious. Imagine they're all naked Henry Cavills. You'll be smiling in no time."

She laughed, her anxiety melting away.

With that I hurried back out. The function room had been decked out in cream ribbons and pretty flower arrangements. It was the epitome of bridal. Tom, acting as Ronan's best man, took my arm to walk down the aisle. As we approached the front, I cast my gaze over the attendees, only spotting Sean when I'd almost reached the top. He sat next to a pretty, willowy redhead. This must have been his younger cousin, Eilish, the one he thought of as a little sister.

I caught his eye but he wore no expression. Despite my best intentions to focus on Ronan and Annie, my heart caught in my throat. I couldn't tell what he was thinking. Goosebumps broke out on my skin as I shot him an unsure smile. His non-expression didn't change. He looked away. I almost got the impression he was embarrassed and my heart took a nosedive to my fancy shoes.

When we reached Ronan I rallied, wanting to be there for my brother. Tom slipped his arm from mine and I went to stand in the section reserved for the bridesmaids. I noticed my brother fidgeting with his cufflinks, so I smiled warmly and gave him a look that said, *relax*.

Jeez, he and Annie were as bad as each other today. Then again, it was their wedding. I couldn't really blame them.

To a string quartet playing at the back of the hall, Annie finally walked down the aisle. Ronan's eyes almost popped out of his head. He stared at her like he wanted to devour her right there in front of all the guests. It was just too funny.

When the ceremony began, I kind of lost focus, my attention wandering back to Sean to find he was already staring at me. Every small hair on my body stood on end as my heart began to pound.

*I love you*, I wanted to say.

*I'm sorry for leaving you last night. It was stupid and idiotic and I wish I could take it back.*

I tried to convey all this with my eyes, but I wasn't sure it was doing the job. In fact, I was certain it wasn't when Sean suddenly looked away, a muscle in his jaw ticking. By the time I brought my attention back to the ceremony it was almost over, and I tried to focus on my brother and Annie for the next few minutes.

They were announced man and wife. They were kissing. Everybody was oohing and aaahing at the loveliness of it all, while I was swept up in a sea of uncertainty.

It felt like Sean was pissed at me.

Was he pissed at me?

I would be pissed at me.

After everything that went down yesterday, it made sense. I suddenly felt sweaty in my dress, as Tom took my arm again and led me outside for pictures. But I pushed thoughts of him from my mind and tried to live in the moment, smiling widely and with feeling.

Basically, my emotions were all over the map. So I allowed myself to float through the wedding pictures, smile and nod during the reception line, make chit-chat with Ronan's childhood friends and all guests associated with the rugby team. It was surprisingly easy to pretend. And pretending to be happy began to feel like reality every time I caught a glimpse of Ronan and Annie.

They were too cute. Seeing them so much in love, blissful even, was enough to make me swallow back tears of joy.

I didn't see Sean until the reception dinner, which was held in a hall almost as fancy as where the wedding had been.

I was seated with the wedding party at a long table at the head of the room that faced the other guests. It felt a little like a feast from olden times, where the royals would sit and eat, watching the revelry of their loyal subjects beyond them in the grand hall.

I spotted Sean and his cousin at a table with a few other rugby players and their wives. I didn't know whether to approach him or just leave him be. All through dinner I glanced at him but never caught his eye.

Once the cake had been cut and passed around, I left the table, making a beeline for the bathroom. It felt like I'd been holding my pee for hours. The wedding band started to play, and lots of couples were taking to the dance floor. I saw Sean rise from his seat with Eilish. It was one of those odd timing things. I didn't know where everything stood between us and the wedding reception wasn't the place to hash it out, so I continued on my course to the ladies' room.

But just as I was passing them he called my name. "Lucy."

I turned and stared at him. He took Eilish's arm in his and led her toward me. I watched him as he approached, struck as always by his handsomeness, but also seeing something new. Something more.

Sean was a smart guy. He was wicked talented and funny and, when he wanted to be, was epically sweet. But one of the things about Sean that made him so irresistible to me was how he looked at me.

He looked at me like I was something wonderful. Not odd. Not embarrassing. It took my breath away. And that's why when he and the redhead stepped in front of me I couldn't quite speak. I was so lost in him, how he looked at me, how I saw myself reflected in his eyes.

And I hoped he saw something similar when I looked at him.

But then the redhead cleared her throat, drawing my attention to her and her warm smile.

"Hello," she said.

"Hi," I replied, still a bit dazed.

She smiled widely. "Forgive my cousin, he's usually much better with introductions. You must be Lucy?"

"Lucy, this is Eilish. Eilish, this is . . . Lucy," Sean offered belatedly, his eyes resting on me for another protracted moment and then falling away.

"So, you're Sean's well-kept secret, eh? I'm quite annoyed with him to be honest. Today's the first time I've heard anything about you."

I laughed softly and gave her a wink. "Don't be put out. Your cousin and I are experts at keeping secrets. It's lovely to meet you."

"You, too," said Eilish, her attention on my chignon. "Sorry. I think I'm obsessed with your hair. It's kind of amazing."

I grinned. "Thanks."

"It is rather," Sean murmured his agreement.

A moment of silence passed between us. I was taken aback by the warmth in his eyes. During the ceremony he'd seemed aloof. Now his gaze, though still guarded, wandered over me like I was a dish he was eager to taste.

"You look very pretty," he added, his voice low and gravelly.

Eilish laughed and nudged him with her elbow. "Oh, come on, Sean. You can do better than that. She looks beautiful. Tell her she's beautiful."

Sean gave his cousin an indulgent smile before he looked deeply into my eyes. "You're beautiful, Lucy."

I trembled, trapped in his gaze until Bryan Leech's voice broke me from my reverie.

"How's it going, Cassidy? Has Fitzpatrick cut your balls off yet for sleeping with his little sister?"

Sean glared at him. I turned around, raising my eyebrow at his audacity, and Bryan suddenly became aware of my presence.

"Ooops, sorry, Lucy." He sound both contrite and drunk. "My mouth gets the better of me when I've had a few. You know how it is."

I shook my head at him and laughed it off. "Indeed I do."

Bryan's attention went to Eilish, his eyes fixating on her bare shoulders, where her dress draped seductively over her flawless pale skin. "Hello," he said, voice deep. "And you are?"

"I'm Eilish Cassidy," she replied with a smile, her tone polished yet friendly, completely unaware of Bryan's heated appraisal. "And you're Bryan Leech. Sean's my cousin. I grew up following the game, so I know all the players' names by heart."

"Do you now," said Bryan with intrigue, but it wasn't a question. "What else do you know by heart?"

Sean suddenly closed his arm around Eilish's shoulders to lead her away. "And that's our cue to leave," he said, shooting Bryan a look that could kill.

I pressed my lips together to keep from laughing just as Sean moved his gaze to me. He narrowed his eyes in mock disapproval, making my heart skip a few beats. Because if he was teasing me then he probably wasn't angry. Right?

Right?

RIGHT?!

. . . I hoped so.

I watched the two of them mingle into the crowd while I stood next to Bryan. Meanwhile, Bryan had completely missed Sean's stare of dismemberment and watched the young Ms. Cassidy with unveiled lust.

"Don't even think about it. Ronan might not have cut Sean's balls off for being with me, but I can tell you with absolute certainty that Sean will cut off yours if you so much as lay a hand on Eilish. He thinks of her as a little sister."

Bryan shot me a wry look and grinned mischievously. "You should stop talking now. You're only making the challenge more appealing." He paused and let his eyes wander to Eilish again. "Forbidden fruits are always the sweetest."

I patted him on the back before heading to the bathroom. "It's your funeral, buddy."

I speed-walked the distance because I now suffered from a bladder emergency. But I didn't care. Sean had approached me. He hadn't seemed at all upset, and had introduced me to his beloved cousin. Things were definitely looking up.

Well, they were looking up until I left the toilet. The first person I saw when I returned was my mother. The relief I felt was quickly squashed when she linked her arm through mine, hijacked my trajectory toward Sean and Eilish, and began determinedly leading me to a table of well-dressed men.

"Let's go talk to these gentlemen, Lucy," she said. "I have it on good authority that they're all single."

"I'm really not in the mood, Mam."

"Oh hush. You're never in the mood. An eligible bachelor isn't simply going to fall into your lap, you know. You have to work hard for one."

"I see. Shall I deck myself out in figure-hugging minidresses and trawl all those fancy bars in town where businessmen go after work in the hopes of securing a wealthy husband?"

Mam pulled her arm from mine, upset now. "Why do you always have to talk to me like I'm stupid? I'm not stupid, Lucy. I just want you to be happy."

"I am happy."

"Happy and settled. I want to know you've found a man who will keep you safe."

"I don't need a man to keep me safe. And anyway, how do you know I'm not already seeing anyone?"

Her eyes lit up, her hurt feelings instantly forgotten. "*Are* you seeing someone? Is it Broderick? He's quite the dish."

"I know exactly how much of a dish you think Broderick is, Mam. You proved that by flirting with him all through Annie's hen party."

"Just because I'm old doesn't mean I'm dead. I like to flirt. So sue me."

"Yes, I know that. And you can flirt with whoever you want, just not my best friend."

"So you are seeing him?" Mam asked hopefully.

"Pardon me," a deep male voice interrupted as a warm arm wrapped around my middle, drawing me completely away from my mother. "With your permission, Mrs. Fitzpatrick, I'd like some time with my lady before the evening ends. Excuse us."

Mam's jaw practically dropped to the floor as she stared at Sean, who was currently standing behind me, holding me to him possessively. He dipped his mouth to my neck and placed a spine-tingling kiss there. Mam didn't breathe a word, just continued looking between the two of us in disbelief, like she didn't know whether to object or jump for joy.

Sean twirled me around, and God, he looked amazing in his tux. His hair was lightly tousled and his cologne was woodsy and fresh. I wanted to sink into his embrace and just savor the feel and smell of him.

Last night felt like a lifetime ago.

The band had just started playing a cover of "Friday I'm in Love" by The Cure.

Sean stared into my eyes, his lips curving in a seductive smile as he asked, "Care to dance?"

# Chapter Twenty-Two

@**SeanCassinova** I'm in love and she is the most perfect, gorgeous creature in the universe.

@**RugbyUnLvr01 to @SeanCassinova** NOOOOOOO!!! #Devastated :-(

@**SeanCassinova to @RugbyUnLvr01** Sorry, love. #OffTheMarket But may I introduce @**THEBryanLeech**? He's single and ready to mingle ;-)

## *Sean*

PERHAPS THERE EXISTED a very small chance that I'm not always right about everything.

. . . Perhaps.

"I told you it was simple," I said.

Then again, perhaps not.

Lucy shook her head, a reluctant smile playing over her delightful lips before she shouted over the music. "There was nothing simple about the conversation I had with my brother last night."

Concern had me slowing my movements as I considered her. "Are you all right?"

She nodded, her smile enigmatic. "I'm okay."

I frowned. "What does that mean?"

Instead of answering, her eyes darted over my face. "Were punches thrown? Because you both seem to be in good health. Or are the bruises elsewhere?"

"Please." I rolled my eyes, twirling her then bringing her back into my arms. "You make it sound like we're savages."

She snorted. The sound made me laugh. I held her closer, but not as close as I wanted. It was a wedding, after all. Children were present.

Regardless, we were drawing stares. Some shocked, most disapproving. I cared nothing for others' opinions. Only Lucy's.

"I'm only savage with you," I teased, liking how her eyes sharpened. Her grin turned wicked as I said the words.

"Are you . . ." she started, then drew her bottom lip between her teeth. Still dancing, she studied me uncertainly.

"Go on."

"Are you angry with me?" she blurted at last, her expression betraying worry and guilt.

I immediately shook my head then leaned close to her ear. "No."

"But you were?" I felt her fingers grip the lapels of my jacket.

I glanced around at the other couples on the dance floor as I spoke. "I didn't see your note. It fell off the side of the bed and I didn't see it on the floor until after the unpleasantness at the shop last night. I'm afraid I wasn't looking very closely when I woke up and you weren't there. I reacted, I overreacted, and I thought you left me last night for good and I . . . I was in a rage."

"Oh, Sean. I didn't leave for good. I just needed—"

"I know." I covered her hands with mine, encouraging her to relax. "We'll talk later."

Embarrassingly, I didn't see her note because I'd immediately jumped to the worst possible conclusion. I wasn't going to admit as such out loud, but when I thought she'd left me, I'd become the ape I'd always despised in Ronan.

"I'm so sorry about the note."

"Don't be. I wish you would stop being sorry." She had nothing to be sorry for. I'd been the ape. And then I'd been unforgivably awkward, unable to return her smile at the ceremony. I was unused to losing my temper, unaccustomed to losing control.

"Sean—"

Before she could continue the thought, we were interrupted. A hand on my shoulder pulled me back and away from Lucy, not roughly. Insistently.

"Come on, Cassidy. Let's go." William Moore stood at my side; his tone wasn't aggressive, just adamant.

I lifted an eyebrow at my teammate. "Where are we going?"

He released my shoulder. "We're having a match."

"What? A rugby match?" Lucy asked, her disbelieving eyes moving between the two of us.

"That's right." William nodded and grinned at Lucy, disproportionately pleased by her question.

"What? Now?" I asked, glancing around the room and seeing that our team plus several others were removing their jackets and draping them over chairs.

"Yes. Now." William pointed to my tie. "I hope that tux isn't a rental."

"Certainly not." I nearly shuddered my revulsion. Renting a tuxedo, the very thought abhorrent.

"Good. Lucy can hold your jacket and cufflinks. You're on my team." He nodded as though everything were decided and left the dance floor, not waiting to see if I followed.

"How'd that happen?" I called after him, "Did you lose a bet?"

"Not at all. I won the coin toss and you were my first pick." William walked backward and shot me a rare grin. "Only today, you're playing hooker."

***

LUCY DID HOLD my jacket and cufflinks, as well as my belt, tie, shirt, shoes, socks, and vest. We played in pants, undershirts, and bare feet—all except for Bryan Leech as he was charged with drop-kicking the ball at the start.

The lines were estimated. Even so, Bryan's inebriated kick made it nowhere near Ronan's ten-metre line. As such, he opted for a scrum at the center of our haphazard field.

I was too big, my torso too long for a hooker, so it wasn't my strongest position. As such, we came out on the wrong side of the scrum despite having both props on our side. I grew frustrated by my inferior skill, but my rising ire was quickly assuaged by the sound of Lucy cheering for me.

I glanced over at the sideline, spotting her immediately due in large part to her rainbow hair. Other than Eilish, I'd never had anyone cheer for me specifically. It was an odd sensation, made me feel as though my performance on the field mattered more, because she was invested in my success.

With renewed determination, I ignored procedure and led the front row, Cain Masey recovering the ball from Ronan's team after an almost-friendly maul. Since the teams were comprised of several non-professionals and retired players, the general tone seemed affable.

Punches were pulled and there was plenty of encouragement all around.

And so the match progressed . . . for a time.

Until I had my first possession.

As soon as the ball was in my grasp, Ronan broke position and rushed forward. He tackled low and hard, knocking the wind from my lungs even though I'd braced for impact. I fell to the ground, mindful of my rucking position and prepared to hand the ball off despite my gasping state.

However, there's a reason ruck rhymed with fuck. Because a ruck is where you're most likely to get fucked up.

Oftentimes, especially when three gigantic rugby players are piled on top of your back, attempting to roll you over in an effort to achieve a turn over, you'd receive all manner of abuse. Punches, bites, pinches, hair pulls—all par for the course. Especially if there wasn't a referee.

Ronan was the bloke immediately on top of me. His fist connected with my eye in a purposeful movement, though he paired it with an "Oops."

Several kidney punches, elbows to the sternum and ribs, and a knee under my jaw later, the ruck was over. I'd successfully saved the ball. Bryan had scooped it up and, through my one good eye, I saw him run toward the makeshift goal with no opposition in his way. This was because, though they were supposed to be limited to three, almost every player on Ronan's team was still on top of me.

"All right, all right," William called just as I felt a second impact under my jaw. "Get off him. You've just lost a score."

"Did we?" John O'Mar's cheeky response came. "I thought Sean still had the ball."

"You did not, you great arsehole," William laughed. Ronan kneed me in my ribs as he stood, then "accidentally" trod on my hand.

"Oh fucking hell," I grumbled, holding my fingers close to my chest as I was freed from the pile.

"Oh shut it, you big baby."

I squinted through one eye and found Ronan standing over me, offering his hand, a small, satisfied smile on his face. When I didn't accept his offer at once he reached down and pulled me up.

Standing in front of him, I flexed my fingers. "Feel better?" I asked, working my jaw and finding it sore, but not broken. I'd bitten the inside of my cheek, though I couldn't tell if the blood dripping down my chin was from my nose or my mouth.

"Yes." Ronan nodded, patting me on the shoulder with a solemn kind of affection. "Ready to have another go?"

I spat blood on the ground and wiped at my nose. "Absolutely—"

"Absolutely not."

Both Ronan and I turned to find Lucy running out to the field, her expression thunderous. "What on earth do you think you're doing, Ronan? What the hell was that? He's bleeding from every orifice. Satisfied?"

Ronan shrugged, fighting a grin. "Not *every* orifice."

Lucy tut-tutted at him and punched him in the stomach. She was strong, but he was clearly prepared for her assault as it affected him not at all.

"Christ, Luce. We're rugby players. This is what we do."

"Really? Twelve men in a ruck?" Her soft hands were moving over my face with gentle, probing movements and her brow was wrinkled with concern. "Jesus, Sean. You're all busted up."

I smelled her—her perfume, her scent. There's just something about getting the shit beaten out of you that gets your blood pumping. If I could have taken her on the field right then, I would have.

I wanted to.

I grew hard at the thought, understanding why ancient marauders were exhibitionists after violent raids.

Meanwhile, Ronan crossed his arms over his chest. "He's had worse. Come on, Luce. You're holding up the match."

Lucy fitted her hand through my arm and led me away, calling over her shoulder, "Well you're just going to have to play without Sean."

"You going to do that, Cassidy? Be led away by your woman?" I heard Bryan Leech taunt from someplace behind me.

"You bet I am," I responded immediately, drawing chuckles from my teammates who'd gathered to watch the sibling standoff.

"Smart man," someone said. It sounded like Ronan, but I couldn't be sure.

I may have only had one working eye, as the other was quickly swelling shut, but I couldn't take it off Lucy.

Wherever she led, I would follow.

***

SHE BATHED ME.

It was a glorious experience, though made frustrating by her insistence I not touch her while she tended my wounds. They weren't terrible, nothing that would leave a scar. I felt entirely mobile, though my left eye was swollen shut and my ribs were sore.

Nothing a week of ice packs couldn't fix.

"Oh! Your face," she lamented, pulling a towel full of ice cubes away from my eye. She was frowning, gazing upon me with pity and concern. I rather liked it.

"Don't worry, none of it's permanent. Now my face matches your hair."

We were sitting on the bed in my suite. Rather, she was sitting next to me and I was laying down, allowing her tender ministrations mostly because I was discovering how much I enjoyed being fussed over. But only if Lucy were doing the fussing. She was still in her bridesmaid dress and I was loosely wrapped in a bathrobe.

"That's not funny, Sean," she said, though there was clear amusement in her words and expression. "I don't want your face to match my hair. I want your face back to normal."

I caught her hand before she pulled it away and admitted abruptly, "I've missed you."

She gave me a small smile like she found the statement silly, tilting her head to the side and allowing me to hold her fingers hostage. "When did you miss me?"

"Until now. Until right this moment." I pressed her palm between mine, studying how we fit together, how my large hand swallowed her much smaller one. "I think I've always missed you."

We were quiet for a moment and I felt her eyes on me as I examined her fingers. Her nails were both perfect and atrocious. The polish was chipped, the edges uneven. She needed a manicure, but only if she wanted one.

"I think I've missed you all my life," I murmured unthinkingly to her knuckles before bringing them to my lips.

She said nothing, allowed me to kiss each of her joints, and then she blurted, "Sean, I'm in love with you."

I stilled my movements, hid my unbidden smile with her hand, and closed my eyes. The room was quiet save for the sound of her breathing.

The silence was soft, unobtrusive, and Lucy surrounded every part of me. I smelled her. I touched her. She was in my mind and in my heart, her warmth obliterating what was once cold.

This was a moment I wanted to savor. To remember. To recall.

Frequently.

"Sean?" Her voice was small, unsure.

"Mmm?"

She shifted on the bed, tried to withdraw her hand. I held it fast, singled out her middle finger and licked it, sucked it into my mouth, ignoring the cut on my cheek.

A tremor shivered up her arm.

"What are you doing?" she asked on a breathless whisper.

"I'm tasting you."

Lucy sighed a nervous sounding laugh. "Why are you doing that?"

"I don't know," I responded honestly. "Because I want to and I can."

"Are you trying to distract me?"

"From what?"

"From that fact that I just spilled my guts to you and you've said nothing about it. Not even a measly, 'Thanks, Lucy. Thanks for being in love with my snobby arse.'"

I started to laugh but then had to stop, wincing. It hurt my ribs. "Don't make me laugh."

"It would serve you right if I tickled you."

My one eye flew open. "Don't you dare."

She wrinkled her nose. "Well, I won't. Because I love you. And I don't want to see you hurt."

I slid my hand up her arm, over her shoulder, threading my fingers in her hair. "I wish I had a picture of us together."

She grinned at me, almost shyly. "I have one, if you want it."

"You have one?" I tried to remember when we'd taken a picture together, or at least one she hadn't deleted.

Lucy reached for the nightstand and handed me my phone. "Type in your passcode."

I did as instructed then returned it to her. She concentrated on my screen as she said, "I'm just going to log into my email. I sent it to myself. You're not allowed to tease me about it, but I made it the desktop image for my laptop."

Finished with her task, she showed me the phone again and my mouth parted in surprise. It was the picture I'd taken that first night, when I'd forced her into having dinner with me, unable to help myself.

She'd ordered the tuna.

"I thought you deleted it."

She shrugged, her smile wry. "I told you that because I didn't want you to know that I fancied you."

"So you kept it."

"Yes." She nodded once.

"And you looked at it every night."

She narrowed her eyes. "Not *every* night."

I wanted to smile at that, in fact I wanted to shout my discovery from the rooftops, but my cheek and ribs protested. I loved that she fancied me, the way I looked, enough to keep the image and risk discovery.

Did that make me vain? Probably. Oh well.

"I have something for you, too. Go look in the closet." I held fast to my phone while she walked hesitantly to the bedroom closet. I heard her gasp as she pulled open the door, allowing my eyes to stray from the picture on my mobile so I could see the happy expression on her face.

"This is the coolest dress! Look how sparkly." She held up the rainbow frock I'd purchased while out with Eilish. "But Sean, it's really short. Is it a dress or a tunic?"

"A dress. The kind you should wear for me with no knickers."

"I'd be arrested for indecency." She grinned, hanging it back in the closet, her hands lingering on the sequin of the skirt. "I love it, but you didn't have to do that."

"I wanted to. It reminded me of you. Will you wear it?"

"What? Now?" She glanced back at the dress.

"Now, later, soon."

"Yes. Of course. But if I go out in it, I'll be wearing knickers."

I made a show of frowning, then motioned to her. "Come here. Please."

She came immediately and leaned over me, looking concerned. "What? Why? Are you okay?"

My attention dropped to her lips. "I want to kiss the woman I love."

They parted with surprise then curved into a huge smile. "You love me?"

I nodded, certain my grin mirrored hers. "I do."

"You're in love with me." She leaned closer, her eyes wide, and happier than I'd ever seen her. I vowed to put that look in her eyes every day.

"I'm so in love with you." I pulled her closer, curling my fingers around the long strands of her hair as she lowered.

She brushed a soft kiss over my mouth, giggling and grinning at me. "I can't believe you're in love with me."

"Why not?"

"I don't know," she said with wonder. "I just, I don't know. It feels funny to say or think about. Like, Sean Cassidy, bubble-butted brute is head over heels in love with flaky Lucy Fitzpatrick. The most mismatched couple in the world."

"We're perfect together." I smoothed a hand down her side and lifted her fancy dress, searching for the edge of her knickers and finding the sweet spot between her thighs.

She stiffened, her smile falling away. "What are you doing?"

"I want to taste you. Sit on my face, let me—"

She tried to back away, but I had a hold on her hair.

"No, no, no. You're all bruised ribs and cuts. I'm taking care of you."

"Then take care of me," I whispered, releasing her hair and bringing her hand to my cock.

Her mouth fell open. "Are you ever not horny?"

"Only when I'm not with you. And even then I'm semi-hard, because I'm thinking of you."

Lucy threw her head back and laughed. I allowed myself to chuckle, enjoying her free and easy smiles. As her laughter tapered off, her hand closed over my erection and stroked once.

"Rest now. More lessons later."

As best I could, I lifted an eyebrow at this news. "You mean there's more? More lessons?"

My Lucy winked at me and grinned, holding my gaze hostage with hers. "Oh Sean, my love, with you and me, there's going to be a lifetime of lessons."

# Epilogue

**@LucyFitz** What's the deal with Yorkie Bars these days? Def getting smaller.

**@BroderickAdams to @LucyFitz** My opinion? Chocolate manufacturers and WHO are conspiring to screw us while continuing to hike prices #candyconspiracy

**@RonanFitz to @LucyFitz** They decided to model them on the size of **@SeanCassinova's** manhood.

**@SeanCassinova to @RonanFitz** Or the size of your IQ.

### *Lucy*

*Some years later…*

"I REALLY LIKE the burgundy one. The flower print is too busy."

A yellow taxi honked in the background as I held my phone up in front of me, multi-tasking hurrying through a busy Manhattan street and video-chatting with Mam.

"But the flower print has a higher neckline. You know I'm self-conscious of my neck these days, Lucy."

"Your neck is fine. Get the burgundy dress. You'll look drop dead gorgeous in it and this date of yours will think he won the flippin' lottery."

My mother worried her lip, a frown marring her forehead. She was seriously overthinking her outfit choice. And before you wonder, no, hell hadn't frozen over. Me and my mother were having a friendly conversation like a pair of old pals. It hadn't become our norm, not yet; but I had high hopes that it would be in another two years.

Therapy was a work in progress. Sure, it took a whole lot of convincing on Ronan's part to finally get her to see the light, but in the end she'd agreed to join me for a few sessions. A few sessions turned into every session, and I'm not gonna lie, in the beginning it had been rough. We had a lifetime's worth of issues to get through, after all.

The first day I stepped into Dr. Hollyfield's office he'd told me about a little thing called the phone test. If a certain person calls you and you just can't bear to pick up and talk to them, then they're probably toxic and you should cut them from your life. If it's a person you can't cut from your life, then you need to find a new approach to dealing with them.

"What if he doesn't like me?" Mam asked. "Or what if we can't think of anything to talk about?"

"Now you're just being ridiculous," I answered. "Look at you, you're a catch. Plus, we both know you can talk for Ireland, so don't give me that."

She wiggled her head and gave me a small grin. "If you say so."

In the case of Mam and me, I started to realize that no matter how much she nagged or how many times she commented on my appearance, there was nothing she could really do stop me living my life how I wanted. She could say whatever she liked, I'd still dye my hair whatever color I chose, date who I wanted to date, and wear the clothes I liked wearing.

As we delved deeper into our issues, we had a lot of breakthroughs. I learned about her insecurities that stemmed back to her relationship with my dad and how his family had shunned her. He'd later died tragically, leaving her feeling helpless and alone. All these things hardened her, but now she was seeing Dr. Hollyfield on her own as well as during our sessions.

"I do say so. Now go glam yourself up. This guy doesn't know what's about to hit him."

Now she laughed, a blush coloring her cheeks that was almost girlish. "He's a builder, you know. Works with his hands…"

"Okay, stop right there. I can give you as many pep talks as you need, but I really don't want to know anything about his hands and what he does with them."

She rolled her eyes at me. Yes, that's right, my own mother rolled her eyes – at me. I thought I was supposed to be the kid here. "Fine. I'll say no more. Give my love to Ronan and Annie when you see them. Tell them I miss them and can't wait for them to come home next week."

"I will, Mam. Enjoy your date. I'll call you tomorrow for all the details."

"Looking forward to it." She paused, her smile growing a little watery before adding, "I love you, Lucy."

I returned her smile and her sincerity. "Love you, too."

Hanging up, I reflected on how things had changed. Our relationship wasn't perfect, but she was happier. I was happier. I was beginning to look forward to her phone calls and that felt like a flippin' miracle!

Oh yes, and I hadn't stolen a single thing in over two years. I didn't even take the complimentary slippers and toiletries when I stayed in hotels. I was a whole new woman.

I slid my phone back in my bag and continued on my way, hoping I wasn't going to be late. Ronan and Annie were in New York all week for business meetings and I was supposed to be having dinner with them at Tom's restaurant.

Whenever my brother and his wife came to visit there was no keeping them away from Tom's. Annie was absolutely crazy about the food there. She even said herself that she'd sell the soul of her firstborn child for the secret recipe to his pecan pie.

Rounding the corner to the restaurant, I glanced in the window to see them sitting in a booth. Ronan had his arm around Annie as he affectionately placed a kiss on her temple. My heart ached as I watched them, so in love, because it made me miss Sean even more than I already did.

Unfortunately, it was going on three weeks now that I hadn't seen him, and though video chat was a godsend, it just wasn't the same as seeing him in person. There were so many nights that I found myself hugging my pillow, wishing it was him. And don't even get me started on cyber-sex. We'd become quite adept at it, both desperate for each other but separated by an entire ocean.

With a heavy sigh, I opened the door and was instantly hit with the mouth-watering aroma of Tom's red wine gravy. There was just something about his food that always smelled like home, and I felt a little less heartsick as I stepped inside.

Ronan lifted his hand when he saw me come in, waving me over, and I began shrugging out of my jacket as I slid into the booth on the other side of them.

"Hey you two! God, I'm starving," I said as I settled into the seat. "I've been chasing after that new Australian singer all day, trying to get pictures for the blog. You know the one who sings that song they keep playing on repeat everywhere? Plus I had a shift at the animal shelter this morning and they just rescued ten puppies, none of which wanted a bath."

"Hi Lucy," said Annie, biting her lip, for some reason not commenting on what I'd just said.

"Luce," Ronan nodded in greeting. I glanced between the two of them, getting the sense that something was up. Annie's mouth twitched, like she wanted to smile but was trying to hold it in.

"What's going on?" I asked, my tone suspicious. When I moved my foot under the table it met with something bulky; I ducked my head to see a suitcase had been shoved under there. I looked back to Ronan and Annie. "What's with the suitcase? Don't tell me you two are going home early! I feel like you just got here."

Ronan lifted a shoulder and took a swig of the water sitting in front of him. "Nah, we're still here until next week."

Annie giggled in barely restrained glee as she pinched Ronan on the arm. He cast her an indulgent look and shook his head with a sigh. "You're such a little romantic."

"Okay, will one of you tell me what's going on before we all die of hunger," I complained. As I said it, something caught my eye on the other side of the restaurant. The door leading to the men's bathroom opened up, a man stepping out.

I stood abruptly, my hip banging off the table in my haste, but I was too emotional right then to feel any pain. Tears pricked at my eyes as I began moving through the room, dodging wait staff and other customers just to get to him.

Sean's eyes found mine and they warmed instantly as he held his arms out. I ran the last few feet, throwing myself into his embrace. He caught me, pulling me tight to him as I buried my face in his chest, inhaling his scent.

"What are you doing here? I thought I wasn't going to see you for another two weeks," I asked when I finally found my voice.

Sean's warm hands massaged the base of my spine as he smiled down at me, smiled at me like I was the center of his entire universe.

"I wanted to surprise you," he murmured, dipping down to steal a kiss.

I clutched his cheeks and began planting kisses all over his face like an affection-starved lunatic. I couldn't believe he was actually here, that I was actually feeling his heat and his body against mine.

"I missed you so much," I said, almost on the verge of tears. "Seriously, I'm not sure how much longer I can keep doing this."

He stared at me, his expression turning serious for a moment. "I know, darling, I know. Let's go join your brother and Annie. We're blocking everybody's way."

I pulled back, suddenly aware that there were several people trying to get by where we stood between two tables. "Right. Yes. Sorry," I said, shooting an apologetic look their way.

Sean slid his big fingers through mine and led me over to the booth. My heart sang in my chest, all of my insides alight with exhilaration and relief. He was here now. I didn't have to miss him anymore. At least until he had to leave again.

No. I refused to think of that. I just wanted to enjoy him while I could, for however long it might last.

"Christ Cassidy, I've seen pile ups on the motorway make less of a disruption than you. I think you need to cut down on those steroids," said

Ronan.

Over the years, my brother and Sean had fallen into a grudging sort of friendship. They'd both accepted the presence of one another in their lives, and honestly, I thought they might even secretly enjoy each other's company. Still, they'd never let themselves admit it out loud. They also couldn't carry out a conversation without at least five insults being thrown back and forth.

The male ego was a strange breed.

"Don't hate me for what I was born with. It's okay to be hobbit sized, Fitzpatrick. Nobody's judging you," said Sean, a big grin on his face.

"I'm normal sized," Ronan retorted. "You're the one whose biceps block out the sun."

"Exactly, my biceps are phenomenal. Thank you for pointing that out."

"It wasn't a compliment, dickface," Ronan bit back with a smile.

"Dickface at the dinner table, really Ronan? I see you have more work to do on your manners." Sean tutted.

I rolled my eyes at them both and tucked myself under Sean's arm, snuggling close and looking across the table to smile at Annie. We both grinned, used to their banter by now.

"Oh my God, would you two just shut up and kiss already? This is getting ridiculous," Annie teased and I laughed loudly. They both instantly quieted their bickering. My sister-in-law was an evil genius sometimes. Ronan frowned and Sean's face formed a grimace. I snuggled closer to my boyfriend and pressed a kiss to the underside of his jaw.

"I'm so happy you're here," I whispered.

***

"CAN WE TALK about the picture you sent on Tuesday?" Sean growled when we arrived home from dinner, i.e. to Annie's apartment. As soon as I closed the door to my bedroom he was on me, hands in my hair, mouth on my neck, nipping, biting, licking.

"The one of me wearing the lingerie you ordered?" I asked coyly, closing my eyes in ecstasy when his hand slid beneath my top to cup my breast. "I thought that was the whole reason you bought it."

His thumb grazed my nipple and I swear I felt it all the way down between my legs. "I opened the message during a meeting with my agent. Do you know how inconvenient it is getting an erection while trying to discuss work opportunities?"

I let out a guffaw of a laugh that quickly transformed into a moan when Sean threw me onto the bed and mounted me, his hard cock pressing between my thighs. The bed creaked loudly. A second later there was a knock on the wall, followed by Ronan yelling, "I don't want to hear that shit, Cassidy. Keep it down."

I giggled and Sean put his hand over my mouth to stifle the sound. "We really should have gotten a hotel room. I want to fuck you loudly tonight, and I can't exactly do that with your brother in the next room."

"Fuck me quietly. Tomorrow when he's out we can be loud," I smiled.

Sean groaned and began divesting me of my shirt and bra. "I'm not sure I can wait that long. I've missed you so bloody much." His eyes travelled over my face for a second. "God, you're beautiful."

That blasted emotion clutched at me again, and I nearly got weepy because I'd missed him so much, too. Then my mind tracked back to what he'd said a minute ago.

I stared at the top of his head as he kissed his way down my body. "Sean."

He glanced up. "Yes?"

"Why were you discussing work opportunities with your agent? You already have a job."

He went still, the muscles moving in his jaw as he exhaled. The quiet went on for so long I began to grow worried. "Damn it, I wanted to wait until tomorrow to tell you. I had a whole day planned."

"Tell me what?" I said, my body tensing and my heart pounding.

Now he looked up at me, those blue eyes of his so bloody handsome I couldn't take it sometimes.

"I'm retiring from the team, Lucy," he said.

My mind reeled. My voice barely a whisper. "You're what? Why? How?"

"I'm getting old."

"You are not old." I smacked his shoulder, making a face at him.

"For professional rugby, I'm ancient. I'm not going to be able to play forever. There are younger players out there more than willing to take my place. It's time."

Suddenly, everything he was telling me sank in, and my heart pounded for a very different reason. This wasn't bad news. It was good news. The best news I'd ever had.

"Are you…does this mean you're moving over here?" I practically squealed.

When he smiled it was glorious. Moving up the bed, he took my face in his hands and kissed me delicately on the lips. "Yes, love, it means I'm moving here. I'll be working with ESPN, New York office, as their international rugby liaison."

"Is this for real? Am I dreaming?" I asked, hardly able to contain my smile. Seriously, I was smiling so hard right then my jaw hurt. Everything inside of me rejoiced. Sean was staying. I didn't have to go through the pain of watching him leave again.

"You're not dreaming, Lucy," Sean murmured and gave me another kiss. "I can't stand it when I'm not with you. I feel like a piece of my heart is missing," he went on and I knew exactly how he felt, because I felt it too.

"God, I love you so much, so, so much," I told him between kisses.

"I love you too, Lucy. It feels like you've always been here, is that mad? I can't remember my life without you. It feels like someone else's life."

"I feel exactly the same," I said, sucking back the happy tears at his murmured declaration. I lost myself in him, his body, his taste. I was a whirl of emotions, so many wonderful thoughts swirling between my head and my heart. Then, the most exciting realization hit me, as I pulled my mouth from his and looked him dead in the eye.

"Oh my God, you do realize what this means, don't you?"

His smile was indulgent. "What does it mean, darling?"

I grinned so wide my face hurt again. "It means we can finally get a dog!"

*\*\**

FOR A LONG time, circumstances had been against us. Annie's apartment building didn't allow pets and Sean travelled too much to be able to care for one properly. So, I volunteered at the shelter as often as I could, giving all my love to the animals that didn't have families while desperately wishing I could take all of them home with me.

Now, two weeks after Sean had moved to New York permanently, we signed the lease on a top floor apartment with a roof garden. The best part of all? Pets were permitted in the tenancy agreement. I wasn't sure who was more excited, me or the big hunk of rugby muscle who currently held my hand as we walked through the kennels at the shelter, saying hello to all our friends.

"Hello Sam, hello Patch, hello Charlie, hello Buddy, hello Hampton," I sing-songed as Sean went to greet his favorite canine.

Being such a large dog and almost six years old, Hampton had a hard time getting adopted into a home. Sean had sponsored him at the shelter and visited with me whenever he was in town. I knew without even having to ask that he was the one Sean wanted, and I was already mentally preparing to purchase a year's supply of lint rollers and some sort of handheld vacuum cleaner to deal with all that long black fur getting everywhere.

"You want him, don't you," I said, grinning down at Sean where he knelt by Hampton's kennel, reaching through to rub him on the head. Hampton barked in greeting and gave Sean's hand a big slobbery lick.

He only nodded quietly and smiled, his attention all for Hampton as he opened his kennel and the big dog came barreling out, knocking Sean off balance and causing him to fall flat on his bottom. I laughed loudly as Hampton proceeded to hop all over Sean, licking his face, delirious with excitement to see his most favorite human.

It was as I was smiling at the two of them that I saw something zipping by me out of the corner of my eye, a little ball of tawny fur. Several more zipped by and I looked down to see four Pomeranian puppies play fighting with one another at my feet.

"They're adorable, aren't they," said Linda, one of the full-time volunteers. "A woman came in with them the other day. She found them in the bushes at the back of her house, thinks the mother abandoned them after giving birth. That being said, I doubt we'll have any trouble finding them new homes."

"Me neither," I agreed as I stared down at the ball of fluff biting and yipping at the toe of my shoe. "I think I've just fallen in love."

Linda smiled as I bent down to pick the puppy up and cradle her in my arms. She was a girl and she was so adorable I could seriously die.

"Hello," I said, staring down at her.

She barked a tiny puppy bark and I was convinced she'd just said hello back. Sean approached with Hampton and I peered up at him, mustering my most pleading expression.

"I have to have her," I said beseechingly.

Sean frowned, then glanced down at Hampton, who made a sort of huffing noise like he wasn't too sure either.

"I dunno. That crazy little face kinda freaks me out," he said but I could tell he was holding back a grin.

"Her face isn't crazy! It's the most adorable face ever created and I'm putting my foot down. I won't leave this kennel without her. I'm sorry, but we've bonded and are now best friends for life."

"You just picked her up five seconds ago."

"Yes, and when I stared into her eyes I silently told her I was her mother. It's a done deal. There's no turning back now."

Sean laughed as he ruffled Hampton's fur. "What do you say Hampton? You okay with sharing your home with a spoiled little furball?"

"She won't be spoiled. She'll be a lady."

Now he smiled at me. "You know I love giving you everything you want. Of course we can have her."

"I'm so happy right now. *So* happy. Can we get her a rainbow-striped kennel with her name on the front?"

"Perhaps. I haven't bought you anything in a while. You're due a gift."

"You just bought me lingerie."

"That doesn't count. Lingerie for you is a gift for me, and is as essential as breathing."

I shook my head at him. "Only you could say that and make it sound normal."

"You know I like to treat myself to something extravagant for you at least once a month. This month you can have your rainbow-striped kennel, with rainbow rhinestones if you'd like."

"And what about next month?" I asked with a hint of flirtation.

His eyes heated up as he gazed at me and there was something about his look that made my tummy do a flip. "You'll have to wait and see," he winked.

"No clues?"

He paused a moment, a glint coming into his eye. "There might be a diamond involved."

My heart stilled and all I could do was stare at him. I'd been joking around, flirting harmlessly, and then he went and dropped a bomb the size of a small country on me.

*A diamond? A DIAMOND?*

What did that mean?

Okay, yes, I knew what it meant, but that didn't stop my heart from trying to leap its way out of my chest. Sean gave a throaty chuckle and shook his head. "Calm down, Lucy. Rest assured that when I do finally buy you a diamond, you'll be ready for it."

I continued staring at him, mindlessly petting the puppy I held as I stood there in silence. Finally, I spoke. "Sean."

"Yes, Lucy?"

"What if I said I'm ready for a diamond now?"

A slow, caramel smooth smile shaped his mouth and his look set a fire burning deep in my belly. "Then, my dear, perhaps it's time to go shopping."

End.

# About the Authors

**L.H. Cosway** has a BA in English Literature and Greek and Roman Civilisation and an MA in Postcolonial Literature. She lives in Dublin city. Her inspiration to write comes from music. Her favourite things in life include writing stories, vintage clothing, dark cabaret music, food, musical comedy, and of course, books.

She thinks that imperfect people are the most interesting kind. They tell the best stories.

Find L.H. Cosway online! www.lhcoswayauthor.com

**Penny Reid**'s days are spent writing federal grant proposals for biomedical research; her evenings are either spent playing dress-up and mad-scientist with her three people-children (boy-9, girl-6, tiny dictator-8 months), or knitting with her knitting group at the local coffee shop. Please feel free to drop her a line. She'd be happy to hijack your thoughts!

Find Penny Reid online! www.pennyreid.ninja

## Please, write a review!

If you liked this book (and, more importantly perhaps, if you didn't like it) please take a moment to post a review someplace (Amazon, Goodreads, your blog, on a bathroom stall wall, in a letter to your mother, etc.). This helps society more than you know when you make your voice heard; reviews force us to move towards a true meritocracy.

# Read on for:

L.H. Cosway's **Booklist** (current and planned publications)

Penny Reid's **Booklist** (current and planned publications)

# L.H. Cosway Booklist

Contemporary Romance Standalones
*Painted Faces*
*Killer Queen*
*The Nature of Cruelty*
*Still Life with Strings*
*Showmance* (coming May 16th, 2016)


Hearts Series
(Contemporary Romance)
*Six of Hearts*
*Hearts of Fire*
*King of Hearts*
*Hearts of Blue*


Irish Players (Rugby) Series – by L.H. Cosway and Penny Reid
(Contemporary Sports Romance)
*The Hooker and the Hermit* (#1)
*The Player and the Pixie* (#2)
*The Cad and the Co-ed* – #3, TBD 2017


Urban Fantasy
Tegan's Blood (The Ultimate Power Series #1)
Tegan's Return (The Ultimate Power Series #2)
Tegan's Magic (The Ultimate Power Series #3)
Tegan's Power (The Ultimate Power Series #4)

# Penny Reid Booklist

## Knitting in the City Series
(Contemporary Romantic Comedy)
*Neanderthal Seeks Human: A Smart Romance* (#1)
*Neanderthal Marries Human: A Smarter Romance* (#1.5)
*Friends without Benefits: An Unrequited Romance* (#2)
*Love Hacked: A Reluctant Romance* (#3)
*Beauty and the Mustache: A Philosophical Romance* (#4)
*Ninja At First Sight* (#4.75)
*Happily Ever Ninja: A Married Romance* (#5)
*Dating-ish* (#6, coming summer 2016)
*Marriage of Inconvenience* – #7 TBD 2017

## Winston Brother Series
(Contemporary Romantic Comedy, spinoff of *Beauty and the Mustache*)
*Truth or Beard* (#1)
*Grin and Beard It* (#2, May 24, 2016)
*Beard Science* (#3, coming 2017)
*Beard in Mind* – #4 TBD 2017
*Dr. Strange Beard* – #5 TBD 2018
*Beard Necessities* – #6 TBD 2018

## Hypothesis Series
(New Adult Romantic Comedy)
*The Elements of Chemistry*: ATTRACTION, HEAT, and CAPTURE (#1)
*The Laws of Physics* – #2 TBD 2017
Book #3 – TBD 2018

## Irish Players (Rugby) Series – by L.H. Cosway and Penny Reid
(Contemporary Sports Romance)
*The Hooker and the Hermit* (#1)
*The Player and the Pixie* (#2)
*The Cad and the Co-ed* – #3, TBD 2017

CPSIA information can be obtained
at www.ICGtesting.com
Printed in the USA
LVOW10s1924281117

557886LV00013B/1133/P